HOTTIE ON A HARLEY

He straddled a Harley. The bike looked like a Heritage Softail Classic. No shiny new machine for this man. He held power and heat between his thighs, a blast from the past when the Harley was all rumbling thunder and bad attitude. Basic black.

"Would you look at that hottie on his Harley?" Flo, one of Camryn's senior partners, rolled down her window to get a better look. "Hope he's one of our targets. I'd like a shot at searching him for weapons. Bet they're not too well hidden."

No kidding. Black shaggy hair touched his shoulders. Hard face. She was a little too far away to see, but she'd bet his eyes were as hard as the rest of him. Black sleeveless T-shirt that exposed tanned, muscular arms. He had some sort of tattoo on his left upper arm, again too far away to make out, but she'd bet it didn't say *Mother*. Worn jeans. Boots. Probably scuffed. And no helmet. A risk-taker.

"As soon as we get to Chance, find out who that man is. He looks like the kind of agent L.O.V.E.R. would send."

FROM BOARDWALK WITH LOVE

NINA BANGS

LOVE SPELL NEW YORK CITY

LOVE SPELL®

January 2003

Published by

Dorchester Publishing Co., Inc.
276 Fifth Avenue
New York, NY 10001

ISBN 0-505-52506-2

The name "Love Spell" and its logo are trademarks of Dorchester Publishing Co., Inc.

Printed in the United States of America.

Visit us on the web at www.dorchesterpub.com.

In memory of the real Meathead,
a cat with courage, loyalty, and
ATTITUDE.
Miss you, big guy.

FROM BOARDWALK WITH LOVE

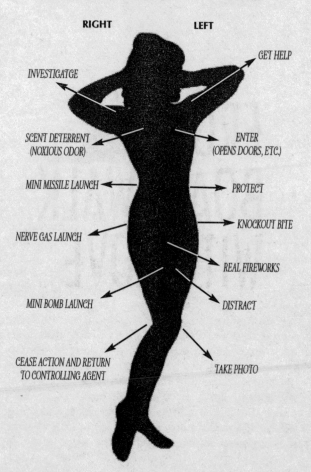

Camryn's Hot Dots—
used to control F.I.D.O.
(Feline Intelligence Defense Operative)

RIGHT   **LEFT**

GET HELP

INVESTIGATGE

SCENT DETERRENT
(NOXIOUS ODOR)

ENTER
(OPENS DOORS, ETC.)

MINI MISSILE LAUNCH

PROTECT

KNOCKOUT BITE

NERVE GAS LAUNCH

REAL FIREWORKS

MINI BOMB LAUNCH

DISTRACT

CEASE ACTION AND RETURN
TO CONTROLLING AGENT

TAKE PHOTO

Chapter One

B.L.I.S.S.

Complete happiness.

Poor name choice for an international crime-fighting organization. The bad guys sure wouldn't buy into the earthly nirvana concept.

Camryn O'Brien cocked her head to get a better angle on the tastefully understated sign perched on Y's massive desk.

Someone in marketing must've taken a poll, analyzed data, and decided that putting dots after each letter would add an aura of danger and secrecy to the agency's name. Perfect.

Camryn did some mental knuckle cracking as she waited for Y to appear. A few lights would make the office a little cheerier. As it was, only the light from Y's computer screen pushed back the darkness. She glanced at the bare paneled

1

walls. Of course, since B.L.I.S.S. headquarters crouched far beneath an innocuous little antique shop at street level, windows weren't an option.

"Welcome to the women of B.L.I.S.S., Agent 36DD."

Camryn swallowed her alarm as she jerked her attention back to the desk. The shadowy figure of a woman now sat behind it. Y. A woman steeped in power and mystery, a legend in the department. How had Y entered the office without making a sound?

Y pushed the monitor aside, so no light fell on her face, then sat quietly, waiting for Camryn to make an intelligent response.

No intelligent response came to mind, so Camryn began to hum. The humming was almost subconscious, an automatic reaction to extreme stress, a calming influence she'd used since she was a child.

" 'Twinkle, Twinkle, Little Star'?" Y's husky laughter filled the darkness.

More like "Tinkle, Tinkle, Little Star." No more Big Gulps before career-defining meetings. Camryn's nervous system was connected directly to her bladder today. But she would *not* run to the rest room. This was her shot at a dream. She wouldn't be able to take a potty break in the middle of saving the free world from destruction.

She'd better say *something*, or Y would kick her back down to Research. "I'm sorry about the humming, but—"

"No need to apologize, 36DD." Y managed to sound almost motherly. "Our psychological testing revealed your need to hum childhood songs in moments of great duress. We have no problem with this so long as you can hum 'Mary Had a Little Lamb' at the same time you're neutralizing an enemy agent."

"Thanks." *I think.* "My humming would never jeopardize an assignment."

Y merely nodded. "How do you feel about being part of B.L.I.S.S.?"

Camryn had no difficulty responding to this question. "Excited. I've lived in this part of Texas all my life. I've even driven down NASA Road One to get to my job, and never guessed that an international crime-fighting agency was right across from Johnson Space Center."

"This is only one of our headquarters. We have several others in different parts of the world. But you'll have contact only with this one, so if something . . . unforeseen happens, you won't be able to compromise the total organization."

Unforeseen? Camryn didn't like the sound of that. "You're lucky to be in this location. If trouble crops up, NASA can protect you."

"No, dear." Y's voice was softly chiding. "*We* can protect NASA. The fake clock tower on the antique shop contains the latest technology and weapons. If anyone threatens NASA, he will be eliminated."

Y leaned back in her chair. The chair didn't squeak. Camryn had the feeling nothing in Y's range of influence would dare squeak.

"I'm thrilled to be part of B.L.I.S.S., but I just started in Research a few months ago. I don't have any training, so what can I offer the agency?" Camryn thought she knew the answer.

"You have a particularly interesting skill, 36DD."

Even though she couldn't see Y's eyes, Camryn sensed that her attention had shifted to the computer screen.

She suspected the monitor displayed the brief and unexciting history of Camryn O'Brien. Age: twenty-six. Education: public relations degree. Hobby: likes to tinker with cars. Job history: unsettled. Useful skills? Only one that would interest Y. But that skill took Camryn out of the "ordinary" and into the "weirdo" category. She'd never thought of it as marketable until B.L.I.S.S.

"My 'skill' isn't a skill at all. It's natural, I can't control it, and it's been a pain in the butt my whole life."

Y's amused chuckle made light of her doubts. "Natural skills are sometimes the most useful."

Camryn decided to put aside that line of thought for the moment in favor of something a little more immediate. "Don't get me wrong, I'm honored to be a part of the organization, but about my agent number . . . Okay, let's be up-front about this. My number's a bra size. Why was I given a bra size? Who's going to take me seriously with a number like 36DD?"

Camryn felt Y's considering gaze and resisted the urge to fold her arms across her chest.

"No one, if you're lucky. An agent who's underestimated by the enemy has a huge advantage." Y slid back her chair, further throwing her face into shadow. "We have one other number available. Would you prefer 20AA?"

Camryn blinked. "A battery size?"

Y offered her a take-it-or-leave-it shrug.

Camryn sighed and accepted the inevitable. "Fine. I'll keep 36DD." She tried for a positive spin. It would *not* be a good thing to look like your agent number. Too easy to identify. You'd stand out like . . . Well, you'd just stand out.

Y nodded her approval. "The numbers are computer-generated. Nothing personal."

Camryn had her suspicions. She'd bet the computer that burped out her number was the victim of a hacker from Victoria's Secret.

Y studied Camryn. "But the letters are significant. The double D indicates you have the right to detain or destroy. That's quite a responsibility."

A B.L.I.S.S. assignment would be the ultimate affirmation of the new and totally revamped Camryn O'Brien, but she had to point out the obvious. "Look, I know you need an agent right now, and I know all the other agents are already on assignment, but I don't think I'm ready for—"

Y's gaze never wavered. "Is anyone ever completely ready?" She leaned closer. "I worked for Mary Kay Cosmetics before joining B.L.I.S.S. They taught me everything I needed to know about self-confidence. Femininity is power, and B.L.I.S.S. agents use their power in any way they must to achieve success."

Camryn frowned. She wasn't quite clear on Y's concept—wasn't sure she *wanted* to be clear on the concept.

5

Y leaned back again. "Mary Kay awarded me a diamond bumblebee pin before I left. Do you know anything about the bumblebee?"

Bumblebee? "Not much." What did bumblebees have to do with anything?

"According to aerodynamic engineers, the bumblebee shouldn't be able to fly. Its body's too heavy. Its wings are too small." Y's soft chuckle filled the space between them. "But no one told the bumblebee."

Message received. Camryn had the uncomfortable feeling Y was breaking her up into basic components, then placing her parts into debit and asset columns. "Tell me what you want me to do, and I'll tell you how ready I am."

Y nodded. "To the point. I like that." She leaned forward and fixed Camryn with a penetrating stare. "You present a kind of wide-eyed naiveté that's deceiving. That's good. And you're intuitive. Excellent. But your most useful skill is what you do to men."

Camryn frowned. Would this one tiny blip in her "normal" rating determine her whole career's worth?

"You, my dear, send men to hospitals in unprecedented numbers. Just being around you is an invitation to an accident for men. In your life you've incapacitated . . ." Y shifted her attention to the screen for accurate information, then shook her head. "We don't even have the complete figures, but I'm sure it's enough men to arm a small developing nation. What a wonderful skill to have." Y's voice rang with sincere admiration.

Camryn's frown deepened. Maybe it wasn't such a tiny blip. "What good is it if I can't control it? Every time I date a guy, I wonder if we'll end up doing the emergency-room rumba."

"Oh, but you *can* control it." Y's tone indicated that the matter was settled.

"Could've fooled me." Camryn hoped her mumbled sarcasm hadn't reached Y. She really wanted this assignment.

Y opened another page on her computer. "Let me tell you what we know about Camryn O'Brien. Your mother died shortly after your birth. You were raised by your dad and six brothers. Six *protective* brothers. You were never allowed to solve your own problems or make any independent decisions. You were smothered by the men in your life, who thought they were keeping you happy and safe."

Camryn swallowed hard. It wasn't easy listening to the essence of your life laid out in clipped, unemotional word bytes.

"The accidents started when you were seven years old." Y scrolled down the page. "First recorded incident: your brother Ben wouldn't let you climb the live oak tree in your yard to rescue your kitten. He went instead. Ben fell out of the tree and broke his leg." She scrolled to the bottom of the page. "Most recent recorded incident: last week Sam Delora took you to the Ragin' Cajun restaurant. He was right in the middle of saying he'd order for you because he knew what was best on the menu when a light fixture fell on him. Broke his glasses and knocked him out.

7

Emergency-room visit for bump on head." Y glanced from the screen. "Do you see a pattern, agent 36DD?"

Camryn closed her eyes. She'd spent a lifetime avoiding a truth she'd probably always recognized subconsciously. "The men who get hurt are the ones who try to make my decisions, the ones who want to take care of me." Managing men drove her nuts. She opened her eyes, surprised at the relief she felt upon her admission.

"Very good." Y was in her approving-teacher mode. "Now that you understand the why, you can control the when."

Was it possible? *A secret weapon.* If she could really control her "gift," she'd have an honest-to-goodness secret weapon. Camryn shut down her burgeoning excitement. She wouldn't know for sure until she tried it.

Y was silent for a moment, letting the implications sink in.

Camryn grinned. "This is so great. I've really wanted to be part of B.L.I.S.S. This is my chance to prove I can handle a demanding job without a man's help. My brothers won't be around to rescue me. I can be *me.*"

Y nodded. "B.L.I.S.S. wants you because you'll approach every assignment with a single-minded determination to succeed. Single-mindedness, total commitment, is what B.L.I.S.S. looks for."

Camryn felt Y's smile touch her.

"Anyone can be taught to shoot a gun, but you bring a lot more positives with you than an ability to use weapons." Y shut off her monitor, throwing the room into almost total darkness. "Now I bet you want to know about your first assignment."

Camryn drew in a deep, steadying breath. This first assignment would probably be insignificant. Something to get her feet wet. But if she did a great job, it would lead to bigger things.

Y was all business now. "You must protect Owen Sitall, the world's wealthiest man. Owen owns most of the free world and a few of the semifree parts as well. He's been marked for assassination by Zed, L.O.V.E.R.'s deadliest agent. Your assignment is to stop Zed." Her tone indicated this should take a few days, tops.

"L.O.V.E.R.?" Camryn's throat had closed in panic, so it was sort of hard to get more than one word out at a time.

"League of Violent Economic Revolutionaries." Y seemed unaware of the monumental mistake she was making. "They plan to kill Owen before the next World Economic Summit. Owen flies to Paris for the summit in thirteen days. If they succeed, the world's economies will face chaos, and life as we know it will cease." She paused to retrieve a disk from a drawer. "You can take a look at this later to get more details. You'll be leaving—"

Urp. She'd wanted an assignment that would showcase the new and improved Camryn, but she hadn't counted on the fate of the world hanging in the balance. "Wait, wait. What if Zed isn't a man? I don't have enough training. What do I do if—"

"Remember the bumblebee, Agent 36DD."

To hell with bumblebees. "But—"

Y held up her hand. "You'll do fine, dear. I wouldn't send you into your first assignment alone. Three former B.L.I.S.S. agents will accompany you. In their day, they were the best." Y offered an aside: "We don't usually call agents out of retirement, but unfortunately we're a bit short-handed. If you think of anything else you need to know before you leave in three days, feel free to contact me."

Three days? Anything else? Anything else? How about, where's the bathroom so I can throw up?

"I'll have an associate take you to meet your partners." Y stood and slid open a paneled section of the wall. "They can't wait to get started on the assignment."

Camryn wondered how anxious they'd be once they found out who their fearless leader was. She tried to distract herself from the tiny but vocal voice of reason screaming excellent advice such as, *Run like hell! Hide your head under your pillow!* and her personal favorite, *Eat Snickers bars!*

"Remember, 36DD, that a woman of B.L.I.S.S. has only two options: she survives and grows wiser"—Y placed her hand on Camryn's shoulder—"or she doesn't."

The woman waiting to escort her took Camryn's mind off the sound of Y's door sliding shut behind her. Big. Tough. Scarred. Silent. Would Camryn be like this after a life of service? "So how long have you been with B.L.I.S.S.?"

The woman stared coldly at her. "Two weeks."

"Oh."

"But I have previous experience." Her accent hinted at time spent in Russia.

Camryn didn't choose to speculate on what that "previous experience" entailed. Their steps echoed in the wide, empty hallway. The white walls looked innocuous, but Camryn suspected there were cameras interspersed with weapons of mass destruction hidden every few feet.

To forestall any temptation she might have to start humming "Mary Had a Little Lamb," Camryn asked a question: "What's your agent number?" She didn't want to be the only one with a bra size for a number.

"I am agent 5455." She cast Camryn a piercing stare. "It spells 'kill' on a touch-tone phone."

"What a great number. Friends and assassin seekers can just dial 555-KILL. I mean, who's going to forget it?" *Oh, boy. Time for another question.* "What does B.L.I.S.S. stand for?"

"All information in the agency is on a need-to-know basis, Agent 36DD."

Uh-huh. "You don't know."

"No." A woman of few words.

"Does anyone know?"

Agent 5455 shrugged. "It is rumored that C knows."

"Who's C?"

"I don't know."

Camryn should've hummed "Mary Had a Little Lamb."

"Do you play Monopoly, Agent 36DD?" Agent 5455's suit jacket gaped open, revealing a shoulder holster and gun.

"Monopoly? Sure. Doesn't everyone? It's part of being American. Mom, Monopoly, and apple pie." Great. She'd aimed for a low, confident tone, but what came out was squeaky alarm.

Agent 5455 followed Camryn's gaze to the gun and offered a slight twist of her lips that was probably her idea of a huge grin. "Your first lesson in survival: be prepared even when you assume you are in a friendly environment."

Camryn nodded, calm enough now to wonder about the Monopoly question. What did Monopoly have to do with anything? But she forgot about Monopoly when they reached the end of the hallway.

The door facing her was as intimidating as if it had been studded with six-inch spikes and a warning sign: *Beware: hungry dragon. Prefers tender new agents.*

"Behind this door waits everything you'll need to complete your assignment successfully." The woman had a warped sense of the dramatic.

"Right. So before I meet my partners in death and destruction, any advice for a newbie?"

"Advice?" Agent 5455 didn't hesitate. "Never trust *anyone*."

Camryn frowned. Not a very positive spin on life, but she supposed it beat being dead.

The door did some kind of secret scan known only to itself and other like-minded doors. It clicked its approval and slid open.

Agent 5455 motioned her into a large, brightly lit room.

Camryn's eyes widened.

"These are your partners. This is your car. And this is your ultimate weapon of destruction." Agent 5455, a.k.a. Ms. Kill, accompanied her introduction with a sweeping gesture of finality.

Camryn stared at her partners . . .

Looked at her car . . .

Peered down at her weapon of destruction . . .

She was doomed.

Chapter Two

Dorothy was a marshmallow if she thought she had it tough in Oz. *Ha!* Dorothy had a lion, a tin man, and a scarecrow as partners. Piece of cake. Camryn had . . . She glanced at the woman beside her, then surreptitiously peeked in the rearview mirror. She had the SKPs.

In nonsecret-crime-fighting language, that meant she'd drawn three members of the Escapees, a group of retired B.L.I.S.S. agents who traveled the country in their RVs.

Camryn was distracted for a moment as one of Owen Sitall's checkpoint guards stuck his head in the driver's-side window.

"Please open the trunk, ma'am."

She sighed. They'd been parked here ever since they'd emerged from the tunnel connecting Owen's island with the Ecuadorian mainland. For fifteen minutes Owen's men had searched the car from top to bottom. They'd found nothing. Would find nothing. B.L.I.S.S. had made sure of that.

"Nice car, ma'am." He grinned.

Right. Camryn released the trunk latch. She'd hoped for something that would fit her new image as secret agent. Maybe a Lotus or Viper. She would even have opted for a tornado used only once by a little girl with pigtails. She wanted exciting, spectacular. She tried to erase the frown lines she knew were creasing her forehead.

So what did she get? A '78 pink Cadillac. A nostalgic reminder of Y's Mary Kay days. Y *loved* this car. Camryn *hated* this car. The only way she would eliminate Zed while she was driving this car was if he died laughing. How did you blend in with a pink Cadillac?

And speaking of *The Wizard of Oz,* Dorothy won the pet war hands down. Dorothy had Toto, a cute little fuzzy dog. Camryn had . . . She glared down at the seat beside her, where a fat orange cat sat sneering at her. Okay, so maybe cats couldn't sneer, but this one was.

Even the yellow-brick road had a sort of exciting sound to it. Camryn stared out the front windshield, where a life-size Monopoly board stretched into the distance, sandwiched between the brilliant blue Pacific and vivid green jungle. She was parked at Go, and she hadn't collected her two hundred dollars.

What kind of man owned an entire island dedicated to his own personal obsession—Monopoly?

"I'll take your cell phones, ladies." Another one of Owen Sitall's minions poked his head in the window.

Grudgingly, Camryn handed hers over. She noted that her partners handed theirs over without comment. Hey, she had a mouth, and she intended to use it. "Why can't I keep my phone?"

"Mr. Sitall's orders. He doesn't want any distractions while you ladies are playing the big board. You wouldn't get good reception here anyway."

His smile did not placate Camryn. She tapped her index finger impatiently on the steering wheel as she continued her point-counterpoint analysis of Oz and Owen Sitall's stronghold. Oz was winning hands down. She glanced toward the forest. *Until now. Hmm.*

What comparison with *The Wizard of Oz* would be complete without considering the villain? Dorothy had the Wicked Witch of the West. Camryn had . . .

She stared at a man half-hidden in the shade of palm fronds and tropical vegetation. The lush jungle grew close to the edge of the narrow road rimming the Monopoly board where a man waited, blending with the cool shadows of the tropical forest.

He straddled a Harley. The bike looked like a Heritage Softail Classic. No shiny new machine for this man. He held power and heat between his thighs, a blast from the past when the Harley was all rumbling thunder and bad attitude. Basic black.

"Would you look at that hottie on his Harley?" Flo, one of Camryn's senior partners, rolled down her window to get a better look. "Hope he's one of our targets. I'd like a shot at searching him for weapons. Bet they're not too well hidden."

No kidding. Shaggy black hair touching his shoulders. Hard face. She was a little too far away to see, but she'd bet his eyes were as hard as the rest of him. Black sleeveless T-shirt that exposed tanned muscular arms. He had some sort of tattoo on his left upper arm, again too far away to make out, but she'd bet it didn't say "Mother." Worn jeans. Boots. Probably scuffed. And no helmet. A risk-taker.

Hard, dangerous. Definitely her Wicked Warlock of the West.

"As soon as we get to Chance, find out who that man is, Sara. He looks like the kind of agent L.O.V.E.R. would send. Bold. Ruthless." Rachel quietly continued to knit. "And if you'd wear the communicator in your ear that B.L.I.S.S. supplied, Camryn, you wouldn't be so bent out of shape about giving up your cell phone."

"You three told the guard you had hearing aids. What're the chances he'd believe I had one, too?"

Rachel sighed. "They *are* hearing aids. The communicator is the flesh-colored insert behind them. Anyone checking our hearing aids would find them completely innocent and wouldn't look any further." She shook her head. "Too bad they're only good for receiving calls. B.L.I.S.S.'s wondernerd needs to come up with a miniature

17

communication system that can send *and* receive messages."

"I can't stick anything in my ears. Childhood trauma." Camryn tried to ignore Rachel's long-suffering sigh.

Rachel put down her knitting long enough to root around in the satchel by her side. She pulled out a book. "Here's my personal copy of *Who Moved My Cheese?* It gives you some great insights into adapting to change"—meaningful stare—"and if you detach the spine you'll find a phone and recorder." She slipped it into Camryn's purse.

"Thanks." Camryn slid a sideways glance at Rachel. "Why does Zed have to be a man?"

Rachel offered Camryn the small secret smile that was beginning to drive Camryn crazy. "L.O.V.E.R. would never send a woman. They think women are too emotional."

Rachel stared at her with the coldest gray eyes Camryn had ever seen. Too emotional? L.O.V.E.R. hadn't met Rachel.

Okay, so unemotional was a good thing. Camryn needed to cultivate some ice and attitude. Become more like Rachel. "I really appreciate that B.L.I.S.S. sent you along to take care of all the . . . equipment."

Rachel's clicking needles mesmerized her. "It's a package deal. I designed everything you'll be using. Even though I retired from B.L.I.S.S. a few years ago, my stuff is still the best. And I go where my toys go."

Camryn frowned. "I thought T took care of supplying everything."

Rachel's voice turned as cold as her eyes. "I created all the gadgets before T came along. I was S." She drew out the letter into a snake's hiss. "I told B.L.I.S.S. I wouldn't take the assignment unless I could use my own toys." Rachel's wintry smile didn't do a thing to warm things up. "I didn't have anything to do with the car. That's T's baby."

"Sure. I understand that." Camryn glanced out the window to see if the man was still there. Startled, she realized he was staring back.

He offered her a slashing grin that had nothing to do with friendliness and everything to do with challenge. Then he pulled onto the road and roared away. At the same time, the guard who'd been checking the trunk motioned that she was free to go. Relieved, she started the Cadillac and pulled behind the biker.

As she passed Mediterranean Avenue, she realized why she'd been fixated on *The Wizard of Oz.* A pair of ruby slippers that looked like they'd just been ripped from the feet of the Wicked Witch of the East rested inside a Plexiglas case. The case was set atop a larger-than-life replica of the slippers that rolled along a single track beside the Monopoly board. "Wow, those look like the real deal."

"Probably are." Sara's mutter didn't sound happy. "Owen uses authentic tokens, but his methods of procuring them are sometimes questionable."

Camryn wasn't about to try to analyze that comment. She turned her attention back to Rachel.

"So tell me more about my ultimate weapon." She sneaked a glance down at the orange cat. He still stared at her with unblinking yellow eyes. *Scary*.

"F.I.D.O.?" Rachel chuckled. "He's my most advanced creation. I asked everyone to keep quiet about what he did because I wanted to be the one to explain his special . . . qualities. Get used to him, because he'll be your new best friend. You'll never go anywhere on this island without him." For the first time, a note of excitement crept into her voice.

"Fido? He's feline, not canine, Rachel." Camryn cast her a frustrated glance. She hated secrets she wasn't in on, and Rachel seemed to have more than her share.

Rachel offered Camryn her trademark smile that said, *I know something you don't*. That smile didn't go with the stereotype of a seventy-one-year-old woman. But then nothing about Rachel fit a stereotype. Tall and slender, with short blond hair and a face that belonged to a senior sex goddess, she was nobody's grandma.

"F.I.D.O. stands for Feline Intelligence Defense Operative." Rachel crossed her legs, adjusted her shorts, and continued knitting. "We couldn't think of anything to go with F.L.U.F.F.Y."

"And?" Only one thing about Rachel said "granny"—her knitting. Until you noticed the electricity that arced between the needles at regular intervals. Camryn decided the bad guys would get a real charge out of Rachel and her knitting.

"I know you've wondered why you had all those

tiny chips implanted just under your skin." Rachel paused in her knitting. "I call them my hot dots." She held out what looked like a diagram. "Each of those hot dots controls one of F.I.D.O.'s functions. This is a body map showing you which place on your body to press to activate a response from F.I.D.O. Guard it well. It wouldn't do to get confused and push the wrong spot. Think of it as a marriage license. You and F.I.D.O. will be one for the duration of the assignment."

And here Camryn had thought Rachel didn't have a sense of humor. *Holy hell.* She was attached to a robot. She slid a sideways glance at her new alter ego. He didn't look friendly. "Give me that map." She took the paper from Rachel and drove with one hand while she shoved it into her purse. She'd memorize the darn thing tonight.

"Stop messing with your purse and speed up, Camryn. You're losing the Harley hunk."

Camryn hoped Flo would bring the same intensity to her pursuit of Zed. In fact, she prayed all three seventy-plus assistants were totally focused on the coming assignment, because they'd probably not only have to save Owen Sitall from Zed, but their trusty leader, Camryn O'Brien, from herself.

Camryn sucked in some courage. That kind of thinking was defeatist. Y had chosen her for this assignment. Ergo Y believed Camryn could handle Zed.

Flo, totally focused on the biker's buns, peered between Camryn and Rachel. "What an ass. It's Italian. Italian men have tight tushes. See how firm it is? Doesn't spread out all over the seat. Great butt. I haven't a clue what B.L.I.S.S. stands for, but right now I'd settle for Babes Love Italian Sexy Studs."

Fine. Time for another defeatist thought. Camryn's chances of survival were dimming by the minute.

"That's disgusting, Flo. He has to be forty years younger than you are. He'd kill you in bed. Besides, we have a job to do. Nothing gets in the way of that."

Camryn brightened. She could still depend on Sara. Rachel might be brilliant, but she was completely involved with her technological wizardry. Her gadgets might get Camryn out of some tight spots, but Camryn wasn't sure how much direct assistance Rachel would supply.

"Young's the only way to go, Sara. Young men are hot, hard, and ready to rumble." Flo's voice held the conviction of a dedicated stud hunter.

Camryn caught Flo's emphatic nod in the rearview mirror. Black hair untouched by gray. A lean face that wouldn't dare sag. Nope, Flo would never earn granny status either.

Camryn returned her gaze to the road. Baltic Avenue. The board's low-rent district. Okay, so maybe her assessment of Flo was colored by a tiny bit of envy. Flo was a true 36DD.

She wasn't too sure what role Flo had in Y's grand scheme, because Flo never stopped talking about men long enough to explain.

"I don't have time for this nonsense. Pass me the layout of Sitall's mansion. I want everything clear in my mind before we arrive." Sara sounded like the professional Camryn needed at her side. "We have an almost square island. Five miles on each side. Life-size Monopoly board runs along the perimeter. Owen's mansion, Chance, sits in the exact middle of the island at the top of a small volcanic mountain. Four roads, located at the railroads, lead to Chance. The tunnel is the only way onto the island other than by boat or helicopter. I'll set up surveillance equipment as soon as we get to Chance."

Wow. Was Sara impressive or what? Sara was the only one who really looked like a grandma. With her halo of white hair and comfortable round face, she could fool almost anyone. Until you looked in her eyes: hard, intense, and scary enough to send kiddies screaming into the night. *Too bad.* Sara would fail the granny test, too.

Flo wasn't to be sidetracked. "You know, Owen Sitall's kind of cute for an old guy. Wonder why he's never married? He has a son out there somewhere, and he's involved with this woman who handles his tokens, so we know he isn't gay."

"Owen Sitall is younger than you, Flo. And he looks like the man on the Monopoly box, for heaven's sake. A guy has to be pretty weird to run around dressed like a character on a game box. I'd stay away from him."

"But he's so rich, Sara." Flo's voice had turned wheedling. "When you have that much money, you aren't weird; you're eccentric."

"Whatever." Sara had evidently lost interest in the conversation. "You're vibrating, Flo."

"Oh, hell. I told them not to contact me on this line."

Vibrating? Contact? Camryn glanced again in the rearview mirror. She narrowed her gaze on Flo. Sure enough, Flo's breasts were . . . vibrating. *What the . . . ?*

Widening her eyes, Camryn watched in horror as Flo ripped off her blouse, took off her bra and— *No.* Camryn wasn't seeing what she thought she was seeing. Flo was pulling off her . . . It couldn't be. She was putting her . . . Headphones. She was wearing her breasts as headphones. No, fake breasts. Because underneath the fakes were the real things, covered by a lacy black bra.

Fascinated by the fake breasts, Camryn swerved across the road. Steering back into her lane, Camryn glanced in the mirror again.

"I told you never to call me on this line." Flo was talking into a nail file she'd pulled from a pocket. As she listened, her expression grew worried. "What do you mean, she ate the Wheaties box? Put her on the phone." There was a pause as everyone listened raptly. "Is my little girl sick? Did you eat the big bad box? Mommy is coming home soon. Crystal will give you medicine to make your tummy feel better. Mommy loves you. Kissy, kissy." Calmly, Flo took her breasts off her head, replaced them and her jumbo-sized bra, and put on her blouse. She glanced defensively around her. "What? One of my dogs is sick. They're my babies. Gotta take care of my babies."

Camryn stared straight ahead, but she couldn't shut out Rachel's amused chuckle.

"Lesson learned, Camryn. When you're searching someone, always check out body parts. *All* body parts. A prosthesis can easily hide a weapon, or as in Flo's case, a communication device."

Static coming from the Cadillac's radio interrupted anything else Rachel might have said. "Whoa, dude. Sorry. *Dudess.* Careful with the machinery. Treat the Big Smooth right, and it'll take you to Jupiter or Mars. No more zigging or zagging unless you're in pursuit." More static. "Later."

T. Camryn did some eye rolling. B.L.I.S.S.'s resident genius was keeping track of his treasure via satellite. "Right, T. Will do." T's snotty comments were going to drive her crazy. One more reason to dislike the Cadillac.

Rachel's eyes narrowed to evil slits. "Eighteen-year-old puny, pimply pissant. I *hate* child prodigies."

Sara calmly continued her conversation as though fake breasts and T's interruption had never happened. "Oh, make sure our rooms are spread out, Camryn. It'll be too easy to eliminate us when we're all bunched together."

Camryn frowned. That didn't sound encouraging. "Do you think Zed is already here?" Her thoughts drifted to the dark-haired man.

"Probably." Sara sounded matter-of-fact. "And right now Zed has the advantage. Zed knows B.L.I.S.S. will send someone, and L.O.V.E.R. can ID all of us except you. You're too new for them to have information on." Sara shrugged. "Y told us to stick close to Owen while you search for Zed."

Camryn had never felt so inadequate in her life. "We don't know anything about Zed. How will I be sure when I find him? Assuming Zed is a him."

Sara smiled for the first time. "Zed will be the one trying to kill you."

"Hey, no pressure." If Camryn was a quitter, which she wasn't, she'd stop the car right now and walk back to the mainland. Sure, she'd wanted adventure, but on a smaller, more intimate scale. She'd wanted something from which she could win a victory to wave in her brothers' faces as proof that she could compete with them on an equal footing. She couldn't gloat if she were dead. "Level with me. Why do you think Y chose me for this assignment?"

Rachel paused in her knitting for the microsecond it took her to consider an answer. "Beats me. Y probably realized that with the equipment I have, anyone with half a brain could take down Zed."

Camryn sighed. With Rachel along, her ego would never survive puberty.

Flo had her own take on Y's decision. "Camryn looks good. With that long red hair and those green eyes, she'll attract a lot of attention." Flo paused for thought. "Her boobs aren't 36DD quality, but she's got killer legs. Anyway, Zed'll spot her right away. And while he's trying to come on to her, we can sneak up and snuff him."

"Thanks for the vote of confidence, guys." This

was definitely not a positive beginning to her great adventure.

Sara threw her thoughts into the ring. "I talked with Y. It doesn't pay to go to war with team members who're unknown quantities. Y said B.L.I.S.S. chose Camryn because her psychological tests showed she was intelligent, quick thinking, and intuitive. Y also said Camryn had a unique skill that qualified her for the job."

Thank you, Sara. Camryn gathered her bruised and battered ego off the car floor.

Sara wasn't finished. "Besides, Y didn't have any other free agents."

Camryn dropped her ego back onto the floor.

"What kind of skill was Y talking about, Camryn?" Rachel again paused in her knitting.

Camryn turned right at the Reading Railroad, and began the winding climb that would lead to Chance. "I can kill with my thoughts." She cast Rachel a lethal glare, then stared into her rearview mirror. "I've already put a white light around Owen. Anyone disturbs the light and I'll know."

Silence. *Good, let them think about* that. One thing Y *hadn't* told Sara: Camryn would lie like crazy when she was mad or scared. Right now she was both.

Okay, calm down. Y had picked her for a reason. She was committed, in great physical condition, and a fast learner.

"One more question." Camryn didn't know if she should try for one more question. Her trusty team of oldies-but-goodies seemed to deal only in crappy answers. "Why am I wearing this dress?

Shimmery, gold, and barely there doesn't qualify as tropical casual day wear." She glanced down. "And what about a gun? There's no place to carry a gun."

"That's one of my babies." Rachel sounded insulted. "Didn't Y tell you? All the clothes you'll wear on this island are my babies." Her knitting needles were a blur of irritation. "You won't need a gun. You'll have F.I.D.O."

Flo made a rude noise. "Don't make her into a clone of you, Rachel. You don't use a gun because you can't shoot straight, Camryn. I've seen you practice."

Camryn frowned. She'd have to explore the F.I.D.O. connection later. "Y told me she'd see to my packing, not to bring any of my own clothes. I thought she was choosing clothes that would help me blend in so I could hunt down Zed without calling attention to myself." *Dumb me.*

Rachel shook her head, her smile once more in place, her knitting needles generating enough electricity to power a small city. "You have a lot to learn, Agent 36DD. Everything you wear, use, or drive is designed to kill, maim, or provide escape." Her smile widened. Evidently, maiming and killing were fun thoughts.

"So what does the dress do?" Camryn wasn't sure she wanted to know.

"Right in the vee where the dress plunges, you'll find a small tab. When you pull the tab, the dress unravels to give you enough steel-strength fiber to rappel down the face of a cliff or the side of a building. The underwire of your bra is really a power hook that you secure to the cord. When you flip a small switch located on the strap of your bra, the hook automatically drills into any surface, no matter how hard, and allows you to safely go over the edge."

"But—"

"Your panties contain a corrosive. When you're ready to tackle the cliff, you knot the panties around the exposed part of the hook and pull a tab in the waistband. Anyone who touches the hook gets their fingers burned off." Rachel shrugged. "That way no one can release the hook when you're halfway down the cliff."

"So . . ." Camryn needed a few seconds to assimilate the mental picture. "As I rappel down the cliff, I twirl like a human top while my dress unravels. When I get to the bottom of the cliff, I'm naked."

"That's about it." The click of Rachel's needles sounded like the Baltimore Express coming in on track nine.

"Great." *Neat dress. Please don't let me ever have to use it.* Surreptitiously, she reached down the front and fumbled around. She had to reach a long way because the dress plunged a long way. *Yep.* There was a tab. And she wouldn't wear B.L.I.S.S.'s panties for the rest of her stay. No way was she wearing acid-lined underwear. She hoped Chance had a store where she could buy ordinary panties.

How to ask her last question without offending Rachel? "Umm, the dress is pretty sexy. I didn't get a chance to see the other things Y packed. Are they all—"

"Provocative?" Rachel nodded. "You bet. We want you to be noticed. Zed won't be looking for the obvious. He'll be looking for someone trying to blend in. And with the clothes Y has chosen, he'll notice you big-time."

Won't be looking for the obvious. Once again, Camryn thought of the dark-haired biker. Maybe Zed had come up with the same plan.

Camryn sighed as the black wrought-iron gates that guarded Chance came into view. Owen Sitall's initials were worked into the elaborate design of the metal. She tapped in the code she'd been given on the small remote and the iron gates slid open. Why didn't they creak? Gates like that should always creak. As she stared down the winding drive leading to Owen's lair, she decided there should be a sign posted above them: *Abandon Hope of Passing Go, All Ye Who Enter Here.*

Jace Sentori got off his bike and stretched his arms above his head to get rid of the kinks. He glanced at the black Jaguar parked next to him. Citra was here. Good. Then Jace watched as the pink Cadillac parked nearby. *Pink.* He smiled.

He stood riveted as *she* opened the door and he got his first glimpse of a smooth, tanned leg that went on forever, followed by a bare thigh that . . . The gold dress ended his hopes of visual ecstasy.

The gold dress. The cloth molded her tight little bottom and blended right into her sway as she walked to the car's trunk. And when she bent over the trunk, the cloth gaped to reveal the swell of her breasts above her bra.

A hunter's dress. The big question: Who or what was she hunting? There'd be plenty of rich men here, so if a multimillionaire was her prey, supply wouldn't be a problem. Something wasn't right, though. The three faces peering out at him from the Cadillac were predators, too. But those faces belonged to a different kind of hunter. More direct. More deadly?

He forced his attention away from the woman. He'd made a mistake meeting her gaze back at the tunnel, calling attention to himself, when one of his prime concerns was anonymity.

Jace studied Owen Sitall's mansion, Chance. Two stories, white pillars, perfectly maintained grounds. Looked like a *Gone with the Wind* knock-off. Any minute now a Rhett Butler look-alike would fling open the door, welcome him to Chance, and admit that he didn't give a damn.

Jace didn't give a damn either: about the mansion, about Owen Sitall. He'd do what needed doing, then get the hell out of here.

His glance returned to the woman. She and her gold dress wouldn't be denied. What if she wasn't hunting a rich man? What if they were hunting the same thing?

Jace smiled. Fine with him. He could get into matching moves with those long legs, that sweet seat, and those tempting breasts.

He blinked. No, he'd meant matching *wits* with her. He couldn't let great body parts get in the way of his master plan. The only problem? He

31

didn't have a master plan. But he'd damn well better get one soon.

The older women got out of the car and started toward Chance's door. One of them was carrying a cat. A cat? Ms. Sexy Bottom lifted her mass of red hair from her neck, then started to follow them.

But she must've felt his stare. Hell, how could she not? Turning, she met his gaze. Green eyes. He'd better say something now or be sucked in and spit out, because if she smiled at him, he might just forget about all this keeping-a-low-profile crap and go for what the gold dress was offering. That would ruin everything.

Jace fixed her with a stare that stripped the gold dress from her body; then he smiled. He made it slow, hard, with everything he wanted to do to her in the slant of his lips. "You bring the heat, lady."

She sucked in her breath and quickly turned from him. His smile widened. Point his. Match his. He knew how to play games, and he *always* won.

He stood watching until all the women had gone into Chance. Exhaling sharply, he lifted his stuff from the back of his bike, then stared up one more time at Chance, Owen Sitall's monument to his lifelong obsession with Monopoly. Jace knew this time his smile was pure cynicism.

"The bastard's back, Owen."

Chapter Three

"Welcome to Chance..." The woman greeting him glanced at her gold clipboard. "Jace."

Her red dress was designed for maximum exposure, and Jace had to admit he would've rated the exposure spectacular if he hadn't seen the goddess in the gold dress first.

"I'm Carla, one of Owen's Community Chest. We're dedicated to making your visit memorable. Do you need help getting to your room?" Her glance slid down his body, hinting at how memorable she could make it.

The word *chest* evoked the automatic male eye shift. The Community Chest was, well ... stocked. "No, I'll be fine. If you'll give me my key, I'll go on up."

Smiling, she handed him the key and left. Jace stepped into the ornate entryway of Chance, then whistled low. *Damn*. Red carpet and gold mirrors. It looked like a whorehouse. No subdued good taste here. But then, Owen Sitall was all about excess.

Ignoring paintings of the Boardwalk, photos of Owen with Parker Brothers executives, and sculptures of Monopoly tokens, Jace headed toward the stairs. The gold-and-glass elevator would've taken him up in style, but he wanted as few people as possible to see him.

Camryn glanced up and down the hallway with its plush scarlet carpet and ornate gold mirrors. *What a rush. Alone in the house that Monopoly built.* Well, not technically alone, but at least her B.L.I.S.S. associates were gone for the moment. They'd hurried off to their rooms right after dumping her. Even as she stood abandoned in Owen Sitall's painfully opulent hallway, they were probably squirreled away plotting Zed's demise.

They didn't need her. So far as they were concerned, she was a wart on the nose of B.L.I.S.S. Someone they tried to ignore in the hope she'd go away. Sure, they hadn't said that, but it didn't take a genius to figure out they thought a newbie was a pain in the butt.

Camryn drew in a deep breath to cleanse herself of the self-pity fumes clinging to her. This was what she'd always dreamed of: a chance to prove her strength and courage to the men of her family, a chance to show them she didn't need coddling. She was independent, self-reliant. She was . . . locked out of her room.

She rattled the gold knob and thought ugly thoughts. The key that one of Owen's Community Chest women had given her didn't fit this lock.

Community Chest. Ha! Owen Sitall was a sexist pig. She hadn't seen any hot hunks handing out keys or greeting her at the door. She drew in a deep breath. Fine, so bitchiness was not a positive trait. Just because she'd met someone who might really fit the double-D category didn't give her the right to act mean and spiteful.

She'd just go back and get the correct key. Unless . . .

She glanced down. "Do you do doors, F.I.D.O.?"

The big orange tabby Rachel had plunked down beside Camryn's suitcase before rushing off to her room stared up at her. "Ow?"

" 'Ow'?" Camryn frowned. "What happened to the 'me' part?" She rooted through her purse for the body map Rachel had given her.

Missiles. Bombs. Scent deterrent. Nope, nothing that said door opener. There was a spot marked *Enter.* Maybe . . .

Missiles? Oh, my God! Her fingers shook as she carefully put the paper back into her purse. "Can you really do those things, kitty?"

"Ow." This time the reply sounded confident.

Sudden awareness slammed into her a moment before the man behind her spoke.

"The door giving you problems, sweetheart?" His voice was a husky murmur, a slow slide of sensual promise that the door was no problem at all compared to him. "Let me help." His soft command carried with it a suggestion that he could help with many things. He reached around her for the key.

Let me help. Fighting words to Camryn. *Zed?* While she'd been busy with the stupid door, L.O.V.E.R. could've staged an assault on Chance, murdered Owen, and taken over the world.

She hadn't studied the body map long enough to remember what was where. Besides, missiles might be considered overkill in this situation. She'd rely on the tried and true. As she swung to face the man, she concentrated on every male who'd ever taken a decision from her, demanded she let him help when she didn't want his help.

Somehow she wasn't surprised. The shaggy black hair and hard face were the same. And she'd been right: she'd never thought brown eyes could be cold, but his were dark chocolate after a night in the freezer. Up close he was all male intimidation: big, muscular, with a smile that said, *I'm a man. I can turn the key better than you, little lady.* Flo was right: Camryn might not know his nationality, but she recognized an ass when she saw one.

She waited expectantly for her "gift" to kick in. Glancing down, she noted that F.I.D.O. was rubbing his orange bulk against the man while staring up at him with feline adoration written all over his fuzzy face. So much for Rachel's ultimate weapon.

Camryn returned her attention to the man's face. Okay, when was it going to happen? Y had assured her—

"Ow!" The man's pained exclamation cut off her thoughts.

Camryn frowned. Whatever F.I.D.O. had, it was catching. She followed the man's gaze downward. *Great. Just great.* F.I.D.O. had locked his jaws on the man's ankle and looked like he was in for the long haul. This was *not* what she'd wanted. She'd wanted something quick and less painful. Just something to discourage any more offers of help. How did you turn the damned thing off?

Frantically she ripped open her purse and searched for the map. Handcuffs, truth gas disguised as lipstick, *Who Moved My Cheese?* Where was the stupid map?

"Look, lady, your cat is chewing off my ankle. So forget the purse." He bent over and tried to disengage F.I.D.O. from his ankle.

Camryn could've told him he was wasting his time.

"What the hell are his teeth made of, steel?" His question was a pained grunt.

"Probably." In her nervous desperation, she dropped her purse, scattering its contents across the carpet. She still couldn't find the map.

"What?" His question was distracted, because by this time he was trying to pry F.I.D.O.'s jaws apart, with no success. "Your cat's a demon, lady. Did you know that?"

"I suspected." Maybe if she pressed as many hot dots on her body as she could at once, it would blow F.I.D.O.'s circuits. Then she remembered the missiles. It might blow more than his circuits. Did her insurance cover total destruction of exotic islands? If she survived, which was unlikely, her insurance company would cancel her for not disclosing a preexisting condition: chronic stupidity.

Rachel. She'd call Rachel for help. Camryn scrambled for *Who Moved My Cheese?* At the same time, the man moved and brought his foot down on the book. She closed her eyes at the ominous crunch.

Panicked, she fell to her knees in an attempt to help with the prying process. Just as she was about to abandon the attempt and run for Rachel, she looked up.

Thank you. Rachel was hurrying down the hallway.

Without a word Rachel motioned for her to stand up, then pressed a spot below Camryn's right knee. Rachel whistled softly as she straightened. Camryn was impressed with Rachel's attitude. She wondered how long you had to be an agent before you could whistle while you fumbled around with missiles and bombs?

F.I.D.O. opened his jaws, sat down, then began to clean his face. "Ow." Camryn would've sworn it was a statement of triumph.

Rachel bent down and scooped up the contents of Camryn's purse. She frowned as she studied the squished status of *Who Moved My Cheese?* Sighing, she pulled the body map from where it had become lodged between the pages of the book. "I bet you were looking for this. Oh, and try to be more careful with the equipment. I'll get you another way to communicate." Her expression said,

One that even a complete klutz can't destroy.

As the man straightened, he studied F.I.D.O. through narrowed eyes. "What *is* that?"

Uh-oh. Dangerous question. Camryn met Rachel's gaze. Rachel shrugged, then turned to leave. Pausing, she glanced over her shoulder. "If for any reason you can't reach your knee, whistling will shut F.I.D.O. down."

"I don't know how to whistle." Another failing. All her brothers could whistle. Her father could whistle the national anthem. She'd bet even F.I.D.O. could whistle.

She finally had Rachel's complete attention. "How totally remiss of you. Perhaps you'd better learn." Rachel walked away.

The man. She turned back to find him leaning against the wall next to her door. He looked a little dazed. She couldn't let him go away hurt when it was her fault. Besides, she had to find out more about him, learn whether he might make her list of Zed suspects. She hurried over to him, pausing long enough to cast F.I.D.O. a meaningful glare.

F.I.D.O. ignored her, evidently choosing to relive his moment of glory.

Camryn started to put her hand on the man's arm, but pulled it back. He might think he'd been the victim of an attack by a deranged cat, but Camryn knew the truth. He'd innocently offered his help, and her personal curse had zapped him. Y would be thrilled that it was working, but Camryn felt guilty. She'd been operating on an adrenaline high since getting to Chance, and she'd overreacted.

His gaze touched her hand, then lifted to her face. "No, I'm not going to sue you. And yes, I'd like to know if your cat has had his rabies shots." Even when his tone was cold, it carried enough heat to bring Camryn to a simmer.

"He's had all his shots." She hurried on before she could lose her nerve. "Come into my room so I can take care of your ankle." This was the right thing to do. Besides, she had to find out as much as she could about everyone at Chance. And she had to do it before Zed made her.

Camryn thought for a moment that he'd turn her down, but then he nodded. While he was retrieving the backpack he'd dropped a few yards away, Camryn sneaked a peak at her map, then took a chance on the "enter" command. Pressing beneath her left shoulder blade, she breathed a sigh of relief when F.I.D.O. put his front paws against the door and it clicked open.

The man cast her a puzzled glance as she pushed the door wide and waved him inside. "How did you unlock it?"

Camryn shrugged as she picked up her suitcase. "Guess I didn't put the key in right." She offered F.I.D.O. another warning glare as he followed them into the room.

Once inside, she stopped dead. She blinked. This was a nightmare. This whole place was a monument to over-the-top. Too much red, too much velvet, too much gold. And reminders of Monopoly everywhere, from photographs of

Owen's life-size board to a framed history of the game. Of course, there was the prerequisite Monopoly game sitting on the gold-and-glass coffee table.

But then, who was she to criticize when her wardrobe made her the perfect accessory for this room? Speaking of accessories . . . There was a gold kitty-litter box plunked right in the middle of the room. As much as she appreciated Owen's staff for catering to the pet lovers of the world, she didn't want to have conversations with guests over a litter box, gold or otherwise. Besides, F.I.D.O. wouldn't need it. Offering the man beside her a vacuous smile, she dropped her suitcase, picked up the litter box and set it down in a convenient closet, then shut the door.

"What if he has to go?" His voice seemed a little slurred.

"He'll have to wait." She glanced at the man, then frowned. Something about him seemed different.

"Cold, lady. Really cold." He blinked and ran his palm across his forehead. "No wonder the big guy has a rotten attitude."

All thoughts of F.I.D.O. fled as the man staggered, regained his balance, then yanked off his T-shirt.

"Damn, it's hot in here." He pulled off his boots and socks, then unbuttoned his jeans. "I'm burning up. Can't stand it."

Camryn knew her eyes must be taking up at least half her face as he pushed down his jeans and kicked them away. She had only a millisecond

41

to take in the contrast of white briefs against tanned skin before he slipped them off and collapsed onto the couch.

"Can't get cool. What the hell did that cat do to me?" On that insightful question, he closed his eyes and passed out.

F.I.D.O.? Poisoned teeth? Would Rachel do that? *Sure, she would.* Camryn glanced at the map. *Yep.* There was a "knockout bite" hot dot on her left hip. She had to get him a doctor. Where the heck was the phone?

The cause of the problem stood and padded over to the closed closet door that held his litter box. Planting his ample behind on the scarlet carpet, he spoke his mind. "Ow. Ow! *Ow! Ooow!"* The volume reached glass-shattering levels in a matter of seconds.

Camryn gritted her teeth. *Phone.* Just as she spotted a phone hidden behind a gold statue of a Scottie dog, the front door was flung open and her sisterhood of mayhem rushed in.

Rachel had almost reached the closet door while muttering "Urgent message, urgent message" in a frenzied monotone when Camryn collared her.

"He's unconscious. What did F.I.D.O. do to him? Why did he strip? How do I help him?" She clung tightly to Rachel's arm as Rachel tried to shake her off.

"Temporary effect. The drug F.I.D.O. injected causes a sensation of unbearable heat and a compulsion to remove all clothing. Makes searching a suspect a lot easier. He'll sleep it off. Now let me go." When Camryn complied, Rachel pulled open the door and dragged out the litter box.

Happy once again, F.I.D.O. proceeded to use the box in the time-honored fashion of all cats. As much as Camryn wanted to concentrate on this weirdness, she now had other things to think about.

Flo crouched just inside the doorway with the biggest gun Camryn had ever seen. "Get out of the way, Camryn. Where're they hiding? Point me at the sniveling cowards, and I'll take the suckers out." She swung the gun to cover the whole room as she advanced, still in a crouched position.

Camryn gulped. At least she now knew Flo's purpose in Y's grand scheme of things.

Sara still stood in the doorway, an impatient look on her face. "Calm down, Flo. Nothing's here. Just an unconscious naked man. I don't have time for this nonsense. I was in the middle of studying diagrams of this place and plotting escape routes."

"A naked man?" Flo's eyes lit with an inner fire. She lowered her gun. "Woo-woo, would you look at this? It's the hottie on the Harley. Unwrapped."

Camryn turned her attention back to Rachel. She hoped Flo wouldn't devour the man whole while she wasn't looking.

Camryn opened her mouth to speak, then froze that way, mouth still gaping. F.I.D.O. had done his thing, whatever that was, but F.I.D.O. wasn't a real cat, so how . . . ?

She couldn't finish her train of thought as she watched Rachel push F.I.D.O. out of the box, then root around in the litter. *Ugh! Gross. Yuck.*

Triumphantly, Rachel sat back on her heels and held aloft something small and black. "The disk, ladies, with Y's latest message."

Weighed down by the bizarreness of her world, Camryn dropped into a red-and-gold-brocaded armchair. "Why didn't you tell me about this, Rachel? And what about the man?"

"He'll be fine in a few hours. Let him sleep it off. Search his clothes and backpack while he's out. And don't forget a full-body search. But if he's Zed, you won't find anything. Too smart." Rachel sounded distracted as she fiddled with what Camryn figured must be a miniplayer. "And if you look at F.I.D.O.'s eyes, you'll see the 'urgent message' code flashing."

Camryn peered into F.I.D.O.'s eyes. Sure enough, a series of dots and dashes were flashing in the yellow orbs. Morse code. This was something she understood. When they were kids, her brothers had learned it so they could send secret messages. She wanted to be part of the message sending, so she'd learned the code too.

Rachel wouldn't leave it alone. "I thought you'd be able to figure that out. Y needs a way of communicating top-secret messages that can't be intercepted. F.I.D.O. is programmed to release the disk only into his litter box. I'll give you something you can use for messages when his litter box isn't within range."

Translation: You are beyond stupid. Camryn was beginning to think growing up with Rachel would've been a lot harder than growing up with six brothers. Too bad her "gift" didn't work on women.

One thing Rachel would have to learn that Camryn's brothers already knew: 36DD might not know much about being an agent, but she never gave up. She'd learn how to do what needed doing; then she'd blow right past Rachel. That was if Rachel didn't manage to kill her with F.I.D.O. and the rest of her toys.

"Okay, listen up, guys." Rachel motioned everyone around her. Sara and Camryn leaned close. Flo edged nearer, but never took her attention from the man. She wasn't about to waste one second of ogling time on something as piddling as an urgent message.

"I have disturbing news, ladies." Y's voice held no emotion. Obviously, disturbing news was a daily occurrence. "Reliable sources have confirmed that Zed is aware of who you are and your connection to B.L.I.S.S. Exercise extreme caution. We also have reason to believe Owen might be in danger from several other unknown persons. It is your assignment to protect him from all dangers no matter what the risk to yourself. Above all, this must be kept quiet. If news of this threat leaks to the press, it will cause panic in the world markets, and stocks will plunge. This would play into L.O.V.E.R.'s hands. Have a nice day."

Rachel nodded. "I'm going back to my room. I was right in the middle of my knitting." She glanced at Flo. "And you don't put your gun down just because you see a naked man. If Zed finds out that all he has to do is take his clothes off to immobilize our firepower, we're toast."

Flo nodded, but before turning away she bent down and pressed the spot right below Camryn's left knee. F.I.D.O.'s eyes turned red and there was a muted click.

"Good. Now I'll have a picture to keep me warm at night." With a wicked chuckle, she walked from the room with Sara right behind her.

Camryn still had questions. "Why did F.I.D.O. act friendly at first? And how did you know each time I needed help?"

Rachel laughed softly. "I have a monitoring device, so I know through F.I.D.O. if you need me. And some of F.I.D.O.'s actions are automatic. He's programmed to rub against unknown subjects, collect DNA, run it through his computer, and decide if the subject might be a danger to you. He then activates his protect mode."

Camryn wouldn't go there. F.I.D.O. was *not* smarter than she was. He couldn't even say *meow*. "There's something the matter with F.I.D.O. He only says 'ow.' "

"Hmm." Rachel crouched down and did some of this and some of that to F.I.D.O.

While Rachel was working, Camryn considered the possibility that she hadn't caused the man's injury. On the one hand it lessened her guilt, but on the other it meant she still wasn't sure if she could control the power Y was counting on.

Absently, she watched Rachel fasten a collar around F.I.D.O.'s neck. Camryn stared. "A diamond collar?"

"Zircons. Budget cuts. The agency had class in

my day." She motioned Camryn closer. "You can use the collar as a regular cell phone, or you can use it to receive Y's messages when F.I.D.O. is out of range of his litter box. The collar has a special fastener that makes it almost impossible to remove." Rachel handed her a piece of paper. "These are the speed-dial codes for Y, Sara, Flo, and me."

Great. Something else to memorize. Camryn hoped she wouldn't have to take any calls when someone was around. Talking into a cat's collar could make people question her mental health. "Oh, and why did F.I.D.O. decide the man was a danger to me?"

Rachel stood. "F.I.D.O. should be okay now." She gazed over at the sleeping man. "I don't know what F.I.D.O. found out about him, but F.I.D.O.'s technology is the best we have. If F.I.D.O. has a problem with him, you'd better be careful." With that warning, she left.

Slowly Camryn closed the door and leaned her back against it. *Goody.* She was now alone with a machine that scared the heck out of her and a man who . . . scared the heck out of her.

Chapter Four

Okay, Camryn could handle this. Alone. She didn't need her three sinister sisters here to help her.

She had a naked man who might or might not be the world's most dangerous agent sprawled across her couch, and a machine of cataclysmic capabilities crouched on the back of the couch watching him.

Hey, things could be worse.

She would worry about one thing at a time. First the man. With any luck F.I.D.O. wouldn't feel a need to protect if the man wasn't moving.

Too bad she couldn't cover him up, but he was still sweating like crazy. She didn't want to make him any hotter. Camryn slid her gaze the length of his sweat-sheened body. She pulled her dress

48

away from her breasts to let some air circulate. Sweating must be contagious.

She needed a cooling-off period. A quick look-see through his clothes and backpack before tackling his ankle should take care of that. Besides, the bite didn't look serious.

Sitting cross-legged in front of his pile of clothes, she examined his boots first. No hidden compartments, no weapons that she could see, just expensive, smooth, supple leather. *Smooth. Supple.* Words to conjure decadent images. She allowed herself a quick glance at the man on the couch. *Expensive.* She'd bet he'd be worth it to the woman willing to pay the price.

His T-shirt didn't reveal anything special, but the pocket of his jeans supplied three treasures. Camryn opened his pocketknife to make sure it didn't conceal any advanced weaponry. Just a pocketknife. She returned it to his pocket along with his room key after making note of the number. She held the third object in her hand. She studied it from every angle, wondered what mechanisms were imbedded in its center. She'd dissect it later. Camryn slipped his Snickers bar into her purse. If she found nothing, she'd eat . . . er, destroy the evidence.

He really needed to ask Rachel to supply his clothes. Unraveling jeans would give Camryn one of life's memorable moments.

His briefs had all kinds of special qualities. They burned her fingers without the help of corrosives. Soft, suggesting images of tanned skin and intimate body parts molded in white cotton, clinging, warm . . .

Camryn dropped the briefs. No corrosives, but loads of superheated fantasies.

Carefully she folded his things and put them on the chair. Okay, now for his backpack. Opening it, she peered inside. Laptop. That definitely needed attention. Some more jeans and T-shirts, running shoes, and briefs. A few white shirts for more formal occasions. Didn't look like he'd packed for a long stay, and he was keeping it casual. Unzipping a small leather bag, she took out his shaving stuff, comb, toothbrush, toothpaste, and . . . a packet of condoms. On the surface nothing looked lethal, unless he intended to use the condoms as slingshots. She replaced the bag.

Strange, she hadn't found any ID. No wallet with a driver's license or credit cards.

Now for the laptop. Setting it up, she faced the man on the couch so she could see if he started to wake. Not much chance of that, since Rachel had said it would take a few hours.

His files were password-protected, but the file names widened her eyes. World Domination. Diabolical Machines. Lethal Attack.

Oh, my God! She shut down the laptop and put it back in his backpack with shaking fingers.

Calm down. Zed would be too smart to label his files with over-the-top titles like that. They sounded like video games, for heaven's sake. Then again, maybe that was what he figured anyone coming across them would think. Zed might be arrogant enough to flaunt his plans to the world. She closed her eyes. This wasn't getting her anywhere.

Camryn couldn't put it off any longer. She had to deal with the body search and the man's injured ankle. Her problem? She had to make sure she didn't enjoy the body search too much. That shouldn't be hard, since she was a nervous wreck.

The computer files and lack of ID were suspicious, but she hadn't found any weapons. Of course, that didn't say very much. If anyone searched *her* suitcase, they wouldn't find any weapons either.

Retrieving her first-aid kit, she knelt on the floor beside him and dabbed at his wound with antiseptic. He had strong-looking ankles. She smoothed her fingers over his foot. Nothing lethal there.

Camryn had a feeling this was the only nonlethal part of his body, even if she didn't find any missiles or bombs. She moved her hands over his legs, trying to block out any emotional reaction, reaching for pure objectivity in her search for suspicious bumps beneath the skin. Nope, just hard muscle. She relaxed a little.

Next, thighs. Camryn kneaded his flesh with the slit-eyed enjoyment of a purring cat. She could feel her objectivity sliding down the slippery slope of sexual awareness.

You are a professional. Act like one. This whole search thing was raising her stress level, and her lifelong reaction to stress kicked in. A song bubbled just below the surface.

"This old man, he played one, he played knick

knack on my . . ." As her fingers reached his buttocks, she closed her eyes at the tactile joy of smooth warm skin. *Bun? Perfect rhyme for one.*

Concentrate on the search. She opened her eyes to make sure she didn't stray into any area that didn't rhyme with *one.*

He was on his back, so she couldn't get an overall impression of his buns, but what she could see was magnificent. Firm, rounded. Flo had been right. She touched a dimple in the one she could see. A tongue could do amazing things to that indentation. No hot dot, though.

Hurry up. He could wake up early. The horror of that thought drove her on to the second verse. "This old man, he played two . . ."

Five minutes later she was almost finished and feeling really cranky. *Chest* and *lips* rhymed with absolutely nothing. And nothing in the way of evidence was what she'd found. She forced back a smile. Okay, so she'd found one very fine body. And she now knew the tattoo on his arm said *Game Master.*

You know you're not finished. There was only one unexplored body part left, and it sang a siren song. Camryn didn't for a second believe she'd find a hot dot there, so she had no justification for touching him. *Yes, you do.*

Camryn drew in a deep breath. While she'd been arguing the pros and cons of her hands-on investigation, her search for hard evidence was bearing fruit. In fact, things were hardening at an amazing rate. This must be a reaction to whatever drug F.I.D.O. had injected.

She bit her lip in concentration. Sure she'd seen a few erections, but none this big or this . . . *big*. Definitely suspicious. She couldn't see the base of his arousal. The only way to find out if it was real or an incredible fake was to touch him.

Remember Flo? Would you have believed where her communication system was? Well, no, but . . .

How could she find out if it was a communication device? *Do you know how really dumb that sounds?* Gritting her teeth, she leaned close enough to feel his body heat and react to the scent of aroused male. She spoke directly into his erection. "Hello. Is anyone there?" If it answered her, she'd run screaming from the room.

Silence. *Talk about relieved.*

One more thing and she was home free. She had to touch him to make sure everything was real, no hidden weapons. She'd seen the Austin Powers movie where the fembots' breasts morphed into gun barrels. Wouldn't fool her with that trick. *Do not touch that man's sexual organs. You'll regret it.* That was her brain. Her brain thought in absolutes. Her brain was also bossy.

Live for the moment. Those were her senses. They had a more liberal view on life. *Besides, it's your job. Touch him.* Her senses could be slutty if the opportunity arose.

The bottom line: it *was* her job. She reached for him. "This old man, he played ten, he played knick knack on my—"

"I don't think 'cock' and 'ten' rhyme." His observation was a husky murmur.

No! Camryn yanked her hand from his body.

53

He wasn't supposed to be awake yet. Rachel had said—

"The rhyme for ten is hen. You're in the right family of fowl, but wrong sex." His voice still held a residue of sleepiness. "How does it end? I haven't heard that since I was a kid."

" 'With a knick knack, paddy whack, give the dog a bone, this old man came rolling home.' " Her voice was a mere ghost of its former self.

"Bone, huh?" He paused. "I usually know the names of women who touch my body." The sleepiness had disappeared, but the sensual remnants remained.

Camryn leaned back, distancing herself as much as possible from her point of contact with him. She would have sat on her hands, but she didn't want to be too obvious. "Camryn O'Brien, and I can explain why I was touching you."

He glanced pointedly at his arousal. "Some things are self-explanatory." He pulled himself into a sitting position. As he glanced up at F.I.D.O., his gaze sharpened. "Is your cat going to attack me again?"

F.I.D.O. returned his glance. "Me?" He blinked big yellow eyes.

The man looked at Camryn. " 'Me'? What happened to the 'ow'?"

Camryn drew in a deep breath, trying to recapture her fleeing patience. She'd have to talk to Rachel about F.I.D.O. But first she had to make this man believe she hadn't been copping a cheap feel while he slept. "He's a halfway kind of cat."

"There wasn't anything halfway about his clamp

on my ankle." His gaze shifted, grew more personal, traced a path of positive energy over her face and throat, then plunged along with her dress's neckline to explore new energy sources. "What's his name?"

"Name?" She didn't want to talk about the damned cat. She had to explain why she'd been touching him. "Meathead." She would *not* tell him her cat's name was F.I.D.O.

"Fits." He stared at the cat. The cat stared back. "Where'd you come up with that name?" He swung his feet to the floor, then walked over to retrieve his clothes. "After you tell me that, you can tell me about yourself and what happened after your cat bit me." His back was a solid wall of smooth, tanned skin stretched over hard muscle; his attitude was smooth seduction stretched over hard resolve. Dangerous.

"I was taking your pulse when you woke up. There's a major artery in the groin area. . . ." Like he would believe that?

He glanced over his shoulder. His lips lifted along with one expressive brow. The word *liar* hung between them. "Let's hear about Meathead."

Make this good, Camryn. She had to convince him that she was ordinary middle America. Hoping that brilliance would strike at a higher altitude, she shifted from the floor to the couch. "He belonged to Dad, and Dad was a huge fan of the old TV show *All in the Family*. So when we got a kitten, Dad named him after one of the show's characters. The name is dorky, but it stuck." *Work on his sympathy.* She lowered her lashes so he couldn't read her expression. "Dad passed away last year. He loved Meathead so much that he made me promise to keep his cat with me wherever I went." Dear old departed Dad was probably out in his driveway back in Seabrook cursing up a storm as he tried to keep his beloved '67 Corvette running.

The man's expression was neutral. "What about your mom? Any brothers or sisters?"

He was digging for information. If he was Zed, he'd be suspicious of everyone.

Camryn shook her head. "Mom died when I was a baby." The one truth in her whole pile of verbal dog poop. "No brothers or sisters. Just me." Good thing she wasn't hooked up to a lie detector, because right about now the machine would explode from lie overload.

"Sounds like your dad and you had a great relationship." His gaze shifted back to Meathead.

"The best." And she would lie until her tongue fell out to keep Dad and her brothers safe.

"Must be nice."

She might not be able to see his expression, but she couldn't mistake the bitterness in his three words. He didn't elaborate.

"So why'd Meathead latch onto my ankle?" Jace had pulled on his briefs and jeans. After putting on his boots and sliding his T-shirt over his head, he returned to sit beside the redhead on the couch.

"He's protective. He sensed you were dangerous."

She watched him out of the greenest eyes he'd ever seen. Colored contacts?

"*Are* you dangerous?" She leaned closer, and the faint scent of lavender and sensual possibilities was a major distraction. "Who are you?"

"Dangerous? Depends on the situation. Everyone can be dangerous." Jace waited as she gathered her resolve to lob the ball back into his court. "Even you."

She crossed those incredible legs, and he watched that almost-nothing dress ride up her smooth thighs. She heaved a sigh of barely contained impatience, dragging his attention up to the swell of her breasts, which threatened to burst free with each new breath she took. Reluctantly he lifted his gaze. Her red hair tumbled around a face dominated by those huge green eyes and a mouth made for sin.

She narrowed her eyes. "Who . . . are . . . you?"

He smiled. *Interesting.* A lot of women's voices got shrill when they were mad. Hers became a throaty purr of warning. "Jace." He'd better tell her something if he expected her to reciprocate.

"Just Jace?" She offered him a smile that would probably act like a truth serum on most men, but he wasn't most men. "So, Jace, why're you here, and what do you do when you're not here?"

Jace rose and wandered over to the wall of glass that overlooked Owen Sitall's extensive grounds. He frowned at the hedges shaped into the various Monopoly tokens. He wondered if insanity ran in the family. "I'm here because my boss is here."

Camryn rose and joined him at the window. "Your boss?"

Jace refused to look at her. If he didn't see her, she couldn't influence what he said, couldn't tempt him to tell more than it was safe for her to know. But he could *feel* her. He hadn't counted on that. "I'm a bodyguard, Camryn. I'm here to see that my boss has a good time, wins a few million, then goes home safe and happy."

"Wins a few million?"

Sliding a glance at her, he could see her chewing on that information, trying to decide whether she believed him. "Yeah. I'm also a game expert. I make sure she comes away a winner." He watched her gaze drop to his Game Master tattoo. Camryn couldn't know all the games he played, or that he never lost.

"Your boss must be pretty famous to warrant a bodyguard. Do I know her?" She frowned down at Meathead, who had plunked his massive bottom on her shoe and didn't look about to move.

He shook his head. "I doubt it. Citra Nella. She's a wealthy recluse. Widow. Her husband made his fortune in oil, died, and left her to enjoy his money."

"Citra Nella?" The corners of her lips tipped up in a smile that would have laid him out flat if he'd been looking at her, which, of course, he wasn't. "What an unusual name." Her voice indicated mild amusement, but her eyes held more than casual interest.

"An appropriate name for an unusual woman.

Citra has some unique talents." He narrowed his gaze on one of Owen's tokens being readied to start its rounds on Owen's giant board. "Looks like one of the guests is about to play a round of Monopoly."

Camryn followed his gaze. "This whole island is amazing. Twenty miles of game board, tokens that are priceless treasures, a man who lives and breathes games . . ."

"Only one game. Owen needs to diversify." Good, he'd distracted her from questions about himself. "But who's complaining? Only select guests are allowed onto the island, and they usually walk away richer for the experience. When they play with Owen, winning is a sure thing. I hear he never wins." He cast her a searching glance, but she only nodded. "Luckily Citra's wealth is her ticket."

"And what's your ticket?"

They were back to him again. "I work for her. Employees are invisible to Owen as long as they do their work." *A big mistake.* Owen would find that out the hard way.

Camryn nodded, but her attention shifted as the token started its trip toward the coast and Owen's board. "What *is* that?"

"The thimble. Onyx with one priceless black pearl. It belonged to Queen Victoria." The oversize replica showcasing the real thing wasn't a cheapie either.

"Wow. Owen must've put down a bundle for that." Her awe sounded genuine. *No hidden agenda.*

"Owen has a talent for . . . acquiring priceless tokens for his Monopoly board." He hoped she was innocent, because he wouldn't let anyone get in the way when he made his move.

Time for him to be out of here, but he found he sort of liked being close to Camryn O'Brien. And not because he hadn't gotten all the information he wanted from her. "Guess I'd better be going." He frowned. In his enjoyment of Camryn, he'd forgotten about several things. "You never finished telling me about Meathead. Why'd I pass out after he bit me? And who was that woman who came by, touched your knee, then walked away?"

He didn't miss the quick shift of her eyes, the way she bit her bottom lip. That lip fascinated his body, but didn't keep his mind from recognizing that Camryn O'Brien was about to lie to him.

"I'm not sure, but it looked like you had an allergic reaction to his bite. Just a guess." She shrugged.

Jace smiled. She needed to practice her lying technique, avoid telltale body reactions that revealed her nervousness. He watched her gaze slide away from him, noting the reflexive twining of her fingers in her lap. "And the woman?"

"She's a coworker." Camryn seemed to relax into her story. "I work with Rachel and two other women for Creature Comforts. We travel to the homes of wealthy clients and provide relaxation services to relieve stress." She smiled as though it should all be perfectly clear now.

Jace frowned. "What kinds of relaxation services?" He didn't know if he was going to like this, or even why he cared.

Her smile was a small tilt of challenge. "You're glowering."

"I'm not glowering." He glowered some more.

"We provide a wide range of services. . . ." She paused, drawing out the tension. "None of them illegal. Flo is a masseuse. Rachel is a feng shui and aromatherapy expert, and Sara is an expert in relaxation techniques involving hypnotism and meditation. Mr. Sitall brought us here to spend several weeks lowering his anxiety level."

Jace thought about that. "Sounds crazy to me." Crazy enough to be the truth? "So what do you do?"

Her expression said she was growing impatient with his grilling. *Tough.*

"I'm a psychologist. I'll be talking to Mr. Sitall during the next two weeks, attempting to help him resolve his issues." She met his gaze. Trying to figure out if he was buying her story?

"Issues? The only thing wrong with Owen Sitall is too much money and time on his hands. Someone should teach him how to win a damn Monopoly game." He drew in a deep breath. *Stupid.* He should've learned by now that emotion didn't change anything. "So how does your husband"—he glanced at her bare ring finger—"or boyfriend feel about you running around the world working as a rent-a-shrink?"

She paused before answering. What was there to pause about? He did some mental head shaking to clear out the cobwebs of suspicion clogging his thought processes. She was probably exactly what she said, even if the three women with her set off warning bells. But just in case, he'd have Citra check her out.

"No husband. No boyfriend. I travel a lot, and I wouldn't want a long-distance relationship." She stared out the window as she spoke.

Jace couldn't read her expression, but he wasn't going to waste any more time wondering about her, no matter how interested he was. He had to do what needed doing, then get off the island. "Well, thanks for . . ." *Don't say it, Sentori. Let it rest.* He was going to say it. He needed to work on his self-discipline. "The laying-on-of-healing-hands thing. If that part of my body is ever bothering me, I'll know who to call." He left her with mouth open, ready to blast him off the island.

Jace dropped his backpack in his room, then ran down the stairs rather than wait for Owen's gold-and-glass elevator. He had to remember to avoid the elevator. The walls were a glass cage, and he didn't intend to be the pigeon caught inside. He wanted as few people as possible to suspect he was around until he was gone. By then it would be too late.

Slowing down as he reached the bottom of the steps, he strode toward Owen's bar, the Water Works. Like everything that Owen did, it was too much: gold, mirrors, and red velvet, with the ever-present reminders of Monopoly everywhere. All lit by Owen's priceless Waterford crystal chandeliers. The chandeliers showed the only good taste in

the room, including the guests. This was a place
to flaunt wealth . . . and other things.

Citra would be flaunting her other things. She
wasn't hard to find. He just headed for the mob
of men clustered in one of the darkened corners.

"Whips and tight leather are delicious, sweetie."
The throaty purr drifted from the center of the
mob. The mob squirmed, flexed, and swelled. "I
still prefer black net stockings and six-inch heels.
Presentation is so important for the total experience." The heat flowing from the center of the
mob was enough to make Owen's air-conditioning
unit self-destruct from pure futility. "Chains are re-
dundant. It's all about attitude. The woman has to
be in total control. Would you like to know what
I'd do with a man in my total control, sweetie?"
The mob's desire to know was a primal groan of
need.

"First, I'd—"

Jace forced his way to the center of the mob.
Men turned to object, then moved aside after
glancing at his face.

He was in a roaring bad mood by the time he
reached Citra. She sat at a table loaded with
drinks offered up by the mob to their new goddess. Lifting a frosted goblet to her lips, she showcased her long, perfect, bloodred nails. They
matched her lips. She took a sip from her straw,
then raised her gaze to Jace. Her dark eyes promised long, hot, sensual nights. The slight curve of
her lips mocked her promise.

"Is it time to go?" Taking a last sip of her drink,
she stood, then lifted her waist-length black hair

off her neck and sighed. The small act of standing drove the mob back with a collective groan of regret.

Jace nodded, then stared hard at the mob. A corridor quickly opened. Jace motioned Citra through the ranks of her devotees, then followed her. She was dressed completely in clinging black silk, and every inch of her shimmered in the chandeliers' light. Jace allowed himself a small grin. The sway of that walk could bring down empires. Probably had.

Jace guided Citra from the building, then stopped in the middle of the long circular driveway. Glancing around, he made sure there was no place close enough for anyone to hide, to listen. "You have a strange way of *not* calling attention to yourself."

Her smile gave away nothing. "Sometimes hiding in plain sight is the most effective. Who would suspect me of being anything more than I seemed back in the bar?"

He would. But arguing with Citra would be a waste of time. "I met a woman, Camryn O'Brien. Room two-fourteen. She's here with three older women." He wouldn't mention his run-in with Meathead. No man wanted to admit he'd been laid out flat by a fat cat. "She might be one of the hunters. We need to check her out."

Citra nodded, all her warm and beckoning sensuality gone. What was left was coldly professional. "You have good instincts, Sentori. I checked the women out as soon as we had word they'd passed through the tunnel. The three women are retired

B.L.I.S.S. agents. I don't know about Camryn O'Brien. Probably a new agent." He sensed her frown. "I wonder why B.L.I.S.S. is sticking its nose into this? Might be something bigger than we thought."

"What the hell is B.L.I.S.S.?"

For the first time Citra looked unsure. "It's an international crime-fighting organization. Very shadowy. No one knows too much about them, but they only come out for the biggest events. They're heavy hitters."

And Camryn was a member of B.L.I.S.S.? He couldn't think about that right now. "I don't care about anything bigger. I just want to collect the things I came to get; then I'll be out of here." He drew in a deep breath of frustration. "And I don't need your help. I like to take care of things myself."

Citra's gaze softened. "Sure you do, Sentori, but the U.S. government has a big stake in your success. Owen is an American citizen, and if you fail, it could mean a diplomatic Armageddon. So they sent me."

A diplomatic Armageddon? Obviously failure couldn't be one of his options. "Are there any more agents in place?"

Her smile was once again mocking. "Just me." Her expression assured him she'd be all he needed.

"Sure." He didn't like working with Citra, but it looked like he didn't have a choice. "I'll pick you up at your room at midnight."

She nodded and started to turn away.

"What happens if any of the hunters we're expecting show up tonight?" At least it didn't appear Camryn would be involved.

Shadows hid her expression. "We kill them." He listened to the click of her heels as she disappeared into the darkness.

Great. Just great.

Chapter Five

"Don't stand there looking like someone just left you at the altar, Camryn." Rachel's order was an impatient hiss. "Smile. Stick out your chest. Make these rich suckers think you're even richer than they are."

"My chest *is* stuck out." Maybe not 36DD stuck out, but she was doing the best she could. She glanced around Owen's crowded game room. The overwhelming glitter and glitz seemed at odds with the game of Monopoly. She'd played the game with Dad at their kitchen table when she was a kid. Monopoly was a wish-fulfillment game. These people didn't need it. They probably already owned their share of hotels. "Where's Owen?"

Flo, who'd slipped into a blue sequined jumpsuit for the occasion, nodded toward one of the monitors that was following the progress of the ruby slippers as they rolled along Pacific Avenue. The slippers stopped, and the man at the monitor vibrated with excitement. "I'll buy it." He turned and beckoned to one of the women circulating with golden trays. "Banker!"

The woman bounced over to him. Okay, so only a specific part of her bounced.

"Humph." Sara's opinion was clear. "You'd think a grown man would know better." She smoothed her hand over her plain black suit jacket, then reached up to fluff her white hair.

"Yeah." Camryn turned her attention to Owen Sitall. "He's old enough to be those women's grandfather. I can't believe he calls them his Community Chest." Owen really did look like the character on the Parker Brothers game: tux, top hat, gray handlebar mustache, and cane. A walking caricature.

Sara cast her a puzzled glance. "I wasn't talking about the women. I meant that buying Pacific Avenue was a mistake. He doesn't have enough cash left to cover the rent when he lands on Park Place or the Boardwalk. And he'll land on one of them. He always does." With a militant glint in her eyes, she strode over to Owen and sent Ms. Community Chest away with an imperious wave of her hand. "Okay, Owen, let's talk strategy here." She bent down and whispered in his ear.

Owen's eyes widened; he grinned, and then he pulled Sara down beside him.

"Would you look at that?" Flo didn't try to hide her disgust. "I've had my hands all over that man's body today, and he didn't smile like that at me."

Rachel cast her an impatient glance. "You're a masseuse. You're supposed to have impersonal hands."

Flo grinned. "Honey, my hands are *always* personal when a man's body is involved."

"Forget men's bodies. We're here to keep Owen Sitall alive and find Zed. That's *all* we're here for." Rachel spun to take in the rest of the area, where everyone was either engrossed in ordinary Monopoly game boards as they huddled at small, intimate tables or seated around the periphery staring intently at one of the many monitors that ringed the mirrored room.

Camryn still found it mind-boggling that the cash the Community Chest carried around like a tray of munchies was the real thing. No play money for these folks.

"I'm going to circulate, try to identify possible suspects. You need to introduce yourself to Owen, Camryn." Rachel strode away with a swish of her flowing red silk gown. Camryn understood the loose and flowing concept. Rachel probably had enough machines under that gown to wipe out an army of Zeds.

"Huh. Forget men's bodies? Why would I want to do that? Just because Rachel's a dried-up old prune doesn't mean I have to be one." Flo looked at Camryn. "What do you think about men's bodies?"

"Umm." She'd thought a lot about Jace's body in the last few hours. Not many men had gotten to the naked stage with her, but the few who had didn't affect her the way Jace did. And since Camryn liked to analyze things, she'd tried to figure out her reaction. Maybe it was the obvious power of his body coupled with his complete vulnerability while he lay asleep on her couch. What woman could resist strength and vulnerability wrapped up in one beautiful package? A purely physical response, but dangerous to her assignment just the same. "Men's bodies are okay."

"Just okay?" Flo made a rude noise. "What a wuss. I bet you didn't even take advantage of that prime piece of manhood you had sprawled all over your couch today." She didn't wait for Camryn's reply. "Think I'll visit the rest room. My knife has shifted, my ammo needs adjusting, and one of my handguns is poking me in the spine." She started to move toward the door. "Oh, after you check in with Owen, you might want to make a perimeter check of the grounds. Sara usually does that." She cast Sara a slit-eyed glance. "But she's too busy sucking up to Owen right now." Flo paused. "Don't go outside by yourself, though. You're a newbie. You need experience riding shotgun for you. Grab Rachel or me when you're ready to leave." She disappeared into the crowd before Camryn could reply.

"Well, how great is this, Meathead?" She looked down at the orange death machine, and he stared blandly back at her. "We so don't fit here. You look like you should be sitting on a fence somewhere scoping out garbage cans, not wearing a zircon-studded collar with a leash attached to it. Okay, so I need a way of communicating with Y and the others, but something a little less weird would've been nice."

Meathead offered her a soundless glance of agreement.

"Yeah, and look at *me*. I'd kill for a dress that's sole reason for being was to cover my body. Do I get it?" Meathead opened his mouth to reply. "Don't answer that. This black nothing I'm wearing is loaded with small transparent bugs. In theory, I rub against a suspect and transfer the bug. See any likely suspects, Meathead?"

"Ow." Meathead was sympathetic.

"Right. *Nada*. Besides that, I didn't bring my purse, and the dress is too tight to hide a toothpick. I can't sit down because I refuse to wear panties capable of eating a hole in me, and they don't sell panties at Chance. I'm tottering around on heels so high they could give me a nosebleed. And do you know how uncomfortable it is walking around with this map of my hot dots stuck down the front of my dress? By tomorrow I'll have it memorized, but that doesn't help me now." *Bring on the padded cell.* She was talking to a robot.

Meathead gazed up at her. "Me."

"Fine. It's always about *you*, isn't it?" She gave Meathead no time to comment on that. Trying for sexy and confident, she walked toward Owen.

She glanced down at her feet to make sure they were still in sight. Walking in these heels made her feel like she was doing the clown-on-stilts thing. So of course she didn't see the brick wall until she slammed into it.

Brick wall? She gazed up . . . and up . . . and up.

Good grief! This was the biggest man she'd seen up close and personal in . . . well, ever. He had to be more that a foot taller than her five feet seven, with a WWE-quality body. The fact that he wore an expensive suit didn't lessen the impact. She lifted her gaze a little higher. Not what she'd expected. This man's face was as close to perfect as she'd ever seen: dark blue eyes, straight nose, sensual mouth, framed by long golden hair that hung past his shoulders. She blinked. Where were the quickened heartbeats, the gasping breaths, the instant attraction she'd felt with Jace? Maybe her reaction was delayed by shock.

"I'm Peter. Peter Bilt. I'm Mr. Sitall's bodyguard, and I don't let anyone I haven't ID'd close to him. Who're you?"

"I'm Camryn. Camryn O'Brien." She offered him her best rich-bitch smile. "I'm one of the Creature Comforts partners. I'm here to make your boss feel better."

"Where's your proof?" He was talking to her, but he was gazing over the top of her head.

"Proof?" *How about the weapon of mass destruction I have on this leash? The one sitting on my foot and just waiting to vaporize you. Or maybe you'd like me to pull out the hot-dot map hidden in my bra? Hot dots that, when pressed, could possibly throw Earth out of its natural orbit.* "Well, silly me. I left my driver's license in my room. But if you ask Sara—that's the lady leaning against your boss—I'm sure she'll verify my identity."

He nodded, but his gaze still didn't meet hers. Curious, she turned to see what was so interesting behind her. Nothing. Just a mirror. *Now why . . .*

"Do you think I should have another inch taken off?" He moved past her to get closer to the mirror.

Another inch off where? She thought of Jace. She smiled. "Keep all the inches you can. Inches impress some women. Call me shallow, but I like a lot of inches on a man."

Peter finally met her gaze. "You think so? Maybe I'll just get the dead ends cut off." He seemed to forget about her completely as he pushed and shoved at his hair, studying the effect in the mirror.

Camryn shrugged. "Looks like Peter found someone more fascinating than us, Meathead. Let's go meet Owen." She tottered over to where Sara was whispering in Owen's ear. With anyone else, Camryn would suspect the whispering involved romance. With Sara? Probably just strategy suggestions.

Sara and Owen looked up as Camryn planted herself in front of them and coughed loudly.

"Oh, Camryn." Sara was flushed and looked a little off-kilter. This was not the face of the duty-at-all-cost B.L.I.S.S. agent Camryn knew. "This is Owen Sitall. Owen, meet my partner, Camryn O'Brien."

Owen glanced up and offered her a perfunctory smile, but Camryn could see he wasn't focused on her. She glanced down. Meathead was sure focused. He was rubbing against Owen's leg and purring to hide his true intent. *Uh-oh.* She remembered what had happened last time he'd done the rub-and-purr thing. She had to get him away from Owen.

"Well, this is really great. I've been a Monopoly fan my whole life. In fact, this is such an adrenaline rush that I feel a little faint. Think I'll step outside for a minute. Let's go, Meathead." She dragged a pissed-off Meathead behind her as she headed for one of the open French doors leading to the patio.

Glancing back, she offered Owen and Sara a finger wave as she stepped onto the patio. She drew in a deep, relieved gulp of warm night air. *Close call.*

Meathead sat on her foot with enough force to squish her toes. She looked down. He glared up. "Me! Ow!"

She glanced at the darkened driveway. "Okay, okay. So you were only trying to do your job. But if you'd clamped your jaws on Owen's ankle, we'd both be kicked out on our fannies."

Meathead's expression indicated that only those with death wishes would try to kick his fanny.

Now that she was out here, Camryn might as well do her perimeter check. She knew she was supposed to have one of the others with her, but she had Meathead for protection. And one of her goals was to learn not to depend on others for help. This was a chance to test her independence. Besides, Owen was inside, and that was probably where Zed was, too.

She strolled to the opposite side of the circular driveway, then paused to decide her direction.

Two shadowy figures moving down the driveway caught her attention.

It was midnight, and there was something stealthy about the figures. They seemed to be hugging the side of the driveway, staying in the darkened patches of shadow cast by overhanging trees.

Suddenly alert, she also moved into the shadows and followed them. She didn't have far to go. They had a car parked around the first curve in the drive. A low-slung black car. An expensive speed machine that rightfully *she* should've been driving as a testament to her B.L.I.S.S. status. Fine, so this was no time for petty jealousy.

With widened eyes, she watched the shorter of the two figures hand a gun to the other. Then they both climbed into the car. This clandestine meeting reeked of covert action. *Zed? Could be.* Why were they sneaking away? She had to know.

For only a moment, she considered calling for backup. *No.* This was her baby, her opportunity to go it alone. Besides, she had Mr. Mass Destruction on the leash beside her.

Camryn hurried to the Cadillac as fast as her demon heels would allow. She touched the handle. A muted click indicated that the computer had read her prints and unlocked the door. Freeing Meathead from his leash, she plunked him in the passenger seat, then climbed behind the wheel.

When she pressed the ID pad on the steering column, the Cadillac rumbled to life. No matter what aspersions she flung at its unique "pinkness" and boatlike dimensions, she had to admit T had made some great modifications to the car. She also knew that behind a small panel on her steering wheel were a few goodies guaranteed to slow down, if not annihilate, life's baddies. Camryn hoped she'd never have to use them.

Following the black car would prove a little harder than she'd anticipated. The driver hadn't turned on his lights. If that didn't prove evil was afoot, then nothing would. Camryn wondered if she was up to the challenge. Gritting her teeth, she turned off her headlights as soon as she drove around the first curve. Luckily there was a full moon and no side roads between Chance and the coast, with its miles of Monopoly board. No opportunity for her quarry to turn off and lose her. Fortunately there were no other cars on the road.

Almost before her eyes could start hurting from squinting at the darkened road in front of her hood, she'd reached the coast. The driver parked the black car in a narrow strip between Pennsylvania Avenue and a cliff that dropped to the sea. The only break in the darkness was a spotlight focused on the board.

Camryn gulped. She was too far away and it was too dark to see the water, but when she opened the car door she could hear the distinctive sound of waves crashing against the cliff and smell the salt air. She'd bet that cliff dropped quite a way. She was sort of sorry she wasn't wearing one of her unraveling dresses.

Leaving her car in the shadows, she crept toward the two figures. Meathead padded beside her.

The shorter of the figures was fiddling with something attached to a pole beside the Monopoly board. Probably a camera. It was hard to see because green and red buildings kept getting in the way. Fewer houses and hotels would make spying a little easier. But on the other hand, they also hid her approach.

Suddenly Camryn heard a strange sound. She looked down. Meathead was growling. Low, rusty, *scary*. Only imminent danger could activate this warning. She swung in a circle, scanning the various shades of black. Forest, buildings, road . . . *Darn it*. She couldn't see clearly because she'd been staring at the lighted board.

The sound of a gunshot followed immediately by the angry-bee buzz of a bullet whizzing past her elicited a startled yelp from her. Never had the word *past* brought such relief.

Reality sank in. Someone had shot at her!

Her feet were in run-like-hell mode, but her body subscribed to the hit-the-dirt-and-curl-into-a-fetal-position response. Compromising, she crouched down and hoped the shooter wouldn't be able to spot her in the dark. She focused her attention on the black car, then scanned the area for its occupants. Everyone had disappeared. Almost before Camryn could register this, a macabre figure burst from the darkness. It stopped in front of her and . . . cackled.

"The ruby slippers belonged to my sister, and now they're *mine*. You can't have them, little girl." With another way-too-authentic cackle, the Wicked Witch of the West tucked her broomstick under her arm and sprinted into the forest.

Camryn stood staring after her with gaping mouth. A real honest-to-Oz witch: black cape, green face, stringy hair, and pointed hat. She blinked. *Wait.* What had the witch been carrying besides her broomstick? Ruby slippers. She'd stolen one of Owen's priceless tokens.

Camryn glanced down at Meathead. He was busy scratching a virtual flea. Strange that Jace warranted an attack, but the witch didn't even rate a flicker of interest.

The gunshot. Who had been shooting at her? Carefully, Camryn advanced toward the black car. Meathead followed uninterestedly.

Camryn saw them as she rounded the corner of the last hotel. The smaller of the two figures lay on Pennsylvania Avenue with the larger one crouched over . . . her. The lighted board revealed that the smaller figure was a woman dressed completely in black.

Camryn must have made a noise, because the larger figure suddenly rose and swung toward her. Camryn's gaze never reached his face; it was fixed on the gun in his hand. The gun he was slowly raising to aim at her.

Reflexively, she reached into the front of her dress and clasped Meathead's map in shaking fingers. Glancing at it quickly, she had only seconds to make a decision. Disabling nerve gas seemed appropriate for the situation. Refusing to second-guess herself, she pushed the hot dot on her right hip, and waited for Meathead's lightning-fast reaction.

And waited . . . and waited. The only reason she wasn't dead was because the gunman seemed fascinated by Meathead. Glancing down, she saw why. Her intrepid protector was busy retching. *Goody.* She was in mortal danger, and Rachel's ultimate weapon was busy hacking up a hair ball.

Camryn couldn't help it: she began to hum.

Meathead finally managed to cough up a small glowing sphere. This was definitely not the launch she'd envisioned. It did not sail in a deadly arc to land at the feet of her enemy. It just sort of plopped out at her feet. *Oh, boy.*

Mesmerized, she stared unblinkingly at it. Any second now it would detonate, sending a cloud of gas into her face. She wouldn't be able to move. Of course, she couldn't move even before it detonated. She hummed louder.

Vague, unrelated thoughts drifted through her mind. She'd have to talk to Rachel about Meathead. Would her lifeless body sprawled across Pennsylvania Avenue ruin Owen's game? And where was the Wicked Witch of the West taking the ruby slippers?

Too bad the gunman wasn't as immobilized as she was. He lunged toward her. No, he was lunging for the glowing sphere. Scooping it from in front of Meathead, he flung it over the cliff.

Her gaze followed its path and watched as it exploded before hitting the water, spewing a yellow vapor into the surrounding air. At least the exploding part worked okay.

The man turned back to her. He moved closer, but she didn't need to go nose-to-nose to identify him. As he'd snatched up Meathead's aborted launch attempt, she'd recognized his Game Master tattoo.

Camryn swallowed. She sort of felt like hacking up a hair ball herself. She fingered the map still clutched in her hand. Tempting, but she didn't think she'd try any more weapon launches until Rachel checked Meathead out. Her shoe? Rachel had explained all about the shoe. Meant for close fighting, it was a weapon of last resort. Well, this was about as last-resort as Camryn ever hoped to get. Bending down, she ripped off her shoe and brandished it at the still-advancing Jace. "Don't come any closer or—"

His smile was grim. "Or what? You'll hum another verse of 'Three Blind Mice'?"

Behind Jace, Camryn could see the woman on the ground starting to sit up. Who were the bad guys in this whole thing? She wasn't sure, but she was very sure about who had the gun. And he still had it pointed at her. She fingered a tiny switch on the inside of the heel.

Her hand shook as a beam of light shot from the bottom of the heel and vaporized a nearby bush. She drew in a deep, calming breath. Rachel had told her what the weapon of last resort did, but seeing it in action was a whole new experience. "I think you'd better put down your gun."

He didn't put it down, but he did drop his gun hand to his side. "We'll discuss this as soon as I take care of my partner." Ignoring her neat little vaporizer, he turned and strode back to the woman in black, who'd managed to get shakily to her feet.

Since her life didn't seem in imminent danger, she pressed the shoe switch to off and slipped the shoe back on. It was comforting to know that at least one of Rachel's weapons could be depended on. She cast Meathead a meaningful glare. He stared blandly back at her. And if she didn't know any better, she'd swear she saw a glint of amusement in those evil yellow eyes.

Jace helped the woman into the black car, then returned to where Camryn still stood. "When she heard the shot, my partner dove for cover and hit her head. She's a little groggy." He frowned. "She seems to have a few memory problems. I have to get her back to Chance so a doctor can take a look at her."

"Memory problems?" Camryn had absolutely no memory problems. She remembered exactly how big he was. All over. She remembered in detail the warmth of his thighs beneath her fingers, the elusive scent of cool danger and hot possibilities. Oh, yes, her memories were sharp and clear. Unfortunately her memory of the whizzing bullet was also sharp and clear. Had he shot at her? Camryn could've sworn he hadn't known she was there.

He almost seemed to have forgotten her as he stared into the darkness. "The witch got the ruby slippers. I hope to hell someone picks her up before she leaves the island with them."

This was so bizarre. "You've lost me. Someone shot at me. Was it the witch?"

His gaze sharpened. "Someone shot at *you?*"

His expression grew shuttered. "I don't think the witch had a gun."

Thinking back, Camryn realized the witch hadn't been holding a gun, just a broomstick and the ruby slippers. Then who had shot at her?

He shook his head as if to clear it, and she watched the play of light over his dark hair. She resisted the urge to reach up and smooth several stray strands back into place. They should stay out of place. He wasn't an every-strand-in-place kind of guy.

"Who was that . . . person who ran off with Owen's ruby slippers?" *Who are you?* "Did you shoot at me?"

"No."

"No? No what?" She needed explanations here. She needed a reason to believe him.

He exhaled wearily. "No, I didn't shoot at you. My gun hasn't been fired." Silently he offered her his gun.

Gingerly she accepted it. Checking it quickly, she handed it back. He'd told the truth: it hadn't been fired. Her relief seemed out of all proportion to the discovery. "So who's the ruby-slipper thief?"

He shrugged, the material of his black T-shirt showcasing the flow of hard muscle across broad shoulders. "Some demented *Wizard of Oz* fan?" His smile was grim. "The Wicked Witch of the West come to claim her inheritance? It doesn't matter. She's just one of the hunters, and I can't let them stop me."

"Stop you from what?" *Who are you?*

She recognized the exact moment his attention shifted from the witchy thief to her. His gaze darkened, warmed. When had he moved so close? She resisted the urge to step back, to shift her glance from the sensual promise of his lips, to admit that she wasn't able to concentrate fully on B.L.I.S.S. business when he focused all that superheated maleness on her.

"From this." He bent down and touched her lips with his. When she didn't retaliate with vaporizing beams or deadly nerve gas, he wrapped his arms around her and deepened the kiss.

The warm slide of his tongue across her lower lip suggested that his tongue needed more room to experiment. She opened her lips to his suggestion. His exploration was all searing excitement and lightning strikes of sensation. Her small, involuntary moan seemed a catalyst as he slid his hands down her back and cupped her bottom, pulling her into him, forcing her to acknowledge his hardening resolve. Her own resolve was turning to mush in direct proportion to his hardening.

Suddenly he froze, his explicit curse a warm good-bye against her cheek. Pushing her away, he looked down.

With a feeling of inevitability and loss, Camryn followed his gaze.

Meathead had chosen a different mode of attack this time. He'd decided that for his encore he'd do a climbing-the-tree routine. He'd wrapped all four paws around Jace's jeans-clad leg and seemed undecided about what to do next. Evidently the material wasn't allowing Meathead to dig his claws in as deeply as he wanted. Meathead looked a little grumpy about this.

Jace raked his fingers through his already unruly hair and glared down at his fat orange attacker. "Between that black dress you're almost wearing and your devil cat, B.L.I.S.S. doesn't need any other weapons."

Camryn almost stopped breathing. *He knew about B.L.I.S.S. How? When?* "Who the hell are you?" *And why does Meathead keep attacking you without my pressing the "protect" hot dot?*

Was she the one causing the attacks on Jace? That thought wouldn't leave her alone. She'd been sure she'd caused the first attack until Rachel had told her differently. But this time? She hadn't even thought about using her gift. Y had assured her that she was the master of her power, but what if under extreme duress it still exploded out of control? Possible.

The evidence? Jace had saved her from the gas bomb. The fact that she hadn't been doing much to save herself didn't matter. Her brothers could've told Jace that saving Camryn from anything was an invitation to disaster. But she still wasn't sure.

Camryn shelved her thoughts for the moment. Her first priority was finding out how Jace knew about B.L.I.S.S. *Zed would know about B.L.I.S.S.* No, she didn't want to believe that. And she wasn't stupid enough to think too deeply about the why and wherefore of her want. She'd just chalk it up to her intuition. After all, Y believed in Camryn's intuition.

Blinking, Camryn noticed that while she had been tossing thoughts of power and want around, Jace had removed Meathead from his leg and started to walk away. He hadn't answered her question.

She wouldn't try to stop him. He had to get his partner to a doctor, so she'd wait for another chance to—

"Agent 36DD, are you alone? This is Y. We have important information on the man F.I.D.O. collected DNA from. Please acknowledge."

Camryn glared down at Meathead. Meathead gazed serenely back at her with the urgent-message code flashing in his eyes. "What's the matter with you? You're supposed to deliver a *secret* message. Secret as in not blabbing it to the world. Doesn't any damn thing work right?"

"Were you talking to me, Agent 36DD? I didn't quite hear you." Y sounded impatient.

She knew Jace had moved back to her. Camryn could feel him. The air shimmered and heated with his closeness. *She* shimmered and heated with his closeness. Camryn recognized on an intellectual level that this was not a good thing. But on a primal level? Hey, it was great.

His breath moved against the side of her neck, and goose bumps on far distant parts of her body sprouted joyously.

"Aren't you going to answer your cat's collar, sweetheart?"

Chapter Six

Jace watched Camryn huff her frustration, then bend down to pick up her cat. He'd swear the orange devil had a gleam of anticipation in his eyes.

Cradling the cat in her arms, she pressed one of the diamonds on its collar. The cat chose that moment to express his joy of living by breaking into a rumbling purr. It wasn't just any purr. It was an eighteen-wheeler thundering down the interstate, a 747 taking off at Kennedy.

"I'm not alone." Camryn was pushing on the diamond again and again.

She was probably trying to disconnect so he wouldn't hear anything. He leaned closer. It was tough hearing her above the cat.

The warning glance she shot his way bounced

right off him. No way was he leaving until he found out what was going on.

"Hello? Hello? Are you there, Agent 36DD? There's a lot of static on the line. Anyway, F.I.D.O. sent us results on the DNA it collected from Owen Sitall and the unidentified male. We're dealing with Jace Sentori, the illegitimate son of Owen Sitall. Sentori has had no contact with his father since he was a child, so I would assume he's on the island for purposes other than a reunion."

Camryn widened her eyes, cast him a surprised glance, then bent closer to the collar. "I'm not alone!" She did some more pressing with no obvious result. Evidently nothing was going to keep this Y person from her appointed babbling.

Camryn's shout was a whisper in the wind. The cat just cranked the thunder up another notch. That was one damned happy cat.

"Jace Sentori could well be Zed, or he could have a completely different agenda. He's a legend in game circles. His board and video games are creative miracles. They call him the Game Master. What we need to know is if he's also the pawn of L.O.V.E.R. If he is, we need to eliminate him."

Jace narrowed his gaze. He didn't like the attitude of this Y person.

"I . . . am . . . not . . . alone!" Camryn's screech would have shattered Owen's priceless crystal chandeliers.

The cat seemed to take this as a personal challenge. His rumble escalated to a meteorite-impact-with-Earth level. Jace would bet that astronomers around the world were scanning their instruments searching for the cosmic catastrophe.

"Here're your classified instructions. Make sure you pass them on to the others." There was a brief pause.

Rumble, rumble.

"Are you sure you're alone, Agent 36DD?"

Rumble, rumble.

Camryn shot him a frantic glance. "Whistle."

"Whistle?" He was losing it. Too many nights spent on the Tricops video game. Wicked Witches of the West, secret agents with names like Citra Nella, devil cats named Meathead, and now the most spectacular agent 36DD he'd ever seen wanted him to whistle. *36DD?* He smiled.

"Anything. Whistle any damn thing you want. Whistle 'Dixie' for all I care. But whistle."

Jace whistled the Notre Dame fight song. Owen used to sing it to him before he decided he didn't want a son anymore. It didn't surprise Jace that he'd thought of the song now. He was on Owen's island, and that was bound to rattle old memories. What bothered Jace was how much emotion the song stirred. He'd thought he was beyond feelings a long time ago.

Rum . . .

The purring stopped. Jace had never realized how great silence could be.

"Here's what you need to do to ascertain how much danger—"

"I'm not alone!" Camryn's voice was still geared to compete with the rumble.

"You don't have to shout, Agent 36DD. You

should've told me sooner. This could have serious repercussions. I'll be in touch."

The click ending the transmission hung between them.

Carefully, making sure she didn't meet his gaze, Camryn placed the cat on the ground.

Jace watched warily as the cat plopped its bottom onto her shoe. At least it didn't have any immediate plans to try another leg attack.

"Okay. I want some answers." Jace stepped away and noted her obvious relief. *Good*. This was one time he didn't feel any guilt at using his power to intimidate. "Who's this Zed? Why're you investigating me? What's L.O.V.E.R.?" He tried to slam the door on his growing anger, but it slipped through a crack and exploded. "What the hell's going on?"

She finally met his gaze, and he read regret there. "Sorry, I can't tell you anything. It's all classified information."

"Do you think I'm this Zed character?" Out of all the questions demanding answers, he hadn't a clue why that particular one took precedence.

She studied him for what seemed like centuries. Then she shook her head. "No. My gut feeling says you're not Zed."

"Do you always listen to your gut feelings?"

"When they're telling me what I want to hear." She offered him a slight lift of her lips, a softening of her gaze. And he felt the shift from deadly serious to sensual.

"But you could be someone much more dangerous." She let the innuendo hang out there to catch the breeze and indicate wind direction.

He wasn't going to let her get away with a diversionary tactic. "If you won't tell me anything that's 'classified,' at least tell me what this F.I.D.O. is that somehow collected my DNA."

Camryn looked down at the cat. Jace followed her gaze.

"Meet F.I.D.O., short for Feline Intelligence Defense Operative. He collected your DNA when he attacked you."

"You're kidding." He stared at the cat. The cat offered him a smug, superior smirk. He could hate that cat.

"You must've known he wasn't a real cat." She edged a little farther away from him. Meathead dutifully followed her and plunked down on her foot again.

"Yeah. I sort of got the picture when he hacked up that gas ball." Jace moved a step closer to her, never letting her put too much space between them. "That's not what I was doubting. You actually want me to believe that F.I.D.O. is a defense weapon?"

She looked insulted. He liked the small, angry pout that reminded him of how sweet her lips were.

"F.I.D.O. is one of our ultimate defense weapons. He can do almost anything."

Jace wondered if he could increase her pout. "Uh-uh. Wrong name. They should've called him D.U.D., for Dubious Ultimate Defense. He almost killed you with that misfiring gas ball."

She now did some lip biting. The wet sheen of

those lips was the real ultimate weapon. F.I.D.O. could've chewed his leg off while he lost himself in the taste, the feel, the—

"He has to have some kinks worked out of him."

Jace saw the exact moment her thoughts changed direction.

"Why're you on the island?"

Offering her a smile he hoped would irritate the hell out of her, he threw her answer back at her: "Sorry. Classified information."

She narrowed her gaze. "How did you know I was part of B.L.I.S.S.?"

He'd hand her a small piece of information, something that wouldn't tell her anything about him. Because no matter how much he'd like to deny it, he wanted Camryn O'Brien to stay interested in him. *Go figure.* "Citra told me." He started back toward the car. "That's my exit line. I have to get Citra back to Chance." He glanced over his shoulder. She hadn't moved. "Oh, and a friendly warning: stay out of my business, and I'll stay out of yours."

"Citra's not your boss. So who is she?"

Jace ignored her shouted question as he slid behind the steering wheel and glanced across to where Citra leaned back against the headrest with closed eyes. "Are you okay?"

"Not quite." She didn't open her eyes.

Jace frowned. He should've gotten back to her sooner. But then who would have saved Camryn from F.I.D.O.?

"I can't seem to remember anything." A frown line formed between her eyes.

Great. "You're a secret agent assigned to return Owen Sitall's ill-gotten tokens to their rightful owners before an international incident erupts." Maybe he needed to tell her something more basic. "Your name is Citra Nella."

"Citra Nella? No joking?" Her throaty laughter mocked the possibility. Then she winced. "God, that hurts. Why would anyone have a name like Citra Nella?"

"Your mother owns the biggest pest control company in California, Nella's Bugbusters, and she has a warped sense of humor." He shrugged. "You told me that citronella is a volatile oil that attracts when it's used in perfumes, repels when it's used against mosquitoes, and controls barking dogs. It can be toxic in its purest form, causing initial stimulation followed by depression of the central nervous system. You seemed to think that your mom picked a great name."

Her smile was dark sensuality. "I like the symbolism."

Strange that Citra's obvious sexual pull didn't affect him, while Camryn . . . Maybe he shouldn't go there right now. He had to think about how Citra's memory problem would affect him.

She'd probably be back to normal in a few days; meanwhile Jace would be able to work the way he liked best: alone.

Jace knew he was wearing his predator's smile, the same one he wore when launching a new game that would flatten the competition. He had no intention of staying out of Camryn O'Brien's business.

Glancing in the rearview mirror, he watched Camryn climb into her pink Cadillac. Putting the Jaguar in gear, he sped toward Chance. Citra's sleek machine would leave Camryn's ancient relic in its dust.

If Camryn weren't driving so fast, she'd be bouncing her head off the steering wheel in angry frustration. *Stupid, stupid, stupid.* Her first real test as a B.L.I.S.S. agent, and she'd failed. She'd stood with her mouth open while a crazy witch stole the ruby slippers, and then she'd watched helplessly as Jace saved her from the plopping gas ball. Her reaction to the gas ball bothered her the most.

Once again, she felt like she had when she was ten years old, waiting for one of her brothers to save her from the huge spider that hid in the garage, Danny Miller in fifth grade who used to jump out from behind Mrs. Jenson's hedge and kiss her, or any number of horrors she'd expected her brothers to handle. She wasn't that child anymore, but she'd felt the same way tonight.

And mixed with her anger at herself was a nagging sense of guilt. She'd made the right decision in not telling Jace anything about her assignment. Just because he was Owen's son didn't mean he wasn't dangerous. But the soft core of Camryn O'Brien, like a pudding that no amount of cornstarch could harden, insisted that he should know his father's life was in danger.

She drew in a deep breath of determination. He probably wouldn't care that his father's life was in danger. He was skulking around the island with his own agenda. And from what he'd said, she surmised the ruby slippers were part of his agenda. She'd tell the others what had happened and see what they suggested.

Reluctantly, she returned her attention to her driving. Staying on Jace's tail like this called for concentration. She was so close to his bumper that if he stopped suddenly, she'd be toast. She patted the Cadillac's dashboard. The old lady could really move. "You're okay."

The radio static warned her she wasn't alone. "You doubted, dudess? The Big Smooth is more than okay. I don't do trash. Since you're not into a pursuit right now, you might want to back off the pedal. Speed kills. And, like, you should put some space between the Big Smooth and whatever you're tailgating. Remember, delicate machinery costs megabucks to fix."

Delicate machinery? The Cadillac was about as delicate as a tank. Camryn hated mean sarcasm. She never used it. She used it now. "Isn't it time for a cookies-and-milk break, T?"

"That's beneath you, dudess. Talk to ya later." He didn't sound flattened. She'd have to work on the sarcasm.

When she reached Chance, she parked beside Citra's sleek Jaguar. The black car looked small and colorless beside the flamboyant Cadillac. Camryn smiled. She needed every perceived edge she could gain against Mr. Sentori.

Glancing around the shadowed parking area, she allowed herself to think about the unthinkable. Someone had tried to kill her tonight. Who?

Someone in league with the thieving witch? Zed? She needed to talk to her partners.

Once inside, Camryn hurried to the game room. A quick glance assured her that Owen had left. Rachel and the others were also gone, probably with Owen. Everyone seemed calm, so Citra must have managed to disable the camera before all the action went down.

Camryn turned to leave. She'd find Rachel and get her to work on Meathead again. He had to understand that when she pushed "launch," it meant more than six inches. She'd memorize the hot-dot map as soon as she got back to her room. If she needed to shut Meathead down, she couldn't depend on passersby to whistle for her.

"Hey, I wanted to thank you for your advice on my hair."

Camryn looked up. She hadn't noticed Peter Bilt standing by the door—which was amazing in itself. A rock would notice this man. He hadn't lost any of his magnificence in the time she'd been gone. "Sure. No problem."

"I was on my way down to the board. The camera went out on Pennsylvania Avenue and the boss couldn't finish his game." Peter shrugged. "Just because he was winning for a change was no reason to get bent out of shape. Anyway, he wants me to personally take care of it." He slanted her a smile intended to send her panting and whimpering to her knees. "Want to keep me company?"

Camryn slid her gaze over Peter's massive frame. She should be jumping at the chance, but nothing hummed when she looked at him. He was a beautiful man and all that, but—

"I'd like to discuss contacts with you."

"Contacts?" Her attention snapped into high alert. "Who're your contacts?"

His smile slipped from sensual to puzzled. "You've lost me. I meant contact lenses. I have blue now, but I thought maybe violet might look better with my tan. What do you think?"

Camryn sighed. "Keep the blue. They're you. I think I'll pass on Pennsylvania Avenue. It's been a long day." Out of habit she scanned the room one more time . . . and spotted Jace standing in a darkened corner with a spectacular woman. Long blond hair, never-ending curves. Camryn hadn't even seen the woman's face yet, but she already hated her.

It was a female thing. She was duty-bound as a woman to hate anyone built like that. Her attitude had nothing to do with the fact that the woman was cozying up to Jace. Camryn didn't give a damn about Jace Sentori other than how he impacted her assignment. "Who's that woman over there?"

Reluctantly, Peter dragged his gaze from his reflection in the mirror. "Huh? Oh, that's Honey Suckle. My sister. She's the keeper of tokens." He grinned, and at least twenty women in the room took fortifying breaths. "Don't you love the title? She's in charge of making sure the tokens stay safe and in good shape. Besides the tokens, she's also sort of morphed into the boss's personal assistant."

Camryn frowned. *Wink, wink* was implied if not stated. This was a woman close to Owen Sitall and also to the tokens that Jace Sentori seemed to covet.

"Honey just got through helping that guy get his boss to bed. Ms. Nella was doing some exploring outside and bumped her head. Doc Nitski is up looking at her now." His gaze shifted back to the mirrors, dismissing anything that didn't involve himself.

With Jace's obvious interest in the tokens, it only made sense he'd be interested in talking to the person in charge of them. But *why* was he interested? "Your parents chose . . . distinctive names for both of you." She forced her attention back to Peter.

He acknowledged her attention with a little-boy grin. "Dad named us. He felt a boy's name should sound tough and a girl's name should be sexy. Honey dropped her last name a long time ago. Honey Suckle Bilt didn't flow."

Camryn nodded. "Makes sense to me. It does have a certain descriptive panache to it, though. Think I'll wander over and say hello. I love her dress. Maybe she'll tell me where she got it." The dress looked like Rachel had designed it: short, silver, and shimmery. She'd bet it didn't unravel so Honey Suckle could rappel down cliffs though.

"Panache?" Peter lost interest once Camryn's attention shifted to his sister. He shrugged. "Yeah, well, I guess I'd better get moving on that camera. The boss went up to his suite, so he should be okay while I'm gone."

Distractedly, Camryn watched him go. She could probably strike Peter and his sister off her suspect list. If they'd wanted to kill Owen, they could have done so a long time ago.

Camryn frowned as she looked back at Jace. B.L.I.S.S. had done background checks on all the guests presently at Chance, and had come up with zip. Everyone seemed legit. Jace and Citra seemed to be the only question marks. Either Zed hadn't arrived yet, or he wasn't a registered guest. All of the island's employees had been with Owen a long time.

As much as her curiosity pulled her toward Jace and Honey Suckle, she had something more important she could do now while he was occupied.

Not giving herself a chance to think about things that could possibly go wrong, she headed for Jace's room. Once outside his door, she stared down at her orange shadow. "Maybe you should stay outside."

Meathead's return glare indicated that staying outside was not an option.

Sighing, Camryn pressed beneath her left shoulder blade. She didn't have to check her map to find the "enter" hot dot. Meathead did his paws-against-the-door thing and she heard the click of the lock. Easing the door open, she slipped inside. She felt the slide of soft fur against her ankle, indicating that her orange stealth machine had also slipped inside.

Closing the door quietly behind her, she pressed a link on her gold bracelet, and a narrow beam of light focused on the carpet in front of

Camryn. Quickly, she scanned the sitting area. Nothing.

She glanced down at Meathead, who sat staring up at her; then she pulled out her map. There it was: "protect." She pressed the hot dot on her left side. Miraculously, Meathead stayed put as she moved from Jace's sitting area to his bedroom. Meathead was unreliable right now, but he was all she had. She didn't have time to find one of her partners to help in the search. She only hoped Honey Suckle kept Jace occupied for a while. She refused to examine her conflicting feelings about that last thought.

A quick but thorough search revealed nothing new. She focused the beam of light on the only thing she hadn't examined: the bed. It squatted in the middle of the room, a monument to bad taste. Covered in black velvet, it blended into the darker shadows. Only its four gold posts gave away its position. Thank heavens Owen had stopped short of the prerequisite mirrored ceiling. Instead he'd opted for a row of naked cherubs marching across the headboard.

After pulling back the covers and finding nothing, she carefully replaced them. Only one more place to look. Getting down on hands and knees, she peered under the bed. Her beam of light picked out a scrap of paper stuck between the inner springs and frame. She wiggled a little farther under the bed to grasp it.

There was no warning, just the sudden slide of a warm hand across her bottom. She squeaked her alarm and tried to wiggle out from beneath the bed. The hand held her firmly in place.

"Scoping out dust bunnies, Agent 36DD? Don't think you'll find any here. But don't let me stop you from looking."

Jace Sentori's husky murmur alarmed Camryn more than any full-throated roar of anger. "Get your hand off my bottom."

His soft laughter mocked her demand. "Now, why would I want to do that?"

He slipped off her heels and drew a fingertip along the bottom of her foot. She curled her toes in alarmed response. "What're you doing?" Frantically she reached for her map.

"It's called self-defense. Wouldn't want those shoes to go off accidentally and vaporize one of my essential parts."

He kneaded her bottom in a seductive rhythm that mimicked the sudden clenching of her own essential parts. As she opened her mouth to issue a cease-and-desist order, he slid his free hand along the back of her leg and thigh, pausing only when he reached the hem of her dress. It was dangerously close to her clenching essential parts.

"I love long bare legs. I'm getting excited thinking about what they'd look like in black stockings." His breath warmed the back of her thigh. "They remind me of the great times I've had with leather, whips, and chains."

Oh, my God!

His soft chuckle almost made her collapse on her face with relief. He was only kidding.

"Let me up." *But don't stop doing what you're doing.* Camryn hoped her brain and body would reach a consensus soon. "Where's Meathead?" Why hadn't he warned her? She glanced at the map. Would the robot work even though B.L.I.S.S.'s wondercat wasn't in the room?

Jace glided his fingers a little higher on her thigh. Heat exploded, racing unchecked from where his fingers touched her. If he moved his hand under the hem of her dress, the heat would probably melt her hot dots, making her questions moot.

"You mean F.I.D.O., alias Meathead?" Jace sounded a little distracted. "When I opened the door he slipped out. Trotted toward your room like a cat in search of a litter box."

The darned cat had deserted her. He'd deliberately left her in the hands of . . . Camryn's focus shifted and blurred. Wonderful hands. Jace Sentori's hands were the hands of a wizard, smoothing sizzling circles on her appreciative bottom. She wondered briefly what those hands could do on even more receptive body parts.

"No panties?" His soft murmur suggested wicked intent. "I understand the true meaning of B.L.I.S.S. now: Bun Lovers Investigate Sexy Spies." He slipped his fingers beneath her hem.

That was it. She was out of here. She didn't have the internal fortitude to stand up to this type of attack. Give her guns and grenades any day.

But how to escape? Her malfunctioning shadow was long gone, Rachel and the others were heaven knew where, and her will to resist Jace's particularly effective attack was fading fast.

Jace didn't hesitate. Pushing her dress up over

her bottom, he drew a line of hot intent with his tongue. She shuddered, for a moment allowing the tactile wonder of his mouth touching her bottom and the soft flesh of her inner thigh to seduce her.

She had to remember something . . . panty hose. She had to buy some panty hose. Rachel had said that in an emergency, panty hose could be whipped off and used to strangle a man. But why would she want to do that? She couldn't recall.

She shook off her growing sensual lethargy. Y had said she could control her power. Now was the time to test it. She tried to concentrate, forcing aside her need to spread her legs further, to invite him and his talented tongue into her house. She focused on one thing: something had to stop him, because she sure couldn't.

His soft curse coincided with his sudden withdrawal from her bottom. Her bottom felt bereft. But she couldn't comfort her bottom now. She wiggled from beneath the bed and sat up.

Jace sat on the floor near her, clasping one leg and grimacing. "A cramp." He forced the explanation through gritted teeth as he rocked back and forth.

The trembling started in Camryn's heart and worked its way to the surface. She'd done it. This wasn't a coincidence or a random cramp. *She'd* caused it. For the first time in her life, she believed in her ability to control her power.

But with the awe came guilt. She should race back to her room while he was essentially helpless, but she couldn't. The B.L.I.S.S. attitude was too new to her. She couldn't walk away from pain she'd caused.

Moving to his side, she reached for his leg.

"I'll take care of this." His words were pained expulsions of breath. "Go find your robot before he nukes the world."

Well, sure, she could do that, but she pretty much suspected that Meathead was crouched in his gold litter box while Rachel, Flo, and Sara hovered in anticipation. She'd rather help Jace. "I think the world will be safe for a few minutes while I help with your cramp."

Camryn felt his resistance as she rolled up his pant leg and started to massage the rock-hard muscles of his calf. Gradually she felt the loosening, the relaxing that signaled his release from pain. Her tightening was in direct proportion to his loosening.

She had to do something about the silence stretching between them, a silence that gave her time to dwell on how good touching any part of him felt. Her job was to find things out. The only thing she was finding out here was how much she wanted to feel Jace Sentori's naked body stretched beside her.

Finally she sat back on her heels and studied him. "Someone shot at me tonight." Probably Zed. "My own cat almost killed me with an exploding hair ball, and I found squat in your room."

He didn't look at her as he rolled down his pant leg. She fixed her gaze on his Game Master tattoo and once again wondered what games he was playing at Chance.

"Tonight has been the pits." Okay, so her foray under his bed had had some up moments. "You could make my night if you'd tell me why you're here."

He met her gaze, and she wished he hadn't. His gaze was heated promise with a savage undercurrent that excited even as it scared the heck out of her.

"I could make your night in a lot of ways, Camryn O'Brien. Let me know when you're ready." His voice was a soft slide of seduction, tempting her, making her want to forget B.L.I.S.S. for just one night of *real* bliss on that black bed.

She wouldn't, of course. Camryn was a woman on a mission. She couldn't be sidetracked by sexy men with secrets. "Don't hold your breath." Scrambling to her feet, she headed for the door.

As she reached for the doorknob, she sensed him behind her. She could feel him, his connection to her a thick layer of awareness slowing her movements, tangling her in a web of what-ifs. What if she didn't open the door? What if she turned to him? What if she slipped the black dress off? What if while they were making love he pressed the wrong hot dot?

What if she got the hell out of here? With grim determination, she turned the knob.

"Don't you want to know why I'm here, sweetheart?"

Chapter Seven

Jace watched Camryn wrestle with her dilemma. Should she escape while she had the chance, or stay and satisfy her curiosity?

Amused, he noted her sigh of surrender. But his amusement was tinged with regret—regret that only curiosity would keep her with him.

Jace turned on the lights and turned off his regret. He didn't care if she stayed with him. Sure, he wanted to have sex with her, but that was it. And he was telling her about the tokens only because B.L.I.S.S. might come across information that could help him. Citra had said they were the good guys, so he'd take her word for it.

"You can turn off your bracelet now. Have a seat." He gestured at the red couch.

Never taking her wide-eyed gaze from him, she gingerly perched on the end of the couch. He smiled. Her eyes grew wider. He'd have to work on his fatherly *trust me* smile.

Jace thought about joining her on the couch, but decided that getting too near her black dress would scramble his brain cells. He wondered if she'd take it off. Probably not.

"So let's hear it, Sentori. I have things to do." She made a valiant attempt at sounding casual.

Wiggling farther back on the couch, she did the tugging thing with the dress hem. The dress didn't respond. *Good for the dress.* He loved that dress.

In lieu of cozying up to her dress and ripping it from her body, he paced. Motion helped to keep him focused. It also kept more primitive instincts from mobilizing their forces and attacking his common sense.

"The only reason I'm telling you anything is because if I don't, you'll keep sticking your nose"—*Your bottom.* He smiled—"in my business. Once you know why I'm here, I want B.L.I.S.S. to leave me alone."

"That depends on what you tell me." She folded her hands in her lap and tried to look stern.

He could tell her she didn't do "stern" well. Jace suspected his grin was bordering on predatory.

Trying to defuse the grin, he thought ugly thoughts. *Raw clams. High-fiber foods. Tapioca pudding.* It worked. He frowned. Strange that all his ugly thoughts were centered on his mouth. Jace glanced at Camryn's mouth, incredibly edible even when she tried for serious. *Well, maybe not so strange.*

"I'm waiting." She looked as though she wanted to tap her foot impatiently, but didn't dare because any motion would impact the position of her dress. She settled for some lip pursing.

He stared at her lips and drew in a deep, steadying breath. *Raw clams. High-fiber foods. Tapioca pudding.* It wasn't working this time. Jace couldn't hold back his grin: hungry, wanting.

He turned away to stare out the French door at the darkness, but he could still see her reflection in the glass. "Owen is bullheaded and stubborn. He's used to getting everything he wants. He's a firm believer that money *can* buy happiness. Except for Monopoly." Jace knew his smile had turned cynical. "That board game has defied him his whole life. It's the only thing that has ever defied him. Ergo this place."

Jace pushed aside the bitterness that still wanted a voice, even after all these years. He hadn't taken Owen's name, hadn't even seen Owen since he was six. And so far as he knew, Owen hadn't wasted a second's thought on his bastard. A secretary in some remote corner of the Sitall empire had written a support check each month until Jace reached eighteen. Jace could never compete with Owen's all-consuming passion, Monopoly.

"You don't sound like a loving son, so why are you here now? And why don't you want Owen to know you're here?" Her words were measured and noncommittal, but in the glass he could see her leaning forward, her interest evident.

"It's hard to play the loving son when you haven't seen your father since you were six." In the door's reflection, he watched her expression soften, turn sympathetic. He didn't need her sympathy—*anyone's* sympathy. He'd long ago stopped wanting a father-and-son reunion.

"I was six years old when I beat him at Monopoly. That was too much for his oversize ego to take. Mom left with me the next day. I haven't seen him since."

A frown line formed between her eyes. "You can't make me believe a man would banish a six-year-old who beat him at Monopoly. There must've been another reason." She drew her bottom lip between her teeth as she thought.

Jace fixed his gaze on the pool of light marking the entrance to the mansion and refused to think about her lip, as thought-provoking as it was. He needed to get this conversation over with and get her dress out of here. "You might have done research on Owen Sitall, but you don't know the real man. He doesn't take humiliation well, and I humiliated him by winning." Jace shrugged. "So I had to go. To be fair, he probably would've sent me packing anyway. Children have never been part of his game plan."

"Okay, so assuming that's true, why did you come back?"

Jace narrowed his gaze on the parking lot. It looked like another guest was arriving. All guests were of interest to him. "I deal in the game world, and word has come down that Owen is acquiring stolen tokens. Very rare tokens. Some of the owners have discovered where their property is, and they're sending people to retrieve it. The owners don't want all-out war with Owen"—he smiled into the glass, and she picked up the smile and returned it—"because when you're the richest man in the world, living on an island that's a veritable fortress, you are for all intents and purposes above the law."

She nodded, and her red hair was a fall of flame around her face. Distracted, he searched for the rest of his story.

"The short of it is, there're hunters out there now who don't care how they make their money. If they have to kill to get the tokens back, so be it."

Her expression sharpened. "Could the shot that was fired have come from someone helping the witch steal the ruby slippers?"

He shrugged. "Could be. All I care about is returning the tokens to their rightful owners so Owen won't be a target anymore because of them." He held up his hand as she opened her mouth to ask another question.

"Why am I doing this? In the Sentori family, blood ties are important. Lucky for Owen we have the same DNA, or else I'd let the hunters have him. And as much as I'd like to sit back and watch Owen get his butt kicked, family takes care of family."

"I see why you don't want him to know you're on the island." Her voice was soft, with a note that puzzled him. "Won't he recognize your last name?"

"He won't see my last name. Employees don't interest him, so he'd never check." Jace watched two men emerge from the car that had just parked. He narrowed his gaze. Kilts? "Looks like two new guests have arrived."

"I can help you, Jace."

Help him? He didn't want help, only information. "Forget it. I work alone. There's not much I can do about Citra's help, but I don't have to put up with anyone else." He exhaled sharply. With that attitude, Camryn probably wouldn't even share the time of day with him.

His diatribe rolled right off her.

She surprised him by smiling. "I guess we're kind of alike. We both want to do it our way. What about your mom? Didn't she help you?"

This was it. This was the last bit of family history he'd share, and he was sharing only in the hope that she'd give him some information in return. He was surprised he'd opened up as much as he had. "When I was eight, Mom married a guy from France. She was too involved with him to worry about what I wanted. He never adopted me, and that was fine with me." He shrugged.

That part of his life didn't bother him. He liked being a Sentori and wouldn't have wanted to be anything else. "She shipped me off to her parents when I was nine." He smiled at the one great memory of his childhood. "I grew up in south Philly with Grandma Sentori and her Italian cooking. Grandpa taught me to play baseball and took me to the Phillies games. They taught me the *real* meaning of family."

She nodded, her expression serious. Camryn O'Brien was cute when she was serious. "Family is important." She looked like she wanted to say something else, then thought better of it.

"So what's B.L.I.S.S. here for?" Jace tried for a hopeful expression. He really didn't expect her to blurt out classified information, but at least she might tip him off if she came across any of the hunters.

"I can't tell you that." Camryn felt awful. He looked so hopeful, and she couldn't tell him anything. "But I'll keep my eyes open for anyone asking about the tokens."

He nodded. "Fair enough. I can guess you're here because of Owen. Citra thinks it's something big if B.L.I.S.S. is involved." He offered her a cynical smile. "Big guns aren't brought in for the little people of the world."

"Little people don't have the power to bring down governments." She shouldn't have said that.

"True." He turned and moved back to tower above her. "I think I'll go down and see what I can find out about the new guests. Seems a little weird that someone would show up at this time of night."

Camryn took her cue and left. She could feel the power of his gaze all the way down the hall. As much as she wanted to wait until he left his room, then follow him to scope out the new arrivals too, she knew she had to check in with the others and retrieve Meathead. Because as crazy as it seemed, she was becoming attached to the orange horror. He did everything wrong, but he sure did try hard. She sighed. Just like her.

She opened her door and stepped inside. Three senior citizens with big guns crouched, ready to blow her away. Ignoring them, she kicked off her heels. "Wow, that feels good."

Meathead spotted her and padded over to plunk himself on her foot. His gold litter box sat in the middle of the room, so he must have delivered his message.

Camryn had to shuffle over to join the others, because now that he was reunited with her, Meathead wasn't about to desert her foot. She blinked to clear her fogged brain cells. *Reality check.* He wasn't a real cat. But she still didn't have the heart to dump him off her foot. "Anything important?"

Three accusing gazes were turned her way.

"Every message from Y is important." Rachel tucked her gun into the waistband of her jammies. "She said you already know Jace Sentori's identity, but she has some new information." Rachel's gaze sharpened. "Who was with you when Y called?"

"Jace Sentori." Camryn steeled herself for the inevitable reprimand. "He heard more than he should."

"That wasn't very wise, sweetie." Flo sounded distracted as she searched for somewhere to tuck her gun. Her gauzy, sexy nightgown for aging sirens didn't seem to have any convenient place to stash a weapon.

112

"How could that happen, Camryn?" Rachel sounded more puzzled than angry.

Camryn shifted her gaze to Meathead, and everyone's glance followed hers. Meathead offered them a silent meow. "He was making so much noise that Y couldn't hear me saying that I wasn't alone. I tried to disconnect, but the zircon wouldn't work." She frowned. "You've got to fix him, Rachel. He almost killed me with a gas bomb that didn't launch. And he started purring without a hot-dot command. If I hadn't gotten Jace to whistle, he'd still be purring."

Rachel looked as though Camryn had slapped her. "He was working perfectly when I gave him to you." Her gaze turned thoughtful. "Why were you with Jace Sentori, and why did you try to launch the gas bomb?"

"I'd followed him because I thought he might be Zed. And the launch was . . . an accident." Camryn wondered at her conscious decision not to tell them any details of her night's adventure.

"We could be talking sabotage here." Rachel bent down to check Meathead's collar.

Camryn shook her head. "He's been with me every minute."

Rachel's glance was impatient. "F.I.D.O.'s a computer, Camryn. Have you ever heard of hackers?"

How did Rachel always manage to reduce her to stupid-newbie status? "So what did Y have to say?"

Diverted, Rachel pulled up the message on her watch. "Jace Sentori is here to retrieve some tokens his father stole from a few very unforgiving people. On the surface it seems he's acting out of concern for Owen's safety. I don't know if I believe that. Owen didn't treat his son well, so there's no reason for Jace to give a flip about his father." Rachel tapped a steady rhythm on the face of her watch with the tip of her finger as she thought. "Jace Sentori is a genius in the electronic game world. He'd have the smarts to sabotage F.I.D.O." She allowed a small smile to lift the corners of her lips. "Jace must've gotten a double dose of brains to make up for what his father doesn't have."

"Owen isn't a stupid man." Sara was still wearing her black suit. Her gun was nowhere in sight. "He's maintained a financial empire. So maybe he made some poor choices in his personal life, but I'm sure he regrets them."

Rachel made a rude noise. "Owen doesn't *have* a personal life. Monopoly is his life." Her smile widened. "Wait. Maybe I'm wrong. He seems pretty cozy with Honey Suckle."

Sara's face flushed a bright pink, an interesting contrast to her white hair. "We don't make assumptions in B.L.I.S.S., Rachel. We deal with hard facts. And I think Owen is a perfectly nice man."

Rachel's eyes narrowed. *Uh-oh.* Camryn had to say something to defuse the escalating warfare. "What should we do about Jace Sentori?"

All gazes shifted to her.

"I'd say keep a close eye on him." Flo was still searching for a hiding spot for her gun. "Citra Nella is with him. CIA. She's no dummy. They could lead us to Zed." With a huff of disgust, she gave up on her search. "Y doesn't seem to think he's Zed, but nothing's a given. Anyway, this whole token business complicates everything. We don't need anyone or anything getting in the way of our search for Zed."

Flo met Camryn's gaze, and Camryn shivered. What she saw in Flo's eyes didn't say *fun-loving sexy senior citizen*. Flo's glance said *deadly professional*. Camryn must never forget what these women really were.

"I guess I'll turn in." A big fat lie. "It's been a long day. Where will you guys be?"

"I'll be in my room. Have to clean my guns. Then I'm going to bed. If I don't get a full eight hours, my reaction time is cut way down. Reaction time is the difference between life and death." With that homey advice for budding assassins, Flo left.

Sara headed for the door. "I have to hook up some more surveillance equipment."

"I bet most of it's in Owen Sitall's bedroom." Rachel's mutter didn't reach Sara.

But it did reach Camryn. *Interesting*. All was not warm and supportive in the B.L.I.S.S. ranks. "Where will you be, Rachel?"

"Here and there." Rachel didn't give Camryn time to tie down the exact location of "here and there." She quickly left, closing the door softly behind her.

Camryn had the feeling that even in a towering rage, Rachel would always close the door softly. Her rage would be a silent, deadly thing.

Camryn stared at the door, trying to decide what to do. She'd lied about going to sleep, and she hadn't mentioned that someone had shot at her. Maybe she was finally starting to think like a B.L.I.S.S. agent, where *everything* was on a need-to-know basis.

When she tried to take a step toward the door, a furry weight anchoring one foot to the floor reminded her she wasn't alone.

"Me." Pause for emphasis. "Ow."

Camryn glanced down and sighed. "I guess Rachel isn't putting you into the shop tonight." The truth? She was starting to have warm, fuzzy feelings for the little guy. It didn't make sense. Meathead was a computer wrapped in orange fur, nothing more. He needed major reprogramming, but she found his flaws really endearing. She shook her head. Those flaws could leave her really dead.

She eyed the dreaded heels. No way would her feet tolerate any more of that kind of torture tonight. And flats would look stupid with the black dress. Hey, B.L.I.S.S. agents had to maintain a sense of fashion while flushing out evil. Quickly she changed into a pair of shorts, a sleeveless blouse, and running shoes.

Rachel had explained that the shoes contained powerful, tightly coiled springs. Pushing a tab on the heels would release the springs, allowing her to cover a lot of ground in giant leaps. It sounded weird, but then all of Rachel's inventions sounded weird. Camryn was wearing the shoes because they went with her shorts. Period. She knew the shorts and top did something, but she was too tired to remember what right now. Snapping the leash onto Meathead's collar, she headed for the stairs.

When she reached the ground floor, Camryn checked out the bar and game room. Nothing. No, there were two men in kilts she hadn't seen before. She glanced down at her orange shadow. "What do you think?"

Meathead burped.

"You're right. We need to ask someone." She made her way over to where Honey Suckle was deep in conversation with a thin-faced man who looked like doing in his granny wouldn't even make him blink. Okay, so she shouldn't make snap judgments based on externals. She'd decided Jace was dangerous the first time she'd seen him, and he was perfectly . . . dangerous. Fine, so sometimes first impressions *were* valid.

Pasting a friendly grin on her face, Camryn butted into the conversation. "Hi, I'm Camryn O'Brien, and—"

"Well, hi, Camryn. I hope you're enjoying Chance." Honey traded false smiles with Camryn. "What can I do for you?"

Gain fifty pounds was the first thing that came to mind. Camryn drew in a deep breath. That was so low. She should be above pettiness. Just because Honey Suckle was perfect in every way did not call for meanness. The fact that Jace had seemed to find Honey intriguing *did* call for a small expression of spite, but very small. Jealousy?

Camryn hoped not. "Have you seen Jace Sentori recently?"

"Jace Sentori?" Honey pursed full, pouty red lips.

Camryn narrowed her gaze. "You know: big, dark, gorgeous."

"Oh, yes." Honey's gaze turned speculative. "He headed out toward the stables a few minutes ago." She didn't seem to notice as the thin-faced man melted into the crowd.

Camryn itched to rush out to the stables, but she wanted to do a little probing first. "Peter told me you were in charge of Owen's tokens. What a fascinating job." *Translation: Tell me everything you know about them.*

"Normally, it is." Even Honey's frown was sensual. "But something disturbing happened tonight."

And?

Honey smiled. "Nothing important."

Damn. Honey Suckle wasn't supposed to be discreet. She was supposed to blab everything to everyone, making Camryn's job simple. *But the tokens aren't your job.* Camryn chose to ignore that truth.

Honey turned to someone else, and Camryn decided she'd better find Jace. He was probably checking up on a new lead. A new lead that could lead her to Zed.

Once out of the building, she unsnapped Meathead's leash. "Hmm, stables." She pulled up a mental picture of Chance's grounds, then headed down a gravel path. She knew Owen kept some horses for visitors who chose to explore his board on horseback. Personally Camryn would choose to do her exploring from behind the wheel of her trusty Cadillac.

As she drew closer to the stables, she moved into the shadows, slowing down to take stock of her surroundings. The barn was dark, but Camryn could see a light in the small cottage nearby. The person who took care of the horses must live there. Bright moonlight lit the area around the barn with a silver glow. She wouldn't have any trouble seeing anyone who emerged from the barn. She'd just move a little closer and—

Someone grabbed her from behind. A muscular arm wrapped around her, pinning her arms to her sides. A large hand covered her mouth, stopping her squeak of protest.

Camryn tried to push panic aside. She rolled her eyes in an attempt to locate Meathead. Meathead wasn't interested. He was too busy scoping out the entrance to the barn to worry about something as minor as an assault on her person. She couldn't reach any of her hot dots. She was helpless.

Well, not quite. Her attacker was male. She'd just focus all her energy on him and—

The crack of a breaking branch in the tree above them sounded like a gunshot in the night silence. Camryn winced as she heard the branch connect with her attacker's head. Must've been a very large branch to make that solid a sound. Luckily it didn't get her too.

The pained grunt behind her was followed immediately by her release. Camryn frowned. She recognized that grunt. With a dread sense of inevitability, she turned.

Jace stood clutching his head and breathing silent curses.

Oops.

She didn't have time to dwell on her mistake, because suddenly a figure appeared in the barn entrance. Huge. Menacing. It stepped into the bright moonlight and pointed at them.

"Come out from your hiding place. Your attempt to sneak up on me was pitiful. I am in a good mood tonight, so I will not break your worthless bodies in half." The figure strode closer. "Skulking cowards."

Jace staggered backward and slid down the trunk of the attacking tree. His poor head. Worse yet, that left only one skulking coward to face . . .

The most frightening woman Camryn had ever seen, over six feet of solid muscle and intimidation. Long black hair surrounded her face in a tangled glory. Her angry gaze alone could have held Camryn immobile.

Her knee-high boots and tan riding breeches were at odds with the tight black blouse she'd unbuttoned, then tied beneath her breasts. Very large breasts. It must be the air on this island. Then why wasn't *she* growing and expanding to fill her agent number?

The woman slapped her riding whip angrily against her leather-encased calf. "Did you hear me, worms? Come out from hiding before I come in and drag you out."

Oh, boy. What to do? Jace must have a gun, but she didn't have time to search for it. Camryn rooted around in her bra for her map. Damn, it had somehow slipped from her bra during her brief struggle with Jace and was now lodged somewhere around her stomach. Frantically she started to unbutton her blouse to get at it.

The need was taken from her. Just as the woman started toward Camryn, Meathead padded between them. Camryn slunk further into the shadows, keeping her body between Jace and the amazon. Jace was now making mumbling noises of pain, which she hoped signaled a return to consciousness.

Meathead plunked himself in front of the frowning woman; then he farted—loudly, melodiously, odoriferously.

The woman staggered back. "Hiding behind a stinky cat will ultimately do you no good." She placed a hand over her nose. "But tonight it is sufficient to keep me from tearing you apart. You are no threat to me anyway. Anyone who would hide behind a cat is unworthy of my wrath."

Camryn gloried in her unworthiness.

"You must already know my mission or you would not be sneaking around in the shadows." The woman edged farther away from Meathead. "I am here to take the horse token, Ramses. Nothing will stop me. When I call Ramses, he will feel compelled to come to me. It is my gift." A slight smile touched her lips. There was something magnificent about her, in a scary sort of way. "You do not work for Owen Sitall, who will soon *not* own

121

it all, or you would not be hiding. If you think to steal Ramses from me, think again. Tomorrow I will take him, and no one will stop me because . . ."

"Who is *that?*" Jace's muttered question seemed loud in the sudden stillness.

Camryn put a warning finger over his lips.

"I am the Horse Shouter!"

Jace covered his eyes with one hand. "Hell!"

Chapter Eight

Now that Xena, Warrior Princess, a.k.a. the Horse Shouter, had gone, Camryn knelt down to see how badly Jace was hurt. "Hey, I'm sorry. I didn't know you were the one holding me." She ran her fingers through his hair, found the bump, and lightly traced its circumference.

"Damn." His exclamation of pain warmed the skin of her stomach exposed by her unbuttoned blouse. "Don't apologize. It wasn't your fault the branch zapped me."

Wrong. "Actually it *was.* . . ." Camryn bit her lip in indecision. She shouldn't tell him anything. But if she hadn't been sticking her nose into his surveillance, he might have stopped the Horse Shouter, and he certainly wouldn't have gotten bonked on the head. A hardened B.L.I.S.S. agent wouldn't care. *She* cared.

"Was what?" His voice had deepened, grown suspiciously husky. The warmth on her stomach heated up. He'd moved closer.

"Nothing." Which was absolutely true. Her growing awareness of his mouth so close to her skin had drained every last meaningful thought from her brain. Who knew that stomach and brain had such a symbiotic relationship?

"Uh-uh. You were about to say that the branch *was* your fault. I'll have to investigate this further." He exhaled deeply. "When I can think clearly."

No kidding. Camryn bent her head, closing her eyes to fully experience the soft brush of his hair against her cheek. *Touch my stomach with your mouth. I want to feel the pressure of your lips there, low on my belly, then the slide of your tongue lower, lower. . . .*

"Do you always undress at the threat of danger?" His lips grazed her skin, the words forming abstract patterns of heat across her flesh.

Depends on the danger. If the danger was Jace? Ripping off clothes would always be an option. "I had to get to my . . . weapon." Weapon? Camryn had no weapon to protect her against his kind of assault. She raked her fingers through his thick hair, inhaling the scent of shampoo and tropical nights.

"I"—he groaned as he wrapped his arms around her waist—"can't"—his tongue was hot and demanding, exploring her navel and surrounding territory—"stand"—he slid his hands under her blouse, and she felt the pressure of his palms against her back, a heated brand she knew would leave the imprint of his fingers there forever—"it"—his lips trailed fire and need across her stomach at the same time he shifted his hands to her bottom, cupping her, pulling her into closer contact with his lips—"anymore."

He slid one hand over her shorts and splayed his fingers across her abdomen. She felt his pause. *Don't stop now.*

"Feels like you have a little bump right here." He touched the spot low on her abdomen with the tip of his tongue, just in case she couldn't find it herself.

Her eyes popped open, the sensual haze clearing as the cool wind of reason blew through. What was it? She couldn't remember. The missile launch? What if he poked at the bump? Meathead might launch a missile that could take out ... Who knew what? Rachel hadn't been too specific about the missile's capability. Worse yet, Meathead probably wouldn't launch it. He'd just plop it in front of her like a dead mouse he'd brought home for his owner's inspection.

She pushed at Jace and he released her. Perversely, that irritated her. He could have been a little more lost in lust, a little more reluctant to let her go. She scrambled to her feet and buttoned her blouse with fingers that seemed to have lost their ability to connect button with buttonhole. "This has been really ... informative, but it's been a long day and I know you want to rest up so you'll be ready for the Horse Shouter tomorrow when she tries to take—"

"I'm going to make love with you, Camryn." He

held up his hand to stop her instant denial. "Not tonight, but it's going to happen. I've made up my mind."

She closed her gaping mouth. "I guess *my* mind has nothing to say about the decision." Her sarcasm didn't even make him blink. She tried to bite back her next words, but they slipped around her clenched teeth and escaped. "Sensual experiences in dark rooms with strange women can be deadly."

"Then we'll have to make sure the lights are on." He grinned up at her, and she had to make a conscious effort to remember why she couldn't end up making love with Jace Sentori. Her career was more important to her than any man. Besides, if she made love with Jace and he pushed the wrong spot . . . *You can't have a career if you're dead.*

Camryn didn't realize she was making a quick touch survey of her hot dots until Jace rose lithely to his feet and placed his hand over hers.

"What's with the silent Macarena thing? If you want to dance we can go back to Chance and find some music." He rubbed a rhythmic circle with the pad of his thumb on the back of her hand, and she happily abandoned her hot-dot check.

"I don't dance." A duck had more rhythm than she did.

"I'll teach you." His voice was strong with his conviction that she would dance. His eyes glinted with the joy of a challenge.

Camryn studied him silently. Insight: This was a man who thrived on challenges, fought them to a standstill, and then pummeled them into submission. Brilliance combined with that kind of competitive nature must have earned him his Game Master title.

"You can try." She wasn't without her own competitive nature. She started to move toward the path, but his hand halted her.

"How'd you stop our Horse Shouter friend?"

His attention had shifted from Camryn, and she mourned the loss. She could get downright greedy where Jace was concerned. She'd better ration her interest, though, because Zed was still out there. "I didn't stop her. Meathead did. He . . . passed gas. It was a noxious-odor attack. Very effective." That sounded totally dumb.

His bark of laughter shattered the night silence. "You're kidding, right? Another technological miracle from Wondercat. Does he have a fart button?"

Camryn opened her mouth to defend Meathead, then shut it. Why did she feel any emotional connection to that cat? He wasn't her creation, and he was a constant embarrassment. But perversely, she did.

Another question surfaced: Why had Meathead done what he'd done? She hadn't given him any command. She didn't even know which hot dot to push. He hadn't touched the Horse Shouter, so he had no reason to activate his protect system. And Camryn's unique skill had no effect on females, so she couldn't have caused the cat's confrontation with the Horse Shouter.

Another mystery. Rachel had made it sound like Meathead's collection of DNA from strangers was automatic, but he'd made no attempt to investigate Peter or Honey Suckle.

A strand of unease unwound from a dark corner of her mind and pushed its way into the light. She'd really have to make Rachel understand her concern. With all those hot dots under her skin, she couldn't just shed the cat when he didn't work right. Technically he was a part of her—a part of her that seemed to be taking on a life of its own.

Camryn suddenly realized Jace hadn't said a word while she'd been doing all her silent analyzing of Meathead. She glanced at him.

His lips were set in a hard line, his gaze focused on the tree behind them.

"What?" But even as she said it, she saw what had attracted his attention. A small dart was imbedded in the trunk—a dart that hadn't been there long, because a small bead of liquid still shimmered at the point of contact. While she watched, the bead started to slide down the trunk.

"If you hadn't bent down to help me, that dart would've gotten you." His voice was hard, refusing to soften the blow.

"The Horse Shouter?" Even as Camryn asked, she knew the answer.

He shook his head. "She isn't exactly a shadow moving silently through the night. I could hear her clumping down the path. She couldn't have gotten back here that quickly. Besides, I got the feeling that poisoned darts weren't her style. If she wanted to hurt you, she'd just break every bone in your body."

Jace studied the dart more carefully. "See how deep it's imbedded in the tree? I don't think a regular blowgun could do that. It looks like it went into the trunk with the force of a nail gun behind it."

Camryn winced at the image. *Poisoned darts.* The words hung between them.

"You know"—his glance was sharp, assessing— "I thought the shooter earlier tonight was trying to take out Citra or me. Were they trying to kill you, Camryn?"

She continued to stare wide-eyed as the bead wended its tortuous path down the rough bark. "That's a logical conclusion."

"He didn't have to worry about making noise when he shot at you, because Citra had disconnected the camera and speakers." He crouched down to get a closer look at the bead. "But this is too close to Chance. He wanted a silent kill. I wonder why he chose a poisoned dart when he could've just used a silencer? Guess he's into exotic weapons." Jace reached for the dart.

"Don't touch it." She took a deep breath and shoved her initial panic away. Reaching inside her blouse, she fished for the map, then pushed the "investigate" hot dot on her right upper arm. *Please let Meathead get it right this once.*

Camryn put her finger close to the beaded moisture and waited. Meathead padded over and touched the bead with the tip of a pink tongue. A series of burps indicated something was happening.

A minute later, the code for "analysis complete"

flashed in the cat's eyes, indicating that the investigative process had finished. She picked up Meathead and pressed the report zircon on his collar.

"Analysis of data complete. Rare deadly snake venom. No known antidote. Death occurs within minutes after contact. Used by L.O.V.E.R. agent Zed to eliminate B.L.I.S.S. agents on June fifth, 2000, and August twenty-fifth, 2001." The flat, tinny voice didn't lessen the impact of the news.

The silence stretched into forever, broken only by Jace's quiet oath.

Zed. He was on the island, and he was hunting her. She scanned the surrounding forest. Nothing.

"He's gone or else he would've tried again by now. I'd guess that in the darkness he assumed you were hit when you bent your head down toward me. He wouldn't want to stick around and risk being identified." Jace's voice sounded calm, but Camryn sensed the coiled tension behind each word.

"Why didn't the cat warn you?" He glared at Meathead.

"I don't know." She'd forgotten to press the "protect" hot dot, and things had happened so fast. She had to learn to have a quicker reaction time or else she'd wind up *so* dead. *Dead.* If she hadn't bent down to rub her cheek against Jace's hair, she'd be dead. The thought chilled her. Okay, so it scared the hell out of her.

"Why is this Zed trying to kill you? I assumed Owen was the main target." He reached up and tiredly rubbed the back of his neck. "And who is L.O.V.E.R.?"

She hesitated. Why not tell him? He knew most of it anyway. And it was *his* father they were trying to protect. He wasn't Zed, and Citra Nella *was* a CIA agent. She'd heard about interagency jealousies, but she was too new at the game to care who led her to Zed.

"Look, if I'm going to help you get rid of Zed, then I need to know the whole story."

Her wide-eyed surprise mirrored his reaction exactly. Now why had he said that? He had enough to worry about without involving himself with this Zed character. *This Zed character is trying to kill Camryn and Owen.* Jace didn't want to examine his motives too closely.

"I don't want your help in getting rid of Zed. Sure, if you have any information, I'd like to know, but he's mine." Her voice held a fervor he didn't understand.

"Want to tell me why it's so important that *you* take him out?"

"Not now." She glanced away, then down at the cat, who'd seated himself on her foot. "L.O.V.E.R. stands for League of Violent Economic Revolutionaries. Zed is their top agent. They want Owen dead so they can destabilize the world's economies and open things up for their domination. Rachel, Flo, Sara, and I were sent by B.L.I.S.S. to stop them."

He nodded. "Aren't your partners a little old to still be out in the field?"

"Ha! Deadly doesn't get old; it just gets more

131

experienced." She turned to stare at the dart. "I need to take that with me to show the others."

"I'll get something to wrap it in." He walked quickly to the barn and grabbed a cloth from a peg. Glancing down the aisle of the barn, he noted the prick-eared interest of the gray stallion that had its head stretched over the top of its stall door. "I hope you're ready for the adventure of your life tomorrow, guy."

Returning to Camryn, he yanked the dart from the tree and carefully wrapped it in the cloth. He handed it to her. She held it well away from her body. "You'll be going with me tomorrow, right?"

She turned from him and started back toward Chance, but not before he'd seen the surprise in her eyes. "Where're you going tomorrow, and why should I go with you?"

"Owen is taking a few of his high rollers out tomorrow to the Reading Railroad. There's a big game going on, and Owen's token is the horse. He'll be riding Ramses. The other players will have their tokens, but most of them will get there on the train." He cast her a searching glance. "I bet the Horse Shouter makes her move while Ramses is away from Chance. If she can take him while he's close to the coast, she can get him off the island fast. It would be a good shot for Zed, too."

Camryn nodded. "The others probably know the details. I'll check with them." She frowned. "I should've known that. Why didn't I?"

He shrugged. "It's kind of hard to ferret out details when you're dodging bullets and poisoned darts. Oh, and don't forget avoiding death by fat cats." He offered Meathead a pointed stare. Meathead yawned at him.

Jace would like a look at F.I.D.O.'s innards. He hated programs that didn't work right.

She gave him a tired smile. "Right. I haven't had time to worry about tomorrow. I just want to live through today."

Jace put his arm across her shoulders and steered her back to the path. Sliding his hand down the cool smoothness of her arm, he felt her shiver. He smiled. He didn't think she was shivering from cold. "Does Owen know about Zed?"

"Not the details. He's been warned about a possible attack, but he chooses to think he has enough defenses in place to protect himself." She leaned into him, and he tightened his grip.

A man could never have enough defenses. "And what about the tree branch? What did you have to do with that?" He could see Chance at the end of the path. *Chance*—a word to conjure intriguing scenarios. Jace wondered what his chances were with Camryn.

What was the matter with him? Both their lives were on the line, and he had time to think about sex? Maybe it was a combination of danger and the woman. The adrenaline rush of possible death combined with a fascination he couldn't shut down.

She stopped in front of the marble steps leading up to Chance's huge double doors—doors that had Monopoly boards carved into them.

Jace's grimace had more to do with the doors than with his pounding headache.

Camryn glanced around. "Let's go inside. Zed might be gone, but I don't like being out in the open like this."

He followed her up the steps, watched the swing and sway of her round little bottom, and wondered at his attraction. Her round bottom was great, but he'd known other bottoms just as rounded. Round bottoms were not unique. Maybe it was her job description. He'd never met a woman willing to do what Camryn did. It took lots of courage and lent her an aura of danger. That attracted him.

She stopped in the now dimly lit hallway, scanned the area, then stepped into the shadows of a tiled alcove. Carefully she set the poisoned dart on the floor. "Okay, here's the deal. My whole life I've had this ... effect on some men. When they try to protect me or manage my life, they have accidents. I thought I couldn't control it, but now I know I can." She cast him an apologetic glance. "When you grabbed me, I focused on something happening to you." She shrugged. "It did."

He narrowed his gaze. "F.I.D.O.'s attacks?"

"Meathead?"

Jace shook his head. "No, F.I.D.O. Meathead is a pet's name. This is a robot."

She sighed. "I don't know. I didn't give him any command to attack you after you saved me from the gas bomb, but my brothers always ended up with bruises when they saved me from anything.

So it could've been me. But then, Meathead hasn't been himself, whatever *himself* is. Rachel has to look at him."

What was it about Camryn? She didn't fit in a box, and he had the feeling she'd never stay in a box long enough for him to tape down the lid. She constantly surprised him. "So what you're saying is that if I spend much time with you, I'd better make sure my Blue Cross is up-to-date."

Her smile tempted him, making a trip to the emergency room seem worth it. "Only if you try to be overprotective or play the managing male. Oh, and of course if I feel threatened." She lifted her mane of flaming hair off her neck, then ran her fingers through the strands. "There are different kinds of threats, you know." She cast him a sideways glance that intimated what kind of threat she thought he was.

He drew in a deep breath and tried to focus on all the reasons he shouldn't answer the siren call of her breasts as they lifted and thrust against the thin material of her blouse. "Got it. No threat, no bruises." He'd rather be black and blue from head to foot than be considered "safe." "Danger comes in many forms, O'Brien." Right now he didn't give a flip about the sheik's horse. "I bet you don't think you're a dangerous woman." She made him forget. And *that* was the real danger for him, and for Owen.

"Me?" She blinked at him.

"You." *Well, hell.* If he was going to give in to temptation, he'd do it big-time.

He moved closer and watched her eyes widen,

135

watched as she dropped her arms to her sides. She didn't move back—a good sign.

He studied the alcove. Yep, the bust of his father in full Monopoly regalia wasn't tottering on its pedestal. His toes were safe. He glanced down. Meathead was busy cleaning his face. No immediate danger there. He looked beyond the alcove. No rabid agents hiding in the darkness ready to launch a poisoned-dart attack.

He stepped closer, and this time she stepped back. The wall was behind her, and he leaned into her, bracing his hands against the wall, trapping her between his arms. "Feel threatened yet?"

"Uh-huh." She slid her tongue across her bottom lip.

"Good." He had to follow the path of that tongue, to taste her, to savor each of the senses with her. And if the roof collapsed on him in the process, he hoped it wasn't during his exploration of touch.

Jace took one hand from the wall long enough to push her hair away from her neck, then lowered his head. His first instinct was to devour her whole. *Not smart, Sentori.* His games would sell zip if he didn't understand how to build excitement. You had to start slow and then intensify the action.

The smooth curve of her neck drew him. Following his bliss, he touched the soft skin below her ear, allowed his lips to linger, sampled the texture of her flesh with his tongue.

Encouraged by her sharp intake of breath, he nibbled a path to the base of her neck. His early warning system for incoming explosive arousal missiles was flashing a code red, affirming his belief that in a previous life he was probably a vampire. Only a vampire could get this excited about a woman's neck.

Sighing, she wrapped her arms around his waist, pulling him closer. He bit back a groan at the pleasure-pain of her breasts and stomach pressed against his chest and groin.

But pleasure was never enough. Jace Sentori had built a reputation by working past just "good" until he reached the ultimate. The ultimate with Camryn O'Brien didn't include a layer of clothing between them.

Pushing away from the wall, he placed his palms on each side of her face, holding her in position as he claimed her lips. He traced her lower lip with his tongue, fulfilling his short-term fantasy. "I want to know all about you, Camryn. What you feel, what you'd *like* to feel."

She opened her lips to him, giving him an insight into what she'd like to feel first.

His kiss wasn't tentative or gentle. *He* wasn't tentative or gentle. He took her mouth the way he'd like to take the rest of her, delving deeply, tasting, letting the moist heat of her mouth fuel his building pressure and need.

When he finally broke the kiss, he had to gasp for air to supply oxygen for his pounding heart. He skimmed his hands down her body until he reached her bottom, then pulled her more tightly to him. Shifting his hips, he let her feel the size and extent of his excitement.

She made a small sound of satisfaction as she worked at the buttons of his shirt. When the last two wouldn't cooperate, she gave an impatient yank, and, surprised, he listened to the sound of them bouncing off the tile floor.

He lowered his head and muffled his soft laughter in her flaming riot of red hair. "Whoa, woman. I only brought a few shirts. Between the bumps, bruises, and torn clothes, there won't be enough left of me to ship off the island."

"Hey, as long as the important parts are in one piece, who cares?" Her murmur warmed his chest and upped the temperature in other body areas accordingly. "And now that you understand what a dangerous woman I really am, you're going to answer a few of my questions."

"Make me." He squeezed her bottom, felt her cheeks clench, then sucked in his breath as she ran her palm over his bare chest and squeezed his nipple in response.

"Torture is certainly an option." She sounded thoughtful as she slid her hand between their bodies, letting her palm rest over his arousal.

"Do it," he said. Her challenge sang through his veins, engorging organs that had just about reached capacity level. He thrust into her palm, groaning at his need to have her hand directly on his flesh.

Camryn sighed. "Have it your way. I've already told you one of my secrets, so now it's your turn." She touched his nipple with the tip of her tongue while her fingers worked at the button of his jeans. He silently urged her to rip it open like she had his shirt. Buttons were expendable.

"Tell me the secret of your success, Game Master." She conquered the button and made short work of the zipper. "I have ways to make you talk." Her fingers lay warm and promising over his erection with only his briefs as a barrier.

"Try every one, sweetheart." He slid his hands down the back of her shorts to get a better grasp on the situation. He froze. No panties. How could he have gotten lucky twice?

He felt her smile against his chest. "Acid-lined. Won't wear them."

"Acid-lined panties? Is there any part of you that's safe to touch?"

She nodded. "A few." Seconds passed. "Very few." She kissed the center of his chest. "Tell me your secrets and I'll tell you where they are."

"Secrets of the game?" He abandoned the inviting possibilities of her bare bottom for another time. "There are no secrets." He undid the top button on her blouse and touched his mouth to the warm vee of smooth skin. "The most successful games imitate life, only more over-the-top." How could he maintain his train of thought all the way to the bottom button? He didn't know, but he was always up for a challenge.

"Umm. Imitates life?" She sounded distracted.

Hell, her rhythmic stroking of his erection wasn't helping *his* concentration a whole lot.

"Give me an example."

"For instance . . ." He undid another button, then pushed the material aside far enough to run his tongue across the exposed swell of her breast.

It was probably asking too much to hope she had acid-lined bras she refused to wear. "Suppose you and I were mole people."

"Mole people?" Her voice was taking on a breathless quality.

Another button and he'd be getting breathless, too. "We've always wanted more than a subterranean existence. We yearn for light, fresh air, the sun's warmth, and seats behind home plate at the World Series." He ran the tip of his finger around her nipple, and she gently squeezed his already overexcited shaft in response. He clenched his teeth to hold back a groan. At this rate he'd be abandoning the mole people to their fates very soon.

"World Series?"

She swayed toward him as he finished the unbuttoning process, then reached behind her to unsnap her bra. As the bra slid down to waist level, he almost lost the mole people. "We plan an escape. Fighting our way through the strangling roots of genetically engineered broccoli and ferocious mutated worms, we reach the surface."

"Do we stop to rest along the way?" She reached inside his briefs and ran the tip of her fingernail the length of him. "Energy renewal is important."

His deep shudder indicated an impending massive expenditure of energy. "Sure. Gotta have rest stops." He couldn't focus on anything except tasting her. Closing his lips around her nipple, he teased it with his tongue, felt her hand clenched in his hair, anchoring them both to a fast-disappearing reality.

Her tug on his scalp should have ratcheted the pain in his head up a notch, but with her magic fingers right *there* . . . *What headache?*

"Tell me more." She wrapped her fingers around his arousal, holding him captive.

Think? She expected him to *think?* "We reach the surface. Our dream is within sight. Then . . ." He kissed a path from between her breasts to where her bra was bunched around her stomach. She pulled in her stomach with a tiny gasp. "Major disaster." He had to touch all of her, with his fingers, his mouth. He pulled her bra from her and flung it to the floor.

"No."

He wasn't quite sure if her quivery "no" was in response to their shattered dreams or the slide of his fingers up the inside of her bare thigh. "A deadly plow driven by a Kelly Ripa clone is bearing down on us. She's busy reading her newest 'Reading with Ripa' Book Club selection, *The Bachelor,* so she doesn't see us in her path. Death is only inches away."

Heaven is only inches away. He slipped his fingers beneath the bottom of her shorts, felt her move her legs apart to accommodate him, and closed his eyes on the sensation of her warm mouth touching the hollow at the base of his neck, her tongue tracing tiny circles on his flesh. His pulse was a heavy beat of readiness.

"What should we do?" She slid her finger around the head of his erection, testing its texture.

141

He didn't care what the mole people did, but he sure knew what *he* wanted to do. Jace drew in a deep, gasping breath. He had to slow the action down. Letting his hand rest on her inner thigh, he felt a small bump beneath his fingers. *Focus.* He had to focus on the stupid story he'd started.

"Our only chance of survival is to go back the way we came. But once we do that, we'll never make it to the surface again. The plow will destroy our tunnels. Our dreams will be dead." *Dead* didn't describe any part of him right now.

"We can't give up our dreams." She emphasized her strong commitment to dreams by nipping his shoulder.

"Sorry, we have about thirty seconds before we're ground into mulch. Gotta go back." He pictured her small white teeth nipping at another body part and almost went to his knees at the explosive visual.

Leaning her forehead against his chest, she breathed hot life into every part of him. He stroked her inner thigh with a promise of what his fingers would do when they reached a little higher. But he returned again and again to the tiny bump. What was it?

"This is your fantasy. What would you do if this were one of your games?" Her question was a whisper of need.

"I'd never create a game with moles. People don't relate to moles. Gamers want weapons, speed, and alien hit men." He paused to slide his tongue into her navel as he undid the button on her shorts.

"Yes." Her one-word response was a moan of pleasure.

He smiled. It was nice to have a woman who agreed with him. "But if I were going to make this into a game, I'd stack everything against our mole people, make it seem like they had no option except going back the way they'd come." He wanted to slide his tongue lower, explore the hot temptation of her lower belly. This presented a painful dilemma. If he did that, he'd have to shift his body position, and she'd lose touch with his erection, which by now had formed an unbreakable bond with her fingers.

While he considered the problem, he unconsciously rubbed the tiny bump on her thigh. "Then I'd do something that would never happen in real life."

"What?" She sounded dazed—probably thinking deep thoughts about the mole people's situation.

"I'd give us a shot at a miracle. The Kelly Ripa clone has just reached the . . . climax, and is so overcome with . . . emotion that she drops the book. We have about a minute to climb from our hole and race out of the plow's path while she's picking it up." Since he couldn't move any lower on her stomach, he settled for tracing a return path to her breasts with his tongue.

"No problem. A minute is plenty of time to get our tiny tushes out of there." She reached under his briefs with her free hand and molded her fingers to his bare butt, probably trying to judge the capability of his buns for instant action. Her sigh indicated he'd passed the test.

"Not as easy as you'd think. Mole people don't move fast. If we take the chance, we probably won't make it." Why was he talking about mole people when all he wanted to do was lay her down on the floor and—

"We'll take the chance. Freedom is worth it." She didn't sound as focused as she had earlier.

Good, because he didn't want to think about the mole people anymore. He wanted to concentrate on the heat and sensations generated by touching her, wanted to lose himself inside her.

"We will, won't we?" Her words came in tiny gasps as he covered her breast with his mouth while his fingers inched higher on her thigh.

"Huh?" What was she talking about? "Oh, take the chance? Not me. I don't believe in miracles. I'd go back the way I'd come."

She stilled. Stopped the wonderful things her fingers were doing to him. "You don't believe in miracles? Ever?"

He raised his head from her breasts and drew in a deep, steadying breath. "Miracles don't happen in real life, but players want them in games. So I give them a chance. Maybe they'll make it; maybe they won't."

She smiled up at him. "I choose to believe we make it out of the plow's path and get those World Series seats."

The intensity of that smile rocked him. He pressed the mysterious bump on her thigh in response to it, prepared to pull her into his arms and get serious about their body contact.

It didn't happen, because Meathead chose that moment to burst into song. His howl rose in volume and intensity even as Jace muttered a curse that should have relegated the robot to kitty heaven.

Jace stepped back from her, allowing Camryn to peek around him at Meathead. While they'd been intent on each other, the cat had managed to climb atop Jace's father's bust. He perched atop Owen's head now, warbling and wailing.

Jace closed his eyes, counted to ten, then opened them. "What the hell is this about?"

Camryn ran agitated fingers through her tangled hair. "You pushed the hot dot. Whistle."

He didn't question. He'd do anything to stop the piercing howls that pounded at the base of his skull. He whistled.

Meathead stopped his serenade as suddenly as he'd started. Leaping from Owen's head, he settled himself on Camryn's foot.

Leaning down, Jace scooped up Camryn's bra and handed it to her. Wordlessly she stuffed it down the back of her shorts, then buttoned her blouse and shorts. He did some buttoning of his own, signaling that the magic moments were over. *Damned cat.*

He didn't have to worry about generating small talk, because suddenly Peter and Honey Suckle appeared in the alcove's opening.

Peter glanced at Meathead. "Thought someone was killing a cat in here."

"It could still happen." Jace glared at Meathead.

Meathead was oblivious. He was busy staring up at Camryn with what could only be described as adoration.

"We were just making a last-minute check of the place. Someone stole the ruby slippers tonight, and Owen's furious. He wants security tightened." Honey Suckle's heavy-lidded survey signaled her willingness to do a bare-body search of Jace anytime he chose.

Honey Suckle was probably a really nice person, but Jace's instincts were telling him something else. He'd gotten the same feeling when he'd glanced over the side of his boat and met the gaze of a great white.

Jace could feel a frown forming between his eyes. He didn't like the way Peter Bilt was looking at Camryn. *He* wanted to be the only one to look at her like that.

Time for a reality check. A brief encounter in a darkened alcove did not constitute right of possession. He didn't want any emotional or physical ties to Camryn O'Brien. Well, maybe he wanted the physical ties.

He watched as Peter and Honey Suckle faded into the darkness. Were they really doing a security check? Was he really getting paranoid?

"Guess I'll turn in. It's been a long day." Camryn yawned as she bent down to pick up the dart.

Jace turned his frown on her. He knew a fake

yawn when he saw one. "It could've been earth-shattering, sweetheart."

She offered him a small secret smile as she turned toward the stairs. "More than you'll ever guess."

Chapter Nine

Camryn might be standing outside Rachel's door, but her body was still downstairs with Jace. What exactly had happened? A few more minutes and she would've thrown him to the floor, ripped off his clothes, and done unspeakable things to his body.

This was not the same Camryn O'Brien who'd sworn no man would get in the way of her job. A whole army of Zeds could have marched through Chance's doors, and she would still have kept her fingers superglued to his body.

She allowed herself a small smile. At least he'd escaped her mauling with no new bumps or bruises. *Bumps.* Her smile faded. She didn't for a minute fool herself into believing he wouldn't touch her again. She *wanted* him to touch her again. But how could she keep his hands away from dangerous body areas? *How can you keep your-self from making love with him?* She didn't know, but she'd have to find a way.

Drawing in a deep, fortifying breath, she knocked on Rachel's door.

"Come in." Rachel's voice was calm and controlled even though she couldn't know who was on the other side of the door. She didn't even keep the door locked. Rachel was a scary woman.

Camryn opened the door and stepped inside. Rachel sat with her back to the door watching a movie. Even as she stared at the screen, Rachel's fingers were busy with her knitting. Camryn glanced at the electrical arcs generated by the needles. How did she do that?

"Don't just stand there gawking. Sit down and tell us what happened tonight." Flo moved into Camryn's line of vision. She had a small gun in her hand. Noting Camryn's attention, Flo nodded at the gun. "This is an FS95."

"FS95?" Camryn had never heard of it, but then she didn't know much about guns.

"Yep. This little baby is a Flo Special. Developed it in 'ninety-five. Most powerful gun for its size in existence. I'm working on a laser variation now." She offered Camryn a conspiratorial wink. "I could let you use it. Why mess with all those fancy gadgets when all you have to do is point this sucker at Zed and blow him into the next century? Works for me."

"Gee, thanks, Flo . . ." How could she explain to Flo that her aim was a little shaky? She'd had only a few days of practice before leaving. She'd be just as likely to blow everyone around Zed into the next century.

"Don't worry about taking it away from me. I'll just move up to the next level with my FA98. Developed the Flo Assassin in 'ninety-eight. Don't need an army, just the Assassin and me."

"I'll pass for now, Flo. Maybe later when—"

"I came into B.L.I.S.S. before Y was in charge. They let you do your own thing back then. I got to pick my own agent tag. I chose 1BA. It means scumbags have one second before I blow them away. Great symbolism." Flo offered Camryn a pointed stare. "I'm the voice of experience, girl. Guns keep you alive."

"She doesn't need a gun with F.I.D.O. around." Rachel glanced away from her movie.

Wouldn't count on that, Rachel.

Rachel took a last look at the screen.

"Titanic?" Camryn smiled. "Great movie."

Rachel shrugged. "I really enjoy watching the ship go down." Abandoning her movie completely, she turned to study Camryn. "F.I.D.O. has the capability of destroying a ship that size within seconds."

Camryn shuddered. She'd started to think of Meathead as just an orange cat. She had to remember what he could do when he was working right. "You need to fix him, Rachel. He won't do me any good at all if he malfunctions when I'm in a tight spot."

Rachel frowned at the implied criticism of her pride and joy. "I'll take care of him."

"And please fix him so I don't have to whistle

to shut him down. Think of a verbal command I can use in case I can't reach my hot dot." Camryn was on a roll.

Rachel narrowed her gaze on the object of their discussion, who had once again plunked himself on Camryn's foot.

Camryn had to ask: "Umm, why don't you lock your door, Rachel? And why'd you invite me in when you didn't know who was knocking?"

Rachel cast her an amused glance. "Zed or anyone connected with L.O.V.E.R. wouldn't knock. No one's coming through that door who shouldn't. Sara put surveillance equipment in the hall, and if the face outside isn't friendly . . ."

She nodded toward the door and Camryn followed her gaze. Suddenly arcs of electricity crisscrossed the opening in a crackling dance of death. Camryn shuddered. She was glad Rachel was on her side.

Flo had tucked her gun away and was studying a map of the island spread out on the coffee table. "We've got to make plans for tomorrow." She glanced at Camryn. "I'm sure Jace Sentori told you his dad was taking a group of players out." Her smile was conspiratorial. "Then again, maybe you were too busy to talk about Owen."

"What do you mean?" Camryn could've sworn no one had seen Jace and her except Peter and Honey Suckle.

Flo shrugged and looked back at the map. "F.I.D.O. sings a mean tune when he gets revved up. Could make the dead rise from their graves."

Camryn relaxed a little. If Meathead's noise had

drawn Flo, then she hadn't seen much. "I know about the game."

Rachel turned off the TV. "Sara will stick with Owen tomorrow." She pursed her lips. "She does that pretty well."

For the first time, Camryn noted Sara's absence. "Where is Sara?"

Rachel's purse became more pronounced. "Protecting Owen. More specifically, making sure no one climbs into bed with him." She put down her knitting needles. "Except her."

"Oh." *Who would've thought?*

"Flo will be out of sight, taking care of any peripheral problems." She studied the map. "I wouldn't ride the train with the rest of the players, Camryn. You need more mobility. Take the Cadillac. I assume Sentori will be with you, and he won't want Owen to spot him." Rachel didn't look up from the map. "Keep in mind that sex with Jace Sentori could be cataclysmic. I think I'll stay here and do some snooping while everyone's away."

Camryn blinked. Had Rachel really stuck in that comment about sex with Jace? "Back up, Rachel. Explain the sex-with-Sentori thing."

Rachel's expression said it should be self-explanatory. "He's a great-looking man and you're attracted. Who wouldn't be? But remember he's only on the island to get rid of Owen's stolen tokens. You're part of B.L.I.S.S., therefore a source of information. He's a master of all kinds of games. Don't let yourself be used." Her expression tightened. "Besides, sex with him would be catastrophic. He pokes the wrong hot dot and we lose half the island."

Something about Rachel's bossy attitude really steamed Camryn. "I can take care of myself."

Rachel relaxed and smiled. "Of course you can. Anyone who can use her mind to kill has the ultimate weapon. When Y first said you had a unique mental ability, I was dying to know what it was. Do you actually have to see your victim, or can you just focus your energy on a mental image?"

For the first time, Rachel seemed impressed with her. Camryn should admit her thoughts couldn't kill, that she could do only a little minor maiming. But a part of her that hated Rachel's patronizing assumption that Camryn was useless baggage on this assignment wouldn't let her admit the truth.

"It depends." Camryn hoped her muttered comment would end the discussion. "Oh, Zed tried to kill me tonight." She carefully unwrapped the dart, then set it on the coffee table.

Camryn ignored Flo's surprised exclamation and Rachel's intent stare. She was tired and had a lot to think about. "See you in the morning."

Checking to make sure Rachel had turned off her deadly electrical cross fire, Camryn stepped into the hallway. Looking both ways to make sure no one lurked in the shadows, and trying to ignore Meathead's bereft "ow" at being abandoned, she hurried to her room. She paused with her hand on the doorknob.

Alone. For the first time since starting on this

assignment, she was truly by herself. No Meathead on her foot, no deadly toys or clothing, and no trio of senior assassins to save her if Zed attacked now. Of course, she still had her "gift," but only if Zed was male.

She was afraid. The knowledge was a soul flattener. During the actual attacks, the adrenaline rush had kept the full impact at bay. She could've been dead two times over tonight. Was this really the career she wanted?

She bit her lip. If she walked away from Chance before proving she didn't need six brothers to save her, she'd never respect herself. And as much as she wanted to hurry to Jace Sentori's room, fling herself into his bed, and hide her head under his covers, she wasn't going to do it. Too bad, because the view under his covers would be an interesting distraction from her current worries.

Camryn sighed. Maybe she'd never really appreciated her family's support system. It would sure feel good to hear Dad's gruff voice saying, "Just tell me where you are, little girl. I'll roust your brothers out of bed, and we'll be on our way. Don't you worry; we'll take care of everything."

Tightening her lips and her resolve, she opened her door. Flattening herself against the hallway wall, she reached around the corner of the doorway and flipped on the light. When she wasn't greeted with a hail of bullets, she stepped inside. A thorough search assured her Zed wasn't hiding in her shower or under her bed.

The only thing she found was a fly on her wall.

Absently, she smacked it with her complimentary copy of *The History of Monopoly.*

Camryn lay in bed and memorized the hot-dot map. Now that she had time to think about it, some of the stuff Rachel said Meathead could do didn't make sense. Like how could you build a missile small enough to fit inside a cat robot that would pack enough punch to do the damage Rachel claimed it could do?

Of course, she'd seen some recent demonstrations of new technology on TV that included robots, and none of the robots could move or react on Meathead's level. So maybe all things were possible.

As she drifted toward troubled dreams, she sought for a logical reason why, when fear struck, she automatically thought of Jace Sentori as a safe haven, not Rachel, Flo, or Sara. Maybe because she'd counted on men to protect her most of her life? Possible, but she didn't think so. It didn't make much sense, but then nothing had made much sense since she'd met the Game Master.

It was a standoff. Camryn leaned against her pink land boat, arms crossed and temper simmering. This had *not* been a bright and cheery start to her day.

Jace straddled his bike, arms crossed and determination oozing from every male pore.

Citra Nella stood nearby. Evidently a bump on her head hadn't affected her basic instincts. A group of men crowded around her, moving as one when she moved, looking like some exotic giant amoeba.

Camryn recognized on an intellectual level that there was no reason for Citra Nella to trigger a super bitch reaction in her. But something primitive and peevish kept her from thinking positive thoughts about Jace's partner.

And she would *not* ride on the back of Jace's Harley. The Cadillac was security. The new and improved Meathead would fit neatly in its backseat. The panel of buttons on its steering wheel offered a comforting array of weapon and defense choices.

"The bike makes more sense than the pink thing, Camryn. It can get into tight spaces, has better maneuverability." The hard gleam of his eyes suggested the same could be said about him.

"Okay, you take your bike, and I'll drive the car. Then we'll both be happy." Not quite the truth, but she wasn't about to admit the truth: she wanted to be with Jace, but she needed to be by herself. If anyone threatened Owen, *she* would be the one to save him.

He breathed out harshly, and his narrowed gaze said he'd never understand her reasoning. Fine, so she didn't quite understand it herself. She just knew if she ever wanted to feel empowered, she'd have to separate herself from her three senior protectors and Jace Sentori.

Jace would now roar away on his bike, convinced she didn't have a lick of common sense. What he *wouldn't* do was ride in the Cadillac. Her six brothers had taught her that once a man drew a line in the sand, he'd eat dirt before crossing it.

Silently Jace got off his bike, walked around to the passenger side of the car, and climbed in. Camryn blinked in surprise. She'd counted on his being stubborn. What was the world coming to when she couldn't count on male stereotypes?

She shouldn't ask, but she had to. "Why'd you change your mind?" Camryn did her male-stubbornness inventory. Determined chin. Shoulders squared and unyielding. Piercing stare that hinted icebergs would float down the River Styx before he gave in. Yep, should definitely be stubborn.

She wasn't ready for the transformation when it came. He smiled at her, a slow, sexy slant of his lips. Leaning back, he flexed his shoulders, and she watched the flow of muscle with an avidity that was totally embarrassing. And when he rubbed his palm lazily across his chest, she followed the motion with unblinking enjoyment. She'd never realized there could be such joy in small motions.

"Why'd I change my mind?" His smile faded, replaced by a predator's intensity. "Here's my life's philosophy, sweetheart: I never let pride get in the way of my goal, I don't believe in miracles, and I go after what I want with all my weapons."

Powerful stuff, even if it was a little cynical. Camryn broke eye contact by glancing down at Meathead, who'd taken his usual seat on her foot. Her temper simmered anew at this reminder of her other reason for being pissed off.

Rachel had shown up at her door early this

morning with Meathead in tow and pronounced him in perfect working order. Camryn would no longer have to whistle to control him. He now would answer to a password. A password not easily guessed and definitely not easily forgotten. Rachel had whispered the word in her ear. Personally, Camryn thought the password was Rachel's payback for all her whining about Meathead.

Okay, so the password was also a payback for something else. Camryn had squished Rachel's fly bot last night. Her Fly Spy. She'd crunched a robotic miracle. Rachel had explained this to her calmly and without anger. What she hadn't explained was why the Fly Spy had lit on Camryn's wall. And just once, Camryn wished Rachel would act human. Scream, cry, get really into her emotional side.

Camryn scooped the cat off her foot, pulled open the back door of the car, and plunked him on the worn bench seat that seemed to stretch the length of a football field. "You can watch our backs, big guy."

"Me."

Yep, everything was back to normal.

Walking around to the driver's side, Camryn noted that Citra Nella had climbed onto the train with Sara and Owen. *Good.* She and Jace would be alone. As she slid behind the wheel, Camryn glanced at Jace's impatient expression. Maybe alone wasn't good. Maybe she needed a buffer zone. "Why is Citra riding on the train?"

He raked her with a hard gaze, and she mentally yanked her shorts a little lower on her thighs.

She should have been wearing her unraveling gold dress in case she went over a cliff in Owen's defense, but since today was a horsey day, she'd decided on something more casual. Something that wouldn't shout, *Yo, everyone! Camryn O'Brien isn't wearing panties.* She'd compromised, though. She *was* wearing her spring-loaded running shoes. And at the last minute she'd put on the big opal ring Rachel had given her. The ring wasn't her style, but Rachel had assured her that if she punched someone, the ring would activate a mini-capsule of knockout gas that would put the enemy under for about twenty minutes. A useful little accessory.

"Citra has her memory back, but she's still a little shaky. She decided she'd be more useful to Owen in close-up action." He shifted his attention to the window. "I see one of your partners with Owen. Where're the others?"

"They're around." Camryn leaned forward to get a better view of the train. Sara was snuggling close to Owen with a really un-Sara-like expression on her face. She had a glow that Camryn suspected wasn't put there by hormone replacements. Talk about disillusionment. Sara was the last one Camryn would have picked to lose her focus because of a man. At least she was staying close enough to Owen to offer protection.

Camryn indulged in some shameless self-congratulation. She would never put a man before her job. Sure, Jace had distracted her a little, but she was still focused on the main game, protecting Owen.

"The train will take everyone to the Reading Railroad station. The other tokens are already in place on the board. Ramses is in the horse trailer. When they get to the station, Owen will mount Ramses, then ride ahead of the train. He always does. Owen has a cell phone so he can keep in touch with who's moving where on the board. I think the Horse Shouter will strike while Owen's away from the train. She'll want to avoid a mob scene. So that means we should drive on ahead of everyone and try to intercept her." He glanced at Camryn. "Does that make sense to you?"

Camryn nodded. She didn't want to think in terms of what good partners they'd make, but she couldn't help it. She was intuitive, and he planned everything carefully. They complemented each other. That was not a good thing. She wanted to work alone. "Rachel is staying at Chance to check out the rooms of any guests she missed yesterday, but Flo is in the wind somewhere. If there's trouble, Flo will be nearby. And I don't think Sara will let Owen get out of her sight."

"Let's get going. I want to be at the train station before the others arrive, to make sure no one's waiting for Owen." He stared at the train as it started moving slowly along the track that would take it the few miles to the board. "We'd better check the station for bombs, too."

"Right." Camryn bit her lip in concentration as she steered the Cadillac down Chance's winding driveway. "But I'd bet that Flo has already taken care of that. It doesn't hurt to double-check, though."

"Uh-huh." Jace eyed the space between them. Bench seats had their advantages. At the first sharp turn, he could slide closer to her and—

A scratching and scrabbling sound drew his attention to the backseat. He turned just in time to watch F.I.D.O. launch his chubby self over the top of the seat and plunk his fat behind directly between them. Camryn's bottom was much more tempting.

"Well, hell." Lethal weapon or not, Jace felt the urge to create some serious downtime for this interfering orange fuzzball. "Why'd you call him up front?"

Camryn cast F.I.D.O. a worried sideways glance. "I didn't. Sometimes he just does things on his own. He's programmed to protect me, so I guess he figures this is part of his job."

"Great. Just great." He didn't need a robot to chaperon his every moment with Camryn. He'd have to get F.I.D.O. alone and lay down some basic ground rules, sort of man-to-Robocat. If that didn't work, he'd take the little sucker apart and reprogram him.

By the time Jace got over his anger, they'd reached the Reading Railroad station. Turn-of-the-century quaint, and perfect in every detail, it was a true testament to what filthy rich could buy. *Refocus, Sentori.* Now wasn't the time to start thinking about Owen's obsession with Monopoly. Jace had a horse to return to a sheik.

Quickly, they stopped and made a hurried check for bombs. Luckily there weren't many places a bomb could be hidden. Their search turned up nothing.

Jace climbed back into the Cadillac with Camryn. "The train's right behind us. They'll stop at the station and wait for the horse trailer to get here with Ramses. Then Owen will ride on ahead of the train." He couldn't think of Owen as Dad. Owen would never be more than an unfortunate blood link.

Camryn nodded her understanding as she continued to drive along the road that paralleled the Monopoly board and train tracks. Within a few minutes they were out of sight of the train. The road leading to Oriental Avenue wound along the edge of the tropical forest with a spectacular view of the Pacific. Too bad they didn't have time to admire it.

She kept driving until she reached Connecticut Avenue, then parked by the side of the road. "If I were the Horse Shouter, this is where I'd hit. From what I saw of Flo's map last night, the board curves right ahead, following the coast. The jail is on the curve; then the shoreline straightens out."

Camryn stared out at the Cadillac's endless hood. "I understand that the jail and a saltwater taffy shop on the Boardwalk are the only permanent buildings on the board. The saltwater taffy shop has some kind of sentimental meaning to Owen, but I don't know about the jail."

Jace cast her an amused glance. "Owen has made the jail as comfortable as possible because he spends so much time there. Remember, he *never* wins. And I agree about this spot. Once the

Horse Shouter gets the horse around that curve, I'll bet she has someone waiting to help get him off the island." He paused. "Oh, and it's Hogan's Saltwater Taffy Shop." How had he known the name? A memory from his childhood? It was possible.

Camryn looked worried. "Will our presence make her change her plans? Maybe I should hide the car."

Jace made a rude noise. "Where you going to hide something this big and this pink? Besides, I didn't get the feeling she had a changeable kind of mind."

She sighed her agreement. Scooping F.I.D.O. from the seat beside her, she climbed from the car. Puzzled, Jace watched her set the cat down, then push at a spot on her upper right arm. F.I.D.O. padded off toward the dense undergrowth. She watched the cat disappear before peering in the driver's-side window at Jace. "Meathead will scope out the area for us."

Something poked at him, memories of her mysterious bumps and her panic when he touched them, her impromptu Macarena. He narrowed his gaze, reaching for something that would pull his thoughts together. What had she just done? She'd pushed a spot on her arm. What had F.I.D.O. done? He'd run off into the forest.

Suddenly the answer was there. He'd wondered how she controlled the cat. Maybe *control* was not an accurate term. The cat seemed to do what he damned well pleased a lot of the time.

Flinging the car door open, he got out and

strode around to where Camryn waited with eyes that had widened in alarm. "Your bumps. They're implants. That's how you control the cat. No wonder you didn't want me to do this." He slid his fingers along her inner thigh, lingering on a bump. Leaning close, he whispered in her ear, "What would happen if I pressed here, sweetheart?"

"You'd make a very big hole in the ground." Her answer was calm, if a bit breathy.

Raking his fingers through his hair, he muttered a curse aimed at whoever had come up with the idea of making Camryn O'Brien a walking remote control.

He had too many other important things to think about: Owen, Zed, the Horse Shouter, the sheik. So why couldn't he focus on anything but one burning question? "How are we going to make love if your whole body is booby-trapped?"

"Carefully. Very carefully." She blinked as though just realizing what she'd said. "Scratch that answer. We can't make love. It's not going to happen. Ever. I have to concentrate on finding Zed before something happens to your father."

He nodded. "And afterward?"

Her gaze slipped away from him as she scanned the surrounding jungle. "I can't think that far ahead."

His stare backed her against the Cadillac. "Can't, or won't?" He started to reach for her, then paused. He glanced around. Nothing near enough to bop him on the head. No F.I.D.O. to chew on his ankle. He smiled and slid his fingers along her jaw.

A wild thrashing in the undergrowth stopped his fingers before they could continue their exploration. He winced as bloodcurdling yowls interspersed with a wide range of curses, some of which he'd never thought could be combined in one sentence, rent the quiet. Birds' screams and the flapping of wings hinted the local wildlife was heading for the hills.

"Oh, my God!" Camryn's comment was followed almost immediately by the sound of hooves, and Owen cantered around the curve on Ramses.

Owen shouldn't be here yet. They must have decided to drive the horse trailer past the Reading Railroad station, and unload Ramses nearby. Owen had arrived too soon.

Jace had no time to react as a shrill whistle followed by a booming, "Come here, horse!" yanked his attention back to the trees. The thrashing was still in full force, so F.I.D.O. must be putting up a good fight.

Out of the corner of his eye, Jace saw Camryn reach toward her right knee. He placed his hand over hers. "No, wait."

"But we have to—"

She got no farther, because Ramses suddenly reared, dumping Owen in the dirt, then trotted toward the trees.

"Check on your dad. I'll follow Ramses."

Jace was hardly aware he'd started running toward Owen until he heard Camryn's voice. He paused in midstride, watching as Owen climbed to his feet and dusted himself off. The huff and puff of the train grew louder. Any second now it would round the curve.

Indecision warred with a need Jace had never thought he'd feel: the need to know Owen was unhurt. And in that moment of indecision, Owen looked up.

Their gazes locked.

Jace watched Owen's eyes widen in recognition.

"Jace?" The older man's voice shook on the one word.

Jace could only nod as he tried to deny his emotion, an emotion he thought he'd banished years ago. He hadn't heard Owen say his name since he was six years old, had never expected Owen to even recognize him.

Drawing in a deep, steadying breath, he forced his attention away from Owen and focused it on the train that had rounded the curve and was screeching slowly to a halt. Camryn's partner, Sara, had already jumped from the train and was running toward Owen, followed closely by Citra. Owen was in safe hands.

Turning, he raced toward the jungle, ignoring Owen's shouted order to stop. He had to catch Camryn. Once inside the jungle he found an overgrown trail barely wide enough for a horse. Churned-up dirt and crushed vegetation told him the Horse Shouter had taken this path with Ramses. Ignoring undergrowth that tore at him, he overtook Camryn within a few minutes.

He noted the relief in her gaze as he joined her. Frowning, he also noted the scratches on her arms and legs from stray branches. "Next time you dress for a hunt, you'd be safer in jeans."

"I didn't pack any jeans, but these shorts are fine. The only thing these shorts do is inflate so I can use them as a makeshift life preserver. Simple, nontoxic. I like them."

Her defiant mutter made him smile. He hadn't a clue how anything could make him smile under these circumstances. Glancing around, he noticed a missing member of the group. "Where's the cat?"

"He's following Ramses and the Horse Shouter. I didn't give him any command to take action because I'm afraid of hurting the horse." She'd resorted to a half run to keep up with him.

Jace nodded. "This path probably cuts across the corner of the island. We'll most likely come out on the coast by St. Charles Place. They'll have a ship waiting to transport the horse."

"Your dad okay?" She cast him a searching glance.

"Fine." Jace needed to tell her something else. "He recognized me."

"Oh."

Unspoken was the worry that Owen would order his son from the island at the first opportunity. Well, Jace would deal with that situation when it happened.

Jace increased his pace as an opening in the thick vegetation promised they'd almost reached the coast. A question niggled at him. "F.I.D.O. was fighting with the Horse Shouter right before all hell broke loose. Did you order him to engage anyone he met?"

She shook her head and offered him a worried glance. "He was only supposed to do a search-and-report. Rachel swore he was fixed, but it looks like he's still malfunctioning."

Jace grinned. "Just what we need, a rogue robot."

"Not funny, Sentori." She was breathing hard in her attempt to keep pace with him. "He's a part of me, and I don't like parts of me doing their own thing."

Jace frowned at her reminder. Making love with Camryn O'Brien would be like trying to tiptoe through a minefield. Was it worth the danger? *Yes.* His emphatic response surprised him. *Damn.* What had happened to his common sense? First deciding to help Owen, who'd erased Jace from his life, now wanting to have sex with possibly the most dangerous woman in the world.

His minimoment of soul-searching came to a sudden end as they burst from the trees onto St. Charles Place. Beyond the Monopoly board, a startling scene was being acted out.

The Horse Shouter had mounted Ramses bareback and was guiding him across St. Charles Place onto the beach. At the water's edge a man waited. Above him a helicopter hovered. A sling had been dropped from the hovering craft. Beyond the breakers in deeper water, a large ship lay at anchor.

A simple but effective plan. They'd put the sling around Ramses and then the helicopter would transfer him to the ship and they'd sail away. Once the horse was on the ship, Owen wouldn't use his gunboat token to blast it out of the water. Owen wouldn't destroy what he considered his personal horse token.

Jace had no chance to put his own plan into operation before Camryn took action.

For a moment he stood frozen as he watched her sprint toward the beach. As she ran, she reached down and pressed a spot on her left thigh.

F.I.D.O. was suddenly a furry blur of motion.

Hell! They were all dead.

Chapter Ten

This was Camryn's chance. She would save Ramses herself with only a little help from Meathead. She'd pressed the "distract" hot dot and was hopefully waiting for her little furry scare machine to stop Ramses in his tracks. Already he was bounding to intercept horse and rider.

Everything was predicated on her ability to get behind Ramses, so when he turned from Meathead he'd come toward her. Problem: she couldn't move fast enough to intercept the Horse Shouter in time. Okay, she could handle this.

The man waiting beneath the helicopter didn't have a weapon in his hand, so he wouldn't be part of the equation. She couldn't take the time to turn around to see what Jace was doing. But it didn't matter; this was her baby.

She had to move faster. Meathead was already

in position and puffing himself up like a feline blowfish preparatory to starting his fright show.

Reaching down, she activated her spring-loaded shoes, then screamed like a banshee as the springs uncoiled with enough force to fling her ten feet into the air.

She was out of control. She could almost hear the *boing! boing!* as the springs catapulted her high into the air, then let her drop, only to launch her into space once again. Her stomach was in crisis mode. Should it run to keep up or just stop and throw up? No way could she control her direction as she bounced a zigzag path in the general direction of the Horse Shouter. She must look like a jackrabbit that'd had one too many margaritas.

Ramses had evidently seen enough. In front of him was an orange ball spouting smoke and flames, and emitting screeches that sounded like an off-key bagpipe. And behind him was a screaming human bouncing an erratic path toward him. Two other humans were racing toward him, waving their arms and shouting.

It was more than one horse should be expected to stand. With a whinny of alarm, Ramses flung himself into the air. Even the Horse Shouter couldn't keep her seat in the face of so much determination. She landed with a curse in the sand.

Ramses hesitated. Which way to run? He must have decided that the orange ball looked less threatening, because with a snort of panic, he laid back his ears and charged Meathead.

No! Camryn watched helplessly as the scene unfolded while the springs flung her high into the air once more. Meathead would be squished, and she couldn't help him. With her arms windmilling frantically to keep from losing her balance, she couldn't reach any of her hot dots.

"Jace! Save Meathead." The words were wrenched from the very heart of her shattered dream of completing this job alone. But she couldn't afford pride right now.

The words had barely left her mouth before the springs flung her in an unexpected direction. She was ejected from her shoes like a rocket leaving its launchpad. She hit the sand with a grunt, then watched as her shoes bounded away and disappeared into the jungle.

Jerking her attention back to Meathead, she was just in time to see Jace fling himself into the path of the charging stallion, grab Meathead by the only part of him that wasn't smoking or flaming—his tail—then heave himself away from the horse.

Camryn slumped on the sand surrounded by her latest failure. Not only hadn't she gotten Ramses back, but she hadn't even been able to rescue Meathead. Distractedly, she hummed a verse of "Old MacDonald Had a Farm." She was darn sure it wasn't the verse about Old MacDonald having a horse.

She didn't have long to wallow in self-pity, because Jace was stomping toward her, holding the still-smoking and flaming cat by his tail.

"Shut this damn thing down."

Camryn pressed the hot dot beneath her right

knee, then watched with a sense of inevitability as nothing happened. Her mean-spirited self suggested this was Rachel's way of assuring she had to use the cursed password.

She closed her eyes and thought of Rachel's password. She had to use it. If she survived her first B.L.I.S.S. assignment, she would *never* work with Rachel again.

Drawing in a deep breath of resolve, she shouted the password: "Orgasm!"

Meathead's smoke and flames immediately disappeared. She tried to shut her ears to Jace's bark of laughter.

"Orgasm? You're kidding, right?" He glanced at the now quiet cat. "Guess not." Breathing heavily from his recent exertion, Jace dropped down beside her and shoved Meathead into her arms. "You know, if I put what just happened into one of my games, they'd call it a fantasy trip."

Failure. She was a pitiful failure. In the distance she could hear the Horse Shouter calling Ramses, and the man from the helicopter was striding angrily in their direction. No doubt her spring-loaded shoes were still bounding through the jungle, scaring the crap out of the local wildlife and creating a new island legend. She wished she could do the ostrich thing and bury her head in the sand.

"Thanks, Jace." He'd never know how much those words cost her, words she'd said over and over throughout her life as her brothers came to her rescue time after time. She was so tired of those words she wanted to cry. Just once she'd like

173

someone to say those words to her. Of course, she wouldn't cry, because she was pretty sure part of the B.L.I.S.S. oath included a no-crying clause.

Meathead leaned his head against her chest and offered consolation. "Me . . . ow." Wow, a whole sentence from Mr. Silent-and-deadly. Sighing, she rubbed the top of his head. This debacle wasn't his fault.

In a sudden show of affection, Meathead pushed his head up under her jaw, jamming Camryn's ring against the point of her chin. A pungent odor drifted around her. Everything went dark.

Every dream should segue into blissful comfort. That was Camryn's first thought as she burrowed her head deeper into . . . *Hmm. Not* her pillow.

She opened her eyes. She glanced up.

Jace smiled down at her. A strained smile, but still a smile. "Enjoy your nap?"

She turned her face into her makeshift pillow to muffle her groan, which immediately changed to a murmur of something else completely as she realized her head was cradled in his lap.

"Where are we?" It was a purely rhetorical question because she knew darn well where she was. Her mouth was about an inch from the taut bulge in his jeans. No, wait. Now it was only half an inch. Things were growing at a surprising rate.

Still in a happy-gas-induced haze, she slid her tongue along the bulge. Strictly to get placement coordinates, of course. She frowned. How could a woman get an accurate reading with all that fabric distorting her data? She'd just . . .

Reaching up, she unbuttoned his jeans and slid the zipper down. Spreading the material wide, she peered inside. Briefs. Huge disappointment.

He sucked in his breath, and she glanced up again. His smile had disappeared, replaced with heat, need, and something explosive moving beneath the surface of his calm. She liked that.

He'd been slowly stroking her hair, a rhythmic glide of comfort. His hand stopped and he clasped her hair tightly in his fist. "You might not want to go there."

"Sure I do." Blinking at him, she resisted the urge to shake her head to clear away the fuzzies. "Why wouldn't I? Lift your hips so I can slide these briefs down."

"This is a big mistake."

Camryn offered him a sly grin as she traced a teasing pattern with the tip of her finger around and around the erection straining even the stretchy material of his briefs. "I want my mouth on your flesh, Sentori. I want to know the taste, the texture, the heat of you." Even as every sensual cell in her body raced to take advantage of this rare lapse in her good judgment, Camryn had a fleeting sense these were not words that would normally come from her lips. She smiled. They felt good, and she was into feeling good right now.

His groan signaled his surrender, and he lifted his hips long enough for her to slip his briefs away from the targeted area.

She didn't know where her inhibitions were hiding, but she hoped they got lost and never came back. Her whole body clenched around the male scent of him, drew the heated need of him deep inside her, made it her own. Closing her eyes, she drew a line from the base of his arousal to its head with the tip of her tongue.

A faint memory tried to fight its way to the surface. Something about not muddying the water with casual sexual contact that might jeopardize an operation as well as destroy large sections of the civilized world. She frowned. She'd think about that later.

As her tongue continued to map his flesh, his gasp shuddered through her. And a need that had nothing to do with gentleness or quiet joining pushed at her. She wanted to devour him alive, to—

"Stop." His clasp on her hair tightened, drew her mouth from him. "Touch me with your mouth again, Camryn, and we'll end up naked on this jail floor."

Naked? She smiled. *Naked* had a fun sound to it.

Jail? She widened her eyes, dispelling the last residue of the gas, but not her need for him. "Jail? Who arrested us?"

His chuckle was a little shaky, but she figured that had a lot to do with the way she was cupping and massaging certain sensitive areas.

"The Monopoly jail. You know, 'Go directly to jail. Do not pass Go, do not collect two hundred dollars.' That jail." He couldn't stand it another moment. He'd mentally recited all the reasons he shouldn't touch her. She was still under the influence of the gas. She wasn't reacting to him because she needed him; she was reacting to the trauma of what had just happened. She would have found comfort in any human touch.

"Guess you don't have a Get Out of Jail Free card?" She'd stopped working that magic with her tongue.

He shook his head. *Put your mouth on me again. Surround me with enough heat to burn your memory into me forever.*

He drew in a deep breath of reason. The most important argument? He wanted to make love with Camryn O'Brien, but on his own terms. No involvement, just fun. But he was starting to get a niggling feeling that sex with Camryn might just come with involvement attached. He didn't need a long-legged, red-haired B.L.I.S.S. agent complicating his life.

She rolled her head away from his erection, and he shivered as her warm breath was replaced by the air-conditioned chill of the cell.

Her gaze was clearing and she was getting that what-the-hell-am-I-doing look in her eyes. *Too bad.*

"How did we get locked in here, and where's Meathead?" Her eyes widened. "What happened to Ramses?"

Jace pulled up his briefs. If you could calm animals by covering their heads, maybe the same method would work on overexcited sexual organs. He didn't have much hope though.

"Ramses is gone, and the Horse Shouter locked

us in here." He'd make this explanation short and sweet, then ignore all his well-thought-out reasons for having no full-body contact with Camryn O'Brien.

Her gaze darkened. "I'm sorry, Jace."

He hoped his smile didn't look as predatory as it felt. "No problem. The Horse Shouter was bringing Ramses to his legal owner. That was the sheik waiting with the helicopter. They put a sling around Ramses and lifted him onto the sheik's ship. He's on his way home. So everything turned out fine."

She didn't look comforted. "So why're we locked in here?"

"Alibis, sweetheart. We can claim the sheik's men locked us in here when we tried to stop them from taking Ramses." He frowned. "Even that might not be enough. Owen will probably try to heave me off his island the minute he sees me again."

Her gaze turned thoughtful. "You won't go, though, will you?"

The lady was beginning to understand him. Maybe that wasn't such a great thing. "I'll leave when I'm damned ready to leave." He made a real effort to relax his clenched jaw.

He watched varied emotions cross her face. If she were ever to be a B.L.I.S.S. ace, she'd have to learn some cloaking strategies for those feelings. Right now she was trying to decide whether to ask more questions or resume . . . other things.

"So where're Meathead and the Horse Shouter?" Her gaze narrowed as something else occurred to her. "And what's to keep Zed from coming in and killing us?"

She'd opted for questions. He was not disappointed. Sure he wasn't. "This is a sturdy building with only one door and window. F.I.D.O. is outside the jail door guarding against a sneak attack from Zed." He cast her an anxious glance. "You did make sure his protect mode was working, didn't you?"

He watched her surreptitiously poke at her left side. "Umm, sure."

"Right." He grinned, and she flushed. "The Horse Shouter is on her way to Chance to register as a legitimate guest."

That got Camryn's attention. "How can she do that? And why does she want to?"

Now it was Jace's turn to look uncomfortable. "She's registering as a friend of yours." He rushed on to forestall her shout of outrage. "Last night she got a look at Peter Bilt and decided she'd like to hook up with him. He's her kind of man." Jace shrugged. "Who am I to stand in the way of true love?"

"And . . . ?" Camryn offered him a narrow-eyed glare.

"And she's offered to help us."

Camryn popped off his lap with enough force to make him grunt.

"You told her about B.L.I.S.S.?" She stood facing him, legs spread, hands on hips.

"Wouldn't do that." He'd bet that without those little sock things she wore, she'd have cute toes. He wasn't a toe man himself, but his arousal was of the opinion that having those toes massaging it would be a sensational experience. "I told her there were subversive elements on the island and we were trying to track them down. No other explanation."

Walking over to the small cell window, she glanced outside. "This isn't getting me any closer to Zed. Where is he, and why hasn't he tried to kill Owen yet? The only one he's tried to take out is me." Turning back to Jace, she fixed him with a worried stare. "Zed has only eight more days before the World Economic Summit. Why is he wasting his time with me?"

Jace shook his head. She was forcing a seriousness on the moment he didn't want. For some reason, locked in this small cell, he felt insulated from the rest of the world, from his questions about Owen, his motives for coming to the island. He wanted to pretend, for even this short time, that nothing else in the world existed outside these bars. "Something about you scares Zed. Scares him enough to want to eliminate you before taking a crack at Owen."

"Sure." Her smile was self-deprecating. "I have the ultimate weapon, F.I.D.O., who works only on odd-numbered days that end with three. And I have a talent for inflicting bumps and bruises on men who . . . get too close to me. Scary stuff to one of the world's most successful assassins."

"Don't put yourself down, Camryn. Y chose you for a reason." Why did it make him mad when she said things like that about herself?

Smiling, she relaxed her stiff-legged stance. "I'll

tell you a secret: I'm good with cars. I'm probably the only agent Y has who can keep her pink baby running. She threw me into the mix with the SKPs so her Cadillac would come back in one piece. Oh, and I can't forget my intuition. Y seems to think being intuitive is a big plus."

Jace's expression turned assessing. "Y is right. When crunch time rolls around, intuition can be a valuable weapon. Someone like Zed can't plan for intuitive thinking, can't predict what you'll do. That must be scary to someone who probably orchestrates things down to the minutest detail."

"You really think so?" Her ego breathed a grateful thank-you.

Jace smiled. "I bet your nontraditional responses are driving Zed crazy, too. The dart thing is a good example. A seasoned agent wouldn't have bent down to help me. A normal reaction for an agent would've been heads-up, in pursuit. The heads-up approach would've gotten you a dart between the eyes." He narrowed his gaze in concentration. "Whatever it is about you that's bothering Zed, he'll have to get over it soon and make a move on Owen."

"I hope I'll be there when he does." Camryn had to work on her positive thinking. She couldn't just hope; she had to *know* she'd be there.

"You will be. Trust me." Jace rubbed his hand tiredly across his forehead. "I still have to take care of a few more tokens so their owners don't join Zed in trying to eliminate Da . . . Owen."

Once again Camryn wondered at Jace's reluctance to call Owen his dad. "Owen will be fine. No one will get to him with Rachel, Flo, and Sara on guard. They're the ones Zed should be worried about."

He nodded and offered her a slanted grin. "It'll take everyone on the train a while to figure out what's happened and head this way. Then a while longer before they discover we're here. We could speed the process up a little by sending Supercat for help. I assume you have a 'get help' spot. I don't think shouting would do much good with the closed windows. What do you think?"

Camryn thought about it. She was over her poor-pitiful-me bout, and she wouldn't dwell on the Ramses thing. That wasn't her mission anyway. Protecting Owen was. She'd consider it a learning experience. She'd never use those spring-loaded shoes again. From now on her feet would stay firmly planted on the ground.

And she'd also stop thinking of her partners as superior to her. Sure they had experience, but Y had chosen *her* to lead the team, even if Rachel didn't act that way. Rachel wasn't all that great. She couldn't even get Meathead to work right. And where had Flo been when the action went down? If she was "in the wind," it wasn't any breeze blowing in this direction.

Her new confident self admitted that since they were stuck here anyway, she wanted to use the time in an educational way. She glanced around. No one in this jail would ever do hard time. There was a bar, a TV, and enough comfy seating to give new meaning to the term *padded cell*. "Where's the jailer?"

"Chance's bartender doubles as jailer, and he's probably on the train. Owen doesn't leave home without him." Jace sounded impatient. *Good.*

"I've done enough screaming for one day, and I think we should give Meathead's fried brain cells a chance to cool down." Her new confident self took a deep breath and put its fingers in its ears so it couldn't hear the pesky voice of reason. "I'm going to be the one to take down Zed, but since we'll be working closely to . . . secure information, I thought you might want to know where my hot dots are." She frowned. That hadn't come out exactly as she'd intended.

"Hot dots?" He laughed. "Sure. Gotta ID those hot dots." He slid his gaze the length of her body. "For future reference."

Every hot dot in her body stood up, waved wildly, and yelled, *ID me first!*

"Get serious, Sentori. There're a lot of hot dots to remember." Even she had to review what was where each night.

He shook his head and smiled a smile that would have had Little Red Riding Hood running for the hills. "Mission impossible, O'Brien. Your entire body is a hot dot."

She tried to work past the silly glow spreading warm happiness through her because of his compliment. "Pay attention. This could be a matter of life and death someday."

His smile faded, replaced by hot anticipation. "Right. But always remember I'm the Game Master. No one is better at working his way through deadly mazes." His gaze raked her body with the promise of a round-trip journey. "And I'm at my best when the risks are high . . . and the reward is at the top of my priority list."

Camryn's world lit up with the absolute joy of having words like *deadly* and *high-risk* used to describe her.

"You challenge me, Jace." She couldn't control her smile, a smile she knew was all sensual invitation. "Watch and learn."

"You've already seen the first three hot dots in action." With her index finger, she touched below her left collarbone. "This is my 'enter' hot dot. When I want to get into or out of a locked room, I press it and Meathead opens the door. Sometimes." Camryn chose not to demonstrate. She was opting for a closed-door policy right now.

Jace stood in one lithe motion and moved close. Too close. She drew in a deep breath to try to slow down her heartbeat, which had accelerated to hyperspeed.

Carefully he unbuttoned her blouse and pushed it aside. She didn't try to stop him.

"You're wrong, lady." He pushed her bra strap away and placed his mouth on the "enter" hot dot. "This is definitely *not* your enter spot. Guys recognize enter spots when they see them." He slid his tongue across the skin of her shoulder, setting up a chain reaction of goose bumps.

"Well, perhaps we need to explore a few deterrents." She'd meant for her voice to emerge strong and firm, but a certain breathlessness kept

Join the Love Spell Romance Book Club
and **GET 2 FREE* BOOKS NOW–**
An $11.98 value!
Mail the Free* Book Certificate
Today!

Yes! I want to subscribe to the Love Spell Romance Book Club.

Please send me my **2 FREE* BOOKS**. I have enclosed $2.00 for shipping/handling. Every other month I'll receive the four newest Love Spell Romance selections to preview for 10 days. If I decide to keep them, I will pay the Special Members Only discounted price of just $4.49 each, a total of $17.96, plus $2.00 shipping/handling ($23.55 US in Canada). This is a **SAVINGS OF $6.00** off the bookstore price. There is no minimum number of books I must buy and I may cancel the program at any time. In any case, the **2 FREE* BOOKS** are mine to keep.

*In Canada, add $5.00 shipping and handling per order for the first shipment. For all future shipments to Canada, the cost of membership is $23.55 US, which includes shipping and handling.
(All payments must be made in US dollars.)

NAME: _____

ADDRESS: _____

CITY: _____ STATE: _____

COUNTRY: _____ ZIP: _____

TELEPHONE: _____

E-MAIL: _____

SIGNATURE: _____

If under 18, Parent or Guardian must sign. Terms, prices, and conditions subject to change. Subscription subject to acceptance. Dorchester Publishing reserves the right to reject any order or cancel any subscription.

creeping in. "Under my right collarbone is a hot dot that causes Meathead to emit an odor so noxious it can make enemies nauseous." *Ha!* Let him try to turn that into something sensual.

"Hmm. Right here?" He slipped her blouse off and circled the spot with the tip of his finger.

Goose bumps spread in ever-widening circles from the point of contact. She shivered. "This jail is cold. Why do they keep it air-conditioned when no one's here?" Just crown her the queen of mindless chatter.

"*We're* here." His warm breath sliding across her skin and the skim of his fingers as he removed her bra reaffirmed *his* presence. "Hot things happen in small places. Cold is good."

"Yes, well . . ." If she thought hard enough, she'd remember what she was going to say next. But how could she concentrate when her breasts were bared to his hard gaze, and her nipples were puckering up for a kiss they darned well weren't going to be denied? "Right here"—she pointed to a spot on her left side—"is the 'protect' hot dot. When danger threatens, but the source is uncertain or none of the other weapons apply, I press here."

"Danger is relative, sweetheart." He pressed gently against her skin, then slid his fingers up to cup her breast in his palm. "Pleasure can be dangerous. But sometimes the danger is worth risking, if the pleasure is great enough." Lowering his head, he drew her nipple between his lips.

Wow! The warm, wet pressure of his lips, the slide of his tongue across her nipple, the rough

185

skim of his palms against her skin from breast to waist, killed her concentration, and she wasn't even half through her presentation. "Stop." *What a stupid thing to say.* "I have to point out the other places you can't press, and you're . . . distracting me." Talk about understatements.

He leaned back and studied her; then he shook his head. "B.L.I.S.S. would expect more of its agent. A B.L.I.S.S. agent would be impervious to physical stimuli, always focused, always keeping her options open." His expression was serious, but his eyes glittered with challenge.

She recognized his manipulation, but rose to it anyway. How pathetic was that? "Actually, you're not distracting me *that* much." Okay, lying was a necessary skill for any good agent. She was honing her lying skills. "I'll finish showing you my no-press zones and we'll move on." There, that sounded like a professional, no-nonsense response.

"So neither fingers, nor mouth, nor visual temptation will stay you from the appointed rounds of your body's hot dots? Do I have that right?" He attempted to mold his features into some semblance of disinterested innocence. He didn't do innocent well.

"Exactly." She frowned. What was she agreeing to?

"Games are my life. Let's make this into a little game." His smile teased, but his eyes had darkened to something Camryn couldn't read. "You raise your arms and hold on to the bars above your head. Tell me where your danger spots are and I'll locate them."

"What's the point?" She thought she saw the point, but she needed time to brace herself, so she'd make him explain the rules.

"You can't let go of the bars." His smile was a wicked invitation to play. "No matter what I do, you have to hold on to the bars."

Her body clenched in anticipation. "What do I get if I win?"

His smile widened. "Nothing. The fun is in the losing."

"Oh." She wasn't quite sure she understood that, but it didn't matter; she was up to the challenge. Her fingers would stay cemented to the bars no matter what he did. At least one thing would go her way today.

Reaching up, she clasped the bars above her head, felt the lift and thrust of her bare breasts, and watched Jace's gaze follow the motion. The touch of his glance alone set off a sensual warning. This might not be an easy game to win, but win she would.

Never letting his gaze waver from her breasts, he clasped the bottom of his T-shirt and deliberately stripped it off in what seemed to Camryn like slow motion.

She swallowed hard at all that muscular male flesh exposed to her view. Had she agreed to this part of the game? Maybe permission to expose his body was in the small print she hadn't bothered to read. Dumb her. "Is that necessary?" Her voice sounded huskier than normal. She coughed to clear it.

"Uh-huh." His grin was a white slash of evil intent. "When a jailer is interrogating a prisoner, he needs freedom of movement."

"Jailer?" Had she agreed to fantasy, role-playing, and all the attendant dangers? She didn't think so. "Now see here—"

"Tell me where your other weapons are, woman, or . . ." He raked her with a gaze that promised things she wasn't ready to contemplate.

"Or what?" She could play a part, too. She offered him her best sneer. "You'll do things to my body?"

He leaned forward and flicked each of her nipples with his tongue. Her clasp on the bars tightened and she just managed to stifle a gasp.

"Uh-uh. I *won't* do things to your body." He turned his back on her, strode across the small cell, and reached through the bars.

She watched the play of muscles across his strong back, imagined them bunching beneath her splayed fingers as he drove into her body.

"What're you doing?" *Why aren't you back here interrogating my body?*

"Turning off the air. Pretty soon it'll heat up in here." He returned to stand in front of her. "We'll see how uncooperative you are when your body's slick with sweat, writhing under my hands, and you can't do a damned thing about it because your wrists are tied to those bars."

And she believed him. As easily as he'd created the world of the mole people, he'd just created a world where she was his helpless prisoner with her wrists bound above her head. "Do your worst." She hoped her expression was suitably defiant.

"No, sweetheart." He slid his index finger between her breasts in a line of shivery reaction all the way to her belly button. "I'll do my best." He slid his finger to the top of her shorts, then calmly unbuttoned them. "Now tell me where the next weapon is."

How could she concentrate on answering his question when all she could think about was the quiet slide of her zipper, the scrape of her shorts against her legs as he eased them off her, the brush of air against her lower belly? She spread her legs to allow air to reach a part of her body that was threatening to incinerate.

"This will not be an easy interrogation." His voice was thick with just a hint of control problems.

Ah, a chink in his armor. Her goal? To cause escalating control problems, culminating in a complete control meltdown. She grew hotter, wetter, just thinking about his ultimate loss of control. "If you press right under my right breast, you'll trigger a missile launch." She was lying. The missile launch was lower on her right side, but a B.L.I.S.S. agent never divulged all her weapon locations. The real reason? Her breast area held more sensually explosive possibilities.

"Hmm." He studied the area as he rolled her right nipple between his thumb and forefinger. "Long- or short-range?"

"Both." He had to do *both* of her nipples at the

same time. She arched her back in a silent plea. When he complied, she moaned, then offered him another tidbit of information. "Range is relative with Meathead. The missile could go a thousand miles or one foot, depending on his mood. You never know with him."

"Yeah. I remember his gas ball went about six inches. You might not want to try any of his launch things too often."

She wasn't paying much attention to what he was saying, because he'd abandoned her nipples to unbutton his jeans, peel them off along with his briefs and shoes, then kick them out of his way.

Her breath left her in an awed whoosh. The small cell was already heating up, and a sheen of sweat covered his broad chest and flat stomach. The force of gravity drew her gaze down his body until it reached his erection. She drew her tongue across suddenly dry lips. Many things might be relative, but Jace Sentori's arousal was not one of them. He was definitely a very big man. And he was into his fantasy with a lot of enthusiasm.

"I don't want there to be any doubt about the areas I'm interested in." He slid his palm from his chest down to his groin.

She certainly had no doubt about *her* area of interest. If she were free, she'd drop to her knees in front of him, cup the male weight of him in her palms, then use her lips and mouth to—

Camryn shook her head to clear it. All she had to do was loosen her grip on the bars and go to him. That was what he wanted. Stubbornly she clasped the bars until her knuckles must be white. "Show me." Her request was made through gritted teeth.

He nodded, then drew his finger across his lower body. "I want to know what's here." He stopped at the point of his right hip.

"Gas bomb." The truth. But that location didn't matter because Meathead had already used up his gas bomb supply. She watched the play of muscle along his hip and thigh as he moved closer.

"Yeah. The plop dud." He touched the inside of his left thigh. "How about here?"

"Distract." *Not.* Not all of Meathead's weapons going off at once could distract her now.

His laughter was low, husky. "You don't need a hot dot for that, lady." Slowly he slid his finger to a point right above his erection. "Anything here?"

The question hung between them. She knew the answer was in her eyes. This had nothing to do with weapon games and everything to do with sex games.

"Fireworks." The truth. She followed the path of his fingers as he traced his own length, touched the head of his erection, then slid his fingers on a return path that left a glistening trail of moisture, proof of his ultimate buy-in to his own fantasy.

"The real deal?" His words were a mere murmur, not needing an answer; he only needed her to come to him, touch him, taste him.

"Real fireworks. Shooting stars. The whole works." Slowly she rotated her hips, thrusting, inviting.

"The whole works." His echo of her words changed meaning, became something else, something totally sexual, something too tempting to resist.

Moving even closer, he lowered his head and kissed her. His kiss was rough, taking what he wanted. His tongue was a deep invasion she welcomed. On a subconscious level, a spark of remaining humor recognized that he assumed her mouth held no danger. He was so wrong.

She met the thrust of his tongue, played with him, taunted him . . . and wished like hell she could take her hands off the blasted bars.

He moved into full-body contact, pressing against her, becoming an extension of her need. Her nipples, already sensitive from his touch, grew more so as they pressed against the heat and slick dampness of his chest.

She could feel the flex of his stomach muscles as though they were her own, and his erection was hard between her spread legs.

Do it! The aching fullness, the growing moisture between her legs demanded he drive deep into her, filling her, easing the demons that clenched her muscles and screamed for release.

When she knew she couldn't stand the touching one more second, he stepped back.

She thrust her hips toward him, wanting, needing. . . .

Holding her gaze, he slid a finger between her legs, touching the one spot that made all Rachel's other spots seem inconsequential. She bit her lip to hold back her scream.

Moving his finger in a circular pattern of temptation, he leaned close to whisper, "Come to me. Touch me the way I'm touching you."

She'd have to release the bars to touch him. Arching her body against her need to let go, she felt a trickle of moisture slide between her breasts.

Slowly he slid his finger into her, let her feel the wet glide, then purposefully pushed in again, deeper, harder. Whimpering, she clenched around him.

He traced the path of moisture between her breasts with his tongue, glided his palm the length of her damp body from breast to thigh as she twisted with her need to release the bars and wrap herself around him.

But something, some trace of reason not washed away by her hormonal high tide, spoke up. "I haven't told you about the stuff down lower." Who cared? He was as low as she wanted him to go.

The warm touch of his laughter curled her toes and everything else that wasn't already tied in knots. "I don't give a damn if you have a stealth bomber down there."

He moved his finger inside her, making her gasp and writhe. She felt the building fullness, the small spasms moving her toward the inevitable.

"Touch me, Camryn." The voice of the devil.

She met his eyes, and in the glittering gaze that mirrored her own arousal she saw something else, something . . .

"Come to me, sweetheart, and let me do it all for you." He took a step back.

Let me do it all for you. She knew those words. Had heard them with different wordings but the same meaning her whole life. *Let me talk to John Wilson, and he'll never tease you again. Let me fix your bike. Let me do your homework. Let me do every damn thing in your life for you.*

The part that made her the maddest? She'd let them. She'd welcomed her brothers' intervention, had shouted for their help at every little bump in life's road.

She felt the familiar frustration building, recognized what was about to happen, and remembered Y's promise that Camryn could control it. Too late. Too late to make her mind blank.

Jace must have seen something in her eyes, because suddenly he moved farther back, just avoiding the large wooden beam that fell from the ceiling to splinter on the cement floor between them.

"A 'no' would've been sufficient." His words held clipped anger.

In the silence Camryn stared into Jace's eyes and recognized first anger at her refusal, then the fleeting something she'd seen earlier but hadn't been able to identify. She understood it now. More than a wooden beam lay between them.

Breathing deeply to restore her balance of functioning brain cells to rampaging hormones, she watched him further distance himself, physically and emotionally. "It's all about the game, isn't it?"

"No." His response was a one-syllable lie. He

bent down and scooped her clothes from the floor, then handed them to her.

She dropped her hands from the bars to take them. Every muscle in her arms ached from the tense grip she'd maintained. Quickly, she dressed.

"You hate to lose, don't you, Jace?" She watched him pull on his jeans as she worked out what she wanted to say.

"I *never* lose."

"You just did." She wasn't gloating. He needed to admit the possibility that he could lose.

He yanked his jeans up over his hips. "This wasn't all about me. This was about you and your brothers. I said something that reminded you of them, didn't I?"

She closed her eyes. If she expected him to admit defeat, she had to be willing to do some soul-baring herself. "My brothers took care of every detail of my life growing up. I never had to make one decision, fight one battle, solve one problem. And I let them. I never want anyone to take care of me again." The saying made her feel suddenly freer. She opened her eyes to his cynical gaze.

"Then I'd say you might have a little problem, because a man would always want to take care of you, sweetheart." With that admission he turned his back to her. In the distance she could hear the sound of the train approaching.

He was trying to walk away from what she wanted to tell him. She followed him across the cell and spoke to his unyielding back. "You're a lot like your father, Jace."

She watched every muscle in his back tense.

195

Reaching out, she touched his bare shoulder. He flinched.

"I'm *nothing* like Owen." He pulled his T-shirt over his head.

She sighed. This wasn't going to be easy. "Your father is obsessed with winning one particular game, but you're obsessed with winning every game. You're not the master of the game. The game is the master of you. Why?"

He turned and cast her a dark stare. She could read nothing in his gaze. Maybe he wasn't ready even to consider what she'd said. *Maybe you need to keep your big mouth shut, O'Brien.*

"Owen is the richest man in the world, but he's a loser. He's made himself a loser by sacrificing everything to a game he never wins, by focusing on the one thing in life he can't have and ignoring all that he could've had. A family. Love." Jace raked his fingers through his damp hair. "I got my Game Master tattoo to remind me that I'm the master of the game, not the other way around. You're wrong about me being as obsessed as Owen. Yes, I want to create the best games, but when someone comes along who's more important than my games, I'll admit it."

In his list of things Owen had sacrificed, Jace had left out the most important one: his son. Sighing, Camryn collapsed onto the cell's one bench. Absently, she hummed "Mary Had a Little Lamb."

He sat down beside her, and she felt the easing of tension between them. Leaning back, he laid his arm across her shoulders. "I'm going to teach you a new song." He hummed a tune.

She frowned. " 'Nobody Does It Better'? That's from one of the James Bond movies. That's not a kid's song."

His smile was a tired grimace. "You need to learn some new songs, Camryn."

"Why?"

"It's time."

Chapter Eleven

Jace was still shaking. Camryn thought he was all about the game. She was wrong. He watched her stand on tiptoe to peer out the small window. He smiled. Sure, some of what just happened had involved his desire to win, but most of it had been raw need. He hadn't wanted any woman this much, *ever.*

"Sara sees Meathead. She's heading this way."

He leaned his head against the cell wall. Great, they were about to be rescued. He didn't *want* to be rescued. What he wanted was Camryn O'Brien spread naked beneath him, her tangled mass of red hair sliding across his bare body, her luscious mouth touching him in all the right places.

The cell door slammed open, and Sara charged through it with F.I.D.O. trailing in her wake. "What happened? Owen is having a fit over his horse, and he's pretty upset about seeing Jace, too." She offered him a pointed stare.

How had Owen recognized him? Newspaper or magazine photos? Probably. "Ramses's owner took him back. I couldn't stop him."

"I wonder just how hard you tried, Jace." Sara's smile mocked his lie.

He wouldn't involve Camryn. She'd hate admitting failure, and he didn't want Owen ordering her off the island. "The sheik locked us in here to give himself a bigger head start."

Sara glanced at Camryn. "I hope *you* didn't try to stop the sheik. The tokens aren't your job. Besides, a battle over the horse could've caused an international incident."

Camryn met Sara's gaze. "I didn't know the man taking Ramses was his owner." She shrugged. "I tried, and I failed. I didn't think things through. My mistake."

Sara shook her head, but she was smiling. "New agents are always too eager, wanting to do everything themselves. I felt the same way on my first assignment. You'll learn."

Jace stared down at F.I.D.O., who stared back at him. Silent agreement connected them. What man could hope to understand the cloverleaf logic of a woman's brain? He felt a gender bonding with F.I.D.O.

Jace shook his head, took a last look at Camryn, who was deep in conversation with Sara, then left the jail and strode to where Owen stood staring across the widening stretch of water separating him from his prized stallion.

Surprisingly, F.I.D.O. followed Jace instead of planting himself on Camryn's foot. Of course, she'd pressed the "protect" hot dot, and considering the cat's wacko operational system, it probably didn't have a clue whom it was supposed to protect.

Jace smiled. Then again, maybe it just wanted to be in on any action going down. Jace had a feeling there'd be plenty in a few minutes.

Owen was alone. Glancing around, Jace noted that Peter Bilt wasn't too far away. Maybe Owen had told Peter to keep everyone away. Then why had Peter allowed *him* to approach Owen?

Jace stopped and joined Owen in staring out at the Pacific. What did you say to someone you hadn't seen since you were six? "Will you try to get him back?"

Owen shook his head, but kept staring out at the sea. "Some things you can never get back."

Jace nodded. "He'll adjust to the change, but he'll remember you. Probably wonder what happened, why he had to leave."

Owen lifted his top hat from his head and wiped his forehead with a handkerchief he'd pulled from his pocket. "I made a mistake with him. Should've kept him safe, let him know he was important to me." He shrugged. "Too late now."

"So what'll you do?" Jace made a conscious effort to unclench his fists, breathing deeply to relax his tight muscles.

"Have to have a horse token, but not another live horse." Owen glanced to where Peter Bilt was talking agitatedly on his cell phone. "I have a line on the stuffed Trigger. Guests would like that."

Jace groaned silently. How could he discourage Owen from stealing tokens that were ticking time bombs?

Owen turned to face Jace for the first time. His eyes had a strange glitter. "Some things can never be replaced, you know."

Before Owen ordered him to get out of town, Jace had to know. "How did you recognize me?"

Owen's smile was sad. "You look like me when I was young."

That made his day. He was going to look like the man on the Monopoly box in a few years. Jace exhaled sharply. Might as well get things into the open. "Do you want me off the island?"

Owen shook his head, and for a moment Jace could've sworn he saw a flash of bitterness in Owen's eyes. "Welcome home, son."

He walked away, leaving Jace staring after him.

Jace looked back at the sea. *Home? Son?* Chance wasn't his home, and he'd never be a son to Owen Sitall, any more than Owen would be his father. Then what had they just been talking about? Not Ramses. He frowned. Jace liked playing games when he knew the rules. He wasn't sure what game Owen was playing, and he sure as hell didn't know the rules.

Since Camryn was still talking to Sara, Jace wandered over to where Citra for once wasn't surrounded by men.

She offered him a tight smile. "I hear the

201

sheik's men overpowered you, then locked you in the jail. What really happened?"

He shrugged. "The sheik is Ramses's rightful owner, so I let him go. The Horse Shouter locked Camryn and me in jail so no one would suspect anything. She left. She's registering as a guest now."

That distracted Citra for a moment. "Will they let her register? Won't they ask questions?"

Jace smiled. "Have you seen her? I wouldn't say no to her." He glanced over at Camryn. Still talking. "She seems like a resourceful woman. I'm sure she has identification that'll get her in."

Citra nodded and followed his gaze to Camryn. Then she looked down to where F.I.D.O. had planted himself on Jace's foot. "So what was Camryn's part in this whole thing?"

"At first we didn't realize Ramses's legal owner had come for him. Camryn tried to stop the Horse Shouter, but she had a little trouble with some of her equipment." You'd think that B.L.I.S.S. would give its agents more reliable stuff.

Citra's gaze turned thoughtful. "B.L.I.S.S. has a reputation for equipping its agents with the best." She looked down at F.I.D.O. again. "Strange."

Jace would second that. Especially F.I.D.O. Sometimes the cat malfunctioned. Sometimes he performed perfectly. And sometimes . . . Sometimes he did his own thing. But that last was impossible, wasn't it?

"Did Owen order you off the island?" Citra scanned the area, missing nothing.

Citra was the perfect agent: efficient, beautiful,

deadly. Jace liked Camryn a lot better. "Nope."

"What did you talk about?" A slight frown marred her perfect face. She didn't like one-word answers. She was into elaboration.

"Ramses." He walked away from her. He'd head into the jungle and hope Camryn followed as soon as she finished talking to Sara. They could take the trail back to her Cadillac.

Camryn watched Jace's interaction with his father, then with Citra. As much as she wanted to rush over and run interference between the two men, she knew this was one time she needed to butt out. Besides, she had other things to worry about.

"Where's Flo, Sara? I know she was supposed to stay out of sight, but I could've used some backup with this Ramses thing." She narrowed her gaze on Citra. The perfect agent. No doubt about it. She'd bet Jace *really* admired Citra. Camryn could dislike Citra with no trouble at all. And she couldn't believe what she'd just revealed about herself. Jealousy? *Nah.* Camryn returned her attention to Sara.

"I don't know. I haven't seen her." Sara looked troubled. "I tried reaching her, but her communicator's shut down. That's not like her."

Things were getting weirder and weirder around here. "I'm taking a shortcut through the jungle to get the Cadillac. Then Jace and I will head back to Chance. Maybe Flo got a call from Rachel and headed home." She left unspoken the thought that something had happened to Flo, that after today there would be only eight days until the summit, and that Zed would have to move soon. Maybe he had moved already.

Sara nodded. "Owen will ride back on the train. I'll be with him, and so will Peter. He'll be okay. Make sure things are secure at Chance before we get there."

Camryn didn't look back as she hurried into the jungle after Jace. She found him waiting just beyond the tree line with Meathead seated on his foot.

She studied the cat. "Just who're you supposed to be guarding, buddy? Or is this a guy thing?"

Camryn could've sworn a sheepish look crossed the cat's face as he immediately shifted his bulk to her foot. She exchanged startled glances with Jace. "He's not supposed to react to verbal commands other than the code word to shut him down. And that wasn't even a direct command."

Jace narrowed his gaze on Meathead. "I'd love to take him apart and see what's happening in that tiny computer of a brain."

Meathead offered him a slit-eyed glare.

They walked the rest of the way to the car in silence. She was glad he didn't question her about what Sara had said, and in return she wouldn't ask about his father.

When they reached the Cadillac, Camryn climbed behind the wheel while Jace sat on the passenger side. Meathead sat between them. *Cozy.*

Camryn started to pull back onto the paved road, but Jace pointed to where the jungle path continued. It widened into a gravel road cars had obviously used. "Let's stay on the trail. It's wide enough for the car, and even if we have to go slower, it should cut some miles off our trip back to Chance."

They'd almost reached Chance before Camryn decided there was one question she had to ask. "Did Owen tell you to leave?"

"No. He even welcomed me. Can you believe that?"

Jace didn't seem bothered by her question, so she asked another. "What did he have to say?" She had *no* self-discipline. She'd sworn she wouldn't ask nosy . . . er, probing questions about his personal life.

His silence lasted so long, she thought he'd decided not to answer. "I'm not sure. We talked in code."

"Oh." That answer was way too vague for her. "Well, at least—"

The bullet smashing into the driver's side of the windshield made her lose her train of thought. She would kiss the toes of the inventor of bulletproof glass. Jamming her foot down on the brake, she opened her door just wide enough to shove Meathead out, pushed the "investigate" hot dot, then flipped open the control panel on her steering wheel.

The radio crackled. "Activate the shield, dudess. Don't want any bullet dings in the Big Smooth. Oh, and note a new and exciting upgrade in the shield. The shield still keeps bullets and other solid symbols of aggression out, but now sound can pass through. Don't know how it works. I didn't develop it. Anyway, you can now trade insults and death threats with the enemy. Out." T didn't seem to think dings in *her* were of any great importance.

Camryn activated the protective shield as soon as Meathead cleared the area of the car. The shimmering transparent shield was a pale rose color. This must be what it felt like to be inside a giant soap bubble. It was big enough to shield three pink behemoths. She blinked as several more bullets exploded uselessly against the shield.

"Talk about looking at the world through rose-colored glasses." Jace's comment was a frustrated mutter. "What the hell is this about?"

Camryn noted that the motor had shut down as soon as she activated the shield. The upside? T couldn't nag her with the motor off. She tried restarting the car. Nothing. They might be safe, but they weren't going anywhere while the shield was up. "I can't imagine Zed shooting at the car. He'd know it was bulletproof." She glanced at Jace. "Maybe the shooter is after you."

He shrugged and peered into the jungle where Meathead had disappeared. "Why? I'm trying to return the tokens to their rightful owners. Besides, no one knows why I'm really on the island except for you and your partners."

"Maybe your secret is out and someone doesn't want the tokens to go back to their rightful owners." That was a long shot, and she knew it. Then why . . . ?

A figure ran from the jungle, then came to a sudden halt. Camryn blinked. Shorts that showed cheek, minuscule top with overflowing boobs, sexy everything. Yep, that was Honey Suckle. The big, deadly-looking rifle she was carrying didn't fit the image. Meathead trotted happily behind her.

Honey Suckle was bouncing up and down excitedly. Camryn lowered her window so she could hear her.

"Oh, cripes, did I shoot at you? I can't believe I did that. Peter called me and said he'd seen two strange animals go past the train. He said the animals were the size of shoes and were leaping at least ten feet into the air. I figured he'd spent too much time in the train's bar, but I came out to investigate anyway. All I saw was some movement, and I guess I overreacted a little." Her giggle was very convincing.

Camryn pushed the "protect" hot dot on her left side.

Jace leaned toward Camryn. "Tell her a pink Cadillac doesn't look anything like a shoe."

Honey Suckle moved a little nearer. "What's that pink shimmery thing around your car?"

Camryn put up her window and reached for the control panel. Better shut the shield off and tell Honey Suckle she'd imagined the whole thing. She reached for the off button. No off button.

Take slow, deep breaths. Okay, she could understand T's rationale. There was a good reason why the off button shouldn't be on the steering wheel. As soon as she stopped hyperventilating she'd think of it. *Where the heck was the stupid off button?* T had probably told her, but three days of training wasn't a lot of time to absorb everything.

"Let me guess. You can't turn it off." Jace sounded resigned.

Camryn nodded. She had the almost over-powering urge to bang her forehead against the steering wheel, but heaven knew what catastrophes that would trigger.

She aimed a killer glare at Jace. "Search."

For a frenzied few minutes they crawled around looking for the elusive off button. Even if they found it, T probably hadn't labeled it, and they'd be afraid to push it for fear of causing eternal night.

She lowered the window again. Thank heavens T had kept the old-fashioned crank-down windows. "Would you go back to Chance and tell Rachel I need her?"

With a last puzzled glance at the shield, Honey Suckle headed toward Chance. *Bounced* would be a better description. Everything about her bounced. Camryn glanced at Jace to see if he was noticing.

"She bounces well, doesn't she?" He sounded admiring.

Camryn frowned. There it was again—that stab of something that felt strangely like jealousy. She'd never experienced the feeling before, but like any primal instinct, it must be imbedded in the human psyche.

"Wonder how long it'll take her to get back to Chance?" He peered out at the shield as he rolled down the window on his side.

Camryn did some mental math involving speed of forward progress minus drag caused by gravitational pull on bouncing boobs. "About fifteen minutes. Then it'll take Rachel a few minutes to reach us."

Jace was still staring at the shield.

"Why is it pink?" He seemed to have dismissed Honey Suckle's bouncing perfection easily.

Camryn felt better. "The color lets me see that it's operational and its area coverage."

"Can't the bad guys see it, too?" His expression indicated he was thinking of something other than the shield.

She didn't trust that look. "Does it matter? It's a protection and a deterrent, no matter what color it is."

"Hmm." Jace turned to study the backseat. "Guess we could be stuck here for a little while."

"And?" Camryn noted that Meathead was still outside the shield. Not altogether a bad place for him to be.

"I'm into time management. Why don't we climb into the backseat and discuss how we could manage this time wisely?"

"No." She had a lot to think about, and sitting in a backseat with Jace Sentori didn't lend itself to deep thinking. "I need to figure some things out. I'll stay right here." She smiled at him. "But don't let me stop you. You could probably stretch out on the backseat and take a nap." The seat was big enough for an army to sleep on.

"Never mind. Backseats are no fun alone." He gazed fixedly out the windshield. "Hope you don't mind being stared at."

"What?" She followed his gaze out the wind-

209

shield, along the mile-long front hood of the Cadillac . . . and met the unblinking yellow stare of Meathead. "Goody." The cat had climbed a tree directly in front of the car and crept out on a limb that didn't look strong enough to support his ample body. He might not be able to cross the shield, but he could darn well still keep watch.

"Why don't you shut him down, or send him out to investigate something?" Jace glanced at her, then returned his gaze to Meathead's fixed glare. "I don't think he likes what he's seeing."

"I don't want to take him off protect." She didn't think anything could get through the shield, but she also didn't want to take any chances with Zed out there somewhere. Besides, there was something funny about Honey Suckle's story. Camryn would rather err on the side of being too careful.

"You know, if we climbed into the back, we could scrunch down, and he couldn't see us over the top of the seats." Jace's glance was hopeful.

Camryn shook her head and laughed. "You are *so* transparent, Sentori." She squirmed a little under Meathead's continued stare. "But you're right. I don't want to spend almost a half hour like this. Let's do it."

Nodding, he opened his door and slipped into the backseat. Camryn did the same. They rolled down the back windows, then scrunched down.

"I can't believe we're hiding from a robot." Jace sounded rueful.

Camryn didn't move as Jace slid closer. He put his hand on the back of her neck and slowly massaged her tight muscles. She sighed her relief as everything loosened. She frowned. She had to keep a tight rein on all that loosening though. Back at the jail she'd taken loosening to dangerous lengths.

"We might not be hiding from just a robot." Camryn hadn't realized the thought had been forming in her mind until she blurted it out. "I know Meathead is equipped with a camera. He could be sending pictures back to someone." Y? Rachel? She shook her head. Paranoid? Not really. If she were truly paranoid, she wouldn't trust Jace. But Y listed intuition as one of her gifts, and her intuition told her Jace was a completely different kind of threat.

"Pictures, huh?" With one fluid motion, he stripped off his T-shirt. "It's hot in here without the air conditioner on."

The backseat suddenly became a lot smaller . . . and a lot hotter.

"I only had three days to prepare for this assignment, and there was no way I could cram in everything I needed to know. I'm sure I missed a lot that Rachel said." She wasn't missing a lot now. No matter how much she wanted to stare somewhere else, her gaze kept returning to his bare chest; she was mesmerized by the rise and fall of his steady breathing, the damp perfection of smooth skin over hard muscle.

"Why the big hurry?" He tried to stretch his long legs, but even the roomy Cadillac didn't have enough space. With a murmured expletive, he shifted until he was half lying across the seat.

Since Camryn was in his way, he lifted her easily and placed her on top of him.

She stiffened into board mode. But she wouldn't make a big deal out of this. That was what he wanted. She tried to relax and remember his question. "The World Economic Summit takes place in eight days. Word is out that L.O.V.E.R. wants Owen out of the way by then. That didn't give me much prep time."

"Why you, Camryn? Why not just send the three women who're with you? They're more experienced."

Her mind might be involved in an intelligent conversation with Jace, but her body had a totally different agenda. She'd allow her body its little triumph. She relaxed against his chest, felt the heat of him seeping into her, savored the scent of hot male, discovered the erotic effect of his body contours molded against her. . . .

"Camryn?" His voice was a murmur of amusement against her ear.

"Hmm?" She blinked. "Oh, why me? I'm not sure, but Y seemed to feel I was right for the job." She'd tried to avoid analyzing too often Y's reasons for sending her on this mission. Tried to dismiss her suspicions that Y's reasons had sounded a little too simplistic. Would Y not give her the whole picture if she thought it would benefit the agency? Camryn sighed. In a heartbeat. "Her reason doesn't matter, though. She gave it to me, and I'll get it done."

"You have my vote." He shifted beneath her.

"So why'd you try to zap me back in the jail? You were the one in control."

She sucked in her breath at his movement. His legs were spread, with one foot on the floor and the other leg propped on the seat. Her leg lay between his. The scrape of his jeans against her inner thigh and the unmistakable evidence of his readiness to take this backseat thing to the next level made reasonable thinking almost impossible.

"I *thought* I was in control, but I wasn't. You knew I wouldn't let go of those bars, so you could do whatever you wanted."

"And I wanted to do a lot." His warm chuckle heated her cheek. "But you always had the power to say no."

She took a deep breath and admitted the truth. "I didn't want to say no." *Tell him the rest.* "When you said you wanted to do it all for me, it reminded me of my brothers and I just reacted."

"Okay, I know there's logic there somewhere, but I don't get it."

He splayed his hand across her lower stomach, and she felt each finger as a point of fire. How could she be so sensitized to this man's touch?

"The truth? It's always been more than a reaction to my brothers' control." Why was she trying to explain this to him? Why did she care if he understood? "It was about me. I hated myself for wanting them to take care of my whole life. Whenever I had a problem, I told myself that I wanted to handle it alone, but I was always relieved when they took care of it for me. This thing with men, it must've developed from my need to control my own life, even when I didn't have the guts to say no to my brothers." She smiled. "Is that deep or what?"

He didn't say anything for a moment, and she concentrated on his steady breathing, his calmness. She let his calm become her own. If he didn't want anything more to do with her because of her admission, so be it. He was a distraction she didn't need. *And you're a big fat liar, Camryn O'Brien.*

"You need time. Eventually you'll have enough confidence in your own abilities, in *yourself*, to realize you don't have to do it all. You can trust a man enough to take his advice, let him help, and know it isn't diminishing you." He frowned. Something wasn't right here. When he'd climbed into the backseat, he'd had every intention of continuing what he'd started in the jail. So where had things gone wrong? Why did he give a damn about Camryn's life when he only wanted her body? That *was* all he wanted, wasn't it?

She wiggled into a more comfortable position on his lap. More comfortable for her, but he almost groaned at the increased pressure on his erection. His erection didn't handle pressure well.

A distant rumble distracted him from thoughts of pressure, volcanic activity, and molten magma.

"What's that?" She sat up on his lap, putting optimum force where force was least needed right now.

"God almighty, woman." He lifted her from his

lap and sat up. He did some deep breathing and silent cursing.

The rumble grew closer. He frowned. He recognized that rumble. "My bike. Someone has my bike." *No one* took his bike. It was sacred. Sort of like the plans for his latest video game.

He pulled on his shirt, rolled up his window, then climbed from the car as Rachel roared into view on his bike. Give the woman credit—she looked completely at ease on the Harley. When he saw one of Camryn's partners like this, it reminded him that these weren't ordinary retired women. There was nothing grandmotherly about Rachel.

"Why my bike? Why didn't you take Citra's car?" He knew better than to ask how she'd started it without a key. He was sure B.L.I.S.S. had a gizmo that would start anything.

Glancing around, he noted that Camryn had rolled up the back window, then climbed from the backseat, but instead of joining him she'd climbed into the driver's seat. She motioned for him to get back into the car.

"I like your bike. It gives me a feeling of power." Rachel was talking to him, but her attention was on Camryn. "I like power."

Jace felt the sudden tension. Unlike the shield, he couldn't see it or measure its dimensions, but he knew it was there. He'd learned a long time ago to trust his instincts in all things.

Walking around to the passenger side, he climbed in. "What's the problem?" He kept his voice low so it wouldn't reach Rachel.

Camryn's answer was a tense whisper. "I don't know. Something doesn't feel right. It's like there's a loose string somewhere, and if I can just find it and pull it, then L.O.V.E.R.'s plot will unravel. But where's the darn string?" She shrugged.

Jace nodded. They agreed on something.

Rachel's smile was enigmatic, and he had the creepy feeling she knew exactly what they'd said. "What happened? I couldn't get anything rational from Honey Suckle." Her gaze touched him. "I suppose I'm free to talk in front of Jace. I'm sure he knows all our little secrets."

Camryn frowned as her gaze slid away from Rachel. "Honey Suckle accidentally took a few shots at us. I put up the shield, and now I can't find the button to make it go away."

"Stupid woman." Rachel's smile disappeared.

Jace hoped Rachel was referring to Honey Suckle, because he wouldn't put up with anyone insulting Camryn. *Listen to yourself.* He was turning into exactly the kind of man Camryn hated.

Rachel's frown deepened. "I can't help you with the shield. T tells the secrets of his car only to the designated driver on an assignment. You're it. I'll have to contact him." She carefully pulled off the driving gloves she wore.

Jace stared. Rachel had a netlike glove on under one of the driving gloves. Quickly she pressed a code into the pads of three of her fingers, then spoke into her palm.

"Agent 36DD is inside the shield and can't find the off button." A few seconds later she nodded, then put her driving gloves back on.

Rachel smiled at Camryn. "Inside the glove compartment you'll find an old Mickey Mouse watch. Press on the face and it'll get rid of the shield."

While Jace got rid of the shield, Rachel expounded on the state of their mission. "I have a bad feeling about this assignment. Little things are going wrong. F.I.D.O. shouldn't have any operational problems. I suspect tampering."

Little things? Jace would hate to see what Rachel considered big things.

As if to underline Rachel's observation, a sudden crack drew everyone's attention to the tree where F.I.D.O. crouched. Well, *had* crouched. He'd evidently tried to back off the limb, and it had snapped under the burden of all that chubby cat. They were just in time to see Rachel's weapon of mass destruction tumble to the ground. Cats were supposed to land on their feet, not their bellies. Rachel glared at F.I.D.O., a large orange testament to her equipment-tampering theory.

Rachel left the obvious unspoken. The B.L.I.S.S. agents were the only ones who had access to the equipment.

One glance at Camryn's face assured him she understood the implications.

Camryn studied Rachel. "How tamper-proof is this car?"

"The car should be okay. Besides its security system, F.I.D.O. scans it before you get in."

They all looked at F.I.D.O. Jace shook his head. "He can't even get off his belly. Doesn't bode well for any heavy-duty explosive detecting." He grinned as Camryn opened her mouth to defend the robot. She was loyal, even to a computer-driven cat that was probably a lot more dangerous to her health than ten Zeds. "Hope nothing important is stored in his stomach."

Camryn glared at him as F.I.D.O. struggled to his feet and staggered to the car. She opened her door, scooped up the cat, and plunked him on the seat between them.

Before starting the Cadillac, Camryn paused to ask Rachel one more question: "Have you seen Flo?"

Rachel looked intense as she prepared to roar away on his bike. She must be over seventy, but if anyone told him Rachel was planning to jump ten parked cars with his Harley, he wouldn't even blink in surprise.

"Haven't seen Flo . . ." Rachel pulled on her driving gloves.

He decided against pissing her off by offering any take-it-easy advice.

"Where the heck *is* Flo?" Camryn looked worried.

"But we did have a little excitement while you were gone." Rachel crouched over the bike in a position meant to minimize wind resistance. "I found a bomb in Owen's bedroom." Rachel roared off, and Jace waited expectantly for the sonic boom.

Chapter Twelve

"I don't need you to help me find Flo. I don't need you to go with me to your father's room to check out the bomb." *The things I need you for aren't listed here.* Camryn narrowed her gaze on Jace, then turned to knock on Flo's door. "Protecting Owen is my job. Go find a token to rescue."

"Owen is my father." His statement sounded as though it were forced through clenched teeth.

"Could've fooled me." Okay, so that was really cold. "Look, I understand your interest in Owen, but Flo is B.L.I.S.S. business." She rapped harder on Flo's door.

"Anything that affects Chance is my business." He was using his Game Master voice. "I care about what happens to Owen"—she could almost hear his mental foot shuffling—"and to *you*."

"Hmm." She let her silent question about his

meaning hover between them. He chose not to answer. She'd pursue her answer later, but right now she had more immediate concerns.

Camryn put her ear to the door. There was some sort of strange whining on the other side, then a voice making shushing noises. What the heck was going on in there? She almost didn't notice when Meathead plunked his chubby bottom on her foot.

The door slowly cracked open a few inches, and Camryn leaped to the side to avoid any laser-beam greetings. Meathead looked offended at the sudden removal of his chosen seat. Nothing happened. Moving back into place, she met Flo's intent stare. "It's only me, Flo. Open up."

Flo's gaze swept past Camryn and settled on Jace. "Send him away; then we'll talk."

Camryn turned to stare at Jace.

He met her gaze for an intent moment, then nodded. "I'll be in Owen's room with Sara. Don't take too long, or I'll be back."

Now that was a statement guaranteed to earn one of her brothers a bump somewhere on his anatomy, but Jace strode away unscathed. Maybe the corner of her brain responsible for punishing dominant-alpha-speak was taking a late-afternoon nap.

Camryn followed his departure with interest. Wide shoulders squared. Definitely a determined man. Long, easy strides. A man at home in his body. And what a body. The view going away showcased the best buns she'd ever seen . . . or felt. She sighed. Back to business.

Flo opened her door just wide enough for Camryn to slip through. "Keep F.I.D.O. outside."

Camryn hesitated. Meathead was her only protection. Then she looked into Flo's eyes. They weren't the eyes of Zed. Y had counted on her intuition, and her intuition said that going into Flo's room alone was okay.

Camryn pressed her "protect" hot dot on the wild chance this was one of Meathead's more lucid moments and he'd actually work as Rachel had programmed him. One could always hope.

As soon as Camryn entered the room, Flo closed the door. "Have to make sure no one finds out about this."

Camryn eyed her warily as Flo casually put her gun back in her shoulder holster. The holster was obvious beneath Flo's cotton blouse, but Camryn didn't think Flo would give a damn.

"I have to keep him safe." Flo's gaze dropped toward the floor.

Camryn followed her gaze down. A Scottish terrier stared up at her with shiny-eyed interest.

"This is Champion Grenloch's Highland Warrior. He's Owen's dog token, and I'm protecting him." Flo's tight-lipped pronouncement boded ill for the person foolish enough to try to take him away from her.

"A Scottie dog!" Camryn squatted down to pet the dog and was met with a dignified willingness to be friends. No leaper and licker here. "What a big name for such a little guy."

"His owner's here. Little, mean-eyed, rat-faced jerk. Going to take Duncan here back to Scotland.

I won't let him." Flo narrowed her gaze on Camryn. "No one can make me."

Camryn believed her. "Duncan?"

"That's what I named him. A lot more to the point than all that other garbage they tagged him with. Besides, always was a big fan of *Highlander*." Her glance touched the dog with a softness Camryn had never seen before. "I'll take him back with me when this assignment's finished."

Uh-oh. "What about his owner?"

Flo made a rude noise. "I did a little investigating. Rat-face was cruel to him. Don't respect any man who'd beat a little dog."

And that was that. Camryn knew there'd be no arguing with Flo. The truth? She wouldn't want the dog sent back to a cruel owner either.

"Don't tell Sentori. Jace would try to make sure Duncan went home with Rat-face." Flo moved to the door and peered out the peephole. Owen had probably had it installed so a high roller who'd decided to dip into the Community Chest could identify his outraged wife on the other side of the door.

"F.I.D.O. is out there scratching instead of guarding. How the hell can a robot get fleas?" Shaking her head, Flo moved from the door.

Camryn drew in a deep breath. She had to ask some hard questions. "Rachel found a bomb in Owen's room." She forced herself to meet Flo's gaze. "Where were you all day? I needed you."

Flo nodded as if Camryn's suspicion were perfectly normal. It probably was. Suspicion was a part of her world now. Camryn didn't know if she liked that.

"I hung around the train to make sure Owen was okay. I didn't follow you because you can take care of yourself."

Camryn's self-esteem did a silent backflip at the implied compliment.

"I scoped out the area and didn't find anything suspicious, so I headed back here to rescue Duncan before Rat-face returned." She shrugged. "I probably should've hung around until Owen was back at Chance, but I figured he was safe with you, Jace, Sara, and that Citra all hanging around him."

Except Jace and she hadn't hung around Owen, but Camryn didn't intend to go into that now. Did she believe Flo? Her intuition assured her the dog story was too bizarre not to be true. She had to go with her intuition until she had hard evidence otherwise. Right now the bomb was on her front burner.

"I'm going to Owen's room. We'll work out the dog thing later." Camryn opened the door carefully. Meathead looked unconcerned. But then Meathead could look unconcerned with all of L.O.V.E.R. marching toward him.

She made her way to Owen's room and knocked on the closed door. Then knocked again. Camryn finally realized she'd have to beat down the door before she'd be heard above Sara's and Rachel's shouting voices inside. She tried the door. Locked. At least they'd retained that much common sense before going at each other.

Sighing, she pressed the "enter" hot dot. "Okay, Meathead, unlock this sucker." She glanced down at the cat, who was busy scratching at a particularly enthusiastic flea. How stupid would a flea have to be to bite a robot?

Meathead, evidently in the mood for the direct approach, paused in his scratching just long enough to stand, stretch, then crash through the closed door amid the noise of splintering wood, blaring alarms, and various cries of surprise. Once inside, he sat down amid the shattered remains of the door and resumed scratching.

Camryn did some heavy-duty gaping outside the door while Sara and Rachel did the same inside.

Rachel recovered first. Seated on the couch, she resumed her interrupted knitting. *What a woman.* Not even heated arguments or splintering doors could stay those needles for long. Camryn watched the electricity arc between them and wondered what would happen if Rachel chose to use them as a weapon. Not a pleasant thought.

"You could've just knocked. Now we'll have to replace the door." Rachel's needles never missed a beat.

Sara stopped her agitated pacing long enough to pull the door's rubble out of Camryn's way.

"Sure. Knock first. Will do." Camryn stepped gingerly around the wreckage, then glared at Meathead. Meathead didn't care. "So what's all the shouting about?"

"Rachel accused me of lying down on the job because I didn't find the bomb." Sara huffed her outrage.

"Ha." Rachel managed to look superior with merely a raised eyebrow. "What else would you call sleeping with Owen Sitall and forgetting to do a room check after you came back from breakfast?"

"I *did* a check of the room before we left for the day." Sara was talking through gritted teeth. "There was no bomb."

Rachel's gaze turned ugly. "If you did a check, then we have a problem, because I came into this room right after you left and found the bomb wedged under the mattress. When Owen went to bed tonight, he'd have been blown to bits."

Sara paled as the accusation hung between them. Either Sara had put the bomb there herself or someone had been watching and as soon as Owen left had gained access to the room.

But that was impossible, because Camryn knew that with the advanced surveillance equipment B.L.I.S.S. had supplied, no one could enter the room undetected.

Camryn's intuition was drawing an ugly conclusion. *One of them?* She hadn't wanted to listen before, but the unthinkable was becoming more possible. No one else at Chance other than Honey Suckle had raised warning signals. And even though she might have a key to this room, Honey Suckle wouldn't have been able to bypass all of B.L.I.S.S.'s safeguards without inside information.

What was her intuition telling her now? Nothing. It was struck silent by her mind's strident reminders that she had no defense against a woman. In fact, she had no chance at all against another B.L.I.S.S. agent.

Rachel shrugged and allowed herself a tight smile. "What's done is done. But you've got to get over this sex thing with Owen. B.L.I.S.S. agents don't get involved during an assignment. It's a distraction, and you see what happens when you take your mind off your job?"

Sara let that pass with only a narrowing of her eyes.

Rachel put her knitting into her satchel and stood. "I'll check to see who didn't go on the train." She stepped over the rubble and was gone.

"Bitch." Sara's one-word description of Rachel said everything. She glanced toward Camryn. "Is Flo okay?"

Camryn could only nod.

"I'll call down and have someone put in a new door; then I'll reset all the surveillance equipment and deterrents with a few new twists. I hope Zed is just really smart." Left unsaid was that a very smart Zed was preferable to a traitor in B.L.I.S.S.'s midst. "Would you go down to the bar and check on Owen? He was upset when he found out about the bomb. I had to tell him about L.O.V.E.R., but I don't think he believed me. I think he's half-afraid Jace is responsible."

Sara twirled a strand of hair around her finger. It was the first nervous gesture Camryn had seen her make. "Oh, Jace stopped by for a minute, but he left when he found out Owen wasn't here."

"Jace isn't responsible. He was with me the

whole time." Once again she felt surprised at her need to defend Jace.

"I don't think Jace is responsible, but try telling that to Owen. Sometimes we distrust the ones we love most, because betrayal by them would cut the deepest." Sara frowned. "I'm afraid he'll start to suspect *me*." She met Camryn's gaze. "I'll do whatever is necessary to protect Owen. He's important to me."

Camryn didn't like Sara's intent stare. Did Sara suspect *her*? Not surprising. Trusting unwisely could lead to sudden death. Even though Jace might not be Zed, trusting him could be just as deadly to her emotions, to her heart. No, that was not true. Her heart was definitely not involved here. She had to keep that straight in her mind. "I'll go down and make sure Owen's okay." She'd probably find Jace in the same place as his father. Camryn skirted the door's remains and left the room.

Once outside the room she took a deep, cleansing breath, put Meathead on his leash, then took the stairs down to the bar. She had a lot to think about. Who was Zed? Did Owen feel as deeply for Jace as Sara implied? Should she tell Jace about Flo's dog?

Camryn paused in the doorway to the bar. She'd left the most troubling question for last. What could she do to keep Jace Sentori from involving more and more of her emotions and jeopardizing her assignment? She didn't know. She really didn't know.

Camryn pushed all soul-searching aside as she

spotted Owen at the bar with Peter beside him. Owen looked a little rocky, but at least Peter seemed sober. Her stomach did some lurching as she noticed Jace watching her from a darkened corner. The stomach lurching was probably caused by lack of food. She'd grabbed a doughnut for breakfast, but that was it.

Jace's smile was a dark invitation as she started toward him.

A firm hand on her shoulder stopped her. Turning, she met gray eyes guaranteed to invite visions of stormy nights.

"I need to speak wi' ye for a moment." His eyes suggested the time spent talking to him would be well spent. "I'm Jamie MacDuff, and I'm searching for a wee dog. I think ye might be able to help me."

Camryn blinked to clear her vision of the steam rising between them. Hair as red as hers framed a face born in every woman's dream of a Highland lover. A white shirt open at the throat fueled fantasies topped only by . . . Camryn glanced down. *Yes!* A kilt. It didn't get much better than this.

Her gaze slid past the Highland dream and locked with the devil's nightmare. Jace had stepped from the shadows and was watching her intently. When he caught her gaze his eyes darkened, promising that whatever the Highlander could offer, he could offer more. Camryn believed him.

"I've seen ye wi' a woman named Flo. I think she has the dog. Can ye help us get him back? I'd thank ye." Jamie MacDuff's voice suggested few women would turn down his thanks.

Just call her one of the few, the proud. She would've made a great marine. One thing was for sure: Jamie MacDuff was *not* rat-faced. Flo was crazy.

"Have ye ever wondered what a Highlander wears beneath his kilt?" Jamie's smile indicated he knew exactly what she'd been wondering.

Of course, she already knew from research, but she always liked to verify the accuracy of her research.

Her gaze once more slid to Jace. He'd moved closer, close enough to hear Jamie's words. He didn't look threatened, but his warm gaze suggested that it wasn't what lay beneath a man's kilt that counted as much as what the man did with it. His eyes promised he could do a lot with his.

"Will ye help us, lass?" Jamie reached out to sweep a strand of hair from her face.

Jace's expression darkened. Storm warnings were out.

A few days ago Jace's unvoiced declaration of ownership would have brought the wrath of Camryn's "gift" down on his unprotected head. Now? Camryn felt almost warm and fuzzy about it. *Go figure.*

Us? Plural? She'd missed something here. "Is there someone else with you?"

Jamie nodded and looked around. "The dog belongs to my uncle. Ranald was here a moment ago." He shrugged. "He'll thank ye as well if ye help."

Uncle Ranald must be the mean-eyed, rat-faced one. Camryn shuddered. She didn't think she wanted to contemplate Uncle Ranald's thanks.

"Will ye help, lass?" Once again Jamie reached out to touch Camryn.

His wrist was caught in a steel grip.

"I don't think so." Jace's voice was hard with an edge he'd never used in her hearing.

Camryn watched the interplay with interest. This was evidently a man thing, and as long as it didn't deteriorate into a brawl, she was satisfied to stand back and observe.

The men locked gazes while they exchanged silent grunts and chest-pounding challenges. Finally Jamie nodded, then glanced at Camryn. "Think about what I told ye, lass." Turning, he strode away.

Camryn released a relieved breath she hadn't known she'd been holding.

Jace turned to her, once again relaxed, secure in his dominant-male status. Camryn wanted to roll her eyes, but a primitive part of her longed to grab him by his hair and drag him off to mate with her.

"What was that about?" His expression was definitely *Don't fool with me, woman.*

This was it. Either she trusted him or she didn't, and considering what they'd already gone through together, the question of trust should be moot. Besides, beyond the trust issue was the undisputed fact the stolen tokens *were* his business. So why did she feel like she was betraying Flo?

"Jamie's uncle is the owner of Owen's dog token. He wants him back."

Jace's gaze narrowed on the departing Jamie. "Great. So all I have to do is find the dog and hand him over to his legal owner."

Camryn shook her head. "Not so simple. Flo has the dog in her room. She did some checking and found out that Ranald MacDuff abused the dog." She lowered her gaze and did some heavy toe staring. "You wouldn't return the dog to an abusive owner, would you?"

She didn't need to see his face to feel his frustration.

"Look, I'll do some checking on my own and then make a decision."

She glanced up and met his intent gaze. "And what if you can't find any proof of mistreatment?"

"Then he should go back to his rightful owner."

Jace slid his fingers along the side of her face, but she kept her jaw stubbornly clenched. "Flo won't like that."

"Flo isn't my conscience." Long pause. "Neither are you."

So he didn't agree with her. Why the hurt? She wouldn't respect a man who agreed with everything she said. "Fine. Just so you understand this goes both ways. When it comes to Zed, stay out of my way. He's mine." She admitted to a certain amount of childish spite in her statement, but she'd been having a lot of doubts about her maturity level ever since she had met Jace Sentori.

His gaze turned thoughtful. "I know you think getting rid of Zed on your own will prove you don't need anyone to take care of you, but there's a greater strength than the solo kind. Sometimes you have to trust enough, be strong enough to admit you need someone else. That's not weakness. That's being self-confident enough to know that accepting someone else's help doesn't mean you're incompetent."

He was striking too close to a part of her she didn't want to examine closely. Her only defense was in attacking. "Listen to yourself, Jace. Maybe you need to admit you need your father. Go and talk to him. Find out why he wants you to stay."

She watched his shuttered expression. He'd left her on the outside, and she almost wished she'd kept her mouth shut. No, he'd needed to hear the truth.

He raked his fingers through his hair. "This isn't about Owen. I'm going upstairs to make a few calls and get some facts about Ranald Mac-Duff and his dog. If the dog has to go back to him, I'll have to do it fast before Owen discovers another one of his tokens is missing."

Camryn watched Jace leave, then turned to find Owen's gaze also fixed on his son's departure. Peter had moved away to talk with one of the Community Chest.

She wanted to do something before going to her room. Walking over to Owen, she touched his shoulder. Startled, he dragged his attention from where Jace had disappeared.

"Jace didn't have anything to do with the bomb, Owen. He joined me before you even left your room, and he stayed with me all day."

Owen merely nodded, but she read the relief in his eyes. Glancing around, she noticed that Citra had entered the bar with her usual entourage of drooling admirers. The agent took a seat near Owen, then offered Camryn a slight smile. Owen would be safe while Citra was here, and no doubt Sara would be down soon to join him.

Satisfied, Camryn headed for the stairs. She needed the physical effort to keep her mind from racing in circles, chasing answers to questions that had no answers. Who was Zed? When would he—or *she*—strike again? Why had Zed felt the need to get her out of the way first? Heaven knew the other agents were more dangerous. Why had Y sent a newbie on this assignment? And what was she going to do with Jace Sentori?

By the time she reached her door, she'd come to the only possible conclusion. "Haven't a clue." She reached for the knob.

"Me . . . ow!"

Camryn paused. When Meathead made the effort to string two syllables together, she listened. She'd barely had time to move away from the door when someone flung it open.

The Horse Shouter stood in the doorway, feet planted apart, wearing a scowl that could send strong men screaming into the night.

Camryn blinked as she took in the total picture. No matter how many times she saw the Horse Shouter, it was always a shock. So tall. So muscular. So scary. Fine, so the woman did have a certain primitive . . . assertiveness that would attract some men. "What're you doing here?"

The Horse Shouter snapped her whip against her boot in a catchy rhythm. "Do not stand there gawking. Come in." She raked her mass of black hair away from her face, then turned from Camryn. She strode to the middle of the sitting area before stopping. "I told them I was your sister, and since they had no more rooms, they said I could stay with you. I will sleep on your couch." Lifting her whip she executed a flurry of fancy snaps.

Sister? "No. Absolutely not. Leave." Camryn followed her in, slamming the door behind her.

The Horse Shouter ignored her order. "My name is Chastity." She lifted her whip high and brought it down with swishing finality. "I do not think Owen would be pleased to know you helped liberate his beloved horse." She stopped long enough to wipe a bead of sweat from her forehead. "Disciplining men is physically demanding."

"Chastity? Disciplining men?" Suddenly Camryn realized what had come between those two announcements. "Are you blackmailing me?"

"Of course." Chastity ran the whip between her thumb and forefinger—probably checking for wear and tear from whacking all those male bodies. "But do not get upset. I will not be around much."

Camryn watched as Meathead disappeared under the couch. *Coward.*

"I have fallen in love with Peter Bilt." Chastity's smile boded ill for the object of her newfound love. "I long to have his naked body draped across my lap so I can spank his tight butt until it glows pink." She offered Camryn a conspiratorial wink. "Have you not had fantasies of doing the same with Jace?"

"Uh, well, actually, no." She was outta here. "Gee, I think I'll go into the bedroom and take a short nap. You can let yourself out."

Chastity frowned. "It is impossible to imagine you have never sampled the sensual joy of having a strong man spread naked and helpless before you, open to whatever you choose to do to him." Her glance turned sly. "There are many types of . . . persuasion that bring pleasure to both."

Camryn tried on an exaggerated yawn. "I'd love to hear all about it, but I can't keep my eyes open."

Chastity ignored her pointed hints. "You are fortunate, because I have just set up my projector so I can enjoy a few of my finer moments."

"No. Really. I wouldn't want to put you to . . ." Camryn was talking to the air, because Chastity was already operating the projector.

"This is Tomas. I particularly enjoy his position here because it shows off the male sexual organs to best advantage. And this is Victor. He has assumed an excellent position for spanking."

Camryn tried to blink, but she couldn't because her eye muscles were permanently locked open in wide-eyed shock. "Hey, Chastity, thanks for sharing these special moments with me." She would *not* think about them. "But bedtime calls."

Escaping into the bedroom, she flopped onto her bed and closed her eyes until she heard Chastity leave. Then she opened one eye. "You can come out from under the couch, Meathead. She's gone. Good thing I didn't need any protecting."

"Ow." Meathead's plaintive explanation sounded like he was still under the couch.

"Right. I can understand your take on Chastity from a male's viewpoint." She closed her eyes and let her thoughts drift. Sometimes if she just relaxed, her subconscious sorted things out for her.

Unfortunately, her subconscious had other issues to deal with.

A scene formed behind her closed lids: a torture chamber straight out of every description of medieval dungeons she'd ever read. There was the prerequisite blazing hearth to heat the instruments of torture, the wall sconces with flickering candles, and of course the torture instruments lined up and ready for use. She moved into the chamber and ran her fingers over her favorites: a turkey baster, a jar filled with Amaretto liqueur, a cup of melted caramel, and a squeeze container of rich, thick chocolate syrup.

Her conscious self interrupted to point out that this was all about the lunch she'd skipped. Too late now.

In the center of the chamber lay her helpless victim: naked, spread-eagled on his back across a raised stone slab, his wrists and ankles chained. The flames in the hearth and flickering candles drew patterns of light and dark across his sweat-sheened body, turned golden by the fire's soft glow. She licked her lips, watching the play of hard muscle beneath smooth skin as he writhed against his bonds. She noted that he was already hard in anticipation of the evil she'd visit on him tonight.

She slapped her whip impatiently against the side of her boot, then frowned. Something wasn't quite right. She glanced down. *Damn.* She'd done it again. In her eagerness she'd forgotten the rest of her outfit. All she wore were her boots. Oh, well, what did a few missing pieces of cloth matter? All that mattered was her interrogation of the prisoner.

She moved to his side and slid her gaze the length of his incredible body, big and powerful, but now captive to whatever she chose to do to it. And she would choose to do a great deal. "You'll tell me all I want to know, Sentori."

Her conscious self made one more stab at reality. This was about lunch *and* payback for Jace's interrogation at the jail. Her conscious self was growing tedious.

He glared his defiance. "Nothing you can do to me will make me answer your questions."

"We'll see." She offered him her most wicked smile. Skimming his bared body with the tip of her whip, she slid the rawhide over his erection, then allowed it to rest between his spread thighs. "We'll certainly see."

Was this what she'd wanted her whole life? Total control where no man could step in and take over? Hey, this was no time for deep introspection. She was into the moment.

"First question, Sentori. Who is Zed?" *Please don't answer. Please make me use some of my toys.*

His hot gaze lingered on her breasts, then

moved down her body in arrogant disregard of
his precarious position. "You'd know if you just
listened to your intuition. Who scares you the
most?"

You do. No, she hadn't thought that. She was in
control. No man scared her. *But what about a
woman?* "Don't talk in riddles. Tell me the answer."

"Make me."

He'd hurled the gauntlet at her feet. Now he'd
pay. She scanned her torture instruments for the
perfect one. "I think we'll start with the turkey
baster."

His face paled beneath his tan, making his
tangle of dark hair a stark contrast to the lean
strength of his features. "Not the turkey baster."

Smiling in grim satisfaction, she dipped the
baster in the container of Amaretto, then climbed
onto the slab. Positioning herself between his
spread thighs, she stilled his thrashing with one
hand against the side of his neck. Then she
squeezed out a few drops of the rich liqueur onto
the sensitive skin beneath his ear and the spot at
the base of his neck where his pulse beat hard
and fast.

His breaths came harsh and rasping as she
stretched out on her stomach, making sure his
arousal pressed against her lower abdomen. Leaning on her elbows to support her upper body, she
closed her eyes and concentrated on pressing
hard against his groin, rubbing and grinding into
his erection. She almost purred with the joy of it.

His low moan spurred her on. She lowered her

head and slid her tongue across the warm flesh of his neck from beneath his ear to his frantic pulsebeat. The scent, the taste of hot male and sweet liqueur, drove her crazy. "Tell me what I want to know. Now."

"Never." His refusal was grated defiance.

"Then the punishment is on your head." Well, maybe not on his head yet, but it was getting close.

She slid further down his body and carefully squeezed drops of punishment on his nipples, his stomach, paying special attention to filling his navel. Then she paused. "Hmm. I have another question. Why is Zed trying to kill *me* when Owen is L.O.V.E.R.'s target?"

He flung his head from side to side, and sadistically she slid even further down his body until his arousal rested between her breasts. She put down the baster long enough to press her breasts tightly around his erection, then slid back and forth until the heat and friction were almost unbearable. Her urge to abandon all her carefully laid plans for torment and immediately finish him off was almost overwhelming, but she was nothing if not a strong B.L.I.S.S. agent.

He arched his hips in a vain attempt to ease his agony. This was so much fun.

But she had to take care of unfinished business. "Answer me, and make sure it's the right answer."

"Maybe Zed's agenda isn't the same as L.O.V.E.R.'s. Maybe Zed wants something more than just Owen's death." He spoke between tortured gasps.

"Not good enough, Sentori." She was glad he was tough and uncooperative. An easy victory was no victory at all.

Camryn moved higher on his body to reach the glistening amber drops of Amaretto. She circled one sweet nipple with the tip of her tongue, then sucked it into her mouth to claim all the rich taste from his flesh. She concluded by flicking her tongue back and forth across the nipple to make sure she hadn't missed anything. She hungrily moved to the other nipple.

"God, woman, finish me off and be done with it." His whisper was agonized need.

"Not until you tell me what I want to know." She hoped he wasn't weakening. That would really ruin her day.

Before he could say anything else, she added a new question to her list: "Why did Y send me on this assignment? I know what she told me, but I don't know if I believe it."

"Maybe Y knows something about Zed that you don't. You don't think she told you everything, do you? Think, woman. She won't even tell you what B.L.I.S.S. means." His arrogance was creeping back. She couldn't let that happen.

"Of course I know what B.L.I.S.S. means. It means . . . umm . . . Bad Ladies Invite Sinful Seduction. No, I think it's Babes Lose in Synchronized Swimming. Wait, I have it. B.L.I.S.S. means Babes Love Italian Sweet Sausage." She huffed. "Oh, who cares?"

Camryn gave him no warning as she licked a path of fire and heat across his stomach, stopping long enough to dip her tongue into his navel and lap out the amber liquid. Still savoring the taste of Amaretto warmed naturally, she watched his stomach muscles ripple and clench. That would teach him respect.

"Since you've told me nothing, Sentori, I guess I have to go up to the next level." She slipped from the slab, replaced the baster, and retrieved the chocolate syrup.

His tortured gaze followed her. "No. Not the chocolate."

Camryn shrugged. "Give me a straight answer and it'll all end." She climbed back onto the slab and once again knelt between his thighs.

He grew still, his glance grazing her breasts, her stomach, her . . . Deliberately she spread her thighs, allowing him to stare, to suffer. Then she touched herself. She slid her finger across the spot that was already too excited for its own good, and when she knew she had to do something else or explode, she lowered herself over him and allowed the head of his erection to press against the same spot.

Big fat mistake. She gulped in a huge, fortifying breath, because the way her heart was pounding it would give out any minute now, and then her lungs would collapse and she'd be dead, dead, dead. At least the extra oxygen might keep her brain functioning after her heart stopped.

"You don't want me to give you a straight answer." His gaze was hot and hungry on the spot where they touched.

"I don't?" Heck, she didn't even remember the question.

"You want to do it all on your own. If I help you get your answers, then you'll have to say I helped you." He slid his tongue across his lower lip, moistening it.

She stared at his lip's glistening sheen, trying to distract herself from the eager clenching going on in areas that had no business clenching during working hours.

I am in charge. Clench, clench. *I am a professional interrogator.* Clench, clench. *I am in complete control of my body and emotions.* Clench, clench.

If she got any more in control of her body she was going to plant herself on top of his arousal and bob up and down like a yo-yo.

Clutching her container of chocolate syrup, she moved over him until she could reach his lips. His mouth was slightly parted, daring her to do her worst.

Slowly she squeezed a thin line of syrup across his upper lip, then did the same with the lower. Before he had a chance to lick it off, she lowered her mouth to his. She slid her tongue across each lip, savoring the taste, the smooth glide of chocolate over the soft texture of his lips.

His lips opened and his tongue plundered hers, taking control. For a moment she was oblivious to the loss, too involved in the heat of his mouth and the dark taste of chocolate.

When she finally realized what he was up to, she widened her eyes, then pulled away. He'd done that so easily. She'd have to make sure she didn't get within range of his lips again.

His lips slanted in a smile of wicked triumph. "Any other questions that I won't answer?"

"Just one." Her voice was a husky ghost of itself. "What am I going to do with you, Jace Sentori?"

His answer was a soft murmur of seduction. "You're going to release me so I can touch your breasts with my mouth, slide my finger deep inside you until you're wet and trembling, use the tip of my tongue on the spot you just touched until you scream with need."

She shook her head, knowing her eyes must mirror the explosive desire she saw in his dark gaze. "Wrong answer, Sentori. Guess I'll have to use my ultimate persuader."

His laugh was shaky. "Hope it works better than your ultimate weapon."

She wasn't sure her legs would support her as she climbed once more from the slab and took the container of melted caramel from the heating element that kept it warm and soft.

Warily, Jace watched her position herself between his legs. "You don't play fair, lady."

"I'll do what needs doing until you give me the right answers." She drew her fingertip the length of his jutting erection, tracing the fine blue veins, imagining the feel of him sliding into her, stretching her, filling her in a way no man had filled her before.

"You want me to tell you that you don't need any man's help, that you can do it all yourself."

She touched the head of his arousal, where a

243

single drop of moisture belied the calmness of his voice.

"But that would be a lie." He arched his hips, pressing his arousal against her finger. "Sure, you can do things by yourself, but they'll never be the best or the most satisfying. You need to share the power, lady, to win the biggest games." This last observation was grated out between shuddering gasps for control.

"Wrong! You've given all the wrong answers." With shaking fingers she lifted the container above his erection. She cupped him, smoothing her thumb across him in a rhythmic caress as she held him still. She attempted a cruel smile, but she knew it probably lacked a certain degree of wickedness. "Caramel apples have always been my favorite." Then she dribbled the caramel over his arousal, watched it cover the head and slide down the long length of him.

His low groan was enough to lighten the heart of even the most discriminating torturer. "It won't work."

"Why not?" Of course it would work. It always worked.

He raised his head as far as he could to see what she'd done. "It can't harden. I'm too hot."

"Oh." She hadn't thought about that. Okay, so she'd simply have to adjust.

Leaning down, she licked away the dribbles of caramel from the base of his erection, then worked her way up. By the time she reached the head, his breaths were coming in hard pants.

She'd have no mercy. He'd told her nothing.

Nothing. Sliding her lips around him, she took him into her mouth, or as much of him as she could. Her mouth would never be that big. Greedily she slid her tongue around and around, sucking every drop of caramel from him. He bucked his hips, trying to drive himself deeper. But she'd learned her lesson. She wouldn't let him set the pace again.

She withdrew her lips and leaned back, watching him twist in a vain effort to free his hands, watching the slick beauty of his skin beneath the candle glow.

It was time to finish it. "I'm going to take you, Sentori. I'm going to do it myself without your participation."

His pained laughter surprised her. "You'd better hope that at least one part of me participates."

That was it. No more talk. She shifted her body until she was positioned above his erection, her spread legs on each side of his hips.

She lowered herself onto his rigid length, felt him sliding into her. Felt her muscles tighten around him, holding him deep inside her.

"Dammit, Camryn, don't do this alone. Release me so I can touch you, so we can do it together." His voice was a last harsh demand, as close to begging as Jace Sentori would probably ever get.

"No. I can do this by myself. I can do anything by myself." *But I want your lips on mine, your hands on my breasts.* To still the traitorous inner voice, she lifted her hips, then slid back down. She caught the up-and-down rhythm, letting it carry her toward its explosive conclusion. At some point she realized his hips were rising to slam into her, pushing him further and further into her until he touched every bare wire of sizzling need. The short-circuit was spectacular. As the sparks of her climax crackled around her, she threw back her head to scream.

"Me . . . ow!" *Meow?* She never meowed during an orgasm. Maybe a little howling, but never any feline sounds.

"Me . . . ow!"

Camryn opened her eyes to meet the yellow stare of Meathead, whose pudgy body was planted on her chest. She didn't react for a moment because she was shaking. *A dream.* The whole thing had been a dream. But deep in some dusty corner of her mind where all truths lived, she knew the layers of meaning in this dream would haunt her for a long time.

Lifting Meathead from her chest, she started to sit up. "You weigh a ton, cat. Your innards must be made of lead."

She'd barely swung her feet to the floor when she heard the pounding at her door. She pushed her tangled hair from her face and staggered from the bedroom. *Please don't let it be Jace.* The dream was too fresh, too real. She couldn't face him. If it was Chastity, she wasn't going to open the door. That dream was all Chastity's fault.

Staring through the peephole, Camryn spotted Flo. Quickly she opened the door. Flo almost fell in.

Something wasn't right. "What happened?"

Flo rubbed the back of her head as she stumbled over to the couch. Dropping onto it, she gazed up at Camryn with glazed eyes. "That mean-eyed, rat-faced jerk caught me by surprise. I was sneaking Duncan out for a walk when Ranald hit me over the head and ran off with Duncan. He and his nephew thought I was out, but I heard them say they were headed for Free Parking. There're some steep cliffs that drop to the sea, and they have a boat hidden at the foot of the cliffs to make their getaway."

She paused as though gathering strength. "Jace found me. He's gone after them. You've got to help Jace stop the bastards." For a moment Flo looked old and defeated. "Don't let them hurt my Duncan."

Camryn nodded. "I'll take care of it."

Flo leaned back against the couch and closed her eyes. "I can't help you. Too dizzy. Here, take my gun." Flo held out the FS95.

Camryn took the gun, then put it in her purse. She'd never use it. If she tried, she'd either send her foot to the emergency ward or deal a fatal injury to some unsuspecting tree.

Camryn didn't waste time. She called Dr. Nitski and made sure he'd come right up to look at Flo, then she went back to her bedroom. Flo said there were cliffs at Free Parking. She hated to do it, but she had to dress for the job.

And this was a job for the gold dress.

Chapter Thirteen

"Doesn't this make you feel involved, Meathead? We're going to help rescue Duncan." Camryn cranked up the wiper blades on the Cadillac as the rain escalated to a downpour.

Meathead sat on the seat beside her. His expression said he'd rather eat dirt than be out on a stormy night trying to save a dog, and the only thing he wanted involvement with was his food bowl. *Food bowl?* Not likely. More and more she was forgetting he was a robot.

Jace was trying to rescue Duncan. They were on the same side, and she hadn't a clue why that made her so happy. She peered through the Cadillac's rain-washed windshield as she raced toward Free Parking. He had to be trying to rescue the dog or he wouldn't have bothered pursuing its owner.

Camryn wanted to help him, and for just a moment the hypocrisy of her intention made her uncomfortable. If the situation had been reversed, she'd be declaring loud and long that she didn't need his help.

She took the sharp turn at the Go to Jail section of Owen's Monopoly board at seventy miles an hour. The heavy body of the Cadillac hugged the wet road and accelerated out of the curve.

Camryn refused to dwell on what would happen if positions were reversed. Jace didn't have her motivation. He didn't have a protective father and six protective brothers ordering his life. The thought brought a twinge of guilt. Jace probably would have loved a protective father.

"Hey, dudess. My road-read says wet. That last curve? A little fast. Like, we want the Big Smooth to live to fight another day." T sounded like he was eating potato chips while he talked.

"I'm busy, T. Can't talk now."

With a crunchy mumble about geniuses getting no respect, he disconnected.

Through the wind-whipped branches and lashing rain she saw the curve that marked the Free Parking spot on the board. *Almost there.* Camryn felt the adrenaline rush of doing something proactive, stopping Ranald before he got Duncan off the island. She was sick to death of sitting around waiting for Zed's next move, then trying to counter it. Fighting Zed was like boxing with a ghost. You couldn't hit what you couldn't see.

She'd stopped the Cadillac, stumbled out, and was unsuccessfully trying to shield her face from the storm's fury when she realized what was happening.

Two men struggled on the very edge of the cliff. Camryn could tell from the sound of the storm-tossed waves crashing against the base of the cliff that it was a long way down. Her heart seemed to pause, then kicked into high gear. The taller of the men was Jace.

Close to them stood a man in a kilt, clutching a small dog. Jamie and Duncan.

She started to run, aware that Meathead was still in the car and probably debating the wisdom of getting his feet wet. But she'd barely taken two steps when it happened.

Jamie dropped Duncan to help his uncle, and everything seemed to switch to slow motion. Both men shoved Jace at the same time, and he flailed his arms in a losing battle with gravity. Then he simply disappeared over the edge of the cliff.

It was as though someone had pushed a pause button, holding the scene in place so she could study it from every angle. But in this scene there was no rewind button.

He was gone. *Jace is gone.*

"Get the damned dog!" Ranald's shout was swept away on the howling wind.

Jamie made a halfhearted attempt to catch Duncan, but the dog scampered out of reach. "Forget the dog. Let's get out of here. A frickin' pedigree isn't worth getting tagged for murder." Somewhere along the way Jamie had lost his carefully cultivated Scottish burr. He turned his back on Duncan and ran.

"No!" Camryn's shriek of denial would have done credit to the O'Brien banshee.

Both men stopped to stare as she charged out of the darkness.

She didn't think about pressing a hot dot to engage Meathead's help. She didn't think about the gun in her purse. Jace was dead. *Dead.* And every primal instinct rose up in a blinding need to hurt, to punish.

Tears stung her eyes as she stumbled toward the two men. A crushing sense of loss warred with an anger she'd never before felt. She focused every shrieking emotion in her soul on one objective: *Kill them.*

A jagged dagger of lightning speared the earth with an explosion of sound that shook the ground. It was followed by another and another. Nearby trees crashed to earth amid earsplitting cracks of thunder and the overpowering smell of sulfur and smoke.

The men fled. Camryn knew they must be screaming, but she couldn't hear anything except the outer chaos and her inner despair.

This then was her "gift." Even when she dredged up every atom of emotion in her soul, she couldn't kill. Y would want to know that.

Camryn felt drained, lethargic, as she walked to the cliff's edge. The pain would come later, but for now she had to look over the edge, face what she might see. Probably not much. In the darkness she didn't think she'd be able to see all the way to the cliff's bottom, but she had to try.

And in her heart she refused to say his name

or try to picture him. She couldn't deal with her feelings and still function. How could a man she'd known only two days do this to her?

Once the men had gone, the lightning stopped and the wind and rain lessened. Distractedly she glanced at her foot as she felt Meathead's weight there. "Thanks for the support, but it's probably best I didn't use you. You might've killed me, or taken out the whole island." She didn't smile. "B.L.I.S.S. will have to take away one of the Ds in my agent number. The one that stands for 'destroy.'"

Not allowing herself time to dwell on her failure, she looked over the side of the cliff.

And for the first time in her life experienced an honest-to-goodness miracle.

About thirty feet from the top of the cliff, a ledge jutted out. Jace lay faceup on the ledge. It was every fictional cliché she'd ever read. Hero falls off cliff. Hero saves himself by grabbing bush as he falls or lands on ledge he didn't know existed.

When it happened in real life? It was a miracle. Camryn offered up a silent thank-you to the maker of all miracles.

How badly was Jace hurt? Her breath caught as it occurred to her that a thirty-foot fall could kill. She had to get help. Bending down, she reached for Meathead's collar.

At that moment Duncan decided it was safe to crawl out from beneath the Cadillac, where he'd taken shelter from the booming thunder and falling trees. Camryn watched the dog's whole body stiffen as he saw Meathead. She could almost see the realization taking form in his brain: *Cat.*

Yapping frantically, Duncan raced toward Meathead. As Camryn watched with her mouth open, Meathead leaped to the only tree that was still standing and clawed his way to the highest limb.

What the . . . ? Meathead was a robot, for heaven's sake. He wasn't programmed to have a real cat's fears. "Get down here, Meathead. I need your collar." Meathead offered her an *Are you crazy* glance and stayed put.

With grim determination, she pressed the "get help" hot dot on her upper left arm. Nothing. Okay, so she'd catch the dog and put him in the Cadillac until Meathead came down from the tree.

Duncan didn't want to be caught. After her fifth trip around the tree Camryn gave up. She didn't have time for this. She had to get to Jace.

She could think of only one solution: the gold dress. She grimaced. This would *not* be one of her finer moments.

Once she'd made her decision she moved quickly. Yanking the dress halfway down her back, she took off her bra, then pulled up the dress. The darn thing had to be completely on to unravel properly. For a moment she mourned her decision not to wear the lethal panties. Any kind of panties would be a comfort in this situation.

Activating the bra's hook, she decided the tree where Meathead was an interested spectator would have to do as an anchor. Digging the hook's point into the tree, she watched the drill

253

do its job. In moments the hook was imbedded deeply into the trunk.

Trying not to dwell too much on what she was about to do, she pulled the starting tab from the vee of her dress and attached it to the hook. Then she looked over the side of the cliff again. This wouldn't be so bad. The top of the cliff stuck out a little from the rest of the cliff face, so she wouldn't do the Ping-Pong thing off the rocks on her way down.

Taking a deep breath and forcing herself to think of nothing but Jace, she sat down and lowered herself over the edge.

Jace opened his eyes, then blinked the rain from them. What the hell had happened? The last thing he remembered was those bastards shoving him over the cliff. He knew he wasn't dead because he hurt in too many places.

But he sure enough must be hallucinating, because he could swear he was a kid again, lying on the floor under the Christmas tree, staring up at a beautiful golden ornament slowly twirling as it hung from one of the branches.

Jace narrowed his gaze. *What the . . . ?* The ornament was dropping lower and lower. And as it descended it was humming "London Bridge Is Falling Down." He blinked again. Why was all the gold peeling off?

He sucked in his breath as his brain finally caught up with his informational backlog. He was lying on a ledge and Camryn was spinning in a lazy circle as her gold dress unraveled around her.

With each circle she dropped closer and was wearing less.

An unraveling dress. His respect for B.L.I.S.S.'s ingenuity skyrocketed. And he didn't even want to think about how much courage it took for Camryn to lower herself from the top of a cliff. For him. The thought touched something inside him he couldn't name. It went beyond simple gratitude. There was nothing simple about it. People didn't take chances for Jace Sentori. People didn't think he needed help. Ever.

Carefully he moved his limbs, making sure they all still worked. When Camryn finally touched down, he didn't want to lie there like a drooling doofus. Since he didn't sense any other action from the top of the cliff, he assumed the two jerks who'd pushed him were gone. *Good. No immediate danger.* He'd relax and enjoy the view.

The rain had finally stopped and the moon emerged from behind the clouds. *Perfect.* He wanted strong visuals here.

Camryn had her arms above her head, clasping the line. This steadied her as well as keeping her arms out of the way of the unraveling process.

The first series of spins exposed her breasts. No bra. After a crappy beginning, the night had taken a definite upswing. Moonlight cast a pale glow on her skin, making her breasts seem cool perfection. Jace knew better. He knew the warm texture of her, the faint scent of lavender as he touched her breasts with his mouth, the taste of aroused woman as he took each nipple between his lips. No, *cool* didn't describe Camryn.

Her stomach. Her lower abdomen. All were areas of interest.

A smooth expanse of skin broken only by the shadowed indentation of her navel. When had navels become fascinating?

She was very close to where he lay now, and the unraveling process was almost complete: her dress *and* his nerves.

A few final twirls and beneath the moon's light he had an unobstructed view of her perfectly rounded . . . ass? No. Cheeks? Hell, who cared. He wanted to hold them, squeeze them, clasp them and pull her onto his . . .

Her body made one last circle and she stood facing him. He didn't stare at the shadowed area between her thighs, because he'd just discovered something. It wasn't her individual parts that made his breath catch, his heart pound, his mouth go dry. It was the sum of all her parts, the total woman. And the total woman was a lot more than he could see on the outside. He suspected it was a lot more than a whole lifetime would reveal.

Jace closed his eyes. She wouldn't want him watching as she came to him, and he needed a moment to draw his scattered wits into viable thought patterns again.

"Jace." Her voice sounded anxious. Her fingers lightly skimmed his face, his chest.

He knew he had to ease her worry. Drawing in a deep breath, he opened his eyes. She knelt beside him, her breasts so close he could reach up and mold them with his hands.

She had braved the dangerous trip down the cliff face to reach him. And it must have taken a lot of guts to do that knowing she'd reach the bottom stark naked.

He owed her. And he could start by keeping his mind off her body. "Where's the dog?" *Great conversation opener, Sentori.* They were stranded partway down a cliff, she didn't have on a stitch of clothing, and he was asking about a blasted dog.

"You're okay?" She patted him down again as though she might have missed something broken. There were tears in her eyes.

That got to him. He swallowed hard. Jace couldn't remember anyone ever crying over him. He'd broken his arm when he was seven. A neighbor's horse had thrown him. Mom had been mad as hell because she'd warned him to stay off the horse, but she hadn't cried.

"Hey, I'm fine." He reached up and wiped a drop of moisture from the corner of her eye. "Tough B.L.I.S.S. agents don't cry."

She nodded and scraped her hand across her eyes. "I thought I'd lost you, Sentori." Her expression said losing him would have been a hard thing to handle. He didn't try to analyze his sudden rush of happiness.

"So what happened to the dognappers?" He ran his hands up and down her arms and felt her shudder.

"I tried to kill them." She leaned back on her heels.

"You tried to kill them for *me?*" He'd seen this woman daring, scared, playful, and angry. He'd

257

never seen her willing to kill. And selfishly, he hoped it had only been because of him.

"I focused every ounce of concentration I had on wishing them dead." She shrugged, then smiled faintly. "I scared the hell out of them, but I didn't kill them. Y won't be happy to know that I can maim but not destroy."

"We do what we can." He couldn't help it—his gaze slid from the wild red glory of her hair down the length of her bare body.

She flushed and crossed her arms across her chest. Not enough. Not nearly enough.

Sitting up, Jace tried not to wince as a dozen parts of his body complained that he'd landed right *there*. Before he could think about the pain, he pulled his T-shirt over his head and handed it to her. "It won't cover everything, but it'll keep me sane."

She grabbed the T-shirt, put it on, then grinned at him. "Can I talk you out of your pants?"

"Anytime, sweetheart. Anytime at all." Even the thought made his voice husky. He coughed to clear it. "So what about the dog?"

He followed her gaze to the top of the cliff, where he could see the branches of a large tree. Two round yellow eyes gleamed down at him from one of the branches. At the same time he grew aware of persistent yapping. "Don't tell me."

She nodded. "Sorry. When Ranald and Jamie ran away, they left Duncan behind. Chasing Meathead up that tree is the only fun the little guy's had today."

Something wasn't right here. "Meathead's not

a cat. Why would he let Duncan chase him? Can't you press something to get him out of the tree?"

She shrugged. "Tried. Didn't work."

The enormity of their problem hit him in the face. "Damn Owen for not allowing cell phones."

Her soft chuckle worked its way past his sexual control center, which was doing a piss-poor job right now. She shifted from a kneeling position to sitting cross-legged beside him. His T-shirt came down just far enough to shadow . . .

"B.L.I.S.S. should design a shoulder holster for cell phones, because once I started down to you there wouldn't have been a whole lot of places to stash it." Her gaze was teasing. "I guess I could've held it between my knees."

Between my knees. He wouldn't let his glance follow her verbal suggestion. "So we're stuck here until someone finds us." His gaze returned to the sheer cliff wall. No way to climb that, and no way he could climb back up the wire-thin line from the dress. "Let's hope the *someone* isn't Zed."

"You know?" She ran her fingers across his bare chest, pausing at a few scrapes and bruises. "Right now I don't care." She offered him a brilliant smile. "I'm just so glad you're alive, not much else matters. Dumb, huh?"

He couldn't muster an answering smile. "Not dumb at all, lady." The brush of her fingers immediately checked in with his groin. That was automatic. But her fingers were blazing new trails to unexplored regions never affected by a woman's touch. He didn't want to name those regions because the whole concept was scary.

He allowed a slow grin to replace his somber expression. He'd learned a long time ago that thoughts of sex could distract him from almost anything. "When we get off this cliff, we'll have to celebrate in a special way and in a special place."

She narrowed her eyes in mock concentration. "I think the Boardwalk would be pretty special." Her gaze suddenly darkened. "Remember I mentioned the little saltwater taffy shop? The island map says it's right across from the Ollie the Octopus pier. I want to make love with you there on the beach right next to that pier."

He sucked in his breath. "To the point. I like that in a woman."

She didn't lower her gaze. "When I thought you'd died, the pain almost doubled me over. While I was on my way down to you, I realized life was too short to play coy games. You take your shot at happiness when and where you have the chance." She grinned. "Besides, Meathead isn't responding to the hot dots, so . . ."

Her recklessness was contagious. "Come here, O'Brien." He opened his arms and she flung herself on top of him. Laughing, he rolled with her, his fingers clasping her exactly as he'd imagined, pulling her hard against his erection.

Her laughter joined his as he abandoned her bottom to slide his fingers through her blaze of red hair. He stilled with her beneath him. Lowering his head, he kissed her. He didn't try to pretend it was anything other than what it seemed, a greedy plundering of her mouth to sate his senses. She tasted of eager woman, her texture hot and smooth, and within the mix was that elusive scent of lavender. He knew that for the rest of his life, no matter what he was doing, he could stop, close his eyes, and remember this.

Without breaking the kiss, he reached down to pull his T-shirt out from under her and . . . *Uh-oh.* He felt around for solid rock. Nothing.

Widening his eyes, he broke the kiss and looked down. *God almighty!* They'd rolled to the edge of the cliff, and he was staring down at open space on his right side.

"Don't move, sweetheart. Don't even breathe. We're right on the edge." He gathered his body to make the roll to his left and take Camryn with him.

Then he looked into her eyes. He didn't see fear, just a wide-eyed acknowledgment of danger, and something else . . . Excitement. Her eyes glittered with it.

Camryn reached up and touched his lips with her finger. "We've *always* been on the edge, Jace Sentori. And when we finally make love, we'll fall off that edge. I haven't a clue where the free fall will take us, but I'll bet the trip will be incredible. That's my intuition talking, and Y will tell you my intuition doesn't make mistakes." She turned her head to glance down.

He took advantage of her turned head to whisper in her ear. "I love it when you talk metaphorically, sweetheart. But we need to get our butts out of here."

She nodded, and together they rolled away from the edge.

Jace had barely caught his breath when he heard a car door slam. He scrambled to his feet and reached for Camryn, but she was way ahead of him. Together they ran to the cliff wall and flattened themselves against it. Anyone glancing down wouldn't see them. He just hoped whoever had arrived said something to identify themselves. Fat lot of good that would do, though. Since Zed could be almost anyone, they wouldn't know whom to trust.

Jace listened as footsteps approached the cliff edge. One person. Camryn clasped his hand and squeezed. She motioned with her head. He nodded, then dropped her hand and watched her silently move away from him along the wall. Separating made good tactical sense, but he still hated to let go of her.

"Camryn? Are you down there?"

Citra. Jace almost sagged with relief. Of all the people who could be Zed, Citra was one of the least likely. Even so, he cursed softly when Camryn stepped away from the wall and into Citra's line of vision.

"I'm down here, Citra. How'd you find me?" Camryn moved further into sight as she tried to see if anyone was with Citra.

"Flo. She came to me and told me what happened. She was worried about you and Jace. I see Jace's bike. Is he with you?"

"Yeah, I'm here." He walked over to stand beside Camryn.

"This is really interesting." He could hear the amusement in Citra's voice. "Maybe I'm wrong here, but it looks like Rapunzel with a twist. Instead of letting down her hair, she let down her dress. And instead of the prince climbing up, she climbed down to the prince. Cool idea."

Suddenly a second pair of footsteps approached the edge. Jace tensed.

"Jace's Harley is here. Where's my son, Citra?" Jace closed his eyes. *Owen. Crap.*

Chapter Fourteen

Camryn was strangely quiet while they waited for rescue. That gave Jace too much time to think. How much did Owen know? If he was with Citra, he might know a lot.

What would Jace do if Owen ordered him off the island? He'd let him throw him off, but he'd be back as soon as he could get a boat or helicopter. Nothing was going to stop him from helping Camryn in her search for Zed and saving Owen from his own stupidity. Jace's stubbornness on these issues surprised him.

When Peter finally showed up in a truck with a winch, and Jace's feet touched solid ground again, he couldn't help his surge of relief. But he'd always have mixed feelings about his time on the ledge. Something had changed in his relationship with Camryn, and he didn't try to fool himself into thinking they didn't have a relationship. Where it went from here was anyone's guess.

He glanced at Camryn. She was busy yanking his T-shirt as far down on her thighs as she could. By the time she finished pulling on it, the shirt would reach her knees. He grinned as she backed toward the Cadillac. Evidently she'd decided her behind was more vulnerable to attack than her front.

"I guess you guys'll be here for a little while, so I'll just run back to Chance and change." Her glance touched Jace then slid away. "I'll bring back a shirt for you, Jace."

Jace frowned. "We can go back together and—"

Owen touched his shoulder. "We need to talk, Jace. Here. Now."

"I'll go back by myself." She narrowed her gaze on him. "You need to talk to Owen."

"I'll give you my key." He fished around in the pocket of his jeans.

She shook her head and continued backing until she bumped into the Cadillac. "I don't need a key." Before he could protest, she slipped into the driver's seat, then stared up at the branch where F.I.D.O. still crouched. "Time to go home, Meathead."

Jace knew she was pressing a spot on her body, and this time F.I.D.O. responded. The fact that Owen held Duncan securely in his arms probably had a lot to do with it.

F.I.D.O. tried to back off the branch, missed his footing, and tumbled from the tree. This time he landed on his back. He still hadn't mastered the cats-always-land-on-their-feet thing.

F.I.D.O, struggled to stand, then padded over to the car and leaped inside. Offering Jace one more brief glance, Camryn slammed the door shut and sped off.

Jace frowned at the Cadillac's departing taillights. Since when had Meathead started jumping into the car? A robot's behavior should be consistent.

He knew that B.L.I.S.S. had done a job on the car, that it wasn't your garden-variety aging Cadillac, but Camryn's speed still worried him. He shook his head. Talk about incompatibility. If he hooked up with Camryn, he'd spend all his time nursing bumps and bruises, because he'd be a protector until the day he died.

Forcing his attention away from Camryn, he turned back to Owen. After Owen had realized that Jace and Camryn were on the ledge, he'd called back to Chance for help in the rescue. Jace was glad to know that someone on this blasted island had a cell phone.

Now Peter Bilt hovered nearby. The bodyguard sure had a lot of energy. After using the truck's winch to get them off the ledge, he'd paced back and forth even when Owen had told him he could sit in the truck and wait. Peter wasn't into sitting tonight.

Owen waved Peter away, and Peter went to stand next to Citra's car. Citra sat in the car working on her laptop. Probably writing up her daily report to the powers-that-be. Peter amused himself by finger-combing his hair while he admired himself in the car's mirror, then surreptitiously rubbed his butt. Jace wondered what that was all about.

"Citra told me why both of you were here." Owen didn't waste time getting to the point.

Here it comes. "Never darken my island again." Jace was uneasy about his ambivalent feelings. Nothing Owen said should bother him.

"Do you know anything about obsessive behavior, Jace?" Owen held his gaze.

Obsessive behavior? What did that have to do with ordering him away? "Not much."

"I'm obsessed with Monopoly. It's an addiction. I've tried to get help, but I don't know if I'll ever have the courage to walk away. I've made progress since you were six." Owen's gaze wavered, and he looked away to study Jace's bike.

"Could've fooled me." Jace heard the ice in his own voice, recognized the hurt he'd thought was safely buried a long time ago.

"I bet when you got here you expected to see the figure of Mr. Monopoly carved into the side of my volcanic mountain." Owen's smile was self-deprecating.

"Well . . . yeah." Jace told himself not to return the smile, but he did.

"Monopoly's been my life. I couldn't take knowing a six-year-old had beat me. I lost it. After you left I realized what my temper had cost me. I wanted you and your mom to move back to Chance, but she turned down my offer. Smart woman. Chance was no place to raise a child." He still didn't meet Jace's gaze.

Jace frowned. "Mom never said anything about that."

Owen shrugged. "We didn't want you involved in anything that would upset you. You'd settled down, adjusted to your new life."

I never adjusted to my new life. The truth of that thought shook Jace.

Owen finally met his gaze. "But I'm not the same man who ordered his son off the island because of a Monopoly defeat." He offered Jace a weak smile. "Age hasn't gotten rid of my obsession, but it's cooled my temper."

"Prove it." Now where the hell had that come from?

"How?" Owen looked nervous.

Good. He'd make his proposition, Owen would turn it down flat, and Jace could walk away secure in the knowledge that Owen was the same bastard he'd always been. And Jace *needed* to know that. "Citra has probably told you about the ruby slippers and Ramses."

Owen's lips thinned, but he didn't say anything.

"The people who wanted the dog back pushed me off that cliff." He speared Owen with his gaze. "No token is worth dying for. So here's the deal. We play a game of Monopoly tonight. On this board." He cocked his head toward Free Parking. "If I win, you send all the stolen tokens back to their legal owners." Jace paused. "Except for the dog. The dog stays here. The MacDuffs don't deserve him. And if they want to argue, they can talk

268

to my lawyer about attempted murder, or they can talk directly to me." He knew his grin was wolfish.

"And if you lose?" Owen's frown said he knew what the chances of that were.

"If I lose . . ." Jace shrugged. "You don't send them back." *Then I'll have to think of another way to return them.* That wasn't much of an incentive, a lose-it-all or status quo situation. No profit in it for Owen. Jace waited for Owen's explosion.

"Fine." Owen's response was terse, tight-lipped, and totally unexpected. "What token do you want?"

Jace didn't have to think hard. "I want the Bond car."

Owen bit his bottom lip and glared at his son. "Ramses is gone. *I'll* take the Bond car."

"*I* want it." Jace took a mental step back and observed the exchange with Owen. The men in the family must mature slowly. Owen and he sounded about the emotional age of ten-year-olds. Tops.

Owen huffed and puffed before calling over Peter. Citra came with him. Jace caught the end of their conversation.

"Whatta you think about my butt?" Peter really seemed to want Citra's opinion.

Citra offered him a blank stare. "I don't think about your butt at all."

This was a new experience for Citra. She'd probably never met a man who thought of his own butt before hers.

Peter nodded. "I guess you'd have to see it to

believe it. I could show you. . . ." He shook his head. "No, it's too open here."

"I don't *want* to see your butt." Citra's message was a deadly monotone.

Peter was oblivious. "Chastity says I have the best cheeks she's ever seen. She wants to marry my ass."

Luckily Owen was busy with a wiggling Duncan and didn't hear the exchange. "Go back to Chance, Peter, and get the Bond car. Jace and I are going to have a little game. Since the dog is already here, I'll use him as my token."

Peter blinked at him. "Now?"

"Now. Make sure the board lights are turned on. Honey Suckle and you can come along to handle the cards and the bank."

Peter nodded, but he didn't look happy.

"Oh, and ask Sara if she'll come back with Camryn." Owen flushed and cast his son a defensive glance. "Sara's my good-luck lady."

Jace caught himself smiling at Owen. He couldn't help it. What an adrenaline rush. At moments like this he couldn't deny his connection to Owen. It was in the playing of the game, a competitive fever that had made him the Game Master. He hoped Camryn would hurry back to share this with him.

When Camryn came to the right-hand turn that would take her to Chance, she kept going. It would only take her a little out of her way to visit the Boardwalk. She wanted to see the place where they'd make love. Besides, it would give Jace more time alone with his father. She hoped he used it wisely.

As she approached the Boardwalk, she scanned it for Hogan's Saltwater Taffy Shop. It wasn't hard to find. Solid and real with its bright blue front, it stood out amid the generic red and green buildings waiting to be trundled onto the board during a game. Any man who had warm and fuzzy feelings about a candy store couldn't be all bad.

Camryn glanced across the board at the Ollie the Octopus pier. A large purple octopus whose tentacles formed an arch guarded the entrance to the pier.

She'd already begun to shift her gaze to the white-sand beach where she'd bring Jace, when something about the pier caught her attention. She looked closer.

Well, what do you know. Rachel sat in a beach chair at the end of the lighted pier. She was looking out to sea while she worked on her interminable knitting.

Camryn parked the Cadillac, let Meathead out, yanked Jace's T-shirt as far down on her thighs as she could, and walked to the end of the pier.

"I assume you've been looking for Zed." Rachel didn't turn to look at her.

"Sort of." Carmryn was ashamed to admit she hadn't a clue where to look for Zed. And no way would she mention the doubts her intuition was whispering to her. "What're you knitting?"

Rachel finally looked at her. Once again she had her secret smile in place. "I always knit a little memento of each one of my assignments; then I hang it on my wall."

Camryn frowned. Rachel was an enigma. Zed had made an attempt on Owen's life. He'd made two attempts on Camryn's life. And Rachel sat here calmly knitting.

"Jace and I just got rescued from a ledge at Free Parking." She didn't go into particulars, because she'd bet Rachel already knew.

Rachel nodded. "You should let Jace take care of his own business. Your business is Zed." Her smile turned sly. "The sex thing will kill you."

Point made. Rachel could very well be right. "Why did Flo send Citra out to rescue us? Why not Sara or you?" An uncomfortable question, but one that needed to be asked.

It didn't seem to bother Rachel. "Flo doesn't trust Sara or me. But that's fine. I don't trust them either." She paused for thought. "In our business, mistrust is part of the game."

Game? Funny that Camryn had never thought of it as a game. Maybe she had more in common with Jace than she thought. Both their occupations had a winner and a loser, only in hers the losing was a little more permanent.

Sighing, Camryn sat on the pier beside Rachel. Without warning, Meathead climbed into her lap, turned around twice, and curled up into a comfortable ball. The whole routine was clumsily executed, but Camryn was sure it was Meathead's first attempt at being a lap-kitty. Shocked, she stared down at the cat, who was happily snoozing. "Is he supposed to do that?"

"No." The word was sharp and succinct. Something had finally wiped the smile from her face. "I'll have to work on him."

Been there, done that. "What're your thoughts on Zed?"

"Zed is playing with us." Rachel's voice held more admiration than fear.

Playing? The bullet, poison dart, and bomb didn't seem real playful to Camryn, but to each his own kind of fun. "What makes you say that?"

"He's done a few warm-up exercises, but he hasn't started his race yet." Rachel's gaze turned distant. "I've tangled with Zed before. Eleven years ago two other agents and I were assigned to stop Zed. I was the only one who survived."

Camryn was fascinated in spite of herself. "Why is he so successful?"

"We've grown up on the James Bond spy prototype. James Bond wouldn't last five minutes in the real world of spies." Rachel was so involved with her speech, she actually dropped a stitch. Camryn was stunned. "It's all about blending, not calling attention to yourself. The best spy is the one whom no one remembers."

Camryn thought of her red hair, her short dresses, her cat with the zircon collar, and her pink Cadillac. Not exactly a gray shadow fading into the background.

Rachel speared Camryn with an intense stare. "I think Zed is planning something big. Soon."

"What can we do about it?" *Hint, hint. Stop the damned knitting and start looking.*

"We never let anyone we suspect out of our

sight." For the first time Rachel gave her a real smile. "But that's difficult when we suspect so many, isn't it?"

Rachel had a point there.

Rachel dismissed her with a shrug. "You could be Zed. I could be Zed. Almost anyone could be Zed. We have to wait and hope he makes a mistake, and pray we're there when he makes it."

Couldn't argue with that. Time for a positive thought. "At least the rain has stopped and it's a calm night." That was pretty weak, as positive thoughts went.

Rachel's gaze turned distant. "I like the wind. Things happen when the wind blows."

Rachel, the queen of cryptic comments. She didn't seem to notice when Camryn picked up Meathead, stood, and walked back to the Cadillac. Only when Camryn had almost reached Chance did she realize she hadn't seen a car parked anywhere. How had Rachel gotten to the Boardwalk? Okay, so that was at the bottom of her worry list.

Camryn managed to get to Jace's room without anyone commenting on what she wasn't wearing. She pushed the hot dot under her left shoulder blade and glanced hopefully at Meathead. "Can we go in the regular way this time, guy?"

Meathead must've been in an accommodating mood, because a click indicated the door was unlocked. Hurrying inside she found a clean T-shirt and the drawer with Jace's underwear. She pulled out a pair of white briefs, then paused. She thought about her acid-lined panties. She pulled out a few more pairs of white briefs, then hurried to her own room.

Pushing "protect," she left Meathead at the door. Camryn did a quick check. No Chastity and no Fly Spies. Life was good. She changed into loose shorts she could pull over her stolen briefs and a sleeveless top. Camryn slipped on a pair of sandals she'd squirreled away in case of an emergency. When she couldn't find Sara, she hurried back to her car.

She was about to pull away when Flo came running toward her. Camryn waited while Flo scrambled into the passenger seat. Meathead rode shotgun between them.

"Thanks for letting me ride with you. Is Duncan safe?" Flo cast Camryn an anxious glance.

"He's fine. Owen has him. He and Jace are talking. I hope they're still—"

"They're going to play a game tonight, Camryn. And something's going to happen. I can feel it. I've been at this work too many years not to sense danger when it's close." She peered at Camryn. "Don't you feel it?"

A skitter of phantom fingertips played up and down Camryn's spine. She shivered. So much had already happened tonight that she wasn't paying much attention to her intuition. Her intuition agreed with Flo.

"Sara went on with Peter and Honey Suckle. I had to get my stuff together first."

Camryn didn't have to ask what Flo's *stuff* was. Flo was dressed for death. All black. Loose so she could carry a full range of weapons. So often lately Camryn had forgotten Flo's part in B.L.I.S.S.'s grand picture. Maybe Zed should worry a little.

By the time they reached Go, Camryn had tuned in to Flo's tension. Once out of the car, Camryn looked around for Jace. She spotted him standing beside . . .

"Oh, my God!" Camryn would've recognized it anywhere. A living legend. Well, maybe not quite living. She ran past Jace to stand in front of it. Tentatively she reached out to touch it with reverent fingers. "Bond's 'eighty-six Aston Martin Volante from *The Living Daylights*. One of the most destructive Bond cars ever. Rockets. Lasers in the tires. Rocket engine." Emotion caught up with her. "Yes!"

Jace leaned close. "You have the same glitter in your eyes that you had when we were lying on that ledge, three inches from death."

He didn't look too thrilled. In fact, he looked . . . jealous. The thought threw her into happiness overload.

"I love cars." She frowned. "Except for the Cadillac. Driving and fixing cars were the only things I did better than my brothers. I never let them know, of course, because they would've taken over." She turned to Owen. "Can this baby do everything it was supposed to be able to do in the movie?"

Owen nodded, while Sara stood eyeing the Aston Martin worriedly. "The person who acquired it not only restored it, but added fully functional weapons to make it do what the movie claimed it could do."

Sara caught Camryn's gaze and shook her head. Sara didn't want Owen anywhere near something that could be used as a lethal weapon.

"Are you driving it, Jace?" Camryn wanted to drive it, but from the possessive look on his face, she knew better than to ask.

"Yeah." He grinned at her. "This is my one shot at being Bond. Want to ride with me?"

"Try to stop me." She did some eye rolling. "I don't have an interesting name. Bond women have memorable names." She brightened. "Have it. Ima Cookie."

"You like cookies?" He climbed behind the wheel.

She ran around to the passenger side, climbed in, waited for Meathead to scramble in behind her, and slammed the door shut. "Chocolate-chip, soft and gooey from the oven."

"Me too." Jace stared at her for a moment. She met his gaze and something intangible passed between them. Exhaling sharply, he broke eye contact to glance in the rearview mirror.

"Owen and Sara are taking the Cadillac. Citra will guard the rear in her car. Peter and Honey Suckle each have a golf cart so they can follow us around and take care of the tokens and bank. They'll have cell phones to keep in touch." He grimaced. "Lucky them."

Flo ran up to the Aston Martin and stuck her head in the window. "Let me take your bike, Jace. I need to be in the wind."

Jace looked doubtful, but he fished his keys from his pocket and handed them to Flo.

"Thanks." Flo started away. "Hope I remember how to drive one of these babies."

Jace's eyes widened in alarm, but Camryn put her hand on his arm. "She'll be okay. Your bike will be okay."

Finally the game began. Camryn could hardly believe she was really riding in *the* Aston Martin. "This car is so amazing." She slid her fingers along the dashboard.

"Your Cadillac can probably do as much as this car." He paused beside Oriental Avenue while Owen took his turn.

"Bite your tongue. The Cadillac has only three buttons: shield, climb, and destroy. Look at all the things this baby can do."

Jace smiled as he watched Owen stop on Income Tax. "Maybe the Cadillac is into strong and silent. The "destroy" button sort of says it all."

She thought about that for four more moves. Was Jace right? Was she being sucked in by reputation and charisma?

By the end of the fourth move, Jace had bought St. James Place and Kentucky Avenue. Owen was in jail.

By the end of the fiftieth move, Camryn was asleep.

"Wake up, sweetheart. The game's over." Camryn made a valiant effort to shut out the persistent whisper, but to no avail.

"What?" She opened her eyes to the first pale

rays of morning light. "My God, how long did the game last? Who won?"

Jace scraped his palm across his beard-shadowed jaw. "All night, and I won."

She blinked awake her still-groggy brain cells. "That's great. Owen will have to return the tokens now."

"We'll see." He sounded grim.

"You don't think he'll honor his promise?" She watched him open the Aston Martin's door and get out.

He stretched cramped arms and legs, and she admired the play of muscles across his powerful shoulders. She was glad Jace Sentori was on her side. Did that mean she accepted that they were a team? For the first time she didn't push the idea away.

Glancing around, she realized they'd ended up at the Water Works. Speaking of waterworks, she needed a potty break. And besides that, she was starving. She glanced at Jace. *For many things.*

Owen was on his way over to Jace. Camryn wondered how he would take the loss. She prayed that he'd honor his promise, more for Jace's sake than Owen's. Not only might it lay at least one plank in bridging the years of estrangement between them, but it would take Jace out of the dangerous job of returning stolen tokens.

Owen stopped in front of his son while Honey Suckle hovered a little behind him. "You won, Jace. Fair and square."

It must be tough for Owen to speak when his teeth were clenched shut.

Jace studied him. "So you'll return the stolen tokens?"

Owen nodded and turned to Honey Suckle. "Tell Peter to start shipping the tokens back to their rightful owners." He paused for a moment. "And tell him to get in touch with my lawyers. I need to make some changes."

Honey Suckle looked a little distressed, but she made no comment as she swayed her way over to Peter.

Camryn watched Jace wrestle with whatever demons fought their battle inside him. "Thanks . . . Owen."

Camryn saw the almost imperceptible sag as Owen turned to walk away, and felt a stab of sympathy for him. She drew in a deep breath and expelled it slowly. She was feeling sorry for the wrong person. One act didn't wipe out a lifetime of rejection.

Owen paused. "Camryn and you can have the Cadillac back. I don't feel like driving anymore, so Sara and I will ride back to Chance with Citra. Peter has the truck, and Honey Suckle can drive the Aston Martin back."

Camryn eyed the Aston Martin hungrily, then sighed as she climbed into the Cadillac. Jace picked up Meathead and joined her. They both watched everyone leave except Honey Suckle. She just sat in the Aston Martin, her face expressionless.

"If B.L.I.S.S.'s sources are reliable, and Honey Suckle had a relationship with Owen until Sara showed up, I bet she's really ticked off." Camryn wondered exactly how ticked off Honey Suckle was. Still considering that thought, she slowly followed the others, leaving Honey Suckle still sitting in the car.

Jace interrupted her musings. "Do you mind going back to Free Parking for a minute? I think I lost my room key there." He leaned his head against the headrest and closed his eyes.

He must be exhausted after the night he'd had. She couldn't believe how much she cared about his exhaustion. A few days ago, if he'd fallen down from exhaustion, she would've calmly stepped over him and kept going. Not now.

Camryn reached Free Parking and stopped at the same spot as last night. What a difference. No rain, no MacDuffs, and no fear. But one thing did remain from last night: the memory of what she'd felt when she'd thought Jace was dead.

She leaned her forehead against the steering wheel for a moment and closed her eyes. No time to analyze her feelings with only seven days left until the summit. Zed had to be stopped, or Jace and Owen would never have a chance to mend fences.

When she felt the touch of his fingers slip through her hair, Camryn knew it felt right. She sighed her contentment with the moment.

"I'll find the key; then we can go home and get some sleep." His murmur was a husky promise of things to come. "Together."

She wanted to tell him they were going to make love on the beach at the Boardwalk, that she'd always dreamed of making love on a beach, but he'd already climbed out to retrieve his key.

He was on his way back to the car with the key when Meathead's eyes flashed the urgent-message code. She felt stupid doing this, but she still hadn't figured out how to remove the collar. She picked up Meathead and pressed the zircon that opened the communication channel.

Jace climbed in beside her and grinned. "Talking to your cat again?"

"Shh." She turned her attention to the collar. "Who is this?"

"Agent 1BA." The voice sounded breathless and had a jerky quality to it.

Agent 1BA? "Flo?"

"Right. Now listen up, Camryn." In the pause there was the sound of a roaring engine.

"That's my bike." Jace leaned close so he could hear.

"I was watching from cover when all you guys headed back to Chance." Flo paused to insert a few four-letter sidebars. "As soon as everyone was out of sight, Honey Suckle ran down to the water. The land drops off a little right there so I couldn't see anything. But obviously someone was waiting in a boat, because she came back lugging some sort of contraption and I could hear the sound of a motor fading away. She put the contraption in the car and spent some time connecting things. Then she slammed the door and the car started moving. It's heading toward Chance without a driver. Whatever she put in there is controlling it."

Flo faded out for a moment and Camryn closed

her eyes. *Please let at least one piece of electronics work right.*

"That's when it hit me: Zed is going to try to take out Chance with everyone in it. If the Aston Martin reaches Chance, and Zed has programmed its rockets and lasers, there won't be enough of Chance left to fill a bucket. I can't catch it with the bike. I'll call Chance and tell everyone to get the hell out of there. You get that Cadillac moving and try to head it off." Silence. No "Good luck." No helpful hints. She was on her own.

"I'm with you." Jace lifted Meathead from her arms. "Let's see what this baby can do."

She *wasn't* on her own. She blinked back tears and jammed the Cadillac into gear.

Chapter Fifteen

Camryn was afraid to floor the gas pedal. She was even afraid to glance at the speedometer. Superfast was all she needed to know about their forward progress.

The radio crackled. *Joy.* T was in the house.

"Yo, dudess. There's a fire, right? Hey, like, I'm not your regular sexist dude, but an older woman might get intimidated driving the Big Smooth at excessive speeds. So why not—"

Older woman? "Shut up." Camryn could learn to hate precocious children.

In the distance she could see the Aston Martin speeding toward the turn that would take it on its final deadly run to Chance. It would get there before the Cadillac, so Camryn would have to catch it on the last winding few miles. Could she make up enough ground to do it? *Not likely.* As soon as she pulled the Cadillac out of the turn, she'd have to floor it.

As though in a dream, she could hear Jace talking into Meathead's collar, making sure Flo's message had reached Chance and everyone was evacuating. But could they run fast or far enough from the building before the Aston Martin loosed death on them? Would everyone hear the warning?

The Aston Martin swung into the turn, almost skidding out of control. For a moment Camryn hoped the solution would be that simple. *No way*. The car leveled out and was gone.

Camryn muttered a prayer as she took the turn right behind it. Every law of physics said there was no way she could make that turn going at the speed she was going, even if she *was* too chicken to look at the speedometer.

She thought they were all goners as the Cadillac made the turn on two wheels, but once out of the turn it leveled out and was in pursuit again. If she survived, she might even plant a big, slobbery kiss on T's cheek. Of course, she wouldn't tell him. He was already too puffed-up with his own brilliance.

"Do. Not. Do. That. Again. You were way too lucky on that last turn, dudess. Another corner like that and the Big Smooth could go to the giant junkyard in the sky. Calculating the angle of the turn and your recorded speed, your chance of making another turn like that is—"

"Not listening to you, T. Can't hear a word

you're saying." To prove it, she hummed "The Muffin Man" as loudly as she could.

Beside her, Jace sat quietly. No shouts of alarm. No instructions on how to handle the car. No demands to let *him* drive. Without saying a word, he touched her with his strength and confidence in her.

Not so Meathead. Small mews of alarm filled the space between Camryn and Jace. Meathead was no dummy.

With disbelief, she watched lasers from the Aston Martin take out Chance's security gate. How could she stop something that had that had kind of monstrous power?

"I wouldn't want to be in the path of that baby. How about blowing it away now?" Jace's calmness propped her up, and she allowed herself to breathe again.

Camryn shook her head. "Can't. With this winding road and the speed of both cars, I might miss." She gripped the wheel tighter. "I don't know if I'll get a second try. Besides, too many things have malfunctioned. If I press the 'destroy' button and nothing happens, I want the Cadillac blocking the road to Chance. Getting past the Cadillac would at least slow it down enough to give everyone at Chance more escape time."

Camryn drew in a deep, steadying breath. It was now or never. She had to floor it even if she knew there was no way she could control a vehicle this size on the winding road. She'd have to give it a shot.

Her last thought before jamming the pedal to

the floor was that she finally saw things from her brothers' perspectives, understood their need to protect. She would do what she had to do. Her only regret was Jace. She wanted him out of this car and safe. Okay, Meathead too.

Do it. Now.

The instant acceleration was explosive. The engine's whine became the whine of a jet just before takeoff; the force of the car's speed pushed her back against the seat, ripped the breath from her lungs. It took all her strength to hang on to the wheel.

Suddenly Jace's hands were on the wheel with hers. Together they fought the demon the Cadillac had become. She didn't let up on the accelerator as the car whipped around curves that should have overturned it. But T had created balance that seemed ultimately impossible.

For some reason known only to the gods of panic, Camryn thought of Y's tale of the bumblebee. Nothing that looked like the Cadillac should be able to do what this car was doing. Kick her if she ever judged anyone or anything again by appearances.

The Cadillac roared past the Aston Martin with only inches between them. Meathead leaped to the floor. He evidently subscribed to the theory that if he couldn't see it, it couldn't kill him.

It was now a race to the spot where the road widened just before reaching Chance. Camryn would make her stand there. "That wide spot just ahead. I'm going to slow down a little and spin the car around so it's facing the Aston Martin."

She sensed Jace's nod. Biting her lip in concentration, she lifted her foot from the accelerator, and with Jace's help yanked the steering wheel to the right.

The car skidded into a circle and came to rest facing the speeding car behind it. "Get out! Get out!" She glanced frantically at Jace. "Take Meathead and run as far as you can before I push the button."

"Can't do, sweetheart." He scooted close to her.

Thank you. She flipped open the control panel. Only one button mattered. "I'm about to destroy a legend." *I hope.*

"You're *driving* a legend, lady." He leaned close, his voice confident. "L.O.V.E.R. is about to meet C.R.A.P.: Can't Run Away, Pal."

She gave a hiccuping laugh. Even now, when she didn't know if they'd survive the next few seconds, Jace Sentori could make her laugh.

Camryn pushed the "destroy" button.

She shielded her eyes against a brilliant flash of white light. No explosion, no flying car parts, no smoke or flames.

When the flash was gone, so was the Aston Martin. Nothing. No evidence the car had ever existed, not even an oil smear on the road.

"Oh, yeah, baby!" T's voice was an exuberant shout of self-satisfaction. "Am I the man or what?" As he disconnected, he was singing an off-key verse of "We Are the Champions."

"What the hell kind of weapon was *that?*" Jace spoke in an awed whisper.

"I don't know." She drew in a deep breath to

try to control her shaking voice. "No one ever told me." Leaning her head back, she closed her eyes.

"How does it feel to be a hero?" There was no laughter in his voice.

She kept her eyes closed. "I learned something this morning. I learned that the hero isn't always the one who pushes the button." *You're my hero.*

Jace watched a smile tip her lips up.

"Owen's going to be really steamed about this." She opened her eyes to glance down at the cat, who'd jumped back onto the seat and was trying to crawl into her lap.

"He'll get over it." Jace frowned at F.I.D.O. The cat's actions were growing more and more bizarre. "He'd be more pissed off if he woke up dead." In the distance he could hear the roar of his bike. Flo was coming. He'd push aside his emotions and thoughts until he was alone. Then he'd take them out to examine.

By the time Flo reached them, Camryn had shut down the Cadillac and climbed from the car. Jace had followed her. Together they examined the spot where the Aston Martin had been and tried to understand what the Cadillac's weapons system had done.

Flo stopped beside them, gun drawn. Jace stared at the . . . gun. He had to call it a gun for want of a better term, but it didn't look like any gun he'd ever seen. He was beginning to realize that messing with the women of B.L.I.S.S. was not a smart move.

"Where's the car? Did it get past you?" Flo's glance swept the surrounding area.

Camryn shook her head. "The Cadillac took it out."

Flo looked puzzled. "So where're the pieces?"

Camryn shrugged.

Flo's gaze was raptly admiring. "It beats me how a pain in the butt with the people skills of a stinkweed can create something that brilliant. I'll go on ahead and let everyone know things are okay." She paused, then cast them an intent stare. "Honey Suckle isn't Zed, but she knows who Zed is."

"Will she talk?" Jace thought he knew the answer.

Flo offered him a thin smile. "Not if she's smart."

"Zed will try to eliminate her." Camryn's voice held no emotion beyond a thoughtful analysis of the situation.

Jace frowned. Camryn had changed since the first time he'd met her, become more the agent she longed to be. How would that affect him? Would he matter beyond her assignment here? He didn't know, wasn't sure.

Flo stared at Camryn. "After I alerted Chance to what was happening, Citra called me to say she was on her way out to pick up Honey Suckle."

Jace thought about the cat collar and Rachel's glove. He had to find out. "I know you don't have a cell phone, Flo, so how'd you call us?"

Flo and Camryn exchanged grins. Flo winked at him. "You don't want to know, big guy. You really don't want to know." She didn't give him a chance to argue as she roared away.

Jace could see Camryn processing the new information. Flo was obviously working with Citra rather than Rachel or Sara, so that meant Flo suspected one of them was Zed. Then again, Flo could be Zed.

No, his instincts said that Flo was the straightforward kind. With the weapon she was holding, Flo could just blow away anyone she didn't want around.

Jace shook his head. All this heavy thinking was giving him a headache. Or maybe the fall off the cliff was responsible for that. Besides, he was so tired he couldn't make a rational judgment. "Let's get back to Chance and see what's happening."

Jace rubbed a hand across his face to try to revive himself. "Let's take the Badillac . . ." What the hell was he saying? "Sorry. I meant, let's take the Cadillac home."

Camryn grinned as they climbed into the car. "No, I like it. That's what I'll name it. The Badillac. Batman has his Batmobile, and I have the Badillac. It rocks. The baddest car on the board, from Mediterranean Avenue to the Boardwalk."

Jace smiled. He owed the Cadillac an oil change after what it had done today. "You're sleeping with me today, O'Brien."

"Hey, love your subtle approach." She didn't say no.

"I'm too tired to be subtle." He leaned his head back as she drove the short distance to Chance.

"Why is Zed doing this, Jace? I mean, Zed could arrange an assassination that would look like an accident: a fall, a drowning, something inconspic-uous. Why something so spectacular?" Camryn parked, got out, and then made sure the security system was activated.

Jace decided the Cadillac would do a lot more than honk if someone tried to mess with it. He followed her into Chance. "We're dealing with a gigantic ego, someone who not only wants to kill, but wants everyone to admire his brilliance. That's his weakness, and let's hope we can exploit it." He'd used the W word again. He waited for a comment.

None came. And better yet, nothing fell on his head.

"We need to get your father off this island until we track down Zed." *She'd* used the W word.

"I'm not going."

They swung around at the sound of Owen's voice.

"No one's driving me from my home." He stared at his son. "I haven't stood up for much in my life, but I'm making a stand now." He shifted his gaze to Sara, who hovered close to him. "Sara and Citra will question Honey Suckle." A shadow of sadness touched his expression. "I can't believe she wanted me dead."

Owen took a deep breath. "Anyway, Flo and Ra-chel will work with my people to secure the grounds. Peter's pretty broken up about what his sister tried to do, but his new girlfriend will pull him through." Owen frowned. "Looks like she could take out a small army without even breathing hard."

Owen glanced around him. "You know, I thought nothing was as important as my Monopoly game, but in the last few days my perspective has changed." He offered Jace a wry grin. "You two go up and get some sleep. I'll have someone wake you if anything important comes up."

No matter how tired he felt, Jace wanted an explanation for something that bothered him. "Hogan's Saltwater Taffy Shop. Why'd you build a replica on the Boardwalk?"

Owen's glance slid away from Jace. "I took you to Atlantic City on your sixth birthday. We stopped at Hogan's, and I bought you a big box of candy. You told me you loved me." Owen shrugged. "It was the last time." He wouldn't meet Jace's gaze. "I wanted to remember that."

Well, why the hell didn't you ever let me know that I meant something to you? Jace figured he had to say something, but years of convincing himself he didn't care about Owen made the words tough. Okay, he'd just spit it out. "Glad you're okay," *Dad.* Even thinking the word felt strange.

Owen nodded and coughed. "You too, son." He flushed and glanced at Camryn. "You keep my son safe, Camryn."

Jace knew he should argue the wording. They'd keep each other safe. But he was too damn tired.

Camryn went to order some food to be brought to his room; then they made their way upstairs with F.I.D.O. trailing after them. Once inside, Camryn checked to make sure Zed wasn't hiding behind a picture frame or inside the lampshade. Then she plunked herself onto the bed.

"You're still tired, aren't you?" He slid his fingers through her tangled hair.

She smiled at him. "Yeah. It's not every day I do battle with a death star."

He lay down on top of the bed and patted the spot beside him. "Let's just relax for a minute until the food comes."

For a moment he thought she'd argue, but then she gave in with a sigh. "Right. Just until the food comes." She lay down next to him, but made sure their bodies didn't touch.

"Could've sworn you mumbled something about making love when we were back there on the ledge." He turned onto his side so he could see her expression.

"Not on this bed." She closed her eyes. "On the beach."

"Sure." The closing-eyes thing was contagious. Lead weights must be attached to his lids. As his lids drifted shut he felt F.I.D.O. scramble onto the bed; then a furry body invaded his pillow space. Worse than that, the furry body was purring. Which reminded him . . . "Guess we're lucky the car worked better than F.I.D.O. does." He felt sleep pulling at him. "Did Rachel have anything to do with the car?"

Camryn's voice was a sleepy murmur. "Nope. T's the genius behind the car. Rachel had nothing to do with it."

As sleep claimed him, he knew Camryn had said something important.

Jace tossed and turned, his dreams filled with every Bond car chase he'd ever seen, and at the end of each nightmare the Aston Martin would be bearing down on him with a shadowy, demented figure behind the wheel.

He woke, startled out of sleep by motion nearby. Glancing around, he registered the darkness outside, Camryn asleep by his side, and F.I.D.O. trying to eat a piece of meat that was part of their uneaten meal. Camryn must've gotten up when someone delivered the meal, and then fallen asleep again. He looked at his watch. Two A.M. Evidently a clear conscience overrode being pursued by a death star, because Camryn was sleeping the sleep of the innocent.

F.I.D.O. was trying to eat a piece of meat. A robot didn't eat. Then he remembered his thought just before falling asleep. F.I.D.O. was a product of Rachel's ingenuity. He'd never worked right. If Rachel was brilliant enough to once have been the chief gadget creator for B.L.I.S.S., then how had she managed to make something so flawed? And why was F.I.D.O. acting more and more like a real cat?

Jace gazed at F.I.D.O. through narrowed eyes. He was going to find an answer to his questions. Climbing quietly from bed, he scooped up F.I.D.O. and left the bedroom. "We're going to get to the bottom of some things before Camryn wakes up."

"Ow?"

Jace shook his head. "You won't feel a thing."

Two hours later, Jace sat cross-legged on the floor with what seemed like a thousand pieces of the robot scattered around him. This whole thing was way too bizarre for him.

He'd managed to get past the built-in defense mechanisms meant to keep prying eyes and fingers out of the robot, but there was something inside F.I.D.O. that defied even his knowledge of high-tech electronics. When he first went in, the chaos inside had blown him away. As far as he could see, nothing inside the robot should work at all. Someone had made a deliberate effort to ensure that this guy either didn't work or malfunctioned. But that wasn't the only problem.

Inside F.I.D.O. was a black box made of some pliable material. He could see the original dimensions of the box by marks on the robot's casing. But something was happening. The dimensions of the box were increasing. It had already compressed most of the robot's original system, which of course contributed to the malfunctioning Camryn had experienced.

He couldn't access the black box. It had no seams. When he touched it, a strange tingle ran through his fingers, warning him that taking a knife to the outer covering could prove painful. Going on the assumption that the tingles were electrical in nature, he held the rubber sole of his shoe to the black box. The same tingles touched his fingers and this time ran up his arm. A stronger warning this time. He left the box alone.

He would put the robot back together and try to repair a few of the weapon connections, but the robot would never be the ultimate protector of the free world that B.L.I.S.S. probably hoped it would be. As for the black box? He didn't know. A suspicion was forming, but he didn't have a clue whether what he suspected was even possible. Maybe Camryn could ask Y about it.

Jace picked up a part from the floor, then paused. *Hmm.* Maybe he shouldn't put it together for a little while. He smiled. There was something on his personal agenda that needed taking care of before F.I.D.O. was operational again.

He started to rise, then stopped. Someone was behind him. An angry someone. He could feel the mad-as-hell waves bouncing off his back. He exhaled sharply. This wouldn't be pretty.

"You killed Meathead." Camryn's accusation was an outraged croak.

He turned slowly so as not to provoke a lethal attack. "He's a robot, Camryn, and I can put him back together in under two hours."

Camryn knelt down beside him and picked up the robot's head. Her shorts were wrinkled and her top rode up to expose several inches of coming attractions. She'd kicked off her sandals before lying down, and even her bare feet affected his circuitry. This was not a good thing. It was too soon, and she was too pissed.

"You never liked Meathead." She didn't look at him. "Okay, so he didn't always work right, but he did the best he could." She sounded like she was about to cry. "I thought he was kind of neat."

Finally she looked at him. Tears of mingled anger and sorrow glistened in her eyes. "What is it with you, Sentori? Owen is never Dad, F.I.D.O. is never Meathead, and I bet the Cadillac will never be the Badillac to you. Talk to me, Jace. I want to know."

He could lie to her, change the subject, but he wanted those damned tears to go away. They bothered him. And if telling her the truth took her mind off the robot, got rid of the accusation in her eyes, then he'd run with it.

"When you name a person or thing, the name becomes an emotional cord that ties you to it. I made sure I never called Owen Dad, because the word 'dad' carried certain expectations. Owen would never be a dad to me. F.I.D.O.? He's a machine. Call him Meathead and he becomes a pet. You bond with pets." He offered her a half smile, but she was too intent on what he was saying to respond.

"I know a lot of people name their cars, but what's the point? It's another machine, and one day it'll end up in a junkyard somewhere." His smile grew wider. "Grandma Sentori had an Olds when I was about seventeen. Called it Candy. She loaned me the car for a date, and while we were in a movie, some drunk totaled it. She cried buckets over that car. Surprised she didn't have a funeral for it."

"You're scared to death of caring, aren't you, Jace?"

Her eyes widened as soon as the words left her lips. *Smart lady.* She knew she'd blown it.

He narrowed his gaze. "You think I'm some sort of emotional cripple, but I'm a realist, Camryn. I don't call a father who's never acted like one Dad. I don't make pets out of machines. Seems to me a B.L.I.S.S. agent should look at things with her mind, not her heart."

Her heart. The two words hung between them, took on an unspoken meaning, and Jace decided he would have been better off keeping his big mouth shut.

Surprisingly, Camryn didn't look mad anymore, but her new expression was unreadable. At least mad he understood.

"What did you find out?" She smoothed the fur between the robot's ears with two fingers.

"Someone sabotaged him. It's amazing he worked at all. I can reconnect a few things, but not many. There's a listening device in there. Do you want me to reconnect it?"

Camryn shook her head. "I don't think I want Rachel knowing what Meathead's doing anymore." She didn't seem surprised by anything he'd said. "What's that black box?"

"I don't know. I couldn't get inside." He wouldn't mention his suspicion without more information. "If you talk to Y, ask her about it."

"Sure." Her gaze turned thoughtful. "You know, it suddenly hit me that I'm free until you put Meathead back together." A smile tilted her lips. "I don't have to be careful about where or how I touch my body."

Or where anyone else touches it. He tried to keep himself from grinning. No use letting her know he'd already thought of that. "Let's go back to bed and relax while you decide where to go from here." He wanted to say *we,* but he respected her need for independence. After all, *he* was all about being independent.

"I guess that makes sense." She cast a last doubtful look at the robot. "Are you sure you can put him back together again?"

"No problem." *But not right now.* "I could put Humpty-Dumpty back together again."

"I'll make some coffee and be right in." She headed for his kitchen area.

Good. That would give him time to take a quick shower. Jace reached the bathroom in a few strides, stripped, and stepped under the spray. He didn't have time to enjoy the warm water sluicing over his battered body. He'd considered cold water, then dismissed it. It wouldn't work, so why suffer?

Stepping from the shower, he toweled himself dry. *Great.* He hadn't bothered to bring anything clean to change into. Camryn was probably still making the coffee, so he'd just slip his briefs back on and go get clean stuff. After stepping into the briefs, he opened the door and . . .

He lifted his gaze in time to see Camryn stride into the bedroom, then freeze to stare at him. She bit her lip as her gaze slid the length of his body, with a pause for thought at the briefs.

"I can't find your coffee." She'd stopped biting her lip. "Can we go to the beach? Now?"

Camryn wanted him *now.* This was no slow curl of desire, no warm-and-fuzzy snugglefest. Uncontrolled need body-slammed her and left her breathless.

"The beach? Why . . . ?"

He stood studying her with that dark gaze that would make even the comment "Pass the corn-flakes" sexy. His hair was damp and curled around his face in wicked invitation. She clenched her fingers into a fist to keep them out of trouble.

She didn't dare drop her gaze below his face too often. Naked except for those white briefs, his body gleamed damply with drops still clinging to strategic parts that begged to be licked, savored. If she spent too much time staring, she might just go into octopus mode. Wasn't lust wonderful?

Camryn knew the exact moment he under-stood. His slow grin that made all kinds of sexual promises transformed him from electronic wizard to sensual magician. And he hadn't even needed a phone booth.

"And the point of *now* is?" He was going to make her say it.

"The beach is my fantasy. It'll be better at the beach." *Uh-oh.* Did she make it sound like maybe he *wouldn't* be great in a plain old bed? Like only the fantasy would make it incredible sex?

She needn't have worried. He wasn't focused on the beach. "Now?"

"Sure. Now." She did some mental knuckle cracking. "Meathead is down, so I'm kind of free."

He nodded, lowering his gaze as though giving her answer serious thought. When he finally raised his gaze, evil intent gleamed in his eyes. "You want me, sweetheart."

Okay, this was it. A B.L.I.S.S. agent didn't wring her hands and make sounds of indecision. "Yeah." This was way too uncomfortable, and she couldn't

301

seem to meet his gaze. She might have the hand wringing and indecisive sounds under control, but she really needed to work on the steady-unflinching-stare thing.

He moved closer, bringing with him the scent of clean, warm male and the taste of anticipation. "But you don't think it'll be too great if you're not on the beach."

Camryn wouldn't let him make her feel defensive. It was *her* fantasy. "I didn't say that. The bed would be fine, but the beach would be great."

"Whoa, babe." He grinned at her. "Sensitive male ego crushed here."

He didn't look crushed to her.

Reaching out, he smoothed a strand of hair from her face. "Can't wait that long."

She glanced down. *No kidding.* "Fine. I want to take a quick shower." Her immediate cave-in surprised her. Maybe he wasn't the only one who couldn't wait.

To his credit, he didn't express any outward signs of triumph.

Camryn paused in the bathroom's doorway. "Lights off."

"Uh-uh. Lights on. I've waited too long for this. I want to see you." He didn't look playful.

"Too long? Three days?" She raised one eyebrow.

"Too long."

She showered quickly, her entire body humming its excitement. Funny—no nerves now that she'd made her decision. Men and sex had always made her nervous. Maybe the nerves had been because she never knew how far into a date she'd get before she had to rush said date to the emergency room.

That wasn't it. The truth? She wanted Jace Sentori more than she'd ever wanted any other man. And beyond that, she remembered how she'd felt on that ledge, knowing he'd escaped death by inches. Nerves had no place in what she wanted to happen between them.

Stepping out of the shower, she dried off, then started to dress. *Hmm.* Tonight she wanted to emphasize how alike they were. Not physically. She allowed herself a sexy feline smile. Physical differences were yummy.

She didn't want to dwell on differences in who they were as people, things that might eventually tear them apart. Because no matter how much she tried to deny it, the thought of walking away forever from Jace left her with a hollow feeling in her middle.

How to demonstrate this visually, since Jace was a visual kind of guy? Did she have the guts? Sure she did. Guts was the middle name of the women of B.L.I.S.S.

She put on one piece of clothing, then stepped from the bathroom. Dimmed lights. He was into compromise.

Jace was stretched out on the bed, still wearing only his white briefs. He glanced up and his eyes widened.

Chapter Sixteen

Camryn resisted the urge to cross her arms over her breasts. *Stupid.* He'd seen her breasts before, so what was the big deal?

Fine, so she had 36DD insecurity.

To keep her hands from automatically going into cover-up mode, she hooked her thumbs into the top of her white briefs and stared back at him. "We have something in common now. And hey, no acid lining. Like them?" She twirled so he could get a back view.

"On you? Love them. But we have another thing in common."

Something in the air shifted, grew warm, touched her with an awareness that hadn't been there a moment ago. He'd moved from the bed to stand behind her. She needed to turn, confront him, but the strength of whatever moved between them was almost physical, holding her in place.

"We have this." His voice was a husky murmur, a slow slide of sensual promise that *this* would be outstanding.

Camryn drew in a deep breath as he wrapped his arms around her and pulled her close. She closed her eyes to focus on the press of his body against her back. Bare flesh on bare flesh except for the hard ridge of his erection against the base of her spine.

"I . . ."

He rubbed the pads of his thumbs across her nipples, and whatever she'd been about to say was trampled by the stampede of senses rushing to the point of contact.

Before she had time to process any more tactile impressions, he turned her around, scooped her up in his arms, and then plopped her on the bed. "This is the way it is. We have a sandy beach here with the sound of waves breaking nearby."

She bounced on the bed, then frowned. "We have a black bedspread, and I'm bouncing. The beach doesn't have inner springs."

He loomed over her, the flex of his shoulder muscles his only sign of annoyance. "You need to work on your visualization skills. What about the waves? Can you hear the pounding of the waves?"

She shook her head. "Nope. No waves." *Just the pounding of my heart.*

"You have to work with me here." Reaching down, he stripped off his briefs. "I'm trying hard to create your fantasy."

Camryn widened her eyes. "Forget the fantasy. Reality is pretty much an okay thing with me right now." *Wow. Total-impact time.* The unbroken flow of flesh and muscle, all that maleness and need, the heated scent of sexual anticipation.

Oh, no. She felt an *I'm not ready for this man* panic attack coming on. *Stress.* She couldn't stop herself. She hummed a verse of "B-I-N-G-O."

Laughing, he put one finger over her lips. "Uh-uh. We need to update your repertoire." Sliding his finger down the side of her neck, he wandered off course as he circled one nipple, then trailed the finger over her stomach, in and out of her navel, and finally stopped at her briefs. "How about Tina Turner's 'The Best'?"

She thought about that as she lifted her hips so he could slip off her briefs. Tried to keep thinking about it as cool air played over her bare skin, and his hot gaze heated things up. "Are you saying *you're* the best? Kind of arrogant, if you ask me."

"Try me, lady. Just try me." The slant of his grin was wicked temptation.

A chocolate smile. It said, *Taste me and you won't be able to stop. Promise moderation all you want, but you'll always come back, and each time will be better than the last.* She grinned. Was that a great metaphor or what?

Her smile faded as she met his gaze. She'd left something out. Too much chocolate made her sick. But that sure didn't stop her every time she met a Snickers bar. Jace would be like that. Was that what she wanted? To enjoy the moment, but regret all the afterwards?

Her smile eased back into place. If the moment was all she had, she'd take it. "Let the trying begin."

He settled onto the bed beside her, pushed her legs apart, and knelt between them. She watched him with avid interest.

"Guess you'll want this slow and sweet. Lots of foreplay." His gaze settled on her mouth. Hungry.

Camryn frowned. That was so *not* what she wanted. She needed bonded lips, frenzied fingers, instant gratification in the form of a merging of assets. She wouldn't survive foreplay that lasted more than, say, three minutes.

Leaning over, he slid his tongue across her lower lip. "I love it when you pout. You stick your bottom lip right out there, ripe for licking." His husky murmur moved over her cheek as he kissed the end of her nose.

"Pouting *always* gets me what I want." Camryn closed her eyes and he kissed each lid. She sucked in her breath at the slide of his arousal across her belly, wishing it were a little lower. She spread her legs farther apart just in case.

It was a meaningless gesture, because he was still focused on her face. He covered her mouth with his, his tongue tangling with hers, exploring the heat, the smooth slickness. And her body clenched at this preview of things to come.

Abandoning her lips, he grinned down at her. "I don't know why B.L.I.S.S. ever thought you needed hot dots. You've got lethal lips. And what is it about your mouth? I'm going to have to spend a lot of time investigating."

She offered him her wicked-woman smile. "Nothing in there, just teeth and tongue." And a whole bunch of tiny taste buds giving him a thumbs-up. She couldn't pin down a particular flavor like mint chocolate chip, or French vanilla. More like the taste of sex and sin with a generous topping of hot, healthy male. Her new favorite flavor. "Don't you think you should start working your way south? My personal enter spot, as opposed to my B.L.I.S.S. enter spot, is a long way off." *Ugh.* That was coy. She hated coy.

"I know the difference." He nibbled a path down her neck, stopping to touch his tongue to the base of her throat. "And your personal enter spot is where?" He glanced up from under his lashes as he kissed the swell of her breast. His eyes glittered with malicious intent.

He wanted her to touch the spot. *Not a chance.* If she touched herself there, she'd go off like one of Meathead's missiles. "I'm sure if you search long and hard you'll find it."

He smoothed his fingers across the skin of her shoulder, setting off a chain reaction of goose bumps. "Long and hard I can do."

Without warning he leaned back, his thighs open to whatever she wanted to see. The proof of how hard he was looking jutted strong and tempting. Of course, you didn't just eyeball proof. You needed to study it more carefully, get a feel for it.

Throwing his head back, he raked his fingers through his hair. She followed the tense line of his neck, watched him swallow hard. Exhaling sharply, he returned his hot gaze to her.

"Can't do this, Camryn. I can't nibble my way down your body. Can't do the sex-talk thing."

He put his hand between her legs, and every muscle in her body spasmed, then melted into a gooey glob.

"I want to absorb you through my skin, pound into you until we both explode, and there's no way I'll make even fifteen minutes of kissing, licking, and sucking." Leaning over, he put his mouth over one nipple, did a slow slide with his tongue across the startled nub, then sucked as Camryn arched her back, inviting . . . *More.*

Good grief, she was already reduced to a one-word vocabulary.

When he abandoned the nipple, the goose-bump parade began again as the cool air touched the nipple still hot from his mouth. She forgot the goose bumps as he transferred his mouth to her other nipple, nipping gently, then closing his lips over it.

Knowing what would come next, she grasped his hair in a death grip and hung on.

Amazing how her hips automatically lifted, trying to make groin contact, when the stimulus was still so far away. She wanted to fling back her head and scream, *Faster, faster.* "Are the fifteen minutes up yet?"

His soft chuckle heated her from breasts to toes. Her toes curled in response.

"Getting there. Definitely getting there."

His voice sounded breathless. And here she'd thought he was in such great shape.

Must be a sudden lack of oxygen, because she was doing some heavy gasping herself. Zed had probably found a way to suck out all the air in the room. Camryn didn't give a damn so long as she made love with Jace before she passed out. "I need to see how much you want me so I can start the explosion countdown." *I need to feel, to taste how much you want me.*

"Don't have much faith in my word, do you?" He slid over her body, straddling her, supporting his weight on thighs roped with muscle. No game-playing couch potato here.

He paused with his erection nestled between her breasts. She beckoned him closer, then took him into her mouth.

His surprise shuddered through him; then she heard his soft moan of pleasure. Slowly he moved his hips back and forth, thrusting his erection in and out, the slide of all those male sexual parts between her breasts an erotic feel-fest, until she closed her lips tightly around him, let him feel the light scrape of her teeth.

He stilled, not moving, allowing her to absorb his vulnerability, his acknowledgment that she controlled what would happen next. His breathing was a harsh rasp; his thighs trembled on either side of her.

Her gaze slid the length of his sweat-sheened torso, noted the hard rise and fall of his chest, the sharp angles of his tensed facial muscles.

Still he didn't move, didn't attempt to take the power from her.

She slid her tongue across the head of his erection, savored the slightly salty drop of moisture that signaled his own personal countdown to lift-off.

He braced his hands on his thighs, his fingers blunt and powerful.

Camryn glided her tongue along the line of a vein, clenching her body at his harsh curse of pleasure-pain.

Revelation: She'd found a new superhero. He didn't live in a Batcave and he didn't swing from a web. He was stronger than that. He was a man who believed that he should always be in control, but he'd allowed her to control their wild race with death, and he was allowing her control now on a much more personal level. How strong was that?

She released him.

"Just in time." He rolled from the bed and yanked open the nightstand drawer.

She watched him pull out a condom. Watched as he slid it over his erection. Then she met his suddenly intense gaze.

"Know this, lady: I'm a protector; I'll always be a protector. I can't change what I am. Accept it." He returned to kneel once more between her thighs.

This *wasn't* about condoms. *Fair enough.* She could work with the symbolism. But she had one question: "What if I don't accept it?"

She wasn't prepared for his muffled laughter. "Then I'll crawl out of here and get medical help. I want you bad, O'Brien."

Reaching up, she pulled him down to her. "I

want you hard, deep, and *fast*, Sentori."

He reached between their bodies and touched the spot between her legs that would launch her own personal rocket. She clasped his wrist and forced his hand away.

"If you touch me there, it's all over. I want you inside me when it happens." She slid her fingers the length of his erection, then glanced up at him, recognizing the moment when he reached his limit of endurance. More than three minutes, but less than fifteen.

He lifted her hips, then plunged into her. This was no gentle entry. This was the primal urge to mate. She didn't think as she wrapped her legs around him and ground her hips against his, trying to take more of him, glorying in the stretching, the fullness.

With each powerful thrust he drove deeper, awoke sensations she'd never experienced, never wanted to live without again. Clasping his buttocks, she dug in her nails, tried to speed his pumping motion, tried to lift her hips higher.

The building pressure was a silent scream, mindless, pushing its way to the surface. She'd abandoned all her senses except touch. She strained toward the moment when the spasms would begin. *Faster. Harder.*

Her orgasm caught her, shook her with primitive release. She screamed her triumph. It was a moment of total selfishness, when no one or nothing mattered except the incredible power of the sensory explosion that locked every muscle,

313

stopped her breath, and changed forever her definition of sexual satisfaction.

Like ripples on a pond, the spasms slowly faded away, leaving Camryn satiated. She liked the word *satiated*. It sounded decadent. She watched through half-closed eyes as Jace rolled off her onto his side. What could be more decadent than lying naked beside Jace's powerful bared body after experiencing the orgasm to end all orgasms?

She'd had only a few sexual encounters, but when the moment came to experience ecstasy, most of the time she'd been busy mentally composing her weekly shopping list or wondering when it would be over.

Not this time. Move over chocolate, because she'd found a new bad habit. Did she want it to become a permanent bad habit? She wasn't emotionally ready to think about that possibility yet.

Camryn turned onto her side with her back to Jace. Putting his arm around her, he pulled her to him. Wiggling her bottom, she worked herself into a more perfect fit.

"Bet I have nail digs in my butt. Marks of glory." He nipped her shoulder. "I think you shouted louder than me. I'm surprised your partners didn't come running."

She glanced over her shoulder. "You shouted?"

His chuckle warmed the back of her neck. "I love a woman who can block out everything to enjoy a world-class orgasm."

She knew her smile was wistful. "It *was* world-class, wasn't it?" Would she ever experience another with him? Could she afford it? Rachel had warned her about this scenario. Look what had happened when Sara let love distract her. *Love?* No, she definitely did not love Jace. Yet.

"I like the spoon thing." He moved his hand to cover her breast.

What a difference a few minutes could make. His touch now felt warm, comfortable, safe. *Uh-oh.* Safe was not a good thing. She'd spent a lifetime with men who wanted to keep her safe. Funny, though—she no longer felt the need to punish Jace when he got all protective. He would never change. Could she? Maybe. If the motivation was great enough.

"Spoon?" Okay, she'd lost something here.

"Lying together like this." He pulled her even closer to demonstrate the spoon effect.

"Got it. I'm the teaspoon and you're the tablespoon." She glanced over her shoulder again to smile. "Different sizes but we do the same job."

"Uh-huh. Think about it." He shifted his weight, putting a little bit of space between them. "I wonder why no one woke us last night?"

Camryn could feel the outside world oozing beneath the door, distancing them from what had happened a short while ago. "My ego isn't happy with this, but I guess they didn't need us."

"Ow." The call came plaintively from the sitting area.

"Meathead." Camryn couldn't deny her relief. Fine, so she'd bonded with the stupid robot. "I guess you forgot to disconnect his voice box."

Jace accepted the inevitable. He'd have to get out of bed. "I'd better get busy putting him back together again. I'll reconnect as much as I can, but I wouldn't count on him for any widespread mayhem." When this was all over, he was going to lock Agent O'Brien in a bedroom and not let her out for a week. World-class sex? Try universe-class. He wouldn't look past the sex, because he wasn't ready to dissect the experience and admit that sex was only part of the equation. He'd do it later. Much later.

Jace slipped into his jeans as Camryn climbed out of bed and headed for the bathroom. He watched her until she closed the door behind her. If God struck him dead at this moment, he could take the memory of Camryn's incredible bottom to heaven or hell, knowing that life had been good.

Now, back to F.I.D.O. Jace sat on the floor and stared at the black box. Contrary to what Camryn thought, Jace knew he'd disconnected everything inside the robot. . . .

"Me." The complaint drifted from the black box.

Except the black box. "You know, F.I.D.O., you're sort of creeping me out. I've been thinking about what could be happening inside your black box, and none of my thoughts are good." Carefully he started reassembling the robot. "Sure, I believe in the *concept* of AI, but I'm not sure how I feel about artificial intelligence as a reality in the here and now. Seems to me it would take a little more computer than could fit into your box."

He reconnected the fireworks. "When I was a kid, Grandma Sentori used to say that the world

316

would end on the day scientists discovered how to create life. Then she'd cross herself."

He reconnected the two tiny missiles. It didn't look like they'd take out any major cities. They'd be lucky to take out a cornfield. "Some of the things happening inside of you would make Grandma kind of uneasy." What looked like a tiny bomb lay amidst the technological ruin that was F.I.D.O. There was nothing he could do to reconnect that, so he left it alone. "Has B.L.I.S.S. created a doomsday machine, robot?"

"His name is Meathead." Camryn's husky voice spun Jace around. "And let's share some info about him."

Camryn sat down next to Jace. "I forgot that my clean clothes are still in my room, so I was coming to ask you to get some things for me when I heard part of your conversation."

He wanted to rip off that big fluffy towel she had wrapped around her and . . .

She grinned at him. "I'd love to, Sentori, but Zed is out there somewhere. Besides, I want to hear what you think about Meathead."

He shrugged. "The robot's exhibiting behaviors that I don't think were originally programmed into him. When I woke up this morning, he was trying to eat yesterday's meal."

She had a line of concentration between her eyes. *Cute.* Everything about her was cute. *Uh-oh.* Cute wasn't usually a turn-on for him.

"He let Duncan chase him up a tree, and he curled up in my lap yesterday." Before he could stop her, she reached down and ran her fingers over the black box. She didn't jerk her fingers away.

"Didn't you feel any tingles from the box?"

She shook her head. "Should I?"

Jace processed the information. Why hadn't Camryn felt anything? Had the robot bonded with her? He shook the question away. *Impossible.* "Never mind."

She looked like she wanted to pursue his "Never mind," but decided against it. "Artificial intelligence?"

"This robot was programmed as a weapon. He was supposed to follow you around and respond to pressure on the implants beneath your skin. Even if B.L.I.S.S. scientists have found a way to make a computer reason, they wouldn't want it to think beyond the parameters of its purpose. That would make the robot a loose cannon." He offered her a frustrated smile. "Do you have a hot dot labeled 'authentic cat behaviors'?"

"No." She bit her lower lip. "Does that mean this could be something beyond AI?"

Jace glanced away. He would *not* look at her lip. "If I believed that, then I'd have to believe in miracles. I don't do miracles. Remember?"

She looked at the black box again. "I wonder if they really know what's happening inside their clever invention?"

"B.L.I.S.S.?"

She met his gaze. "Not necessarily."

Camryn felt great. Incredible lovemaking and a warm shower were better for a healthy start to the day than a dozen multivitamins. Jace had returned from her room with all of her things. She didn't have to think long about his message. Great minds thought alike.

She stood with Jace in front of the door. He smelled of the soap he'd used to shower and the male scent that was his alone. Who said modern humans had lost their sensory abilities? She'd be able to find Jace in a pitch-black room filled with strangers.

Meathead's familiar weight rested on her foot. All was right with her world. She frowned. Maybe not. Zed was still out there, with just a few days until the summit. Why only a couple of sporadic attacks? The attempts seemed only halfhearted given Zed's reputation as a killing machine. Fine, so the Aston Martin hadn't been that halfhearted. But why such exotic attempts? Why not a straightforward sniper takedown? Even with Flo in the wind and others guarding Owen, Zed would have had plenty of opportunities. Or was Flo that good?

It was almost as though Owen wasn't at the top of Zed's agenda. Her intuition was shouting in her ear, but she wasn't quite ready to accept what it was saying. She'd never depended on her intuition for anything this important before.

"Looks like you're thinking serious thoughts." Jace pushed back a strand of her hair.

She sighed. "I haven't been an agent long, but I'm getting confusing vibes about this assignment. Why hasn't Zed taken the direct approach in trying to kill your father, and why the attempts on *my* life and not on my partners' lives?"

"Maybe Zed fears you more. What could be out there about your abilities that might make Zed cautious?" He reached for the doorknob.

Camryn offered him a guilty smile. "I did a little truth stretching with my partners. I told them I could kill with my thoughts. I told them I'd put a white light around Owen, and if anyone tried to mess with him I'd know." She didn't state the obvious, that unless one of the other agents had blabbed, no one else would have that information.

Meathead lifted his bulk from Camryn's foot long enough to scratch at the door. Jace pulled open the door, then glanced up and down the hallway. He closed the door again. "Nothing. Have you pressed 'protect' yet?"

"What's the point? From what you've said, he doesn't have much left to protect with." She pressed "protect" anyway.

Jace let his hand rest on the knob. "So assuming Zed thinks you can kill with your mind, he or she wouldn't want to assassinate Owen up close unless you'd been taken out."

Camryn nodded. "Okay, so why not a sniper attack?"

He shrugged. "Maybe Zed can't shoot. Zed seems to prefer the more unusual assassination methods."

So simple, so logical. Why the hell hadn't she thought of it? "I have to change my clothes."

She left Jace standing there looking puzzled as she ran back to the bedroom, pulled out two

dresses, the black and the green ones, then carefully transferred three tiny clear chips from the
black to the green dress. As she changed into the
green outfit, Camryn thanked heaven Rachel's
clothing had performed well so far.

It was short, light, flowing, the perfect summer
dress. Also the perfect dress for what she needed
to do today. Camryn slipped on her sandals. Ever
since the debacle with the spring-loaded shoes,
she'd been leery of Rachel's footwear.

Hurrying back to Jace, she picked up Meathead. Too bad she'd forgotten to tell Jace not to
put Meathead's collar back on. "I have to call Y."
She pushed the appropriate zircon.

"Yes." Y's voice.

"Agent 36DD. Activate the tracking chips. I'll
notify you to identify each subject." She didn't
wait for Y's reply before hitting the disconnect zircon.

Jace leaned his head against the door. "Do I
want to know about this?"

"This dress has chips attached to it. When I rub
against a person, the chip attaches itself to the
subject. B.L.I.S.S. can then monitor their movements. A lot less obvious than planting a bug, and
a lot less likely to be detected." Rachel would
probably expect the chips to still be attached to
the black dress. Camryn smiled as she picked up
her purse.

They'd just stepped into the hallway when they
spotted Flo hurrying toward them. They stopped
to wait for her.

"Glad you guys are out of the sack early." Flo

was once again wearing flowing black, a dead give-away that she was carrying—everything. She probably had every weapon she owned stashed somewhere on her body. "Let's go down and get some breakfast while I tell you what we've done."

As Camryn fell into step beside Flo, she rubbed her sleeve against Flo's sleeve. "How did you know I'd be in Jace's room?"

"It made sense. You went into his room yesterday afternoon and never came out. I checked." Flo's expression was matter-of-fact. "Besides, what woman in her right mind wouldn't spend the night with Jace?" She grinned at him. "You have one hot Italian—"

Urp. "Did Honey Suckle have anything to say?"

Flo nodded. "She admitted she started the ball rolling by putting out feelers for someone to off Owen. Seems Owen wrote her into his will when he was boinking her. Left her a measly million, but Honey wanted to hurry along the collection process."

Camryn noted Jace's pained expression. He might say that he cared nothing about his father, but he was fooling himself if he believed it.

"When L.O.V.E.R. took Honey Suckle up on her offer, she thought she'd be in control. But once Zed arrived, she realized L.O.V.E.R. was her worst nightmare. Zed terrified her, and she did anything Zed told her to do." They'd reached the dining area, and Flo chose a table far from any window and next to a wall. She sat with her back to the wall. "She's still terrified. Won't tell us anything about Zed. Smart girl."

Silence fell for a few minutes as they ordered. When breakfast arrived, Camryn and Jace sat fascinated as Flo pulled out a small metal wand. She touched each of her foods with the wand, then studied a gauge at its base. She repeated the process with their food. "Enjoy. No poison. Got this when I was on assignment in Moscow a few years back. It was all hush-hush back then. Probably available on eBay now."

Camryn decided this was as good a time as any to visit the rest room. She hoped Flo wouldn't scarf Jace down along with her grapefruit. "I'll be right back." She scooped up Meathead.

"You're taking *him* with you instead of the gun I gave you? Bet you have the gun stashed in your purse." Flo's unspoken comment: *B.L.I.S.S. needs to run this woman past another shrink.*

Camryn nodded and hurried off. Making sure the rest room was empty, she stepped into a stall, then called Y. "Subject one, Flo." Pushing the disconnect, she went back to the table.

Rachel, Sara, and Owen had joined the group. During the next twenty minutes of conversation, Camryn managed to knock over Rachel's glass of milk, then bump against Sara as she fumbled to help Rachel clean up the mess.

"I assume we all agree on what has to be done today?" Rachel stared directly at Camryn.

Camryn returned her stare. "Chance is secured, right?"

"I have my security force patrolling the buildings and grounds. They're in groups of three." Owen's gaze never left Jace.

"I've drafted the cleaning force, and we're doing a continuous sweep of the area for explosives. In fact, I'd better get back in action." Sara pushed her chair away from the table.

"I wish you wouldn't put yourself in danger, dear." Owen's gaze was warm on Sara.

Sara's return gaze laid her feelings out for everyone to see. "It's what I do, Owen. And this is all about keeping you safe."

"Then I'll come with you." Owen's tone said that nothing would change his mind.

"I'll be where I'll be." Flo was still plowing through her huge meal. "And I'll be there alone."

Rachel cast Flo a considering glance. "I think I'll keep an eye on Owen's yacht and helicopter. I'll have to check out the tunnel too. If anything happens, we need a way of getting off the island." She offered Owen a thin smile. "I know you already have guards in place there, but I'll feel easier if I check up myself."

"Where's Citra?" For the first time, Jace realized he hadn't seen the agent since yesterday.

Rachel shrugged. "Her car's gone, so maybe she left the island."

Jace considered this. It was possible. Now that Owen was returning the tokens, her job was finished. She didn't owe him any explanation. But something still didn't feel right. He raked his fingers through his hair. Except for Camryn, nothing on this blasted island had felt right since the moment he'd set foot on it.

He realized everyone's attention was focused on Camryn.

"Where will Jace and you be today?" Owen voiced the question for the others.

Camryn smiled brightly at everyone. "Since everything seems to be under control, Jace and I are going to the beach."

Sara and Owen looked disapproving. Flo looked uninterested. And Rachel laughed softly.

As Jace and Camryn stood to leave, Owen stood also. Their gazes locked.

Jace steeled himself. "Stay in the building, preferably in a room with no windows. Keep yourself safe"—he took a deep breath—"Dad."

Then he turned from the sheen of moisture in his father's eyes.

Chapter Seventeen

While Camryn waited in the Badillac for Jace to join her, she contacted Y again. "Subject two, Sara. Subject three, Rachel."

There was a moment of silence on the other end of the line. "Turn on your windshield wipers, wait for them to make three sweeps, turn them off, then pull down your sun visor. A monitor will appear. I'll transmit the locations of the subjects you requested on that monitor. Good luck, Agent 36DD." No exclamations of surprise.

Camryn wondered if anything could shock Y. Or maybe this didn't come as a surprise at all. Camryn would explore that possibility later. "Wouldn't it be easier if I could activate the chips from here?"

"Of course." Y sounded distracted. "But B.L.I.S.S. maintains as much control from this end as possible in case an agent is captured or eliminated. For example, your car . . ."

Camryn didn't think she was going to like this.

"T would destroy your car from here before we'd let it fall into the wrong hands."

Camryn could hear the sound of paper shuffling. Probably Y dealing with another world crisis. Y, the queen of multitasking. "T wouldn't do that with me still in the car, would he?"

Talk about disturbing mental pictures. T swatting at a fly that had landed on his phalanx of buttons. His distracted mutter of, "Oops. Sorry, dudess."

"We do what we must, Agent 36DD. There's no self-destruct command on the car's control panel. That command has to come directly from me. Sometimes an agent is not aware of what needs to be done or is incapable of executing it." *Executing* had a sinister sound to it. Y's soft chuckle sent an icy shiver down Camryn's spine. "The chips and the car are the only things we control from here."

And Rachel controls everything else. Camryn disconnected, followed Y's instructions, and watched as a three-dimensional image of the island and Chance appeared on the sun visor. Flo, Sara, and Rachel were all still in Chance.

Camryn glanced down at Meathead, who sat beside her. "I don't know, guy. If it wasn't so hard to get your collar off, I could take the collar with me and leave you home."

"Me?"

There was something pathetic in Meathead's

reply, and Camryn immediately felt guilty. "But you know, even without your weapons, you're a lot of fun to have around." *Not always true, but what the heck.* The lie was for a good cause.

Jace slid into the passenger seat beside her. "Nothing like a relaxing day at the beach before the apocalypse." He shut the door and grinned at her.

"Smart-ass." She returned his grin. Just a few days ago she would have told him this was *her* assignment, and she didn't need his help. Now? She wanted him here beside her. *Always?* She wouldn't go there now.

"Any particular beach in mind?" He glanced at the monitor. "Handy tracking system. Looks like one of your partners is on the roof."

"There's something I need to check out at the Boardwalk." She steered the car down the driveway, then glanced at the monitor. "And that's Flo. She's probably setting up her antiaircraft guns in case Zed launches a hot-air balloon attack."

Jace had the feeling she was only half kidding. He watched Camryn drive, her hands sure on the wheel. She concentrated on the road ahead, but he sensed the question she hadn't asked. "You want to know why I decided to call him Dad."

She cast Jace a quick grin. "Right."

He turned his head to stare out at the passing scenery. "I didn't know I was going to do it until it happened."

"Why?" She glanced at the monitor, where Sara was moving from room to room at Chance.

"I'm not too sure, but I guess it had a lot to do

with seeing him as real. For most of my life he was just a name. I guess I demonized him. But now . . ." He shrugged.

Camryn nodded. "I know what you mean." She glanced away. "I've changed my opinion about some things, too." She didn't elaborate, and he didn't push her.

"I'll always resent his choosing Monopoly over me, but at least I know he wanted me back. And as much as I don't like to admit it, I understand his fascination with games. I'd never let one take the place of family, but I can't imagine not being involved in creating games." And for someone who loved games, what could create more of a rush than the game of life and death?

Camryn parked by the Ollie the Octopus pier and climbed out after glancing at the monitor. All her partners were still at Chance.

Before following her to the end of the pier, Jace stared across the board at Hogan's Saltwater Taffy Shop, and thought about what his father had said. Next time he visited Atlantic City, maybe he'd check to see if the original was still there.

Turning away, he watched Camryn lie down on her stomach and lean over the end of the pier. "Find anything?" He squatted down beside her.

"Yep." She sat up. "There's a small boat tied under the pier. No one would see it unless they did what I just did." She slid off her sandals and wiggled her toes.

"Sexy toes, sweetheart."

She grinned at him. "I bet you say that about all the girls' toes."

"Only yours, O'Brien. Only yours." He glanced around. "So we wait?"

Her smile faded. "I think today's the day, and I think Zed will come here."

"You're sure this is where she'll come?"

"My intuition is screaming it loud and clear. As far as I know, the only other boat on the island is Owen's yacht. I'm sure this is the boat Zed used to take the robot device to Honey Suckle so she could put it in the Aston Martin. Zed will try to leave the island in this." She glanced out at the sea, empty of all other boats. "Common sense says a helicopter or escape through the tunnel would make more sense, but there's something about this pier . . ." She shook her head. "I hope Y knew what she was doing when she counted on my intuition."

"Since we have to wait anyway, I'll drive the car onto the beach. We can kick back and enjoy the sun and breeze while we wait for the harbinger of death to arrive." He took the keys from her, drove the Cadillac to a spot not too close to the waterline, and parked it so the driver's side faced the water. The tide was coming in, driven by a strong breeze blowing off the sea.

Climbing from the car, he watched her walk toward him. Her green dress lifted and swirled in the wind, exposing those incredible long legs and sleek thighs. Her hair was a tangle of red flame, and her eyes glittered with the same excitement he'd seen as they lay at the cliff's edge.

Leaning back against the car, he crossed his arms over his chest and let the slide of his gaze suggest what he wanted to do in the sun and surf.

Once she'd reached him, she tilted back her head and closed her eyes while the breeze played across her parted lips. "I could spend my life on this island if every day I could come to this beach and feel what I'm feeling now."

"What're you feeling now?" Her answer was important to him, on many levels.

"Excitement and . . ." She glanced away from him. "Hand me my purse. I have to put something on my lips if I'm going to be out in this sun. Too bad I didn't bring any sunscreen." Her gaze shifted to the pier, where F.I.D.O. still sat. "Guess Meathead isn't taking any chances of getting wet."

She wasn't going to tell him. He covered his disappointment by reaching into the Cadillac and retrieving her purse. Before closing the door, he swung the sun visor to the side so they could see the monitor easily. "Looks like everyone's still safely in Chance."

Camryn studied the monitor as she reached for her purse. "Flo's outside moving around the perimeter of Chance, and Rachel's in her bathroom. Sara's in the bar now. Good. She and Owen are away from any windows."

"Smart choice. It has a built-in supply of courage." With his attention on the monitor, he thought she had the purse and let go.

Her exclamation of dismay shifted his attention to the sand, where the contents of her purse lay scattered.

"Sorry." He bent down to pick everything up.

"*Who Moved My Cheese?* Having adaptation-to-change issues?"

She dropped to her knees beside him. "I'm adapting just fine. The spine has a cell phone and recorder. Too bad a big klutz stomped on it the day I arrived."

"Ouch." He grinned at her. "And what do we have here? Another pair of my white briefs. How many did you steal?"

Her face grew pink under his amused gaze. "I forgot that was in there." She offered him a belligerent stare. "Well, I couldn't wear mine. And after the cliff thing, I knew I had to wear *something.*"

"Not necessarily." His mutter came from the heart. Or maybe not. Another body part might be expressing an opinion. "Handcuffs?"

Camryn stared at him from under her lashes, an erotic invitation to play. "Chastity convinced me of the joys of bondage. I'd like to strip you naked, handcuff you to the pier, and do unspeakable things to your body." Purposely, she slid her tongue across her lower lip.

"Sounds like fun." Every sexual cell in his body was on high alert. "Have to explore the possibilities after this Zed thing is over."

Their gazes met, and he realized he was suggesting there might be an "afterward" to their relationship. He exhaled sharply. "We need to talk. Later."

She nodded and glanced down at the things still on the sand: a gun and some makeup.

He picked up the gun. "Know how to use this?"

"I can shoot it." She smiled. "I just can't hit anything. My marksmanship is problematic. But after this assignment, I'll work on it."

He nodded and absently picked up a lipstick that must have fallen from the small makeup bag she'd had in her purse. "I wonder what color a B.L.I.S.S. agent would wear? Assassin apricot? Terminator tangerine?" He started to open it.

"Don't!" Her eyes widened as she leaned forward to grab it from him.

Too late. He'd pulled the top off, and a bitter smell that felt like it was burning its way down his nasal passages filled the air. "What the hell is that?" From the look on her face, she'd gotten a good whiff of it too.

Camryn gazed at him with wide, horrified eyes. "Truth gas."

He frowned. "Never heard of it."

"B.L.I.S.S. has lots of things you've never heard of." She scooped the rest of the things from the sand and crammed them back into her purse; then she stood.

"So no half-truths, prevarication, or avoidance tactics after inhaling this junk?" Maybe it wouldn't work. He didn't *feel* any different.

He met her gaze. He said nothing. She said nothing. If they both said nothing, then no truths would be revealed. "So what do you feel like doing while we wait for someone to make a move?" That seemed like a pretty safe topic.

She backed away from him, her eyes wide. "I feel like ripping off my clothes and having depraved sex with you while the waves wash over us."

Slowly, provocatively, she slid her dress over her head and dropped it on the beach. Her white bra and briefs were a stark contrast to the smooth, creamy expanse of her skin, the endless invitation of her long legs.

Lifting her arms above her head, she did a sensual rotation and thrust with her hips while she continued to back toward the incoming waves. She moved to an erotic rhythm only she could hear. "Come play with me, Jace."

"Tell me you're not dancing to 'The Muffin Man.' " He frowned. "Wait. You said you couldn't dance."

Her husky laughter spoke to the part of his body in charge of sex play. His body listened with growing interest.

"Not 'The Muffin Man.' This is hot, sexy, and makes me want to take you deep inside me." She paused to meet his gaze. "I thought I couldn't dance, but I guess love gave me rhythm."

A frown line formed between her eyes. "Did I say that? Why did I say that?"

Jace leaned against the Cadillac and studied her from beneath half-lowered lids. How did he feel about what she'd just said? He couldn't lie to himself. He'd felt an instant stab of joy followed by doubt. Even with all that truth gas floating in the air, he wasn't ready to tackle the joy part of his feelings. The doubt part was easier. Could he trust anything she said under the influence of some gas B.L.I.S.S. had concocted? He'd read somewhere that truth serum wasn't reliable, more like the effect of too much liquor; it loosened lips but didn't guarantee any truths.

Camryn couldn't believe the things she'd said. Out loud. Maybe the truth gas was one more of Rachel's malfunctioning gadgets. Maybe the words coming from her mouth were mad babblings, meaningless. *Who're you kidding, O'Brien?*

She shifted her glance from Jace's intent stare to Meathead. The cat had turned his back to them and was gazing toward Go. *Good.* She didn't need an audience for this debacle.

Camryn wasn't going to give Jace a chance to ask any more questions. It was her turn. "What about you? Any other ideas to while away the minutes?"

He straightened and moved toward her. Each step was deliberate, a quiet stalking. His dark gaze never left her. The breeze whipped his hair away from his hard face and plastered his T-shirt to the muscled planes of his chest.

The first time she'd seen Jace Sentori, she'd known he was dangerous. Nothing had changed. When she closed her eyes and thought *Deadly secret agent,* she pictured Jace: a man capable of explosive emotions held in check by a steel will.

She tried for an innocent smile, but she suspected it had *hungry* written all over it. "Well?"

He didn't answer. Instead he stopped, got rid of his shoes, stripped off his jeans and T-shirt, then continued toward her. Naked.

His smile didn't soften his face. "Someone stole all my briefs."

He reached her, invaded her space, and she

backed up a step. But he still towered over her, his hard body an unbroken line of tanned perfection.

He glanced over his shoulder, and Camryn followed his gaze to the monitor. "Everybody's snug and safe in Chance, so I'll *show* you what I want."

Oh, boy. Talk about unleashing the beast.

Scooping her up in his arms, he laid her down in the shallow water, just as he had earlier in his bed. Reaching behind her, he unsnapped her bra, then quickly disposed of the briefs. She watched them float away from her but couldn't summon the will to scramble after them.

For a moment, panic intruded as she thought about someone pulling up to admire Ollie the Octopus and getting a completely different eight-appendaged eyeful.

Her expression must have clued him in, because he put his finger over her lips before she could voice her concern. "Shh. No one will be doing any sight-seeing today. Everyone's holed up in or near Chance." He glanced over his shoulder at the monitor. "Your three partners are still there."

Camryn thought she'd explode with the joy of the moment. She opened herself to every sense: the cool lap of water around her bare body, the subtle shift of soft sand beneath her, the sensation of her hair floating free around her, and the tangy saltwater scent of the sea. The glare of sunlight on water would've blinded her, but Jace's large body blocked out the sun. Was that symbolic, or what?

"You have that glitter in your eyes again, lady." He knelt in the water beside her, then without warning splashed her stomach and breasts. "Tell me what excites you."

With a squeal of protest, she splashed him back. In a moment they were rolling in the surf, her legs tangling with his. She'd never win fairly, so what was a woman to do? She knew how to play dirty.

For a moment she was on top of him, and without a flicker of pity she rubbed her knee back and forth between his legs. When he gasped and fell back, she reached between his thighs and clasped him. Slowly, deliberately, she met his gaze as she used her hand on him, feeling him grow hard and thick, ready for her. He bucked beneath her and she gloried in his strength.

"You want to know what excites me? Danger. You. They're one and the same." She leaned over him, sliding her breasts across his chest, enjoying the pleasure-pain of her sensitized nipples against his flesh. "If I live to be one hundred I'll always remember you as the most dangerous man I ever knew." *Ever loved. Loved?* The thought rocked her world.

Unexpectedly, he clasped her buttocks and effortlessly lifted her to his mouth. "I guess this isn't going to be long and sweet either. You're still not working with me on this."

"The hell with long and sweet, Sentori. We can do long and sweet when we're eighty." The shock of her own words took away her breath. Could she really be thinking in terms of forever with this man? The cold splash of reality wasn't far behind. It didn't matter what she thought; Jace Sentori wasn't a forever kind of guy.

Then she ceased to think. Pulling her to him, he put his mouth on her.

Her moan was an affirmation of wish-fulfillment on a planet-exploding level. The heat of his mouth, the slide of his tongue across a spot so sensitive that she gripped his muscled shoulders to keep from screaming. She could feel her moist slickness, the building heat, the wanting for more, *more.*

He slid his tongue into her, an erotic glide of promise. Her nails dug into his shoulders as his tongue mimicked the rhythm of sex, touched again and again the spot that was driving her toward . . .

"Please." *Please make me feel complete.* She slid down his body, then lifted herself above his straining erection. "You asked me what I wanted to do."

Slowly she lowered herself onto him, panting as she forced her muscles to remain rigid while she savored the press of him, the feel of the head of his arousal opening her, sliding inside her, and the clench of her body around him, welcoming him.

Her thighs quivered from the tension of taking him inch by inch. She ceased to breathe as he filled her, stretching her body beyond what seemed possible, giving her joy beyond what seemed possible.

With a triumphant cry she settled completely onto him, taking all of him as she thrust down, moved her hips forward to feel the shift and movement of him within her.

His sharp exhalation was her only warning that he'd reached the end of his endurance. He erupted beneath her, driving up with enough force to lift them both from the water.

At the same moment, a large wave washed over them, tumbling them over in the surf. Wrapping his arms and legs tightly around her, he held her steady as the wave receded.

Camryn didn't know whether she was laughing or crying as she looked up at Jace. His hair seemed blacker, framing his face with strands wet from the sea, while water dripped from his chest onto her breasts. His gaze was dark intensity thrumming with sensual need, held in check by only a thread. Still buried deep within her body, he licked the moisture from her nipples, then took one between his teeth and tugged gently.

She followed the tug, arching her body to bring every inch of her flesh in contact with his skin. The heat from his skin, his need, was an instant combustible, and Camryn wondered why steam didn't rise from them as the cool sea lapped at their bodies.

"You bring the heat, lady." His husky murmur was an echo of the first words he'd ever said to her.

Did he remember? "I always will, Sentori. Believe it. When you need a hot memory on a cold night, remember this moment." Wrapping her legs around him, she met his pounding rhythm, clasping his back, his buttocks, to help drive him deeper, so deep that his imprint would be with her forever.

Her orgasm hit her with the explosive force of the waves washing over them. She closed her eyes to the intensity, joined her cry of release with Jace's shout.

Behind her closed lids fireworks sparkled and shimmered; rockets boomed. And as she slowly settled into the limp aftermath of her sensual overload, she opened her eyes to find that Jace had flopped onto his back beside her. She watched the next wave wash over him and sighed at the cool relief as it reached her.

"You are a wonder, Camryn O'Brien."

His tone didn't sound like a *Wow that was great sex* comment. It sounded like a *You are a wonder in everything you do* tone. Was that wishful thinking on her part?

She turned her head to smile at him, and she knew her smile had *sappy sentimental* written all over it. "I don't have a very big sampling to judge by, but you're the first man who ever made me see fireworks and hear rockets exploding."

Camryn wasn't prepared for his laughter. Standing, he pulled her to her feet.

"I'd love to take total credit for that, but the fireworks and rockets were F.I.D.O.'s contribution."

"What?" She looked at the pier to find Meathead sprawled on his tummy, all four legs splayed out in a pathetic picture of complete exhaustion.

Jace put his arm around her waist and pulled her close as he led her toward the Cadillac. "You make me lose control, woman. I forgot about him and pressed just about every spot I could on your hot little body."

Camryn smiled. She liked the "hot little body" description.

"Lucky for us, he only had the fireworks and two minimissiles still in working order, and he let loose with both." Jace glanced over to where Meathead was making a feeble attempt to stand. "I think he's down for the count."

Returning his gaze to Camryn, Jace studied her. "These last few days have proved something. I think we can safely say that shared responsibility is the way to go. In all things. Life isn't a one-woman job."

His wicked grin captured her instant attention, but she noticed the smile didn't reach his eyes.

Suddenly a rumbling explosion shook the earth. Camryn and Jace glanced at each other, their idyllic moment destroyed.

Camryn turned toward Go. "The tunnel?"

Jace nodded as he picked up his jeans and jerked them up over his hips. Slipping on his shoes, he didn't bother with his T-shirt. Then he bent to yank Camryn's gun from her purse. "I *can* hit something." He shoved it into the waistband of his jeans.

Frantic, Camryn pulled her dress over her damp body. She couldn't believe she'd let her underwear float out to sea. Stepping into her sandals, she glanced at the monitor. "Sara, Flo, and Rachel are still in Chance."

Jace stood beside her, staring at the monitor.

"Can you think of any reason why Rachel would still be in the bathroom?"

Camryn frowned. "You're right. Either she has Montezuma's revenge or she's found the chip. We have to find out—"

"A car's coming." Jace raced to the pier, scooped up Meathead, and sprinted back to the Cadillac.

Camryn slid into the driver's seat, and as soon as Jace closed the passenger door she drove back to the road. Then, with windows up, they waited. Camryn's fingers hovered over the panel so she could press the "shield" or "destroy" buttons instantly.

The black Jaguar stopped beside them and Citra climbed out. She had on her secret-agent persona as she motioned Camryn to roll down the window.

Camryn's intuition was saying that Citra was okay, but she surprised even herself by glancing at Jace to get his take. He nodded, and she rolled down the window.

Citra leaned in, her eyes wide in her pale face. "Zed planted a bomb in the tunnel. The tunnel's gone. I was planning on getting an early start back to the mainland, but I decided to stick around for a while to see if anything would go down. I'd finally decided nothing was going to happen, but just as I reached the tunnel, it exploded. We're cut off from the mainland."

Camryn glanced at Jace, then turned to Citra. "Go back to Chance and make sure everyone's okay. Tell everyone to stay there."

A few minutes after Citra drove away, Meat-head's urgent-message code flashed. Camryn could feel Jace's tension along with her own. The call had to be from one of her partners or Y. And whatever it was, it wouldn't be good. She answered it.

"We have a situation, Agent 36DD." Rachel had on her official B.L.I.S.S. voice.

"Where are you, Rachel?"

Camryn almost didn't hear Rachel's soft laughter.

"You didn't think I'd walk around all day wearing that chip so you could track me, did you?"

"I had hopes."

"You'll learn." Now Rachel sounded patronizing. "I wouldn't count on tracking Sara or Flo either. They're both B.L.I.S.S. agents. They know the game. They've probably already put the chips on other people."

Great. Leave it to Rachel to make her feel like a failure. It was about time she fought back. "You supplied the chips, Rachel. If they're that easy to spot, I'm surprised you didn't come up with something a little more . . . unique."

The momentary silence on the other end of the line vibrated with menace. "Here's an update. Zed has incapacitated the yacht and helicopter. We can't keep a lid on this any longer. We've called for backup, but it'll take a while to get here."

Camryn added her bit of news. "Zed blew up the tunnel."

"We have something more urgent at the moment."

Camryn blinked. What could be more urgent than being trapped on an island with evil incarnate?

"Flo was on the roof setting up her antiaircraft guns when she spotted someone on Jace's bike heading toward Free Parking. The rider was wearing some kind of black hood, so Flo couldn't ID the person even with her binoculars. The rider turned off at New York Avenue and rode down that narrow path that leads to the bottom of the cliffs." Rachel paused, probably getting in a few more moves with her knitting needles.

"As soon as I got back from checking out the yacht, Flo told me. When I mentioned it to Peter Bilt, he and that Chastity woman ran off to investigate. I couldn't stop them." Another pause, probably to contemplate the stupidity of all people on earth except her.

"And?" Camryn glanced at Jace. He wasn't looking at her. His brow was furrowed as he quietly stroked Meathead. Amused, she wondered what he'd say if she asked him why he was petting a robot.

"That road's just wide enough for one vehicle. At low tide there's a narrow strip of beach. At high tide there's nothing."

Rachel stopped talking long enough to take a bite out of something. Sounded like an apple. Camryn had heard about calm under fire, but this was ridiculous.

"A few minutes ago Peter called on his cell phone. When they reached the beach, the person surprised them and sprayed something in their faces that knocked them out. When they came to, the rider was gone and they were tied hand and foot. Strange thing is that the attacker left Peter's cell phone in his hands so he could call for help. I wonder what that's all about?"

Rachel paused for another bite. "The tide'll be completely in within the next fifteen minutes. The Cadillac is the only vehicle fast enough to get you there in time to save them."

Camryn listened to the disconnect click. Rachel didn't expend energy on extended good-byes. Immediately Camryn called Sara. "Did you get a call from Peter, too?"

"Yes. Owen took the call. You need to get to them fast." There was quiet whispering. "Owen said to be careful. A bunch of houses and hotels are parked on the track above those cliffs. We don't know what else is sabotaged."

Briefly Camryn filled Jace in on the details even as she started the Cadillac.

"My bike, huh? I'm about the only one not using it." He studied her grim expression as she floored the gas pedal and the car rocketed toward New York Avenue. "You know this is a ploy by Zed to draw you away from that pier?"

She nodded and kept driving. And her decision told him what he'd always suspected about Camryn O'Brien: the perfect B.L.I.S.S. agent would have stayed at the pier and left Peter and Chastity to their fate.

Camryn would never be a perfect B.L.I.S.S. agent, but she *was* a perfect, warm, and caring woman who couldn't excuse the deaths of two people as collateral damage. He hadn't admired too many people in his life, but he admired Camryn. The scariest part? He was starting to have selective memory loss. He couldn't seem to remember any of her faults.

All intense introspection stopped as they reached New York Avenue and the narrow road leading down to the beach.

Jace eyed the row of red and green buildings lined up on the rail along the edge of the cliff. "They aren't all that big. The houses are about six feet tall and the hotels are maybe twelve feet."

Camryn didn't look reassured. "Ready?"

Jace glanced at her and grinned. He hoped it didn't look as forced as it felt. "I'm up for anything, but F.I.D.O. looks a little anxious."

She didn't return his glance, but her lips tipped up. "Thanks for being here, Sentori."

"No problem." He wanted to touch her, to share whatever strength he could give her through physical contact. But she didn't need the distraction of physical contact now. "What're you going to hum on the way down?"

Her smile widened. "I thought 'Three Blind Mice' might be appropriate." She steered the car skillfully down the path.

"Great. That'd be my choice, too." The bottom looked a long distance away. "I'll hum the harmony."

Chapter Eighteen

Not only was the path bumpy, but it was a lot narrower than it had looked from the top of the cliff. Jace could see Peter and Chastity on what remained of the beach, but the beach was disappearing fast.

Camryn bit her lip in concentration, never losing her white-knuckled grip on the steering wheel. Jace mentally steered with her, mentally jammed his foot on the brake.

Suddenly radio static broke the silence. "Yo, dudess. Don't want to do the knuckle-cracking, teeth-gnashing thing, but the message I'm getting is that there's megaspace straight down on the Big Smooth's left. The Big Smooth doesn't bounce. Like, I have real concerns here."

Jace narrowed his gaze on the radio. "Get off the air, T, before I put my fist through the radio."

"Whoa, dude. I'm outta here." T's devotion to his car evidently didn't extend to physical violence.

"Thanks." She never took her attention from the path.

Jace could see the tension drain from Camryn when she reached the beach. She leaned back and sighed deeply. He and F.I.D.O. offered up a silent sigh, because males didn't do the out-loud stuff.

Jace smiled at her. "No humming on the way down?"

Her smile didn't reach her eyes. "No humming. I guess it's time to put away some things in my life."

Scrambling from the Cadillac, Camryn and Jace raced to where Chastity and Peter sat back-to-back. Their attacker had made certain they couldn't escape the tide by tying the end of the rope around a large boulder. Their car was nowhere in sight.

"I've almost chewed through the rope, but it wouldn't have been in time to save us from the sea." Chastity speared Jace and Camryn with an intent gaze. "No matter where you are in the world, if you ever have need of help, call me and I'll come. The Horse Shouter never forgets."

Camryn glanced at Jace. "Wow. She must really be upset. Contractions."

Jace hadn't a clue what Camryn was talking about, but he decided that any woman who could chew through rope that strong was a woman he wanted on his team. Maybe he'd recommend her as a B.L.I.S.S. candidate.

Jace pulled out his pocketknife even as the incoming tide lapped around his ankles. He'd barely finished cutting Peter and Chastity loose when another explosion shook the ground.

Looking up, he watched in horror as the green and red buildings tumbled over the cliff. Some fell into the sea, but most landed in shattered heaps on the path. Better and better. Trapped on the frickin' beach.

"Okay, O'Brien, tell me that the pink wonder has some buttons you didn't tell me about, like 'fly,' 'swim,' or 'time travel.'" Jace gazed down at his feet, where the swirling water had reached midcalf.

Camryn motioned to the Cadillac. "Everyone in."

Once inside she glanced at her choices. "The shield might keep the water out, but I don't know. Even if it did, we'd have to wait until the tide went out before we could escape. I guess that leaves just one choice. Climb."

Everyone's gazes shifted to the sheer cliff that rose straight up for at least a hundred feet.

"Sounds good to me." Jace glanced down to where the water would soon be seeping into the car. "Now."

"I don't think I want to be a bodyguard anymore." Peter said his first words.

"When this is over we'll leave the island, my beautiful one, and I'll take care of you forever." Chastity sounded determined. "Of course, I'll have to discipline you occasionally to keep you satisfied."

Jace was *not* listening to this. He turned to look at Camryn. "Go for it."

Camryn drove the car forward until the front bumper touched the cliff; then she pressed "climb."

With an ominous whirring noise, the Cadillac rose straight up until all four wheels were touching the cliff, then clung to it like a big pink burr. Jace swallowed hard as he was flung back in his seat. Lying on his back staring up at the sky through the windshield did not feel like a secure position.

Then the car simply rolled up the cliff face.

"Oh, my God!" Camryn's exclamation of shock was repeated with interesting variations by Chastity and Peter.

Jace unclenched his jaw. When he was a kid, he'd had nightmares about driving on a bridge that went straight up. Not a great feeling, but he had to know what was happening. He rolled down his window—well, not technically "down" anymore—and hung on to the roof of the car while he leaned out as far as possible. "I think we have Velcro tires." As he started to pull himself back inside, the gun in his waistband caught on the window. Jace watched as it fell to the beach below. "Hell. A crappy day just got crappier."

"Not totally crappy." Jace heard the smile in Camryn's voice.

The crackling radio warned that T wanted some input. "Yes! I knew all those test failures were flukes. I knew the Big Smooth would come through when it counted." Pause. "It's not actually Velcro. It's—"

"Are you telling me *this* is the first time the car has climbed anything?" Camryn's voice had a screechy quality Jace had never noticed before.

"Calm down, dudess. This is the only time that matters, right? When you reach the top, press 'climb' again, and the Big Smooth will put the regular tires back in place. Think I'll celebrate with a Big Mac and fries. Maybe rent *The Spy Who Shagged Me* for some new inspiration." T's maturity level was peeling off in layers.

"When I get back from this assignment, I'm going to hunt you down, tear you into very tiny pieces, and then scatter your remains over a million miles of wilderness so your DNA can never be replicated."

Wow. Jace believed her. Evidently T did too, because the radio went dead.

At the top of the cliff, Camryn pressed "climb," and the car returned to a horizontal position.

"There's our car over there." Peter pointed to the blue Civic hidden among some trees. "We'll drive back to Chance and let you guys do your thing." He climbed from the car and, while he waited for Chastity to join him, studied himself in the Cadillac's mirror. "Damn, salt water is a killer on blond hair. I just had the color done last week, too."

"Why'd you decide to go down there after Rachel warned you not to?" Camryn sounded casual, but her tone didn't fool Jace.

Peter looked puzzled. "Warn us? You have it wrong. She's the one who insisted we go. She said Mr. Sitall wanted us to investigate."

Camryn nodded. "Oh. I guess I misunderstood."

Jace stuck his head out the window. "Let me have your cell phone."

Peter handed over the phone, then walked hand in hand with Chastity to their car. Camryn drove toward the Boardwalk.

Jace shook his head. "You know, I admire a man who can escape death by inches and still worry about his color job."

Camryn's smile was tight. "You don't have to do this with me, Jace. I can let you off at the Short Line, and you can walk back to Chance."

"Do you want me to stay?" This was it. Jace knew he could tell her he was staying, and she'd probably just shrug. But he wanted more than that. He wanted her to say the words.

"Yes. I . . . need you to stay." She glanced over at him. "But I don't want you to get hurt."

He knew his grin was triumphant. "I'm indestructible, lady."

Camryn didn't have to look when she pulled up opposite Ollie the Octopus. She knew who would be waiting. As she opened the door and climbed out, she heard Jace doing the same. It probably would make more sense to stay in the car so they could defend themselves, but her intuition said that Rachel would have covered all the possibilities.

Rachel leaned against the octopus arch, calmly

knitting, her trademark electrical arcs going full blast. "You got back sooner than I expected. I barely got everything in place. You know you should've left those idiots for the tide to take."

"How'd you manage it, Rachel?" She hoped she sounded calmer than she felt.

Rachel shrugged while never missing a stitch. "I made sure I took Jace's bike when I knew Flo was on the roof. Flo would spot me as soon as I hit the board. I came back along the jungle path so Flo would think I was still on the beach; then I told Peter that Owen wanted him to investigate. He was stupid enough not to check it out with Owen. I took the shortcut to get back to the beach before them."

She offered Jace a smile that never reached those cold gray eyes. "Wonderful piece of machinery, Jace. Too bad I can't take it with me. Anyway, no one suspected I'd been away from Chance. People are generally a lot dumber than you give them credit for."

"You don't respect anyone, do you?" Camryn reached out to Jace with her heart. He wasn't touching her, but she *felt* him, his strength, his belief in her. A weight settled on her foot. Meathead.

"I only respect someone who's smarter than me. I haven't found anyone who qualifies yet." Rachel didn't look up from her knitting. "You might want to move away from the car."

Camryn scooped up Meathead and moved with Jace to the side. As soon as they'd cleared the car, Rachel pointed the needles at it. There was a crackle of electricity and every hair on Camryn's head felt as though it were standing on end.

A muffled boom came from under the Badillac's hood, then a thin stream of smoke.

"You have no idea how satisfying that was." Rachel allowed herself a thin smile. "That little pissant, T, thinks he's so smart. He'll never come close to achieving what I did for B.L.I.S.S."

Rachel's gaze narrowed. "You wasted a lot of my time, Agent 36DD. I could've finished this a little sooner if I hadn't spent time trying to figure out how to keep you from killing me with your mind." She nodded her head like a queen showing approval to a subject. "A very creative lie. If I hadn't been listening outside Jace's door this morning, I'd still be worrying." She continued her knitting.

"Why're we talking, and what're you going to do?" Jace's voice was hard, dangerous.

"Why're we talking? I enjoy chatting with my victims before I kill them. Someone has to appreciate my brilliance. B.L.I.S.S. never did." Her needles were a blur of anger. "What am I going to do? I'm going to destroy everyone on this island."

Her words were no surprise, but hearing them spoken out loud deflated Camryn's courage, made her want to run screaming away from the evil that was Rachel. "What is this *really* about, Rachel?" Camryn put Meathead down and he immediately plunked himself on her foot.

"Very good." Rachel nodded her approval again. "Owen Sitall is merely a sidebar for me. I only put the bomb under his mattress to draw suspicion away from me. The car and blowgun were mere amusements." She frowned. "I was embarrassed about how badly I missed when I tried to shoot you. I never could hit the side of a barn. Don't know why I keep trying. Of course, L.O.V.E.R. doesn't know any of this. They think I'm totally focused on *their* agenda." She smiled. "I know you'll never tell them."

Rachel stared intently at her, and Camryn shivered in the hot sunlight. Rachel's eyes were flat, emotionless, dead.

"This was always about B.L.I.S.S. They didn't appreciate me when I worked for them, and then they put me out to pasture because they thought I was too old. They're finding out the hard way that I'm not getting older; I'm getting deadlier. I intend to keep killing B.L.I.S.S. agents, and I won't get caught because I never leave witnesses behind."

Jace moved restlessly beside Camryn. "So how do you intend to wipe out the island?"

Jace was right. They had to know Rachel's plans before they could act. *She can kill you before you take one step. How're you going to defend against that, big bad agent?* Camryn pushed the thought away. She had to believe there was something they could do or else panic would take over.

"Really anxious to die, Jace?" Rachel sighed. "I haven't even explained my name or shown you what I've been knitting."

"Okay, get on with it." Jace wasn't pandering to Rachel's ego.

"Young people are so impulsive." If she hadn't been looking into her eyes, Camryn might have thought Rachel's comment almost grandmotherly. "I chose Zed as my agent name because I wanted to be the last person B.L.I.S.S. agents saw before they died. And my knitting?" She held it up for them to see.

Camryn had always thought that when someone said, *My blood ran cold,* it was simply a cliché. It wasn't. The message on the knitted square read: *Agents 316, 1BA, and 36DD eliminated on July 24, 2003.*

"When I get back to my RV, I'll hang this beside the other ten." She smiled at them. "Now you want to know how everyone will die."

She nodded her head toward the end of the pier. "I'm going to back down this pier, and you're not going to do a thing, because if you do I'll zap you with my needles. When I get to the end, I'll put on a gas mask, then release the gas from that canister you see. The gas will spread over the island within minutes. The wind will be blowing away from me, so I'll simply get in my boat and escape to the mainland. The gas kills within ten seconds. Nothing can stop it, not a volcanic mountain or a house built in the name of Monopoly. It'll seep into every crack, cling to every surface. And to make everything quicker, right before you arrived I called and told everyone to evacuate Chance because bombs had been planted at different places beneath the foundation." She shrugged. "You can try to rush me and die now, or wait a few minutes until the gas gets you."

She offered them another of her humorless

smiles. "I'll tell you a secret: this is my lucky day. The wind is strong and blowing in the perfect direction. And best of all, today is my birthday. What better present than getting a chance to wipe out three B.L.I.S.S. agents and a whole bunch of innocents? I love collateral damage."

Jace reached down to pick up Meathead.

"I wouldn't do that, Jace." Rachel's voice was full of sweet reasonableness. "I know you want to use his collar to warn everyone, but I can't let you do that. And beyond the collar, he's useless. I'm surprised he can still move. I hated having to create such a failure. F.I.D.O. is a stain on my reputation. But a woman has to do what a woman has to do." She took a step back as Jace put Meathead down.

"One more question, Rachel. Why was that black box inside him?" Camryn could feel Jace gathering himself, getting ready to rush Rachel. She put her hand on his arm.

Rachel shrugged. "Who knows? L.O.V.E.R. insisted I include it. Said they were testing something new. Whatever it was, it didn't work." She took another step back.

Camryn locked gazes with Jace and let him see everything she felt for him. "You're a miracle to me, Jace Sentori. I've spent my life denying I needed any man, but I need you." She ran her fingers up his arm. "I love you." She glanced away so she wouldn't have to see his reaction.

He placed his warm hand over hers. "I once told you I didn't believe in miracles. But for the first time in my life I'm going to give a miracle a try, because I have too much unfinished business with you, O'Brien."

Rachel had paused to listen. "That is so sweet. You know, this isn't a bad way to go, in love and all that. It's sort of good to go out on a high."

Jace didn't even glance at Rachel. "Talk to Meathead, Camryn. Don't push any hot dots, just talk to him. Tell him what you want him to do."

Camryn looked down at Meathead. Jace had called F.I.D.O. Meathead. Funny how momentous shifts in attitude and belief came wrapped in short sentences.

"Meathead, I want you to stop Rachel from reaching the end of the pier." She held the cat's unblinking stare.

"Me?"

"Yes, you. I want you to do this for me." She drew in a deep breath. "Love you, guy."

Camryn looked up to see if Jace thought she sounded crazy. He gave her an encouraging smile and a thumbs-up.

They both held their breath and watched Meathead.

The cat padded purposefully toward Rachel. Rachel laughed and shook her head. "I won't even waste my needles on him unless he comes too close. You must be pretty desperate."

Jace glanced at Camryn. "He has a small bomb, but I couldn't hook it up. It's not big enough to do much damage. It's just lying inside him."

They all watched as Meathead padded around Rachel, then stopped halfway down the pier. He turned to stare at Camryn. "Meow."

Rachel dismissed the cat and took another step back.

The explosion rocked the pier. One moment the whole pier was there; the next it was gone. At least the middle was gone. The end of the pier with the gas canister was still intact.

The force of the blast flattened Rachel. Ollie the Octopus teetered, then fell on her. Rachel's knitting needles skittered away, and Jace quickly scooped them up before looking at Camryn.

"She's out cold." He gathered Camryn into his arms and held her. "It's over."

Camryn nodded but didn't speak as she moved from Jace's arms to get the handcuffs from her purse. Methodically she cuffed Rachel to Ollie, then searched her for other weapons.

As Jace went to the car to get Peter's phone to call Chance, he watched Camryn. She was fighting back tears. He walked to her and put his arms around her again. "Flo and Sara are coming. They're contacting Y right now."

"T will be upset about the Badillac." Her voice was wooden.

Jace exhaled sharply and tipped Camryn's chin up so she'd meet his gaze. "Meathead loved you." *Just like I love you.* "He destroyed himself so you'd be safe. He was a unique being far ahead of his time, and we should be proud that he touched our lives."

The tears came. "I don't care about all that unique-being crap. He was my cat and now he's dead."

Jace touched her lips with his. "And that is his

359

greatest achievement. He lived, Camryn. He was really *alive*."

She nodded as she bit her bottom lip. "I'll miss him."

Jace stared out over the gaping hole in the middle of the pier. "The last laugh is on L.O.V.E.R. They created him, and their creation defeated them."

The silence was broken by the sound of Jace's Harley, followed by other vehicles. In a few minutes the area was teeming with people. Flo guarded Rachel, while Camryn talked to Y. Peter carefully removed the gas canister.

Owen walked over to Jace, and they exchanged self-conscious hugs. "This has taught me a lot, son. While we were waiting for something to happen, I didn't worry about Chance or the board. I worried about you and Sara."

Owen glanced toward Camryn. "I'm giving the island and Chance to you, Jace. Something tells me you've found someone special. I know I have." He drew Sara to his side. "Sara and I will be married here; then we'll travel the world in our RVs. We'll have one on each continent. I want to play Monopoly with world leaders, see what they're made of. Sara's coaching me, and she's a sneaky lady." He leaned over to kiss Sara's cheek. "I might just take a few of them."

"I'm happy for you and Sara, Dad." Surprisingly, Jace was sincere. *Nothing like a near-death experience to mellow you out.* "Owning this whole island is a little overwhelming, but thanks. I need a favor, though. I want a list of all the companies you own that are doing any kind of experimental work with artificial intelligence." Jace glanced over to where Camryn was walking toward him.

"No problem, Jace." Owen wandered away with his arm wrapped around Sara's shoulders.

When Camryn reached him, he couldn't miss her exhaustion, a tiredness that went beyond the physical. She offered him a weak smile. "I think I'll have the fit of hysteria I've been saving for the right moment."

Her glance touched the pier, then slid away. "Y said she suspected one of my partners was Zed, but she didn't know which one. Y felt my lack of experience would drive Zed crazy because she couldn't read me, couldn't predict what I'd do next. Y admitted that *she* was intuitive, too. Her intuition told her to go with me."

Camryn pushed back her hair with fingers that still shook. "Y said I'd saved untold numbers of B.L.I.S.S. agents. She offered me a promotion." Her glance again wandered to the missing section of the pier. "I told her I was interested if I could bring a partner. Everything's up in the air right now."

What partner? He'd never realized how ugly jealousy could feel. Jace drew her over to where Citra was standing beside the Jaguar. "Citra, would you drive Camryn back to Chance?"

Citra nodded. "Sure. I have to make some reports anyway."

Camryn looked at Jace, and he saw the questions in her eyes: *Why aren't you coming with me? What do you feel for me?* She didn't ask them, just

Chapter Nineteen

Camryn sat on the bench where Jace had written that he'd meet her. She hadn't a clue what she was doing in Atlantic City eating saltwater taffy while she waited for Jace Sentori to show up. This was a far cry from Owen Sitall's Boardwalk. The only familiar thing was Hogan's Saltwater Taffy Shop.

Chance seemed a million light years away. Hard to believe it had been only three months. So much had changed. Jace had given B.L.I.S.S. permission to use his island as one of its headquarters, and then he'd fallen off the face of the Earth. She was training for a new position in B.L.I.S.S., and Rachel was knitting pot holders in maximum security.

One thing hadn't changed: she still loved Jace Sentori. For three long months she'd waited for his call. Sure, she knew now that she could handle things alone, but she didn't *want* to handle them alone. She wanted Jace with her. Too bad he didn't feel the same.

"You bring the heat, lady."

The sexual slide of his husky murmur made Camryn close her eyes, remembering it all: bare bodies touching, connecting on a sensual level she'd never forget. On an emotional level? She didn't know.

Camryn opened her eyes, then turned to where he'd quietly eased down beside her. "Those were the first words you ever said to me. They scared me then. They don't anymore. Know why?" He looked good enough to bring tears to her eyes. "Because they're true. And that makes me feel damned good."

The wicked slant of his grin tore at her. After today she wouldn't meet him anymore. It hurt too much.

"Pretty sure of yourself, aren't you?" He fiddled with some sort of carrier he'd set on the bench beside him.

Camryn sighed. "About our sexual compatibility, yes. About other things, no." She tried to look around him to see what he had, but he blocked her view.

He put his arm along the back of the bench and played with the ends of her hair. "I've spent three months having sexual fantasies about your red hair sliding between my legs, across my cock and belly. I've imagined your mouth on every part of my body. I've buried myself inside you every night in my dreams." He leaned over and touched his lips to the sensitive skin behind her ear. "And afterward we've lain awake having long philosophical discussions." His breath was a warm promise of pleasure.

Camryn smiled. He could always make her smile. "So what's been happening for the last three months? Why no calls to ask how the weather's been in Texas?" For the first time she noticed the tired lines around his eyes.

He gazed across at the saltwater taffy shop. "Love is hard for me, sweetheart."

Love? He'd used the word *love.* She widened her eyes as she stared at him and tried not to hope.

"I guess the words have never been enough for me. I felt love had to be proved. Most of my life I spent waiting for Dad to prove how much he loved me." Jace slid her a sideways glance. "I needed something tangible, something I could hold on to." He shrugged. "It never happened, at least not when it really counted."

Exhaling deeply, he finally faced her. "I love you, Camryn O'Brien, and you're going to marry me if I have to haul you kicking and screaming to the altar." He picked up the carrier beside him and put it in his lap. "I brought something for you."

Camryn bit her lip to keep the tears at bay. "You never have to prove your love to me, Jace Sentori."

"But I want to." Carefully he opened the carrier and motioned for her to look inside.

Glancing down, she gave a small cry. "An orange kitten. It's a mini-Meathead."

She reached inside and lifted the kitten out. "Thank you, Jace." Tears clogged her voice. The kitten would never replace Meathead, but she'd treasure him because he was a gift of love from Jace.

"Put him down." Gently he lifted the kitten from her arms and set him on the boardwalk.

"Jace, no. He's just a kitten. He'll run away and—"

Her breath caught in her throat as the kitten planted his bottom on her foot, then gazed up at her with round yellow eyes.

"Me." After his brief greeting, the kitten began washing his face.

Reaching down, she scooped the kitten into her arms and held him tightly.

"Ow."

Camryn loosened her grip even as she buried her face in the kitten's orange fur. "Meathead?" She blinked madly, but to no avail. Tears slid down her face. "*How*? How did you do it?"

"I found Meathead's black box. I figured whatever genius created the box would've also made sure it was pretty indestructible. Then I worked with some very talented scientists. Meathead is living proof you *can* put Humpty-Dumpty back together again."

Camryn had seen Jace's full range of sexy grins,

but never the open, boyish grin on his face now. She loved him so much she felt she'd burst with it.

"I love you, Jace." She didn't touch him. If she touched him now she'd end up doing something that would get them thrown into jail without a Get Out of Jail Free card. "We need to do some negotiating, though."

"Negotiating?" He looked wary.

"Yep. B.L.I.S.S. has promoted me, and I'll be living at Chance. Think you could create your games there?" She crossed her legs so her shorts rode up her thighs. Hey, a girl used what she had to get the job done.

He grimaced. "I hate red and gold."

"No problem. B.L.I.S.S. has totally redecorated it." She took a deep, hopeful breath.

His gaze duly noted the lift and thrust. "A few of the scientists who worked on Meathead want to continue their AI research in a secure location. Chance would be perfect. And I'd like to stick around to see how they do."

"Of course, there's a downside. You'd have to live on an exotic island and have sex with an insatiable woman. Often." She wiggled her bottom on the bench.

"Hmm. Sex? Often?" He narrowed his gaze on her bottom.

"Uh-huh. And did I mention that said insatiable woman is also unpredictable? She could demand hot sex at any time of the day or night, in strange places and unplanned positions." Camryn bent down to pet Meathead, who'd scrambled back to her foot, and to provide Jace with a view of things to come at the same time.

"What *is* your new job?" His voice was a dangerous murmur.

"Y feels that some members of B.L.I.S.S. lack the prerequisite people skills to represent an international organization. I mean, look at T. Would you want him representing your company in a public forum? I don't think so."

She leaned into Jace and slid her tongue down his neck. "Y says I have an intuitive grasp of how to handle people." She pushed his open shirt aside and nibbled at his shoulder. "I'll be teaching B.L.I.S.S. members how to interact in a professional way with fellow agents, as well as those outside the agency. I even got to choose my new agent number. I'm now agent 4663. That spells 'Good' on your touch-tone phone." She circled his nipple with the tip of her finger. "I'm good at many things."

His breathing quickened and she could feel the pounding of his pulse as she touched her lips to the hollow of his neck.

"Tell me again what I get if I agree to the deal." His husky demand suggested he'd expect to get a lot.

Camryn pretended to think about it. "Every day I'll drive you down to the Boardwalk in the new and improved Badillac." She slid him a provocative glance. "Then we can play."

"Done." The slant of his grin promised that a lot more of her bras and panties would float out on the tide.

"Me . . . ow!" Meathead agreed.

LISA CACH

DR. YES

Dr. Alan Archer doesn't seem evil. But Rachel Calais knows the insidious truth: The doc is down in Nepal searching for the lost city of Yonam—and a plant that, when properly refined, will have every female in the world on her knees . . . or her back.

Rachel's mission: Stop Archer at any cost. B.L.I.S.S.—an international organization fighting such dastardly villains—has given her a kit to help, as well as a dangerously sexy man who knows how to watch a woman's back. With a stun gun, infrared goggles, and other less conventional forms of protection, Rachel is a regular Jane Bond. She doesn't know that playing spy will make her pay the ultimate price: her heart.

LYNSAY SANDS
THE LOVING DAYLIGHTS

Shy Jane Spyrus loves gadgets. She can build anything B.L.I.S.S. needs in its international fight against crime—although agents aren't exactly queuing up at her door. Some of them think her innovations are too . . . well, innovative. Like her shrink-wrap prophylactic constraints. But they just don't realize that item's potential.

Of course, you can't use wacky inventions to fix all your problems. Jane will have to team up with another *human being*—and Abel Andretti arrives just in time. He will help Jane find her kidnapped neighbor, stop the evil machinations of Dirk Ensecksi, and most of all he will show her how to love the daylights out of something without batteries.

THE PLEASURE MASTER

NINA BANGS

Stranded by the side of a New York highway on Christmas Eve, hairdresser Kathy Bartlett wishes herself somewhere warm and peaceful with a subservient male at her side. She finds herself transported all right, but to Scotland in 1542 with the last man she would have chosen.

With the face of a dark god or a fallen angel, and the reputation of being able to seduce any woman, Ian Ross is the kind of sexual expert Kathy avoids like the plague. So when she learns that the men in his family are competing to prove their prowess, she sprays hair mousse on his brothers' "love guns" and swears she will never succumb to the explosive attraction she feels for Ian. But as the competition heats up, neither Kathy nor Ian reckon the most powerful aphrodisiac of all: love.

___52445-7 $5.50 US/$6.50 CAN

Dorchester Publishing Co., Inc.
P.O. Box 6640
Wayne, PA 19087-8640

Please add $2.50 for shipping and handling for the first book and $.75 for each book thereafter. NY, NYC, and PA residents, please add appropriate sales tax. No cash, stamps, or C.O.D.s. All orders shipped within 6 weeks via postal service book rate. Canadian orders require $2.50 extra postage and must be paid in U.S. dollars through a U.S. banking facility.

Name_____
Address_____
City_____ State_____ Zip_____
I have enclosed $_____ in payment for the checked book(s).
Payment <u>must</u> accompany all orders. ❑ Please send a free catalog.
CHECK OUT OUR WEBSITE! www.dorchesterpub.com

AN ORIGINAL SIN
NINA BANGS

Fortune MacDonald listens to women's fantasies on a daily basis as she takes their orders for customized men. In a time when the male species is extinct, she is a valued man-maker. So when she awakes to find herself sharing a bed with the most lifelike, virile man she has ever laid eyes or hands on, she lets her gaze inventory his assets. From his long dark hair, to his knife-edged cheekbones, to his broad shoulders, to his jutting—well, all in the name of research, right?—it doesn't take an expert any time at all to realize that he is the genuine article, a bona fide man. And when Leith Campbell takes her in his arms, she knows real passion for the first time . . . but has she found true love?

___52324-8 $5.99 US/$6.99 CAN

SUSAN SQUIRES
BODY ELECTRIC

Victoria Barnhardt sets out to create something brilliant; she succeeds beyond her wildest dreams. With one keystroke her program spirals out of control . . . and something is born that defies possibility: a being who calls to her.

He speaks from within a prison—seeking escape, seeking *her*. He is a miracle that Vic never intended. More than a scientific discovery, or a brilliant coup by an infamous hacker, he is life. He is beauty. And he needs to be released. Just as Victoria does. Though the shadows of the past might rise against them, on one starry Los Angeles night, in each other's arms, the pair will find a way to have each other and freedom both.

Improper English

KATIE MacALISTER

Sassy American Alexandra Freemar isn't about to put up with any flak from the uptight—albeit gorgeous—Scotland Yard inspector who accuses her of breaking and entering. She doesn't have time. She has two months in London to write the perfect romance novel—two months to prove that she can succeed as an author.

Luckily, reserved Englishmen are not her cup of tea. Yet one kiss tells her Alexander Block might not be quite as proper as she thought. Unfortunately, the gentleman isn't interested in a summer fling. And while Alix knows every imaginable euphemism for the male member, she soon realizes she has a lot to learn about love.